What if You Made It Up?

What if You Made It Up?

A Novel

Kathleen S. Kolze

All the best!

Kathleen Kolze

Make It Up Press / Lake Zurich, IL

Library of Congress Control Number: 2011944454

Published by Make It Up Press, Lake Zurich, IL 60047.

Book editorial, design, and production by
Diligent Editorial and Book Production Service
http://diligenteditorial.com

ISBN: 978-0-9848806-0-7

Printed in the United States of America

interior illustration: © iStockphoto.com/bubaone

What if You Made It Up?

1

Spy scope grip in one hand, coffee mug in the other, Eva locked in on a bull moose. Sporting the unmistakable horned rack, the animal bent to feast on vegetation beneath the surface of the black lake. As Eva spied on the creature, the doe moose crept into sight and the pair ate with leisure, immune to the arctic weather.

Sidelining her love of nature, Eva moved to her office to prepare for work. Groggy despite caffeine, the flat ring startled her, and she transformed into professional mode. "This is Eva," she answered on the second ring.

"Eva, this is Martin," he said, his voice deep.

"Hello, Martin. It's good to hear you."

"And you."

"What's on your mind today?" Eva asked.

"Well, I think I have not been so good," Martin replied in a thick Eastern European accent.

"Not so good? Please elaborate," she asked gently, glancing out the window at the pines, tiny green triangles against the snow-capped mountains.

"Well, I was irritated at work," he said gruffly.

"Hmm, why so, Martin?"

"My coworkers can be so annoying. I didn't hold back my feelings."

Eva heard his self-deprecating tone, a strong clue. "Martin, you're human."

"Huh, whatever."

"Did you learn anything?"

"Who knows," Martin said.

"Would you do something?" Eva asked, hearing the rare abruptness in his response.

"I guess so."

"Good. Okay, take a deep breath."

Quiet. A fuzzy sound came over the phone caused by his inhale, then a heavy exhale. His breath was joined by a concise puff, likely caused by his weight shift on the chair cushion. Eva relaxed as well. "So, Martin, how's that?"

"Better," he replied.

She imagined him crossing his legs at the ankles, calming his body. "You mentioned being irritated." Eva mirrored his words. "What was that about?"

"No one is ever prepared and they waste my time." He sighed, agitated. "Leaders don't make decisions. Which wastes time." Martin stopped, his frustration returning.

"Hmm," Eva surmised simply, "this time thing is an issue."

A brief inhale came across the phone. "It is. Yes."

"Martin, when time is wasted, you have to work late. Is that right?"

"That's right," Martin said wearily. "Their incompetence steals my free time."

"Steals your free time," Eva mirrored, again.

Silence.

"What's stolen?" she asked, catching a glimpse of a hawk swoop low over the lake looking for prey.

"Time with my sons." His voice caught slightly as he continued. "They are my treasure."

"Go on," Eva prompted.

"See, every day I plan to be understanding with people at work, and then it all goes to pieces," Martin answered.

Eva nodded to herself with empathy. "You're irked about work and ticked off at the way you react. Is that it?"

"Yes."

"Alright, let's play a bit here. Is that okay?"

"I guess," he yielded.

"First, let's say you're not in control of everything at work."

"True," Martin said, his eyes connecting with the busy schedule he had printed earlier and placed next to the phone.

"However, you can control your actions," Eva said.

"Well, I suppose."

"You suppose?"

"I want to rise above, not be ... how do you say? Trivial," Martin responded.

"Understood." Eva said; she definitely tracked with this point. "Imagine how you want to be at work. You—not considering everyone else."

There was quiet as Martin considered the situation. "I don't have to approve of the way they act."

"Sounds interesting. Go on." Eva said, duly impressed at his insight.

"Their conduct needs to be their problem."

"Meaning?"

"Meaning, I won't judge based on how I think they should act. I might be more, ah, flexible," Martin said, and a certain peace settled on his voice.

"Such as?" Eva asked, wanting him to deepen this personal discovery.

"If I sense someone is not ready to discuss an issue, I'll suggest another time to meet."

"Good option. What else?"

"I'll reread my emails before I hit send. We've talked about that before." Martin erupted with ideas. The little stuff, yes, it is the big stuff.

"Being more flexible at work," Eva highlighted his point squeezed in earlier. "What will that do for you?"

"I don't have to be rigid," he replied shortly.

"So, is it loose?"

"Not loose. Free. I want to be free of the need to control things at the office."

"Martin, stand up and move around," Eva directed. "What do you notice?"

"I feel lighter. Like a buoy floating in the ocean."

"What would it be if you acted lighter, like the buoy?"

"I think I might like that. It might suit me," Martin answered, noticeably more relaxed in his tone.

"Would you commit to act this way, lighter, not just *think* about it?"

Martin was quiet, considering the request. "My sons, they live in each moment happily. I'll use them to remind me."

"Beautiful." A brief pause sealed the affirmation, and they moved to other matters in their coaching and ended the call.

Eva swiveled in her chair as she opened the file labeled Martin Hlinka. Not that long ago he, coaxed an oxen team to plow the land outside of Prague, Czech Republic. The Velvet Revolution had transported him from working the fields to exploring his own education. More than two hundred thousand students in Prague came out into the streets, unified in a demonstration that marked an end to their communist confinements. Hearing of this courage moved Martin so deeply he left everything he knew to find out more. His love and aptitude for symmetry led him to mathematics. "Would you consider how we *are* as people more vital than what we *do* as a profession?" she had asked him almost a year ago. After the words had escaped her lips, the irony stung. Did her brain actually form that question? Was it for Martin or for her?

Changing gears, Eva prepared for Lauren, her next client. The girl was making up excuses and letting goals slip away, pretending she didn't care. Eva knew otherwise. Eva was curious what would surface in the call with the guarded lady from Arizona.

2

"Stand still, please, child," Grace Cartwright said as she expertly measured the hem for the bride-to-be.

"It's just that, Miss Cartwright, I can't believe I'm getting married," Sandy said, woozy with excitement.

"Put your arms out to the side," Grace instructed, leaning back on her heels, pins in mouth. "Mmm, looks pretty. Here now, try on this cape. I want to see how the hood lays," Grace commented, more to herself than her young client. "This white faux fur turned out nice around the hood and sleeves."

"Ooh, it's soft and warm. I should be riding in a sleigh, you know, with snow falling down."

Grace lightly chuckled, as she shaped the hood around the girl's innocent face. That was exactly the image in her mind when she designed the gown. Grace had sketched the dress from a portrait of her grandmother's when she was a teen herself all those years ago. A lifetime. "Sandy, spin for me," Grace asked after a brief silence. "Gorgeous," she said, reshaping the hood around Sandy's face. "This piece will keep you warm for a January wedding."

"Thank you Miss Cartwright. I know you don't sew dresses much anymore and, well, I'm grateful."

Touched, Grace took the girl's hand. "It's your beauty, child, which makes it so lovely."

"Do you think Nick will like it?" Sandy asked shyly.

"Mmm, do you like it?"

"I adore it," Sandy said, swishing the gown from side to side. "It's dreamy."

"I think your beau will melt at the sight of you." Grace said, resting on the overstuffed ottoman. "Sandy, do you love this Nick?" She asked, helping the girl step out of yards of fabric.

"Oh, yes. We mix like chips and salsa. Have for three years."

"I see," Grace said as she bit back a smile. "Just no salsa while you wear this gown."

Sandy laughed. "Don't you know that's just what Nick would want to eat, too!

We're having a banquet with all sorts of food my Mom helped me pick out. No salsa."

"Good. You know, marriage starts for you and Nick after that fancy party is over and this gown is packed away. Do you hear me child?"

"Yeah, I get what you mean," Sandy said petting the fur trim.

Grace wasn't convinced.

"I have a cookbook," Sandy slowly added, seeming to grasp part of Grace's message. "And my Dad showed me how to get the hair out of a drain. Some normal life stuff."

"That's my girl," Grace said, hoping marriage would suit her as she reached up to balance the heavy gown and hanger on the edge of the crown molding.

"Wow," Sandy said, eyeing the built-in cabinets and crystal doorknobs, "It would be so romantic to live in a house like this. All these different rooms and storage. Places to hide and find treasures. We're never too old for that, are we?" Sliding on her coat, Sandy leaned into Grace for a hug. "Well, thanks. I'll see you soon."

Grace watched Sandy dance down the street. She was barely out of high school. It was hard not to wonder if Sandy shouldn't be out shopping with friends instead of planning a wedding. But who was she to judge?

In the kitchen, Grace placed the package of Russian teacakes into a bag and pulled on her warmest coat. Her niece, Lois, made the treats for the bake sale, and it was her job to make the delivery. As she turned to leave, Grace noticed Lois left a plate of teacakes by the toaster for them to share after dinner. Bright child.

Eva felt the four eyes bore into her from across the room. As soon as she removed her headset, Dash and Scout responded with growling and spinning around her legs. "Okay, you two. Walk time," Eva said, keeping her balance in the melee.

The dogs frolicked into the laundry room, to the basket full of dog leashes. Unable to control their speed on the wood floors, they slid, stopping with a metal thunk as their collars hit against the dryer. Eva stretched out her back as she watched. They were hopelessly devoted to her and she loved them for it.

"We have to drop off those brownies for the bake sale," Eva said aloud as she rummaged through the closet. She pulled out ski gloves, a face mask, and hat. Eva finished by pulling boots over flannel-lined jeans and slipped on the backpack, brownie tin in place.

"Okay, you dogs, sit," she said. Dash plopped a curly bottom to the ground. He lifted a paw with serious intent. Eva held the rough pad before putting on his leash.

"Scout, you too, honey." The female positioned herself with just enough obedience to avoid reprimand and slow enough to show Eva that she would do what she, Scout, wanted to do. After this exhibit of a minor power play, they left. A day without a walk resulted in irritable behavior from human and beast at the Eva Marie Karlsen household.

Moving in unison, the animals shared a long knotty branch Dash grabbed off the ground. The goldens jawed it like a horse bit in their mouths as they trekked toward the minor bustle of town. Eva read the city limit sign out loud, as she always did, "Bear, Wyoming, established 1879, eleven years before the state entered the Union." If it was the new frontier, Eva wondered, how did it become the Old West? She mused, curious if the real progress was in the suburban sprawl of the cities she knew so well, or if it was in the quiet hamlets like Bear that thrived across the nation.

Passing the school, Eva spotted snow forts and sculptures. Overnight, the cold air transformed the outer packed snow into icy armor. The playground equipment sported a layer of snow, ready for mitten-covered hands to brush it aside.

She spied a pile of snowballs hidden behind a tree, knowing that industrious snowball fighters arrived before the first bell. Smiling, she knew that minutes later students would gallop out to breathe life into the frozen yard.

Eva stopped at the Now and Then Dress Shop and lashed the dogs to a post. As she opened the door, she almost toppled a patron coming out at the same time. "Oh my," gasped the older woman, as the door just missed hitting her face.

"I'm sorry," said Eva. "Are you okay?"

"Yes, dear, I'm fine, just startled. There now, have a lovely morning," she said, and walked with innate poise down the street.

Eva watched the woman for a moment, struck by her elegance. And her clothes. The dark purple tailored coat and matching hat was nothing of the sort one normally saw in Bear. Classy, Eva thought as she entered the breezeway into the shop.

"… she's just an old maid, crazy, really. Do you remember the tales?" The two sixty-ish women stopped their conversation when Eva entered. Eva's eyes narrowed at them as she realized they were gossiping about the graceful woman who just left.

Clearing her throat, one of the women reached her hand out to Eva, attempting to change the negative aura.

"Here are some brownies for the fund-raiser," Eva said as she handed them over. She felt part of something bigger when she supported the community; however, the women's gossip spoiled her moment.

"Thank you, Ms. Karlsen, we appreciate your generosity." Somehow Eva was not sure she believed her.

"And take a look around if you like. One side of the store is a resale shop, and the other is new."

"Maybe next time," Eva said, motioning toward the dogs waiting outside.

Eva stepped out into the cold and collected the dogs, their tails wagging furiously at the sight of her. As she was crossing North Street, a green truck barreled around the corner, the speed just aggressive enough to make a statement as it smoothly held the sharp turn. Steve Mason offered her a crisp wave as he drove past. Eva stopped mid-stride. Her abrupt change in momentum confused the dogs, who received a solid jerk as they continued their gait while leashed to a stationary leader. Embarrassed by her reaction, Eva glanced up and down the street.

Her heart raced. Eva's rapid pulse wasn't from the 7,000-foot elevation. The elevation she had adapted to; her erratic reaction to Steve, she had not. His confident nature set off her male radar to caution. Beware of men! Do not be vulnerable. Do not engage in male relationships. Chiding herself, she couldn't explain her irrational trigger to the man who drove the truck. And such a man at that. She'd seen Steve in and around town; his stellar reputation among the locals preceded him. They never socialized but crossed paths regularly, his virile looks pulling her gaze every time.

Pushing back a haunted memory, Eva sucked in air to keep her equilibrium. Geeshe, move on. She lived in Bear, Wyoming, now, which was almost as far as one could get from Arlington, Virginia, and stay in the lower forty-eight.

"Eva, hello!" Jana's voice whistled as she bounded across the street. "I see those mutts pestered you enough to come out today. Brr, it's cold!" Jana Eberly's hair poked out from beneath her orange cap, eyes sparkling. "You're nuts, girl."

Disoriented at the disruption of crushing together her past and present lives, Eva drew a blank for conversation. On autopilot, she pulled down her face mask, turning it into a chunky neck scarf that outlined crimson cheeks.

"Nice mask," Jana teased, breaking ice that she didn't know existed.

Eva touched her face mask protectively, feigned contempt in response to the rib. Past relationship trauma swept away unseen. "Oh, Jana, what's in that bag?" The two hugged and immediately focused on the package. "You've been shopping at Bear Claw Quilts. I'm jealous."

"Wait till you see. I'm starting a new project for Christmas."

"Really? What is it?" Eva asked, resisting her urge to pull out the contents.

"A flannel quilt top using the new Thimbleberries Christmas fabric. I've never made a flannel quilt. It's time," Jana answered, clutching her treasure.

"Aren't you ambitious?" Eva said, admiring the fabrics nestled in the telltale pink wrapping. "Christmas is next month." Her insides warmed talking to Jana. She had suppressed the pleasures of female friendships for more than a decade, seeing them as frivolous. She hadn't had time for such things as she climbed the corporate ladder. Undeniably, she had been wrong.

"Yes, well, that's the plan."

"You just might inspire me to make a flannel quilt, Jana. We can commiserate!" Both women laughed, knowing that their sewing skills involved a lot of unsewing, the art form of taking out misplaced stitches.

"I'm in a tizzy to get back to the library. I took an early break to shop at Bear Claw. Sure hope Steve remembered to drop off my lunch. I'm starved. So, are we still on for Friday?"

Eva nodded a yes, and before she could speak, Jana kept on talking. "Okay, Eva, perfect. Got to go. Those dogs are being patient. Talk to you later!" She was off, leaving Eva to collect her thoughts in the wake of Jana's whirlwind.

Energized by Jana, Eva quickened her pace home. The minor interaction with Steve Mason slipped her mind until Jana brought him up. Jana roomed with Steve's cousin Heidi, and the three women were fast friends.

Oh, I see, Steve had to drop off food for Jana. He has such a curious schedule. I wish stopping to talk to me was part of it. Oh, Eva, stop!

Rubbing her temples, Eva conceded that her "simple" home business was complex. Acquiescing to the paperwork, she knew it was worth it. No one to tell her what she could or couldn't do, what she was or wasn't worth. Freedom.

Her eyes locked in on the client column of the spreadsheet. Coaching was a service that people didn't realize they wanted, or needed, until exposed to it, which had been exactly her experience. It was Eva's own life coach, Trina, who coaxed Eva to peek under the carefully tended layers of protection. Trina's relentless perseverance opened Eva up to find new enthusiasm for life. Ironically, Eva had hired a coach to help her career advancement, but instead coaching had led her to give up her corporate career entirely. Trina, not attached to the minutia of Eva's daily troubles, was expert at pulling Eva up to look at the bigger picture of her life. Eva was living a businesswoman persona that didn't match her dreams. But it was working on the outside, so Eva kept going with it. Trina tenderly and firmly exposed these conflicts when they came up. No wonder Eva had felt so unsettled. Living outside your values is uncomfortable business. The experience of coaching with Trina, so pragmatic and simple, changed Eva's outlook—and she wanted to help others experience this as well.

Eva considered her newest client, Debra Maretta. Debra had lost her zest for life, and a close friend was wise enough to notice. He gave Debra a year of coaching as a birthday present. Then there was Charlie Cunningham. Eva had met him at a local Chamber of Commerce meeting. Charlie, with his white hair and goatee, looked like a tall, thin Colonel Sanders. Having read her sticky nametag, Charlie had asked, holding firmly to her hand, "What, pray tell, does a life and professional coach do in Bear, Wyoming?" Charlie left their conversation high on the fact he was going to experience life coaching.

As dusk loomed, her stomach grumbled and she decided to stop working. As she shuffled papers into stacks on the uncluttered desktop—no complicated roll-top desk for her—there was satisfaction in knowing the decision to stop working was hers. She looked across her desk nestled between huge plate glass windows and solid walls filled with bookshelves. Contentment. This open–close combination gave her a balance of security and adventure.

After a dinner of angel hair pesto, salad with raspberry vinaigrette, and, of course, a couple nips of Dove's milk chocolate, Eva's mind wandered to the speech she would deliver at the local junior women's club. Was everything in the vicinity prefaced with Jackson Hole Area? Duly noted, the Hole, Yellowstone, and the Grand Tetons did rank high on the inspirational scale.

Heidi had pleaded, as much as Heidi Daniels could plead, when she asked Eva to speak about how she landed as a life coach in Bear. "Keep it real, darling," Heidi advised. Lacquered red nails flashed as she tapped Eva's shoulder, "You'll be great." Heidi was the queen of procuring favors, and Eva was not one to resist her charms. Eva hoped she could share her corporate life without publicly exposing her personal crash.

Curled up in a comfy chair, Eva warmed her hands on a mug of chamomile tea. Her move to Bear had liberated her, but she still feared a poison waiting to contaminate her new world. She knew holding onto bitterness would hold her back. Didn't she work this painful drill candidly with her clients? A way past the hurt in life was to accept it and *move on*.

Eva's thoughts drifted to the incident with the women at the resale shop. She'd known the clerks were gossiping about the older woman, but she chose to ignore it. During the near collision, Eva had connected with the woman. It was a split second yet it was real. There was something familiar to the message in her eyes.

After a long stretch of wrestling with her thoughts, Eva cached the ever-looming feeling of betrayal to outline her speech. She was, after all, a professional.

5

"Is this the right place?" he asked in a squeaky whisper.

"Yes, it's the right place." The response came with a slap on the head. "What, do you think I'm stupid?"

"It's dark," he said, rubbing his head.

"Exactly why we're here. Come on." The second voice was deeper, cocky.

"Are you sure? She's just an old lady."

"Exactly. No one will care," the teen said. "It'll be fun. Like carrying on a tradition." He smiled, the darkness gave him power.

"This house is pretty nice," the younger one uttered, his voice shaking.

"Are you in or out? I'll tell and win the bet if you bail."

"Fine," he said, acquiescing.

They fumbled at the back of the truck, pushing and arguing, when a rapid movement immobilized the instigator.

"Hey!" His arm was yanked behind his back. "Let go of me!"

"What seems to be your business?" The voice was calm, authoritative.

"Don't hurt me," said the one who was free, frozen with fear, arms in the air.

"Let me go!" The other's bravado leaked out as his arm grew numb.

"Shut up," the stranger said, void of emotion. He saw ten dozen eggs sitting on the gate of the pickup. "Who put you up to this?"

"Just us," said the leader with a muffled voice.

"Just you." He'd heard the talk about a bet. "I don't take to being lied to."

"Tell him the truth," said the younger one, his voice now an octave higher.

"That is the truth, nimrod. I made up the whole plan," he said, cockiness gone.

"What?" The younger kid almost wet himself.

"I thought it would be cool. You know, act on a feud. My mom and aunt always talk about how that old lady thinks she's so special. Well, she never had any proof."

"There's no bet?" his protégé said in disbelief.

"No. Let me go? We won't do it."

"Keep talking, punk." Sander knew the harm hadn't been done yet. He needed to uncover if there was anything more than stupidity. A link.

"The eggs, see, she used to talk about gold eggs and stuff. I thought it would be funny to egg her house. Get it?"

"Wait, you mean this is the lady who reads at the library? I heard her talk about those jewel eggs or something." The high voice changed to child-like anguish. "Ah, crap, we're in it deep with Judge Jerry for sure."

"Okay, that's enough. Come with me." Force wasn't needed when fear took hold. The would-be vandals marched in front of Sander the few blocks to the police station.

Sander leaned in the corner taking in the scene. Hair flopped around the teens' bowed heads as Judge Jerry spoke. *Lucky for them they didn't start throwing*, Sander thought to himself. One step onto the dark side was all it took to get brave—in a bad way. He would know.

After the kids were collected by apologizing parents, Sander looked at Judge Jerry. "So, are we done?" Sander was anxious and ready to leave. He had that feeling of being watched, and experience taught him to trust his intuition.

"Seems so. Not sure telling Grace and Lois Cartwright is the best option. Might scare them."

"It's your town, sir," he answered. Sander didn't know how these small towns handled intent to commit crime. Plus, he didn't want any attention. He'd play it light.

"It's a long, old story," the judge, who was also chief of police, said wearily.

"I don't need details. Just separating the boys from their dumb decisions," he said, almost to himself.

At this, Jerry examined Sander. Different. Hard to read. He'd heard about him and the girl living at the trailer park. Didn't seem like the trailer type.

"So, I'll be leaving," Sander said and walked out, glad the judge didn't ask him questions. If there was an undercurrent of resentment for two single women, what else lay hidden in this town? He just might be in the right place.

Eva's stomach fluttered as she stepped into the large hall. The Civic Center of Weber, Wyoming, neighbor to Bear, was buzzing. The name of the club was Jackson Hole Area Junior Women's Club, but any gender and age were permitted to attend. There weren't many single men able to stay away from the gathering of mostly available females.

Surveying the hall, Eva was impressed how the club transformed the room. The space was decked out in evergreen branches and all types of natural ornamentation, including pinecones and orange bittersweet berries. The pine smell was the epitome of Christmas, even though it was just the week before Thanksgiving.

Up on the stage, the speakers' podium, a glass of water, and a tiny silver lapel microphone were set and ready. Next to the podium was a table decorated with a basket woven in the shape of a cornucopia and overflowing with white pumpkins, gourds, pomegranates, and Indian corn. *Someone remembered to slip in a taste of Thanksgiving after all*, Eva mused, pleased that it coordinated with her turtleneck and autumn-motif scarf.

Heidi Daniels, club chairperson, stepped up to the podium, gavel in hand, and brought the meeting to order. It took three loud clacks and a few assisted whistles to silence the chatter and still the tangible, electric tension among the men and women.

"Hello and good evening," Heidi rang out in her polished presenter's voice. "For guests or those new to the Jackson Hole Area Junior Women's Club, welcome. My name is Heidi Daniels, and we're honored to have your attendance." After a short dissertation regarding next years' fund-raiser and upcoming charity events, Heidi cleared her voice.

"Tonight our guest speaker is Eva Karlsen. Eva lives in Bear and has been a resident of the Jackson Hole area for over a year. Maybe some of you can convince her to join our club in the networking session." Heidi raised one eyebrow toward Eva. There were cheers from the audience at the mention of networking and the challenge.

"Tonight Eva will give the first of a two-part lecture series, to conclude in

January. She's a certified professional life and executive coach, and she comes with twelve esteemed years in our own Corporate America. Please, all, let's give it up for Eva." Thundering applause erupted as Eva rose to make her way to the podium.

"Well, thank you, Heidi, and everyone. Heidi, are you sure you wouldn't like to tell my story for me? It might be *much* more interesting from your perspective." Eva winked at her friend, procuring laughs from the audience. "I'm humbled to tell you this tale of mine. It's my hope you'll find a thin parallel to something in your life." Eva took a breath and plunged ahead.

"Today I want to lay out experiences that formed my early career. Next month, I'll take you along on the wild ride I took to pursue my dream. It's true, I'm a professional coach. 'What is that?' you might say. Coaching can sound a little *out there* or California chic. A simple analogy is that life or executive coaching does for a person's whole life what a sports coach does for one's athletic prowess." Eva paused to let the comparison take hold. Speaking to crowds had once been her forte; she sank into that memory.

"First, my backstory. I was a driven youth. This stemmed from my first real job, detasseling hybrid corn. For those of you unfamiliar with the fine art of detasseling corn, you walk through rows of seed corn and pull out the yellow tassels coming out the top of the female corn. You do this so the nasty male corn doesn't pollinate them and mess up the whole crop." Eva fluttered her fingers to illustrate the word *mess*, to both recognition and bewilderment from the crowd.

"Well, here I am in a cornfield at 5:00 A.M., wearing a black Glad garbage bag in a weak attempt to keep off the early-morning dew. Bugs are crawling up and down my arms, across my neck, and into hidden places we won't mention. I can tell you, as a fifteen year old, I knew then I was going to go to college, earn a degree, and never again detassel corn.

"That first night at the dinner table I announced I wanted to quit. My dad, who worked the assembly line at the tractor plant, bribed me with a fried shrimp dinner at the local diner if I would stick it out for the six-week season. Much to my continued astonishment, his bribe worked.

"As a teen I knew I needed to get into a field of work that didn't involve bugs, lightning, sunburn, and mud. In my high school, I was one of two girls in advanced math. Yup, it was Lily Smith and me. Lily, of course, was the perfect, petite, blonde, *val-ed-ic-tor-ian*.

"It wasn't Lily that Mr. Cochran called on to do a calculus problem on the blackboard; it was me. I'd stand up there, humiliated and confused, unable to see the writing eight inches from my face because I was holding back tears. I think even my male classmates pitied me.

"What's the point? Let's review. If I quit detasseling corn on that first day, I'd miss my dad's fried shrimp bribe. Perseverance, even through unpleasantness, was positive.

"Well, I earned a degree in computer science, and it opened many doors. And I had to prove I could do it without tears in my eyes at the front of class." Eva softly cleared her throat. "The lesson? Think about the *why* behind your decisions so you are clear of your motives."

"You got that right!" sprang from a rambunctious young woman wearing a bright striped alpaca sweater and matching knit hat. Eva tipped her head toward the woman.

"All our choices add up to where we are *right now*. Those that we liked and that turned out well, and those that we didn't like and that didn't turn out so well.

"My friends were real impressed with me. Sorry thing." Eva slowed down to loosen the catch in her throat. "I was impressed with me. I defined myself by my job. I woke up one morning after earning a coveted promotion, and I realized it didn't matter. The promotion was something I thought would change my world. You know—my reputation, how people perceived me, my impact on others. Well, it *generously* gave me longer workdays, less time for friends, and no time for hobbies."

Eva paused for a drink of water, nodding her head as she set down the glass, careful not to spill it. "See, I started to realized that I was lopsided. Just working. Stressed out. Not enjoying anything. Lonely. Living the American corporate dream," she said sarcastically, throwing her hands into the air.

"One day a teammate was telling a hysterically funny story. I started laughing, you know, a big belly laugh. After the hilarity of the situation was over, I realized that I hadn't laughed in ages. My face hurt. My muscles weren't used to it. I was a mirthful mess." Eva scanned the audience. Her hands were clammy; she knew she had to get personal. "I realized in that second that I wasn't living even close to my personal values. I wasn't having any fun. Never was around friends. And I lived in a place void of eagles' nests. As you can see, there were some choices I needed to start making." Fervently Eva turned anxiety into zeal as she engaged the audience in details of her experiences with personal choice. She highlighted the importance of balancing the needs of other people, special relationships, and personal goals.

"In summary, your life is a culmination of choices. You make a choice. You take action. Both, of course, are necessary. Next time I'll tell you about how I took action to change the direction of my career—and my life—to end up with you all here in middle of these awesome mountains. Thank you." Eva inhaled as Heidi waltzed over, giving her a quick hug as they changed places.

"Thank you, Eva, for sharing your experiences and wisdom. We'll look forward to hearing the second half of your story in January. Everyone, please let me direct you to the refreshment tables, and let the networking begin." The group erupted in conversation as they migrated toward tables laden with delectable holiday morsels of mincemeat tarts, cut-out turkey sugar cookies, and frosted pumpkin cake.

The woman with the alpaca sweater made a beeline toward Eva, bounding with adrenaline. "Eva, I'm Marlo. Liked your talk," Marlo said, bobbing her curly head.

"Marlo, nice to meet you. I'm glad it's over and that food has taken the spotlight."

"I admire your message. If more people would talk about the choices we get to make in life and that we are free to change, the more honest we'd be." Marlo said, her eyes sparkling with a natural cheer.

"I agree," Eva said, grateful at least the young woman had listened.

"Without conscious choice I'd be in Wichita, Kansas, waiting tables. But here I am, soon to be waiting tables in Bear, Wyoming." Marlo laughed with a touch of melancholy, tugging at her hat and smashing wayward curls in the process. "Way sweeter."

Since Marlo was fussing with the hat, Eva skipped the waitress comment. "That's a great hat, Marlo. Where'd you get it?"

"This is my prize for achieving the summit at Machu Picchu," Marlo answered, moving her hand to touch the hat again. "Now that is some *serious* climbing."

"Impressive. That makes our Gros Ventres look like rolling meadows."

"Completely. I bought the hat on the way down to base camp as a reward. The women crafters were amazing. It was impossible to resist." Marlo tilted her head to the side and gave a shy smile. "Thanks for noticing."

Eva sensed there was a lot to this young woman, who looked all of twenty-four years old. "I'd love to hear about that trip, Marlo. What an adventure."

"It was dreamy. One of these days we should meet for coffee."

"Perfect. Let's do it. We can swap stories," Eva said.

"We transplants need to stick together," Marlo added mischievously.

"I agree. What brought you to Bear from Wichita?" Eva blurted, then hoped it wasn't too personal for Marlo. She realized it probably wasn't, based on Marlo's comments during the speech

Looking pensive, Marlo furrowed her brows and made solid eye contact with Eva. "Bad love," she said. Despite the answer, Marlo didn't appear forlorn or regretful, just factual.

"Ah, bad love. Hmm, clearly another story."

"Yup, you got it. Bad love doesn't have to hold you down." Marlo winked with perception that belied her years. "We best meet for coffee," she said, her large brown eyes yearning for friendship.

Momentarily caught by the woman's astuteness, Eva held out her hand. "It's a deal. I'm free on Fridays. Here, take my card and call me." She watched Marlo melt into the noisy fray.

Eva turned, bumping straight into Jana, who was talking to Steve Mason. She focused on her girlfriend for composure. "Hey, Jana. How goes it?"

"Eva! Doing good! You were awesome up there tonight. This is so much fun. I just love these events around the holidays. Did you try the mincemeat? Yum. You must have some, and the shortbreads. Someone even took the time to cut them in the shape of those little Scottie dogs, you know?" Merriment flowed out of Jana's pores. Eva's head spun, keeping pace with Jana's effervescence.

"Thanks. I'm about to make my way for the sweets. I can't break their pull," Eva said, knowing she needed to address Steve. Turning slightly, she strained for fluid speech she wasn't sure she could pull off. "Hi, Steve. Good to see you."

"Ms. Karlsen." Steve offered a roguish grin, raising his eyebrows in appreciation. "You did yourself proud. It's hard to keep this crowd interested when dessert and—well, shall I say—potential liaisons are waiting." His dark hair was a perfect complement to his forest green plaid-flannel shirt. Eva forced her eyes not to stray down to admire his jeans and boots to relish the complete package.

"This group is driven on food and hormones!" piped in Jana, waving to an acquaintance across the room. "Junior Women's Club, my eye—well, that's why we like it!" There was a hint of moving toward an awkward moment when Jana unknowingly came to the rescue again. "So, Eva, what are you doing for Thanksgiving?"

Eva stared at Jana, forcing her brain to translate the question. The distraction of Steve was more than a little disconcerting, and his blue eyes bored into her at Jana's question. "I guess I hadn't thought about Thanksgiving. Right now, I'm probably sharing some turkey with Dash and Scout. No formal plans."

"No plans? Beautiful. It's a date then. Come over to our house. So far I have a handful of us strays coming together. No holiday can pass without celebration."

Before Eva could get a word in, she looked at Jana, then Steve, who put up both his hands in a sign of resignation that Jana ran this one. "Jana, do you want all the trouble?" Eva asked, a bit curious about just who were "all of us strays."

"No trouble at all. It'll be fun. What do you like to cook for Thanksgiving?"

"Mmm, I'm flexible. What don't you like to prepare?"

"Well, how about hors d'ouevres? Anything is fine. This crowd isn't allergic to nuts or wheat, there are no vegans, and we're not counting carbs. Can you work with that?"

"That I like," replied Eva. "Real eaters. I'll come up with something ... wouldn't want to outshine the chef." She jabbed her elbow gently into Jana's side, teasing her, a gifted chef. "How many people?"

"Let's see, there'll be you, me, Steve, Heidi, Gianni, Dale, Marlo, and her guest." Jana counted out on her fingers as she spoke, lifting her head to Eva. "Eight."

"That's manageable. I appreciate the invite." As she sensed a possible strain with Steve, Eva made her move. "Well, I best do some networking so I don't seem too much like a newbie. Later." Eva hugged Jana, tilted her head to Steve, and entered the crowd. Her head was whirling. An invite to Thanksgiving dinner with

Jana and a group of new friends, including the alluring Steve Mason.

The meeting adjourned, and the parking lot began to empty, Parked near the back corner of the lot, a truck like any other in the area started its engine. It went unnoticed that the driver had not joined the meeting. It was just another pickup, and the unlit parking lot was an added bonus. The figure inside was dressed in dark clothes and wore a baseball cap void of any logo. The handful of vehicles had all been searched and all were dead ends. Nothing. Just mountain junk like gravel, blankets, shovels, and granola bars. No clues on which vehicle might be owned by the professional. But at least these dopes left everything unlocked, which made things easier.

Warm enough to roll, the truck crept out of the lot unnoticed in the midst of the departing revelers. Everyone looked alike in their winter gear. It was impossible to tell them apart. Who would've thought it would be hard to find, let alone follow, a known lead in no-place-ville Wyoming.

7

Steve noticed the Shop-N-Save lot had thinned since the morning. He slipped out of his swamp-green SUV, affectionately known as the Green Hornet. Sauntering into the grocery store, he wondered what the crowds must be like in the cities with the looming Thanksgiving holiday.

"Good afternoon, Lois," Steve said, tilting his head toward the red-haired, freckled woman as he selected a shopping cart. "Townies have you ringing up food like nuts, eh?" He noticed a slight red cover emerge on Lois's cheeks and was touched by her innocence.

"You got that right, Steve," Lois offered softly. "Where are you headed for Thanksgiving? I hear your folks are still away." The townies, which included both Lois and Steve, were familiar with the senior Masons and their escapades speaking at universities around the globe. Long-time Bear residents made it their business to ensure that one of their favorite sons, Steve, was well cared for despite age and self-sufficiency. Lois Cartwright's family was no exception.

"Well, this year it's dinner with a group of displaced singles. Heidi and Jana invited an entourage, assigning us specific dishes." Blue eyes sparkling, Steve gave Lois a lopsided grin. "It should be an interesting Thanksgiving." Including the appearance of the lovely Eva Karlsen, he thought, his mind momentarily wandering.

"What dish did they muster up for you?" Lois asked, knowing his sophisticated yet fun-loving cousin well.

"For me it's, of all things, shrimp cocktail. Only the best will do for our fair Heidi." Steve crossed his left arm behind him and gave her a long slow bow as he swept his right arm out across his body, mimicking approval needed for the Heidi they both loved.

"Ah. Special recipe?"

"Of course. And that's the reason I'm here," Steve said and tossed Lois a salute. "Catch you later." Rounding the corner toward the fresh produce, Steve's cart nearly clipped a woman who was pondering the green beans. His memory flashed. "Hey, Marlo, remember me? Steve Mason?"

"Hi there, Steve, sure," Marlo said.

"What's up?" Interesting, Steve thought, he'd never seen Marlo around town before, now twice in one week.

"I'm gathering ingredients for our feast."

"Ah, yes, me, too. What's your task?"

"To bring that obnoxious green bean casserole with the crunchy onions on top," she said, scrunching her nose.

Steve chuckled. "Heidi wouldn't let a holiday meal pass without the perfect combination of traditional dishes and nouveau cuisine." Nodding toward the seafood counter, he added, "I'm off for shrimp intended to be spiced up by a secret recipe. I suppose she assigned me shrimp because she associates it with trout fishing."

"Yum, I love trout. Best fish ever."

"Absolutely. Cold streams do the trick. I just lure them in."

"I'd like to see you and Gianni whip us up a meal suitable for *Bon Appetite*." Marlo paused, adjusted her knit hat, and scrutinized her surroundings. "Fine sir, duty calls. I look forward to the big event." And off she went.

Gianni? Steve had only heard of Gianni from Jana. He was the new guy opening that Italian place. How does Marlo know Gianni? Raising his eyebrows, Steve anticipated this to be a Thanksgiving to remember. God knows, he needed to bank some new memories. Regrounding. It was an odd thing for him. His parents were grounded, but never in the same place. For him, it was different. He wanted to be grounded in one place, with people he knew, in Bear.

Startled out of his thoughts by the *Singing in the Rain* music warning attached to the new vegetable misters, Steve quickly gathered sweet onions, red bell peppers, tomatoes, and cilantro, and he picked up thirty-six ounces of shrimp at the fish counter. Taking advantage of being in the Shop-N-Save, he tossed in his bachelor cooking essentials—bacon, eggs, flour, milk, butter, syrup, potatoes— and headed for the checkout.

Walking right up to Lois's register, he unloaded his cart on the conveyor. "Lois, how's Grace? I haven't seen her out on the porch with this weather."

Glancing up at Steve as she scanned the items, Lois's sigh was barely audible, holding a distant yet content tone. "Auntie Grace is Auntie Grace, Steve." Lois pronounced the word "auntie" as it was intended, forming the "awe-nt" sound typical of British pronunciation, not the American prounciation, "ant." "She's healthy and her mind sound. We plan to spend Thanksgiving together, cooking a turkey breast with a new recipe she found in the *Bearly News*."

Steve's mind flew to the world of Grace—certainly some secrets they would all like to solve. Like many tales, there must be an element of truth and an element of fantasy to the life story of Grace Johnson Cartwright. He'd sure like to solve the mystery and settle the score with those locals who think Grace invented her own past. Equally as frustrating were the negative vibes that affected Lois, the salt of the earth. "Give her my love, Lois. And back at you, too." Steve left the store in a swirl of memories.

Watching Steve drive away, the driver of the dark pickup truck flicked a toothpick onto the gravel. Earlier, the clandestine figure had purchased dry goods without conversation, a ball cap pulled low over forehead and eyes. Empty candy wrappers and soda cans were strewn inside the rusted vehicle, the processed snacks a far cry from Michelin-star-graded restaurant fare.

This bloody town was a bad dream. No creature comforts. The only warmth came from the burning cigarette despite the running engine. Fricking heater was broken. There were too many people involved. Couldn't these do-gooders keep to themselves? Or stay home? At least mind their own business.

"Sarah, I'm so proud of you," Eva said, having sensed the powerful conviction from her coachee. "Have a happy Thanksgiving." Placing the phone in the cradle, Eva dabbed a tear of happiness. Sarah's success in her new consulting business was beyond her wildest dreams. Last week's coaching homework to contact ten Fortune 500 marketing executives secured two meetings. The courage came when Eva asked Sarah her favorite coaching question, What if you made it up? Eva loved the way this simple question made her clients relax. It always opened up room for actions and ideas that never seem to come up if they had to be "right" or "real." Making things up was easy, and the made-up stuff usually worked into real change for her clients.

Twelve months after earning her degrees, Sarah had married her boss and found herself trapped in a life of lies and violence. On the late morning of a purported sick day, sporting a ponytail and large Jackie Onassis sunglasses, Sarah visited the local police station under the guise of inquiring for "a friend in domestic trouble." The balding policeman at the station told her if the friend's husband was arrested, yes, he could make bond and come right back to harm the friend, if he was so inclined, yes, restraining order or not. No, the police didn't guard homes after an initial report for alleged domestic abuse.

A beleaguered Sarah, dignity not completely stolen, escaped to the women's shelter that day. After pulling herself back together, she created a new life for the second time in two years. She was a poster woman for resolve and courage.

Eva's coaching clients had so much chutzpah and strength, she wasn't sure she was a qualified guide. Sure, she had the credentials, but they had the wherewithal to move on with their lives. Sarah took a negative hand and turned it into a positive; not harboring hate. "Oh, God, why can't I do that?" Eva's voice trembled, barely escaping her lips. *I'm a wimp. Fudge. If my clients knew they'd all fire me.*

Glancing out the kitchen window, she read the thermometer registering in at two degrees Fahrenheit. Wyoming winter had taken hold. Meandering to her office, she watched Scout and Dash, who were the vision of bliss, lying like mirror images in the sun, backs touching, with the gorgeous mountain vista behind them. Eva squinted to spy a moose across the lake but couldn't readily spot one of the bulky creatures. Duty called.

Eva was barely situated at her desk with headset in place when the phone rang. "Hello, this is Eva," she answered, knowing it would be Debra, the homemaker from San Francisco. Last week Eva proposed homework that Debra accepted with mild reservation.

"Eva, good morning. This is Debra."

"Debra, good to hear you. What's on your mind today?" she asked with apprehension, knowing Debra might have been frustrated at the messy ending to their last call. Even being her own boss, Eva still needed approval.

"Eva, I did it! I wrote out the two lists and it was so great. My list of what to remove from my life was easy to write. My list of what to add to my life was equally exciting. Oh, thank you."

Phew. "You sound energized. Tell me more." Eva held her curiosity at bay and didn't ask Debra to read the lists. Eva's role was to nudge Debra into the life of her dreams, not check the details of her homework.

"I feel liberated. I'm taking steps good for me and my family."

"What are the steps like?"

"They're so simple. And good, not bad." Debra, like many of the women that Eva coached, subconsciously reverted to view herself as good or bad, back to the days of her youth when she was a good girl, or not so.

Eva skipped the bad route. "So, Debra, what's good about them?

"They make me feel like a real person, like a woman. They give me back 'me.' This process made me realize that I'm living an almost non-life, going through the motions. I love nurturing my family, but I somehow evaporated in the process. These steps are going to change that." Debra said, confident, happy.

"What actions do you have in mind?" Eva synchronized with Debra's energy to keep it moving forward. Debra gave Eva short descriptions of new tough love family rules. After a smidgen of white space, Eva spoke her mind. "Debra, these rules for home are great. Something tells me you want more than some rules. Is that true?"

After a pregnant pause, Debra quietly inhaled. "Yes, I suppose it is."

"Let's suppose you tell me."

"Eva, I'm considering a complete makeover. Me. New makeup, new hair, and a trainer." Taking a deep breath she continued, "I also researched personal shoppers from Nordstrom who will come to my house to go through my clothes. Talk about lifestyle, budget, etcetera. Then we go shopping together. Eva, now that I voiced it, I'm going to do it."

"That's a yeah! Debra, you're definitely a woman to be reckoned with."

"That's me. Changing from the ugly duckling into the swan." Debra answered, holding her elbows, rocking. "I'm watching the sailboats on the San Francisco Bay. Life is floating all over the place."

"Now that you're flying, what else is there for you?" Having no concept of what Debra looked like, Eva stayed away from any physical comment.

A gulp came from the other side of the phone. "Well, I'm going to pop the question regarding my dream vacation. The dream is for my childhood friend Sue and me to take a trip with our husbands. When we were young, while swinging at the park, we would imagine our future husbands and the marvelous places we'd visit. Our best dream was to go to Paris. I'm so excited I can hardly stand it. My husband, Roy, is a great guy and I can tell the more I am myself, the more he loves me."

"And for good reason." Eva said, loving her client.

"Thanks."

"Paris. What do you need to keep the momentum?" Eva's experience in project management prior to training as a professional coach would've led her to rattle off the five things Debra should do, by when, and how. This is Debra's life. Debra needs to determine the steps.

"Let's see, I'll commit to hair, trainer, and personal shopper. Gosh, I'm a whiz at family appointments. I should be able to schedule mine. I'll also plan a dinner with Sue, her husband, and Roy. We'll discuss Paris. How'd that be?"

"Debra, you're remarkable. Congratulations."

"Merci, Eva. Must brush up on my French for Paris, oui? There is something to this odd thing of coaching, isn't there?"

"I'll talk to you next week, Debra. Until then, au revoir." Disconnecting the phone and removing her headset, Eva's skin prickled, that sense of something bigger busting into her reality.

Strutting at the water's edge, the bull moose left rings of icy water rippling in his wake across the lake. On one side of the bulky animal was a yearling male and on the other the doe. Oblivious to the appearance of her beloved moose, Eva was propped on her kitchen stool, feet aflutter as she intently flipped through the cookbooks stacked on the island. *Decisions, decisions.* Satisfied, Eva patted the stack of books, convinced that old standbys were best for Thanksgiving.

Dash, watching her every move through close-set eyes, instantaneously materialized for a head pat. He used this strategy to jockey for undivided attention when Scout was sleeping around the corner. Eva automatically stroked the soft, silky pet. Dash plunked a giant paw on her knee in an attempt to garner additional accolades. It worked. His fur was so luxurious it was only natural to fuss over the animal.

"Okay, Dashy Baby, we're making hot artichoke dip using the real stuff. Mayonnaise—whole fattening, and flavorful—real grated parmesan cheese, and minced artichoke hearts, served up with gourmet crackers." She paused, scratching ears to his doggy delight. Then, continuing aloud, Eva said, "As for the second one, it's spinach dip with chestnuts, sour cream, and cream cheese. Hmm, I'll buy sourdough bread in a two-pound round at the bakery and make it look special. Done. Simple, good, and don't need a cookbook. So, is that enough information for you, my darling Dash?"

Observing the dog–master adoration between Eva and Dash, Scout unwound her sturdy body, stretched her back up like a cat, and came over to Eva. Ignoring Dash completely, Scout slid in close and put up two paws on the front of Eva's legs dangling from the kitchen stool. "Okay you two, I love you both." Sliding off the stool, Eva knelt on the floor and put one arm around the neck of each dog. "You two are such fur balls." Hugging the animals, they happily sat and let Eva indulge in their soft fur and devotion.

Eva doted on them, savoring their warmth. When cuddling them, her troubles faded. Dogs were Eva's "enjoy life" trigger. It started when she was training to be a certified coach. A colleague, Dorothy, hit a nerve for Eva during a practice session. Dorothy noticed that Eva rarely took time for happiness. Her coaching homework one week was to notice when a grim attitude took over. Then, Eva could choose to accept and keep the negative vibe, or she could change it. Dorothy forced Eva to consider her emotions as she went through her day. All of this living in the moment was foreign to Eva. For a decade, Eva had plodded through life as one big grind, one onus after another.

Dorothy relentlessly grilled Eva on ways to manage this shift from acceptance to choice. "You must have a structure, Eva," Dorothy insisted. "A fun one." To bring it to a playful level was an exotic challenge for Eva.

"Well, I see my dog Zip lying here on his side like a big old log. What about using Zip? He's the role model for living in the moment. I can pet him any time and see what rubs off on me." Admiring Eva's response, Dorothy loved the idea. From that time forward Dorothy used the phrase "Eva, you dog, you," whenever she noticed Eva enjoying life and living in the moment.

Extracting herself from memories and the emersion in her rather large puppies, trigger intact, Eva considered Thanksgiving. Her vision was to look stunning, but not overstated. She was after the ambiance of a French woman, put together with style and polish, not fuss or flash. Truth be told, Eva confessed inwardly, she wanted to look sexy and catch the attention of a particular Steve Mason. How long had it been since she wanted to fix herself up to snare male attention? A long, bitter time.

Maybe she should drop the whole idea of romance; she wasn't good at it. It'll gain her nothing but angst. Maybe this was an excuse. What benefits did her clients reap when harboring grudges? None, they would say, when asked. Who else cared about their self-pity? No one, they would say. In other words, she would suggest, they held themselves prisoner from living their best life? Yes, maybe, they would say. Is that what you want? No, they would say. *Is this what I'm doing?* Eva asked herself, *Yup, Eva, get a grip.*

Distraught with the brief epiphany of her reality, Eva had an image of Debra. Debra recreated herself in a specific and public manner. "Mmm," Eva murmured, "I should call Debra in San Francisco for some recommendations." If her clients knew that she got as much or more value out of the coaching sessions than they did, they just might charge her.

Debra would consult her Nordstrom's shopper for her wardrobe makeover, but Nordstrom's, that remarkable retailer, wasn't yet in the enclave of Bear—and unfortunately likely never would be. "What if I made it up?" Eva said aloud. Smirking in spite of herself, Eva stepped into her closet and took on a persona of a French woman, spontaneous and refreshing. Her inspiration begot a casual-chic look, with a touch of allure á la Français.

"Heidi, come on down! See all this great food," Jana roared up the stairs, flushed from her jaunt to her favorite gourmet grocer in Weber. "We have it all. Turkey, day-old bread for cornbread stuffing, yams, pumpkin pie, wine, fresh cranberries. Oh, did I say a big, twenty-two pound, fresh—*not* frozen— turkey?"

Gliding into the room, Heidi skimmed the grocery bags from Jana and effortlessly had everything in their proper places on the counters, in the ample pantry, and in the fridge.

Drats, the thrill of the feast waned as Jana watched her skeleton-thin roommate glide around the kitchen. Cooking as a hobby had a rather, er, "heavy" downside. While she knew how good food tasted if you used butter, sautéed in oils, and allowed only the freshest of real cream in special soups, Jana ached for the svelte shape of Heidi. She wasn't jealous—no, rather, envious of the ease that Heidi's zest for life didn't register on the bathroom scale. Jana decided to lift her own spirits away from her struggle with her weight. Cooking for friends was her passion, even if it came with a few extra pounds.

"Heidi, we have all necessary ingredients for a proper holiday. What do you think?" Jana said.

"I think we've got it, lass," Heidi boomed in a rough Scottish brogue.

"Yes, ma'am, I think we do," Jana said without the brogue, rubbing her hands together in excitement. Accustomed to Heidi's erratic voice-overs, Jana was impressed how the sophisticated Heidi pulled it off.

"So, Ms. Chef, what's next?" Heidi asked, emerald eyes ablaze. "Your wish is my command."

"We need to turn this," Jana said, motioning to the array of products strewn and stored around the kitchen, "into a delectable, unforgettable meal."

"Let's do our pilgrim ancestors proud," Heidi said, weaving history into the conversation whenever possible.

"Take a look at this." Before shopping, Jana had created a chart that outlined the entire meal, including the times needed for cooking and appropriate oven temperatures. "Don't say I didn't learn administration in culinary school. They harped to us about planning meals like nobody's business." Eyebrows raised, Jana passed Heidi the coveted plan with a grave stare. "Thanksgiving included."

"Marvelous, darling. Great decision to have everyone over early. Like Mom always said, preparing with a houseful is the most fun of all," Heidi said, eyes brimming with tears.

"Indeed, indeed," Jana answered, as she walked to hug Heidi. Jana knew the independent Heidi had an empty longing for her mother. *The nut doesn't fall far from the tree*, Jana thought, contemplating the holiday. Yes, Heidi's mother would be proud and would gush over their Victorian bursting with aroma.

The grand home was a mainstay in Bear. Built by the first mayor at the turn of the nineteenth century, Heidi had purchased it when she settled from her travels east and abroad. Lucrative business deals secured the capital for the home known in town as the Painted Lady. Its intricate exterior paint was in hues of blue and cream. A beautiful lady indeed.

When Jana moved to Bear six months later, she rapped on the front door and pointed to the "Room for Rent" sign in the window. Not missing a beat, she pointed at herself and gave an exaggerated praying gesture, all in the seconds before Heidi opened the door. Heidi was hooked, and they'd been roommates ever since.

10

Blustery weather aside, beads of sweat peppered Gianni's brow as he took the lasagna out of the oven. The Italian sausage, basil, mozzarella and parmesan cheeses, and freshly homemade Roma tomato sauce were bubbling in a mouth-watering aroma of flavors. *Why am I nervous? This lasagna is perfect. The recipe only gets better with age, Grand Mama assured me of that. All that's left is for it to sit while I shower, then off to Heidi and Jana's.*

As he dried off, Gianni Giabaldi filled the space in the small bathroom, his burly muscles courtesy of pruning the olive groves. Before immigrating to America from Sicily on the brink of adulthood, he stood a head taller than the other boys in his village. Local soccer coaches jockeyed for Gianni, but his interest lay in pursuing the edible arts. Sports were fun, and yes, he was strong from the chores of life. But it was the fusion of ingredients that hooked him, and the lure of the tales told by grandparents and uncles around old stone ovens.

He remembered the thrill of hearing the sagas in the kitchen told by generations of Giabaldis. If made into scripts, the stories would sweep American prime-time television with their tragedy and humor. It was the creativity and family traditions that enticed Gianni into the kitchen with savory results. He was possessed. That obsession brought him to this place, the town of Bear.

Then why was he uneasy? Gianni swiped the mirror with a towel and stared at himself through the fog. The reason for his mood struck him between the eyes. His family wasn't here. There was no one to tell him to add more garlic or red pepper to a recipe. He was nervous. And worried.

That's it—this lasagna is my job interview. What if no one likes it? These new friends of mine, their contacts and families combined, they know everyone in town. Dio. I'm serving them my best dish as a sideline to their traditional Thanksgiving dinner. Oh Momma-Mia, please help me.

Unaware, Gianni crossed himself and roughly dried his dark curls with a white towel.

Dale Sawyer exhaled, holding the picture to his chest. A smart-looking couple. A beautiful wedding. Three loving years. Two relocations. One quilt shop. No children. A funeral. Three short years ago? How could that be? Three years was noteworthy. One thousand and ninety-five days. Beth and Dale were married for three years, and now she had been gone as long. Loving, spunky Beth. Her disease was always lurking. Unpredictable.

Beth, at least you didn't suffer in spite of the tragedy.

His wife died two days after slipping into a type 1 diabetic coma. The disease took her in darkness, at night. Life must go on. Isn't that what everyone says? He saw this in the sympathetic eyes of his friends.

Until now I was comfortable to wallow in memories. Lately, dear Beth, my grief has subsided. I'll cherish you always, but life runs through my veins. So my life must continue. This is what she would have wanted, if she had a chance to tell him. There seemed to be no better time to start living than Thanksgiving, the herald day of the holiday season.

Dale was by trade a construction designer. He and Beth had moved to Bear five years earlier. His young wife loved the mountains and dreamed of living where she could physically see them "live," not just in pictures. When Dale had an offer to work on resorts in the Jackson Hole area, they accepted and tangoed around the kitchen in celebration. Beth had been a textile artist. The Bear Claw Quilt Shop was all Beth. Her business acumen, combined with love of fabrics and art quilting, was a reckoning force. One night at dinner, nervous but smiling, she presented him with a business plan that wouldn't conflict with their relationship. Her smile sealed the deal. Such was their short history.

Dale's friend Heidi Daniels bribed him into accepting the Thanksgiving invitation by saying he only need bring himself and a festive beverage to share. He had neither another invitation nor an excuse not to attend. The gathering had the formula to be most entertaining, and this wasn't lost on Dale. Steve Mason would also be there. Steve had been a true friend to Dale, pestering him with social invitations, offering quiet companionship, and never being pushy to rush Dale's grieving process the last three years.

"Time to go," Dale said quietly into the silent living room, and he set down the photograph. He gently lifted the box filled with an assortment of wine and settled it on his hip, swooping up the keys to his truck.

Marlo and Sander sat in the aged Ford Explorer. They weren't arguing exactly, just seeing the world though different lenses. "Let's do this, Marlo," Sander said flatly, with mild detachment, his mind elsewhere.

Exasperated, Marlo turned to Sander sympathetically. "It will be fun. There's no playing charades, no interviews going on here. We don't want to spend Thanksgiving in the trailer, and they're excited to have a house full of guests. Come on, Sander, smile?"

Her pleading voice was convincing.

"If we go home," she signaled with her head to the pan in her lap, "this is all we have to eat."

"Since you put it that way," Sander said, lightening up, catching himself in his own foul mood.

"Besides, this will give you a chance to meet Gianni. I'm going to start working for him next week. Admit it, Sander, that double entendre of the name The Sicilian Ball is pretty good." One of Sander's diverse hobbies was world geography. Sicily, an Italian domiciled island, sat directly in the Mediterranean west of southern Italy. Italy, shaped like a boot, looks ready to kick Sicily, thus the play on words for the name of the restaurant. Marlo's large brown eyes bored into Sander. Producing a broad and sincere smile, Marlo cocked her head in such a fashion of complete vulnerability that Sander visibly let down his guard and mentally connected with her. Sander slowly shook his head and laughed to himself. *This girl knows me pretty well.*

"Fine. But only because you continue to wear that ridiculous hat and because I want to see you actually eat that stuff." He tweaked her nose as Marlo let out a yelp of pleasure, bounding out of the vehicle carrying her eleven-by-thirteen inch dish of green bean casserole with crunchy onions on top.

The doorbell rang and Jana raced to get it. "Eva, we were wondering about you— are you okay? It's not like you to be late. Are the dogs sick?" Eva looked incredulously at Jana. Her firing off of questions never ceased to impress.

"Happy Thanksgiving to you, too, Jana." Eva responded.

"Well, you know, just want to make sure everyone is alright and gets here safe and sound. Then we can start the party. Where have you been? Did that old truck break down? You should get something manufactured within the last five decades, you know," Jana said, never seeming to take a breath.

Eva bowed her head in mock despair. "Scout pulled a power struggle and wouldn't come in. So we played a sitcom routine around the porch until she was ready. Incorrigible canine. The International is running fine, thank you anyway. Sorry I'm late, since I have the appetizers." She raised two baskets, one in each arm, and handed them to Jana. Sliding out of her coat, Eva was stunning in a V-neck silk sweater that matched her amber eyes. It draped elegantly over her slim waistline and was a rich contrast to the black wool crepe slacks. From her ears dangled chandelier earrings with beads of gold and rust, the perfect accessory for an autumn affair. Magnifiqué.

Freeing Eva of the baskets, Jana continued, "I forgive you. Come on in, and I'll make introductions." Eva stamped the loose snow off her black ankle boots and followed Jana.

11

The stately home glowed with nostalgia. Fancy boughs had been made with combinations of Fraser firs, white pine, and balsam, berries and all. The greens garnished the banisters and entranceways leading into the living and dining rooms, a warm complement to the ten-foot ceiling embellished with white painted molding. A beautiful wreath hung above the fireplace complete with red bow, and a wooden crèche, animals and all, was arranged on the hearth.

Bowls of gold, silver, and red glass ornaments adorned the fireplace mantle and side tables, a sharp contrast to some rather gauche Santa Clauses and reindeers strategically placed to add whimsy to the room. When asked about a Christmas tree, the Heidi and Jana in unison shook their heads and stated, "Not until after Thanksgiving."

In the living room, Steve and Dale knelt in front of the ornate fireplace. They were in a quiet conversation as they worked to ignite the perfect fire. Having moved the camels, cows, and sheep from the crèche over to the floor so they could manipulate the fire, they conspired to tell their meticulous hostesses, if asked, that the animals needed more space to graze. Marlo and Sander organized the beverage bottles from shortest to tallest despite bottle contents. They hadn't vocalized the method for arrangement, it just materialized between them.

Having heard the unmistakable whoosh of an open front door, Heidi rushed from the kitchen to give Eva a welcoming hug. "Darling, so glad you could find it in your heart to come," this time using the most uppity, high-class accent she could rally with a serious demeanor.

"Yes, Ms. Daniels, it was hard to fit in with *my* social calendar," Eva said, exaggerating for effect. "This week has been a dull nightmare."

"Dull—Thanksgiving?" Heidi held Eva at arm's length, black hair shining under the hall light.

"My coaching clients cancelled most of this week. All this spare time is exhausting. I alphabetized cookbooks and spices, which took up half a day," Eva rambled on, catching herself as she realized how Jana was rubbing off on her. Sighing, she added, "I'm overwhelmed with my nonproductive funk."

Heidi pursed her lips and guided Eva toward the fray. As the friends entered the party, Eva acknowledged the group with a general hello and royal wave. For a two-second count, Steve's words caught in his throat with her entrance. He noticed Eva nervously scratch the small space behind her ear as she fluffed her hair and gently flexed and released her shoulders. Mesmerized, Steve took in her every mannerism. She was complex, a mixture of impetuous actions. Brave and demure. Modest and confident.

"Everyone, this is Eva. Eva, this is everyone." Jana chimed in, always the social butterfly, breaking the spell Eva had unwittingly cast on Steve. After a few guffaws targeted at the general introduction, Jana properly introduced Eva. She then proceeded to set up Eva's dips next to the shrimp and cocktail sauce on the ottoman. Jana smiled contentedly. Ambiance was the crown to any meal, imperative at Thanksgiving.

The small crowd gathered in the living room and sat among the two couches, chairs, and floor. In the corner, a vintage reading couch was snuggled against the wall and fireplace, a natural look for the Victorian home. Marlo and Sander made that seat their own. The crackle of the fire, the group of people, and the smells from the kitchen made the scene like a modern-day Norman Rockwell painting.

"A unique holiday, eh?" Heidi said as she nudged herself onto the end of the percale flowered couch occupied by Dale, Steve, and Jana. "You know, none of us are family—well, except for Steve and I being cousins and all."

"Maybe that's why we're getting along," Dale said glibly, surprising himself by the ease with which he contributed some humor.

"Yeah, friends like each other more than family because we don't know each other so well," Marlo added.

Jana piped in, "Thanks for the lead in, Marlo. To get things going so we don't talk about what we do for a living all day, I planned a little game."

"Oh, Jana, this is supposed to be a holiday!" Eva objected.

The ensuing groans only egged her on. "Here's the deal. First, it's not charades."

Sander and Marlo turned to each other. Sander winked, remembering her earlier charade comment. Unaware of the interchange, Jana continued.

"You all need to keep your answers to yourself. Don't talk, but consider three facts about yourself. The clincher is, only two are true. So you come up with two true facts about yourself and one lie, and we all have to guess which one is the lie." She smiled, receiving blank stares from her seven friends.

"So you want us to lie?" Gianni asked.

"Believe me, it ends up the truth is more interesting." Jana pleaded convincingly.

"I'll speak the truth, the whole truth, and nothing but the truth!" Heidi added with the cadence of a military witness, getting raised eyebrows to her benign pleasure.

"Who wants to go first?" Jana queried, rubbing her hands together.

Sander coyly replied, "My hostess, I'd be indebted for you to begin." Various agreements prompted Jana to proceed.

She sighed loudly. "Sure, that's fair enough. Let me think for a minute." An expectant pause filled the room while everyone racked their brains on what to say, or not to say.

"Here goes. One, I was trained as a chef in New York City; two, I'm an avid downhill skier; and three, I attended boarding school in Vermont." Satisfied with herself, Jana pursed her lips, waiting for feedback.

Gianni peered at her and a lightbulb went off in his brain. "Janice? Are you the Janice from Mr. Bonhomme's sauce class?"

Jana looked at Gianni as if for the first time. "Yes." She paused with quizzical reflection. "Why are you asking, Gianni?"

"It's me, John. At the time, I went by John, but now I'm Gianni. I tried to make myself be so American, but now I realize I'm American and also proud of my Italian heritage."

"Oh, my gosh! Of course, how could we not have known? That was ten years ago. We both changed our names back to their original form, aged a decade, and landed in Wyoming! Who would know? You look great, Gianni. Do we have some catching up to do or what?"

"We certainly do," Gianni said, amazed at the revelation.

It was Heidi who had invited Gianni to Thanksgiving dinner, and who had spent time chatting with him over coffee the past months. Heidi, in addition to being a middle school world history teacher, was the owner of the Grizzly Tracks coffee shop. This liaison was a solid commercial endeavor for them both. Gianni inquired if Grizzly would provide coffee for his restaurant, and Heidi was ecstatic to provide the goods.

Dale broke into the uncanny coincidence and brought the conversation back to the present. "Jana, you look like you could handle the black slopes at the Hole, but I don't believe you went to boarding school in Vermont."

Jana's shoulders crumbled in exaggerated anguish as she hung her head low, then up again to speak. "Correct. I'm the prodigious result of the Pennsylvania state public schools. Good Pennsylvania Dutch stock!"

"That makes perfect sense, Jana. I wouldn't peg you for a prep school girl. You just don't, well, just don't have the personality for it," Dale said.

Heidi leaned back into the chaise longue at his comment, her heart softened at his perception. Dale and Jana knew each other through dealings at the quilt shop and through the friendship that Jana had with Dale's deceased wife. He was a new acquaintance for Heidi and rather intriguing.

"Eva, since you were last in," Steve said in a deep drawl as he shifted, perched on the hearth, "how about you go next?"

Eva matched his razor-sharp eye contact and managed her nervousness by changing positions on the couch opposite. "Sure." She audibly cleared her throat and forged ahead. "This is harder for me now that I gave that talk at the women's club last week." Holding up her hand, she counted on her fingers. "One, I wanted to join the Peace Corps right out of college. Two, I studied to be a chef but never finished. And three, I took piano lessons for twelve years."

Again, silence settled in the room as the group pondered fact from fiction. This time it was Marlo who tendered a comment. "I don't think you wanted to go into the Peace Corps. With that Corporate America drive you had, I think that's the lie."

Looking around, Eva coquettishly replied. "Nope, that one's true. I yearned to do the Peace Corps stint. In fact, I suppose I still do." Smiling broadly, she caught pensive blue eyes quizzically examining hers.

"I say, Eva, you never studied to be a chef," Steve said, holding eye contact with Eva steady.

"Correct. I never studied to be a chef but would love to do that too." Oh yes, the way he said *Eva*, so comfortable and natural, made her swallow to clear her throat.

"Not sure where you would have sneaked in that chef training," Steve said as he watched Eva with a heightened interest. "Now, I'd like to hear a little *Greensleeves* later on the piano, perhaps?" He noticed a tinge of pink cover her cheeks, but she said nothing. Nice. This friend of Heidi's and Jana's was a curiosity. *Such penetrating eyes. And full rose-colored lips.* Shaking his head back to reality, ever so slightly, Steve adjusted his gaze from Eva.

Ignoring the piano comment, Eva broke the explosive connection with Steve, willing the blush from her face, and addressed Gianni. "Gianni, maybe you can teach me a dish or two. I have a dream to go to Tuscany one day. You can stay in these old stone homes, walk to the market in the early morning, and cook until noon. Then you're free to wander the hills. After an afternoon of hiking, you come back, freshen up, and finish your cooking. Heaven." As she spoke, Eva kept her eyes mobile, looking around the room, trying to speak her little dream without the distraction of those gorgeous baby blues. The close proximity of Mr. Mason made her anxious. Was she attracted to him or just curious? *Careful, Eva.*

"Eva," Gianni replied, "your dream could be realized in Tuscany, but also in Sicily, or maybe here in Bear. You give me a good idea for a cooking class series. I'll talk to you about that later." He raised his glass of wine and toasted the group. "Centi-anni." To one hundred years.

The game continued engaging all participants. It was full of surprises and an excellent way to carve relationships—even if a third of the conversation was just made up! Jana, relishing her ice-breaker success, noticed by smell it was time to shepherd the party into the kitchen.

"Alright, everyone, the food beckons. You chef types and chef wannabes are most appreciated!" The small entourage obediently moved into the kitchen, bringing in leftover appetizers, plates, and wine glasses. The kitchen was a phenomenon in culinary organization. There were stations around the counters for almost every dish. One had a towel laid out to function as a trivet with butter, cream, salt and pepper shakers, and a big old fashioned potato masher lying alongside.

Eyeing Sander, Jana called him over. "Sander, your job will be to mash the potatoes when they're done boiling. I'll empty out the water and put the pot on this towel. All you need to do is add the ingredients right there and mash away. Got it?" Sander eyed his reasonable challenge, clicked his heels, and gave Jana a sharp salute.

"Steve, you're in charge of carving the turkey. Heidi told me of many family Thanksgivings when her Uncle Tom carved the turkey, then handed over the honor to you, Cuz, when you turned seventeen." A blanket of well-being swept over Steve with the task, then an overwhelming flood of memories caught him off guard. He recalled the big family events, the laughter, food, and exquisite decoration his Mom arranged around the house with the keen guidance of her sister, Auntie Mary, Heidi's mom. He quickly gained composure, still raw under a thin veneer of macho bravery.

Steve pulled Jana to his side with a warm hug. "Jana, I'm honored to carve a turkey roasted in this fine kitchen." Jana clapped her hands in glee and pointed to the knife and cutting board awaiting his artistry. She gave him a peck on the cheek and moved to the next assignment.

"Gianni, that warming oven holds your prize lasagna. Please take over from here. It smells like Italia. Yum. I can't wait to eat it!"

Chiming in, secretly wishing she could pull off a convincing Italian accent in the moment, Heidi instead took to her favorite French. "Cherie, Jana, may I have le proper instructions from you to assist with les drinks and condiments?" Jana responded in kind, "Mais oui, oui. C'est bien, ma bon ami. Merci," and Heidi headed off to perform her duties.

Eva, Dale, and Marlo stood together in a cluster like a group of kids on a playground waiting to get picked for a team game of kickball. "You three, well, we have a lot going on right now, but I'll need your help for dessert. Pumpkin pie, turkey cutout cookies, and raspberries with cream. It'll need set up and cream whipped. Here, Eva, take that bowl and beaters and find a place in the fridge. Must be cold before the cream is whipped or it won't be as good," Jana said, queen of the kitchen.

A long, rustic table was adorned with a variety of dishware coordinated like a beautiful patchwork quilt of contrasting colors and shapes. The table was roomy for ten, so it was spacious set for eight. An array of candles on the table sent firelight glittering off the crystal stemware. Heidi had arranged evergreen boughs, holly, and pinecones in the chandelier, transforming it into a halo of winter warmth with boughs protruding all directions.

The smells wafting from the kitchen, the laughter of the friends, and the beauty of the table was a recipe for a memorable Thanksgiving dinner. The feast was divine. The combined group of eight new and old friends found common ground and camaraderie. Embracing the present was a tribute to those they once loved. The thrill of the day was heightened, unconsciously, with the knowledge that life is precious. One must live it well.

As the sun set, Steve found himself drying dishes next to Eva in front of the large stainless steel sinks. She was chattering with Heidi as she passed him pots and pans. Eva laughed and occasionally shook her head to remove loose strands of hair from her forehead, hands encased in soapy blue rubber gloves. She was so real. Yes, he could have easily brushed away those uncooperative strands. Eva performed the trivial task of washing dishes with a simple ease.

And the apron she wore—who would ever have thought that a full apron with a tie at the waist could be so flattering? He noticed tension in the air that emanated between them. It wasn't lost on Steve that she offered a few stolen looks as the group bantered back and forth making jokes in the kitchen. This would be a Thanksgiving to remember.

Deep into the night, Marlo sat up with a start. Shivering, she looked around the small trailer. All was quiet and dark. She had a hollow feeling. Shaking her shoulders, she looked over at Sander, sound asleep next to her, emitting a slight, even snore. Quizzically eyeing Sander, Marlo was curious about the change in his demeanor during the Thanksgiving get together.

He was attentive, funny, and affectionate to her, showing no insincerity in his behavior at the dinner or on the way home. Strange, considering his reluctance to attend the dinner, Marlo thought. A regular chameleon. Who was this guy, really? What made him tick? She hardly knew him, but lived with him. *Living in sin. It doesn't seem wrong to be with Sander. We have such a connection when things are good. Mind-blowing sex aside. What was the reason we were brought together in Machu Picchu?* Quieting her mind, Marlo took refuge that this place, Bear, Wyoming, was a long way from Wichita.

Lois Cartwright was up late, the wee hours of the morning being her favorite time of the day. Everything was quiet, her work complete. Auntie Grace was sound asleep. Dear Auntie Grace. Lois watched her aunt sleep and quietly closed the door.

Hungry, she walked into the kitchen. Who gets hungry later in the day on Thanksgiving? She smiled a sad, bittersweet smile. *Someone who dined early and sensibly with her aunt, having eaten more than eight hours earlier.* Without any self-pity, Lois snooped in the refrigerator for a snack. Cornbread stuffing warmed in the microwave, cranberry sauce, and pecan pie made it to her plate.

She looked out over the calm street. One street lamp illuminated the whole block from the corner. They had a fine flat. The arrangements couldn't suit her and Grace any better. Large living area, two bedrooms, two bathrooms, a grand kitchen, closets, and separate outside stairway access down to the street. They were the blessed inhabitants of the beautiful upstairs floor of the Victorian manor that housed the Bear Claw Quilts hobby shop, a rival structure to Heidi's Painted Lady.

Comfortable in the large easy chair, feet up on the ottoman, Lois cuddled into a large quilt made a half century ago by Grace. Classic wedding ring pattern, her aunt had so advised, a staple for newlyweds and a must-make for serious quilters. Lois closed her eyes in peaceful thought. She loved the warm quilt and could almost hear the soft lilting voice of her aunt retelling memories behind every swatch of fabric.

The townies, those folks living locally for probably too long, were fond of telling tales and making Grace out to be a crazy woman. Lois trusted her implicitly. Complete faith. She also knew there wasn't a crazy thought that came out of her mind or mouth. There was, Lois knew, still much to learn about her aunt and the fanciful stories that made up her life.

Grace and Lois had been living together only a short time. Lois finished junior college south of Wilson toward Hoback Junction three years ago. She loved the studies, earning an associate's degree in business administration. She couldn't muster up the money for more schooling, wasn't interested in procuring student loans, and didn't have the drive to consider a big career and a move away. This place was her soul. Lois had lived in Bear her entire life. After the tragic car accident that took her parents' lives, Lois and her brother James, ten years older, were able to live together in the rented family home until Lois turned twenty-one years old.

It was the kind and wise Judge Jerry who ruled that the rent and utilities should be paid for by the Bear Volunteer Fire Department as part of her late father's death benefit. In addition, the underwriting of living expenses until Lois turned twenty-one would come from the petty cash fund provided by the village of Bear. Most people knew that meant Jerry's own bank account, but the stern and loving man wouldn't have wanted to admit that in a court of law.

Only after James was solidly convinced that Lois was well established in her new home with Auntie Grace and making a salary that provided for her essentials did he take the plunge to go after his goal. James loved Bear, but he had a thirst for more, a desire to experience living and learning in another place. James wanted to be a doctor. He had insight and the unique combination of brains, brawn, and a gift of intuition, formed by ten years of raising his younger sister.

It was a mystery to town folks how James could up and leave, how he could finance an education, especially being past normal college age. But frankly, it was none of their business. One day last August, James had loaded his things in his car, hugged his sister for a full ten minutes, kissed his beloved Auntie Grace and held her hands as he gazed without words into her eyes. Before driving to the University of Southern California, he had stopped at the Mason residence. The parents of his friend Steve were role models to James, and he had an intimate farewell with them before he left on his journey.

James had called Lois earlier in the day to wish her and Auntie Grace a good Thanksgiving. They talked for more than an hour about Bear happenings and his new life at the university. He was absorbed in studies, breathing in the knowledge. If James was anything, he was arrow focused. If that meant taking care of his sister in the best possible way under the worst of circumstances, then that was what he did. If it was driving toward the future of his dreams, he'd avoid all collisions.

Lois's conversation with James was bittersweet. She missed him desperately but at the same time was grateful he was away at school. This was his childhood dream, and because of that, she couldn't imagine him being in Bear any longer. He had given the years of his young adulthood to her, without regret, remorse, or complaint.

Considering her relatively new life living with Auntie Grace, Lois smiled and stretched out lingeringly in the comfy chair. Her small frame was absorbed by the soft cushions. Looking out across the night view of Bear from her second story window, she considered this town and its growing pains.

One hundred years earlier, the Jackson Hole area was a place of reckoning. It wasn't the group of pristine towns with attractions for pampered tourists and the western resident villages that it was today. Living in the Hole was geographically harsh. This rough living was aggravated by the reckless abandon of those who came to the area to find fortunes, change their identity, or homestead property. It was the varied decisions of these predecessors who molded the life of Grace Johnson Cartwright. And it's their descendents who don't believe her story. Lois dozed off to sleep as she considered this sad paradox.

There was a third person awake and alone, pondering on the same Thanksgiving night. Farther up in the Gros Ventres above the village of Bear, a lone figure resisted the strong urge to shiver from the cold, not permitting a show of weakness, even while alone.

Food today consisted of stale peanuts, Fruit Loops without milk, a small package of pecan pie, two over-ripe bananas, and a fifth of Jack Daniels. Thank God for that. Thanksgiving, my ass. Placing the binoculars down on a barren wood table, the dark sinewy silhouette settled back into the swayed chair of an ancient rocker and silently rocked, solitary, into the night.

12

"Heidi, this is Eva."

"Hello, darling," Heidi answered, stifling a yawn.

"That was quite the crowd yesterday, eh?" Eva leaned toward the speaker-phone as she pet Scout's long nose, stroking the white spot with her thumbs.

"You know it. We must start a monthly dinner night to jump-start our social calendars in this godforsaken place," Heidi said, knowing she wouldn't move back to New York for a closet of Prada suits.

"That's a great idea," Eva answered, recalling the comfort she experienced at being part of the group, not to mention the delicious food.

"So, what do you think of the gang?"

"Well, thanks to Jana's game, I learned a lot in one short evening." Eva said, still bubbling from the holiday, a satisfied Scout curled up on the floor by her feet.

"That game was great," Heidi said in agreement, "We are quite the astute liars."

"What about Dale? Wow."

"I would've never pegged Dale Sawyer as a top gun pilot and high school all-state football player. He's so mild mannered, or appears so." Heidi said. "To think I fell for the false fact that he learned construction consulting from his father. There's nothing obvious about him."

Taking a swallow of coffee, Eva went on, noticing the interest Heidi held for Dale. "And who would know Sander has a master's degree in finance and studied in South America. A numbers man."

"Smart guy, I'd say. Mysterious."

"There's something with him that doesn't add up, Heidi. I'm not sure what, but it's like he's hiding something."

"He has that transient aura. Not saying that's bad, but I understand what you sense. He doesn't physically do it, but it's as if he's looking over his back to make sure someone isn't there. His tall, dark, slinky body doesn't help the stereotype," Heidi said, tucking her phone under her chin as she pulled open her briefcase.

"Sort of like Johnny Depp in the movie *Chocolat*."

"Having said that, he's kind of cute in that *he's-too-young-for-you-Heidi* kind of way."

"Especially since he's Marlo's," Eva said teasingly, filling her mug with more coffee.

"Ah, yes, existing romantic knots in the way again," Heidi said, pulling out a pile of invoices.

Pausing only for effect, Eva continued. "Then there's Marlo. Born on the rich side of Wichita, not the cowboy side, and fluent in Spanish. For such a young girl, or I should say woman, she's had quite the life."

"Women ten years our junior seem to have so much going on. I wonder if back when we were that age older women viewed us in the same light. Know what I mean?" Heidi asked. "That zest and drive and *I can do and be anything* attitude."

"Marlo's insight sets her apart from her peers," Eva added, stepping over Scout to sit back on the stool.

"Makes me feel inadequate," Heidi said, licking her forefinger as she flipped through the documents.

"Heidi, did I just hear you say the word inadequate?" Couldn't be. If anyone topped the adequate scale in Eva's mind, it was Heidi.

"Darling, a mere expression," her laugh haughty in spite of herself as she sat in the parlor, gazing out onto Main Street through lace curtains, a soft layer of snow on the sidewalk.

"When I left the corporate world to live in Bear I sensed the same thing. These young twenty-somethings new on the scene were so polished."

"I am woman, hear me roar?" Heidi quipped.

"Ugh, something like that," Eva said. "Maybe, Heidi, most of us don't realize our own achievements until someone shines a light on them."

"Hmm, are we in coaching mode?" Heidi teased, recognizing the tone.

"Hah, should I be?" Eva laughed, then went on, "It's that in our twenties we have no limits, no barriers. Just a big old life ahead of us."

"My future's so bright, I need to wear shades?" Heidi said, recollecting lyrics from her past.

"Something like that," Eva admitted. "Okay, we're off track from dinner gossip. Let's table this philosophical talk for some morning at Grizzly."

"To get back to your intuition on Sander, I hope he's not using Marlo in any way. She's fresh and ready to take on the world," Heidi added, expressing her teacher's eye for potential.

"And equipped, I might add."

"Might we be paranoid? I didn't notice any abnormal behavior on Sander's part." Taking a breath, Heidi continued. "Eva, were you surprised that Steve has a doctorate in history and *declined* the department chair at UC Berkeley?"

Taking a sip of coffee to stabilize a quivering voice at Steve's name, Eva lightheartedly continued, suppressing brewing feelings of attraction. "Seems like his earthy attitude is out of sync with that intense education."

"I'm his cousin and didn't know about the UC Berkeley offer." Heidi's voice held a sisterly concern for Steve as to why he kept it a secret.

"I may have him pegged wrong, Heidi, about being low key and all. Too quick to judge. Me, a life coach and all." Chastising herself, she went on, "It's a blemish to my profession to draw conclusions. Yet, I still can't see him at Berkeley, at least the stereotype of the place. Steve's casual in the western way, not the, shall I say, liberal sense?"

Heidi laughed, "To think that his lie was that he grew up dreaming of staying in Bear and driving a pickup truck. Gosh, that's what he does now. Well, that and a whole lot more."

"I wouldn't have pegged him for an academic. He doesn't fit the label." Eva's thoughts zeroed in on the memory of Steve's muscular chest covered by the soft flannel shirt—and she was interrupted by Dash shaking his body, tail last part to move.

"I couldn't really comment too much on his part of the game. We were raised practically like siblings. My dad had to put his foot down to have our moms stop giving us a communal bath as we approached adolescence."

"Heidi, that's a little too much information," Eva laughed, shaking her head. Focusing back on Heidi, she went on, "What a fun day, Heidi. Thanks for your hospitality. How's Jana?"

"The hygienic freak stayed up until the last glass was washed and put away. Typical. She had to fuss and clean up the entire kitchen before she could rest easy. Then she woke up this morning to open the library at nine o'clock."

"Maybe I'll stop over. I could use a new book, something light and easy. Last night I finished an epic by Edward Rutherfurd, *Sarum*."

"Sarum, as in Old Sarum from the mother country?" Heidi asked, British accent engaged.

The two women chatted about the saga of ancient through modern civilization on England's Salisbury Plain before ending their call to get on with their weekend activities.

13

Steve leaned back and the chair angled just short of tumble range. Rubbing his temples, he blew out a puff of breath. He was in it deep this time. Eva. Eva with her wide smile. Eva with her unusual past. Eva who walks her dogs in any kind of weather. Eva with that sexy golden silk sweater and luscious soft lips. *Enough*.

Getting up from the chair, Steve walked around the room, picked up his calendar, and tossed it back down on the desk in disgust. He had work to do. He needed to establish his schedules for the upcoming season. The white paper for his academic credentials on the Gros Ventre Indians was coming due. This sudden fixation on Eva Karlsen was a distraction. Taking a methodical approach to get practical, Steve recalled what he knew of her.

Eva had lived in Bear almost two years. She was a professional, athletic woman. Good friend to Heidi and Jana. Had a strange job. Doing what, life coaching? Never dated locally, from what he knew. Unusual for such an attractive, single, self-sufficient woman. Not to mention alluring. Maybe she has some medical condition and howls at the moon? Mmm. A real conundrum.

Steve needed James. He'd have words of wisdom, having raised Lois for all those years. Considering the differences between romantic anticipation and sisterly devotion, Steve realized that, no, he supposed it wasn't the same, and James would relish his quandary. This distraction by a woman was new. He'd had romance across the continents, thanks to his parent's meanderings, but never before had a female taken his mind off work. And such a female, at that.

"What to do?" he spoke aloud. *Do all single people talk to themselves?* As he considered this phenomenon, Snowball jumped off the bookshelf and wound herself around his ankles, purring. Steve leaned down, picked up the charcoal cat, and scratched it roughly between the ears. Snowball closed her eyes, purring as the skin ruffled on her forehead. Steve bent over and gently launched the animal in the general direction of the carpet in the center of the room. When his parents left on their worldly tours, Steve was the most convenient—and almost willing—caregiver for the cat. It's odd how much he fancied the lively fur ball. Steve grew up around horses that his Aunt Mary and Uncle Tom bred and raised. Magnificent creatures, the large muscle-bound quarter horses were a natural fit for the inclement Wyoming weather and rugged terrain. Steve never would've imagined himself sharing a human abode with a feline. Cats were meant to catch mice in the barn.

Pacing around the room, Steve contemplated what anchor might temporarily sink thoughts of Eva so he could finish his work. He stopped mid-step in the middle of the room. Out the window, he caught a glimpse of the frozen creek, the stark juniper trees, and the sand-colored boulders that lined the back of the property. The imposing rise of the Gros Ventres set off the view. The big picture. What was the big picture of this issue? The Gros Ventres, the GVs to the locals, are hardly a recognizable name unless you live in the area. Yet they're huge and inspiring, a reckoning force. Their ancient rounded peaks with rolling foothills full of sagebrush are in a particular contrast to the jagged tops of the ever-popular and much-photographed Tetons. The GVs hold the locally esteemed Sleeping Indian, officially known as Sheep Mountain. If you look at it from a distance, Sheep Mountain cuts a silhouette across the sky of a Native American, lying down on his back, arms crossed over his chest.

Switching into academic gear, Steve contemplated his dilemma, observing the relatively unknown mountain range. The GV's held secrets of the early settlers and were home to some of the most diverse and ferocious wildlife in America. Is there something like the Gros Ventres in this situation? Am I really missing the point on this distraction of Eva? Should I be doing something different, more? Is it even her? Academics were a curse to simplicity. How the hell could he make this situation more complicated?

He recalled a theme that old Professor Blake drilled into him over and over when writing his thesis. "In history, young man, human societies that don't look at the bigger picture of their existence and the impact of change don't last long. Then they die out, lose land to enemies, are taken prisoner and forced to conform." Ouch.

Steve plopped into a worn leather couch, arms and legs spread to fill up the space. The couch was of buffalo hide and had been in his family for generations, at least as long as he could remember. It had deep, wide cushions, sturdy armrests fashioned with rounded corners, and a line of brass-topped tacks. The legs of the couch were flattened circles of dark mahogany.

In Christmases past, the senior Masons would seat at least five to six cousins on the couch in a row and just as many cross-legged on the floor in front of the couch for an annual holiday picture. Luxurious memories. Steve acquired the couch when his parents remodeled and chose thick tweed-covered couches and ottomans instead of the traditional stressed buffalo leather.

"I'm making this hard. Better bite the bullet and see if Ms. Karlsen is interested in coffee." Keep it simple stupid, as they say. KISS. Ah, yes, a kiss. Clearing his throat, Steve continued his litany to no one in particular. "Keep it at a high level." Unbelievable coward. *At least now I can finish my work and call Eva tonight.*

14

Gianni, Marlo, and Gianni's sous-chef, Enrique, were huddled studying the menu for The Sicilian Ball's grand opening. Enrique, deep in concentration, scratched a balding crown that sported a wispy ponytail pulled low in the back and trapped by a hairnet. Gianni stood with his bulky arms crossed and perspiration beading at his hairline. Marlo was perched atop the counter, shapely legs moving to an internal tempo. Turning slowly around, Marlo eyed Gianni, then looked at Enrique and swung off her perch. Without any warning, she yelped, put an arm around each of the surprised men, and squealed with abandon.

"This is great. This is great. This is great! Oh my, this is great."

"She's right. It's brilliant." Enrique said in crisp agreement, stealing a glance at his mentor.

Gianni wiped his brow with a towel that had been tucked in the front of his white apron. He barely twitched pursed lips as his muscular arms released their tension and came down from their protective guard at his chest. Who would have known the unlikely trio of transplants would share such a moment of goose-bump bliss. He was speechless.

"To the GEM squad." Marlo did a mini snake dance and stuck out an outstretched hand, palm down. Both men tentatively placed their hands atop hers with confused looks on their faces. "Oh brother," she said rolling her eyes, unruly auburn curls swaying. "It's going to be a long row to hoe training the two of you. GEM, you know, Gianni, Enrique, and Marlo—GEM, the first letters of our names. Like a team?"

"Ah, but of course, Marlo. I get it. To GEM then." Enrique acknowledged, beaming. The three cheered GEM and threw their hands up in the air. "So, this celebration and mutual appreciation is good. However, my team, we must now figure out how to pull off the grand opening. You see, we must get going on preparation and setup."

"You telling us to get to work, boss?" Marlo said, beaming but giving an exaggerated sigh.

"We have to bring all this, what do you say, chaos, together, to make a restaurant." Gianni's voice was laced equally with excitement and fear.

"I'll double check the menus against the pantry to make lists for ordering and shopping." Enrique said, his Italian accent indistinguishable in contrast to Gianni's heavy Sicilian lilt.

"Dear Marlo, you use those talents of yours to set up the ambiance in the dining room."

"Thank you Gianni! I can't wait to get going. Which boxes have the wares?" Marlo asked.

"The supplies are in the boxes over by the bar. You'll find scissors to open them in the kitchen drawer. That big crate in the corner, that's the hostess stand." Unbeknownst to Marlo, Gianni's grandfather Dario had saved the ornate stand from his own restaurant in Sicily and shipped it as a surprise, then alerted Gianni to look out for its arrival. Gianni, sensing Marlo's nostalgic nature, wanted her to open the crate. Her reaction was worth the wait.

As fate would have it, Marlo didn't get to the large crate until late afternoon. She arranged tables and set out the ivory cloths adorned with silverware packets tightly wrapped in purple cloth napkins. The tables had small olive candles set in wrought iron holders fashioned with grape leaves and curly vine stems that cradled the candles.

Cruets of delicate green olive oil sat on each table. A year earlier, Gianni heard a fellow New Yorker exclaim, "Don't you just hate those Italian restaurants that don't leave the olive oil on the table?" It had never occurred to Gianni before he heard that comment, but from then on, he knew his restaurant would have the olive oil cruet on the table so his patrons could indulge.

Gianni put the hostess stand out of his mind as he organized his kitchen just so. He strategically hung stainless steel pots and colanders, cast iron frying pans, and large pasta kettles on the commercial pot racks suspended from the ceiling. An old crock was stationed next to the stove to hold utensils, the hairline crack barely noticeable to an untrained eye. It reminded Gianni of his childhood pet cat, Leo, who had frolicked around the kitchen and knocked it off the window ledge all those years ago. Memories. This contemporary space in the new world had a charming, old-world feel. The commercial kitchen sparkled.

The aged building that housed The Sicilian Ball had been a restaurant, so major remodeling was kept to a minimum. Gianni instinctively created an Italian ambiance in the kitchen and dining room. He and Enrique had plastered the walls and painted them rich mustard. On the wall with the massive white ceramic sinks they built out a large greenhouse window bordered with Italian tiles in varieties of plums, yellows, greens, and blues, and they filled it with pots of herbs. Gianni could close his eyes and see the deep blue of the Mediterranean at the horizon.

The state-of-the-art stainless appliances stood ready like centurions awaiting combat. The three sets of ovens, all double deckers, were arranged side by side, so a chef could view the contents of all ovens with barely taking a step. Two of the kitchen walls were wrapped with shelves and racks filled with stock ingredients, spices, large pouring tins of balsamic vinegar, olive oils, chopping devices, pottery bowls, and spatulas. A desk across from the butcher block was equipped with a computer, telephone, printer, and a variety of cookbooks. The spiral notebooks housed notes and recipes that, when all put together, could tell the story of Gianni's culinary journey.

The tiled entrance in the front of the restaurant matched the exquisite tile in the kitchen. Just inside the door was a long, sturdy dark wooden bar with ten leather and wrought iron bar chairs. Enrique convinced Gianni to go the extra yard and buy chairs with "backs so customers can sit at the bar and eat. Or men can lean behind their dates, sipping Chianti as they wait for a table. Si, the right picture, Gianni?"

As the trio worked diligently on their tasks, the merry noise of clanging pots and Marlo's humming filling the rooms. A sudden intrusion of loud knocks came from the entrance. Startled, Marlo gathered her senses and sang out, "I've got it!" Standing in the frame under the small rounded green awning stood a cat-that-got-the-canary grinning Jana.

"Jana! What a surprise!" beamed Marlo, cheeks flushed from physical activity. She embraced Jana in a bear hug. "Come on in, come in, we're working fervently under the rule of Gianni, the Italian drill sergeant." Waving her arm proudly across the dining room, she exclaimed, "What do you think?" Letting out a slow, low gasp, Jana scanned the enchanting space. It was a walk through the wardrobe to Italy.

"Marlo, this is awesome. It's so, well—Italian! So unexpected in Bear. I can taste the garlic sauce already. Hey, when did the mural appear? Was it a local painter? That's really good." Jana put down a large, awkward box and moved across the room to inspect the grandly painted mural that filled the back wall. The arched door, incorporated into the design like a rolling Tuscan hill, marked where the staff would exit the dining area into the short hallway to the kitchen.

"Gianni had some tie with an art student he met in New York City. The guy, Rich something-or-other, had a typical starving artist story that gave Gianni the idea. After Gianni came out here to view Bear and the property, which he found in some restaurant magazine, he called on Rich and offered to fly him out, all expenses paid, to paint the mural. Nice, huh?"

"Whoa, I would say so, and boy, aren't you just a font of knowledge? That Rich is going to be rich if he keeps up this kind of work. Look at the detail. I just want to jump in, walk those hills, and taste the grapes growing on those vines under that sun. Delicious."

"I'm so excited for the opening that I'm going to burst." Marlo said, swaying to her own thrilling beat, her hair piled up on her head with an oversized scarf.

"Hey, we should have a party for Gianni and watch that movie, *Under the Tuscan Sun*. Do you think he'd like that? This mural just brings me right to that place."

"Oh Jana, that's a great idea. Let's do it." Then Marlo looked at her new friend, cocking her head. "So, what brings you to The Sicilian Ball anyway?"

"Ah, now *that* is definitely a surprise. You'll soon see. Where's Gianni?" Marlo tilted her head toward the kitchen, and Jana picked up her box from the door and obediently followed Marlo.

"Gianni, Enrique, break it up back there. We have company," Marlo said, winking at Jana mischievously. "It's Jana."

Looking at each other and patting down their hair self-consciously, both Enrique and Gianni walked toward the women as they entered the kitchen.

"Jana, hello. Why, it's great to see you." Gianni was on autopilot, wondering if he sounded as excited as he was to see her, not sure he wanted her to notice. Stepping up to Jana, Gianni gave her a traditional kiss on each cheek, laid his hands on her shoulders and held her at arm's length.

"What brings you to these parts?" Gianni asked.

Jana grinned, raising her eyebrows rapidly as she firmly pointed to the large box on the floor. "That, my friend, is a restaurant-warming present. For you. Please, open it."

Enrique automatically handed Gianni a blunt, worn, black-handled Buck knife that he'd been using to open boxes of dried food. Gianni opened the seal on the box with a pop and proceeded to dig inside around a veritable sea of wood shavings, looking quizzically up at Jana. Finally his hand hit something hard and smooth and, he discovered after touching the surface for a second or two, curved and round. He instinctively knew what it was and jumped up to hug Jana.

"Jana, I can't believe it. Where did you find one?"

Jana, pleased at his response, didn't answer and let him continue to unravel the mystery of his gift. Enrique and Marlo, totally in the dark, exchanged glances and took in the scene. Gianni was finally able to lift out the contents of the large box, wood shavings flying everywhere. He carefully lifted out a large, old, green glass olive jar.

The jar was twenty-four inches tall with an opening lip of three inches. The neck of the bottle was four inches until it blossomed out quickly to become a huge exaggerated pear shape before it curved in slightly at the base. The bottom half was in a customized crate made of soft wood planks with straw padding. *Slightly Italian!*

"This, my fine colleagues," he puffed his chest, "is an authentic Sicilian olive jar. It's a beauty. Picture perfect. Oh, Jana, this gift is amazing." Setting it down, he walked over to Jana, struggling to control his pent-up Italian fervor. Gianni kissed her three times on alternating cheeks, then, breaking the tradition, gave her a bear hug. Again, he pushed her back at arm's reach, piercing her with brown tender eyes. Jana was momentarily speechless.

"Thank you so much. I love it." Squeezing her deeply, Gianni stood back, curious. "Let's have it, where did you find such a piece?"

"Well," Jana said, starting on her tale, grinning broadly. "Do you remember Monty back in New York?"

"Monty? Monty, yes, I rather think I do."

"After Thanksgiving I called Monty to pick his brain about a reduced balsamic vinaigrette dressing recipe—oh, I digress. Well, I told him about your new restaurant and how I wanted to find you an olive jar. You know, like the one your grandfather used to have back in Sicily. As true fate would have it, his Uncle Nick worked on the docks in Jersey and found one."

"Nick, he's the one who helped me ship my gear from Sicily. That's my Monty connection. Go on."

"Ah, well, the night before Uncle Nick found it, Monty was at his mom's for Sunday spaghetti dinner. Of course, Nick was there, since it's an Italian family and all. Well, he told them the story about us both ending up in Bear and you starting a restaurant and me wanting to find the olive jar."

"You've been on a mission finding this, for me?" Gianni's neck turned a deep pink, barely touching the bottom of his ears. Jana either didn't hear or ignored the comment and continued on.

"Believe it or not, the next day Uncle Nick was unloading the hull of a cargo ship, and the jar was nestled in the back of a shipment of wine from Italy. No olives or olive oil, just crates of wine and a lone olive jar, with your proverbial name on it!" Flushed, Jana stopped to catch her breath after her exciting soliloquy. "Is that fate or what?"

"This olive jar will hold the place of honor in my restaurant, Jana. My faithful assistant Marlo will find just the spot."

Marlo rubbed her hands together, enchanted at the intoxicating story more than the olive jar itself, shaking her head in agreement. "Yes, sir, I will. I think if we find some of those long decorative grasses that look like wheat, they'd contrast with the hardness of the green glass and soften it with authenticity of nature, you know, accenting the curved line of the jar sort of like the gentle roll of a hill." Marlo abruptly stopped speaking as the men stared at her dumbfounded. She surrendered with her hands up but grinned a self-satisfied smile all the same.

"Right," Jana said huskily, amused by the interplay. "The three of you have work to do. I couldn't focus on anything until this jar was delivered, just too darn excited. See you soon." Jana beamed at Gianni, Marlo, and Enrique, slipped her handmade felted purse over her shoulder, and waltzed out of the restaurant as abruptly as she entered.

Gianni managed to clear his throat enough to squeak out a rather shaky "ciao" as she departed, adding silently to himself, *my dear Jana.*

Marlo eyed him as he watched the door a split second too long. Saying nothing, she went back to work, softly humming as she set up the dining room for the grand opening of The Sicilian Ball, Bear, Wyoming. The comfortable hubbub was broken by another scream of pleasure as Marlo unpacked the dusty crate in the corner. "Gianni. Gianni! This sculpture. This wooden piece of art. Hey, this is an antique hostess stand! You were holding out on me!" In Marlo fashion, she fled to confront her favorite chef.

A nondescript truck drove slowly by The Sicilian Ball, oblivious to the joy inside the walls of the old building. The lanky figure scanned the street with photographic intensity. Not slowing or parking, just driving. Irritated. The truck continued to pass over the streets of Bear as if working the monotony of a bus route. After several hours of traversing the roads in and around Bear, the vehicle left for higher ground, unnoticed in any memorable fashion.

15

Arriving at the law offices of the esteemed Mr. Charlie Cunningham, Esquire, Eva was thankful she didn't have to parallel park her big, too-old-to-discuss aqua International pickup. She grabbed her quilted satchel and made swiftly for the door, clasping her coat tight to block out the biting wind. Taking a glimpse at her parking job, Eva absentmindedly took in her aged truck. A fleeting thought ran through her mind that a working girl couldn't have both an amazing cabin in Wyoming and a nice pickup; *something* had to give. Besides, she loved the clunker. The truck had its own personality and made her feel unique in a quirky way she liked.

Rosalyn Ryan, consumed by her role of law office receptionist-cum-secretary, peered at Eva over the tops of her rectangular red glasses. Every morning Rosalyn told her pet parakeet, Pete, the character she'd play that day as she went about her business of dressing in costume and persona. As she left the house, eyeing the parakeet with ruffled brows, she made an exaggerated sigh, fluttered her eyelids, and told the bird he was hardly worthy of her gracious care.

"Charlie, your eleven o'clock is here," Rosalyn sang out a little too loud for the space. She smiled sincerely at Eva and went about her business at the computer. The contemporary upscale decor took Eva by surprise. Shame on her. She expected an office lost in the 1960s, full of gray file cabinets and old ivy plants, and spattered with stained cut-glass ashtrays.

The office was a decorator's showcase. Small, but exquisite. Warm natural paint colors of taupe and sage green covered the walls. Rocky Mountain maple made up the cabinetry and reception desk, and plush couches with beige and maroon paisley invited patrons in the waiting area. The beautiful wall photographs were of flora from the surrounding mountains and valleys, large hymenoxys, goat's beard, and Indian paintbrush, tastefully done for a local naturalist to love. No kitschy overdone tourist scenes to be found.

The click of the doorknob interrupted Eva's examination of the elegant room and Charlie, full of effervescence, strode into the room. "Eva, thank you for coming," he said, shaking Eva's hand rapidly.

"It's great to see your offices," Eva said honestly.

"Miss Rosalyn over there has me booked all afternoon, and I wanted to be able to fit in with you, eat some vittles before tending to my clients. Some ski collision, he-said-she-said arbitration, and a bit about landlord roof repairs over yonder in Moose."

Laughing in spite of herself, Eva immediately felt at ease. It was clear in seconds that Charlie embraced life despite his more than sixty years.

"Charlie, my pleasure—and frankly, it's good for me to get out of the house. I'm impressed. This is a lovely place."

Beaming, he meticulously took in his familiar office with hawk-like focus. "Well, thank you. We like it here. Have to change with the times, right?"

"That we do."

"Can't have clients coming to an old dilapidated place." He grinned at Eva, rubbing his hands together.

"Why do you think I coach over the phone instead of at my home?" Eva joked.

"If I didn't redecorate like you womenfolk change fashions, ah, I'd be left in the dust by young flashy lawyers over in Jackson taking all the good business."

"Jackson can have that effect."

"My clients come to see me in Bear, and I can't have them thinking we're a two-bit operation. No-ooo, ma'am. They walk into comfortable surroundings decorated up to their normal standards, and they think it must be a better deal because they're working with a small-town lawyer, which it is, of course."

"Good thinking," Eva said, taken by his charm.

"It gets us business, thus keeping Miss Rosalyn in proper costume." Rosalyn eyed Charlie over the top of her glasses without missing a beat on her computer or giving Charlie any satisfaction by responding to the jovial gibe. The two were tied at the hip.

Charlie was well groomed and stylishly dressed. He wore his trademark bow tie, but even that wasn't an old tie. It was of elegant silk and done up in winter colors of deep blue, cream, and purples, clearly something he must have ordered for this season from Brooks Brothers on the Internet.

In their first session, Eva had gathered background information on Charlie, knowledge she would use to challenge him in their coaching. From that session, she had quickly ascertained his core values and the things that make him tick positively and trigger negatively.

"Well, then, before we start, would you like some coffee?" Charlie offered.

"Sure, that'd be great. It's well before three, which is my coffee cut-off time if I want to sleep at night."

"Okay then. Rosalyn, would you please run over to Grizzly?" She happily affirmed and in a fluid motion swung on her coat and materialized at Charlie's side. Eva froze, mouth slightly agape, at the theatrical scene. Rosalyn and Charlie took cues from one another like a perfect staged production.

"The normal for me, Ros. Eva?"

"Oh, um, small cappuccino, sugar-free vanilla, and skim milk, whipped."

Charlie raised his eyebrows and signaled to Rosalyn, who swept out of the office as if on a magic sleigh. Calling after her, he added, "Please get whatever it is you might want," which, of course, was a given, yet a courtesy played out dozen of times.

They sat in a small parlor behind the reception area adjacent to Charlie's office, situated on two plush chairs arranged in a corner to promote conversation.

"Charlie, let's check in. This gives us a chance to speak to whatever is on our minds and clear it to enable us to become present to coaching. No multitasking of the mind. Make sense?"

"I think I've got it. This morning I was feeling rushed, but now as I reflect, I'm prepared for my appointments later today. There's nothing more to do until I meet with my clients. I suppose I can relax and focus on our talk. So, does that mean I'm checked in?" Charlie was enjoying this new thing called coaching and slowly tapped his fingertips together like a steeple as he leaned back in the chair.

"Yes, you're sufficiently *in*. Typically, I coach over the phone, so I need to make sure not to be distracted by the surroundings. So I'm in."

Settling into the cushion, Eva turned slightly to face Charlie. "As we mentioned last time, change happens in our life when we make conscious choices. You said you want to have change in your life. When you say you want change, Charlie, what does that mean to you?"

Charlie sighed and stretched out his legs, crossing them at the ankles. He took a long look toward the window and contemplated the question. With ease, he glanced back at Eva. "Eva, I want to make a difference. To your comment a few minutes ago, I want to be 'in' all the moments of my life."

"Tell me more, Charlie."

"I may be perceived as somewhat of an old codger when folks look at me. My life has been full and varied and, through my midlife years, satisfying and successful. Inside, I feel young. I want to do worthwhile things, and in this second half of my life I want to live my dreams."

"You said you still feel young. Tell me about that."

"Young is fun. Young is exciting and new. Young is allowed to laugh, explore, and learn. Young allows me to be a learner and a doer."

"Sounds like when you're young, life is a canvas that you can paint in any way you want."

"Exactly. That's it, Eva I want to continue to paint."

"What do you want to paint, Charlie?"

"Bright colors. Big pictures. Strong messages."

"Tell me about the colors."

"Colors vivid and pure, like this grand land. I want to use green, yellow, and blue. Giant swatches of brilliance for space and growth." Charlie spoke with his eyes closed, emitting a deep exhale as he used his hands to express the vision.

"Mmm, sounds wonderful. What about the messages?"

"Oh, the messages are saying to keep moving forward and try it. Whatever *it* is. The messages are positive and constructive. They're uplifting and objective; not mandated by the media." Charlie abruptly stood and moved anxiously around the room.

"What can your messages do when not mandated by the media?" Casually, Eva got up to be in step with Charlie. She heard the media barb loud and clear.

"The messages promote individuality. My concern for society today is that the media tells people what to do, how to think, dress, exercise, and eat. Much of the media distorts the truth to propagate what their idea of our popular culture should be. They do this to sell products or get high ratings. As I see it, the media likes to blow minor incidents out of proportion or has a penchant to tell a piece of the story out of context."

Agitated, Charlie paced. Eva decided to let him vent his frustrations a bit longer before interrupting.

"Take war, for example. No matter what the situation, let me say, it's always horrific, but sometimes necessary. However, the media will choose to publish a picture of an injured child on the cover of a national magazine." He turned, roughly pointing his finger into the room. "This then gets popular culture in a mode of thinking that the human, societal, and political reasons for the war were wrong to start with. Soldiers hurt children, etcetera, etcetera.

"From my perspective, this is conscious bias propagated by the media without giving fair coverage to the balance of the story. For instance, regarding the topic of war, I'd like to see the details on the good outcomes, the freedoms, and how our soldiers are fighting to improve the long-term lives of citizens in a foreign land and, therefore, upholding our freedom in America."

Eva allowed a long pause; she imagined that, as a trained trial lawyer, Charlie would pull his thoughts back to the topic at hand. Shaking his head in small movements and holding his lips in a grim line, Charlie concluded his thoughts. "The colors, Eva, stand for the freedom for people to be themselves. To be who they are and not who they think they should be for someone else."

"Charlie, what do you want to do with the colors?"

A giant grin covered his face and deepened his well-deserved laugh lines. "Well, spread them around, of course!"

"What would spreading the colors around be like?"

"Unleashed individuality."

"You're bubbling, Charlie. I have this image of you with a black beret painting the morning sunrise over the Gros Ventres."

"No, Eva, it's not that I necessarily want to paint them. I see it now. I want to be able to give canvas and paint to others so they can paint." Charlie was bobbing his head and pacing when Ros opened the door with the coffee. As if it was script-ed, Charlie put out his hand to take his cup, and Ros turned to Eva to deliver her cappuccino.

"How would giving paint and canvas to others change things for you?" Eva asked, opening her drink and licking the sweet foam from the lid.

"I do things. I go after a task and make it happen. In my sixty-three years, I've been able to do things my way. I don't sway to what others think and say. Of course, I consider opinions and then use them to make my own. By giving paint and canvas to others, I'm a change agent. That's it, Eva. The change that I'm after is to be a change agent for others. To be the cog in the wheel that can alter some of this societal dictation for others."

Eva was absorbed in Charlie's dream; this man cared about having a legacy. "Charlie, that's huge."

"Yes, ma'am, that's what I'm after, something huge."

"Will you keep that vibrant picture alive?" Eva asked, then painfully realized the question was not what she intended.

"Meaning, what exactly?" Charlie asked, swirling the coffee cup in his hand, nonjudgmental in his query.

"How can you keep that image of you as the change agent real?"

He paused to consider Eva's request. "As you might have seen in the reception area, I'm a photographer. I love my colorful surroundings, and framing a small white paper will be out of place and will remind me of this vision of change."

Eva didn't need to say anything just yet; the white space spoke volumes. Coaching works when you stay with your client, dance to their music. Eva kept his thoughts alive with a purpose of expectation that sizzled in the quiet room. After a few moments she continued. "When will you tack it up?" No loose ends.

"Right now." He reached under the coffee table and pulled out a drawer. It was filled to the brim with photography supplies. Charlie took a small sheet of photo paper, showed her, and raised his eyebrows in a grin. "This will do the trick."

"Charlie, your zest for life is contagious." Accepting her acknowledgement with a gentleman's humility, they completed their session and made arrangements for their next session. Eva found herself driving her International home without ever realizing she made the exit from the building.

Taking in the scenery with the companionable rumble of the not-too-smooth rig, Eva contemplated Charlie. He was no old stodgy. No doubt, he had his fair share of disappointments along life's journey. Yet he lives with such a positive out-look.

What about her?

Choking down tears, Eva knew it was time to move forward. Here she was a life coach carrying around more baggage than all her clients combined. Intellectually, she knew that by holding negative garbage in her head she couldn't live life to its fullest. It took up too much room. Weighed her down too much. It was time to claim her life. Could she do it? Could she open herself up for more living? Could she be vulnerable and put herself out there and risk failure and disappointment? It had never been her nature to give freely of herself, except that once. That once with Seaton.

Kathleen S. Kolze

16

Seaton Andrew Rushmore III swept Eva off her feet. They met in San Francisco at an industry conference where they both were panelists for approaches to selling technology services. His stand was on broker selling, and her bent, direct selling. Never having met until the panel, the two had an immediate intellectual camaraderie and electricity that wasn't lost on the crowd. Their jostling brought attendees to bouts of laughter and subsequent standing-room-only sessions over the four-day event. On the fourth day, Seaton invited Eva, his "conversion challenge," as he called her, out for a truce dinner, his treat.

It was a classically flawless evening. They dined at The Palm restaurant; the service was sublime, the lobster perfect, and the chardonnay bottled in nearby Napa Valley. With all her senses lit, Eva was glowing as brightly as the candles. Seaton dished out more compliments to her than the restaurant served entrées. Everything Seaton said was seeded with sincerity and his own brand of intrigue. Their reciprocal interest in one another was an adventure. A relationship at last. Her mouth hurt from smiling, laughing, and talking. To add to the thrill, Seaton sported American good looks—thick, blond-streaked hair, a dark tan, glassy blue eyes, and a fit, football-player physique.

This was a new experience, one of intellectual connection and sexual tension. Fun hadn't been prevalent in her life, especially in business settings, and meeting Seaton was definitely fun. Eva was heady with romance when Seaton caught her in a needy, brutal embrace at the end of the evening as the elevator took them up to their rooms.

"You'll meet me next week in Atlanta," he murmured to her as he released her punished lips.

"I'm not traveling."

"No if, ands, or buts about it, feisty Eva." Shushing her reply, he continued. "I know you can arrange it. I'll be at the Ritz." As if on cue, the elevator door opened at his floor and he was gone. Gone. That's where he was now, too. Seaton was gone from her life, along with trust for any other male companion. This was her self-imposed prison. He'd moved on to other relationships. Ha! If that's what you call them. Flitting from one ripe woman to another. Luring them into his lair with stories of Ivy League schooling, old money, and international travel. Add his sex appeal, and any sane woman didn't have a chance.

It wasn't just the fact he had new relationships or that theirs ended that tore Eva apart. That Eva could understand. That, like it or not, was life. It was how it happened. The betrayal. The raw rotten lie of the whole ordeal. The one small detail that Seaton didn't tell Eva that beautiful night in San Francisco—or any ensuing evening over the year they rendezvoused in Atlanta, Phoenix, London, Toronto, New York, Munich, and Chicago—was that he was married. There was a full-blooded Mrs. Seaton Andrew Rushmore III living and making his mansion a home in Arlington, Virginia.

Seaton's wife was the only way Eva could think about her. The idea of labeling the woman with a real debutante name—which she surely had, like Buffy or Beatrice—wasn't possible. No ditzy, harmless girl would be the object of her fury or the cause of her pain. It was all Seaton.

A year into their relationship, Eva headed to Washington, D.C., for business. She had a day layover, and even though Eva and Seaton hadn't talked about their schedules, she chanced that he may be grounded and at home in Arlington. How perfect to surprise him. Throughout their whirlwind months of weekend courtships, emails, and airport cell phone conversations, they had never once met each other in their own homes or cities.

Eva's heart was beating out of her chest with excitement. This would be so much fun! She was being spontaneous. Now *that's* new. She had found his home address through her network, and now she was driving her rented car to an exclusive mansion-row neighborhood in Arlington. Seaton's lineage and status was impressive. A man like this loved her! To say it wasn't part of the allure would be dishonest. He *cared* about her, made her laugh. He appreciated Eva's hard work and encouraged her career. Seaton humored her as she shared her new love and foray into the world of coaching. Bliss. It was too good to be true. She had goose bumps as she turned onto his street.

Then, right in front of her, her dream crumbled. One obscenely large house away, a man—undeniably Seaton—stood with his arm casually over the shoulders of a beautiful, petite woman. Two children were riding bicycles on the driveway, and a large black standard poodle stood by the front door. He was married. It was all a lie. Shaking with consuming, immediate grief and disbelief, Eva drove away with hot tears in her eyes. When she realized she had no idea where she was going, she quickly pulled into the parking lot at Harris Teeter and crumpled in the seat, hunched over the steering wheel.

How long was she there? She realized rain was pouring down in buckets. An hour must have passed when basic hunger and fatigue kicked in. Survival instinct took over. Eva drove on autopilot back to her hotel at Washington's Dulles airport and checked in like a robot. After sitting motionless for another hour on one of the two double beds in her hotel room, Eva knew she had to act. It was over. She had to sever the relationship with some dignity, if that's what you would call it. Eva sent a final text message to Seaton: *Nice poodle*. She never heard from him again.

Blowing audibly, Eva breathed loudly, self-regulating at the memory. Phone poles stood like centurions protecting the desolate stretch of roadway as she drove.

"It's time," Eva said, suddenly convicted, white knuckles on the steering wheel.

Bitterness is not only a hard pill to swallow, it's a hard pill to keep down. She cleared her voice and sat up straighter, relaxing her hands, still racing along the Wyoming highway.

"What price is it to harbor distrust of all men because of Seaton? Eva Marie Karlsen, its time to move on." The release of tension in her neck was physical. "It's time to take a risk." If she had used drugs as a youngster, which she hadn't, she would have said the rush was akin to a chemical-induced buzz. Torrents of tears streamed down her face.

Coming to terms with her demons was easy. There was a sick sort of comfort in storing them away and using them as convenient reference points to justify living out of harm's way. Her demons were like those old tools shoved in the back of the kitchen junk drawer. They were easy to find when she needed an excuse, but safely hidden from others.

It was habit to hold back from new relationships for self-preservation. Don't let history repeat itself. Nope, it was time to bury her perfectionist identity, those self-imposed shackles that said she must get it right, no matter what *it* was. One failed relationship did not mean a life sentence of failed relationships. Besides, she wasn't the one who failed. He did. Rationally she knew it was true. *Give up the drama, girl*. It was time to liberate from the torture device of perfection.

Gritting out a smile underneath tears that had run down her neck to dampen her shirt, Eva felt free. Her shoulders were wobbly from the release. This idea of dusting herself off and moving forward wasn't a new concept. Hadn't she had this conversation with Trina? Perfectionism, or fear of failure, raised its ugly head time and time again. She hadn't been completely straight with Trina about her progress on this point. It was the one topic she avoided full disclosure. Dumb. It's so stupid. So limiting.

"Note to self," Eva said aloud fondly thinking about her mentor who coached her toward a fulfillment, a greatness, Eva stubbornly resisted. "Call Trina."

17

Bear Claw Quilts was empty except for Heidi and Eva fawning over the completed quilt top that a beaming Jana held out for their viewing. Heidi shook her head in amazement.

"You wouldn't believe it, Eva. Jana has been a quilting maniac, piecing, and appliquéing this top like a wild woman."

"Jana, how did you make this so fast? It's absolutely gorgeous." Eva muttered the words and reverently idolized the stitches and the fabrics in greens, blues, and creams with highlights of red. The result was a mastery of compliment and contrast.

"I couldn't sleep knowing a block was unfinished or an appliquéd border was cut and ready to sew," Jana bubbled. "Thank God for Thanksgiving leftovers. I didn't want to take a minute to cook."

"I must get going on my new quilt. I've made it as far as deciding what I want to make, so now I need a color scheme and fabrics. Oh, Jana, how can I sew a quilt using this pattern when you produced this magnum opus?" Eva put on an exaggerated bleak face and laid her forehead on the table.

"Okay, girlfriend," Heidi clipped. "Enough groveling, no quilting for you!" Eva peeked up from the tabletop to look at Jana, then at Heidi. She was in character, this time mimicking the Soup Nazi from an episode of *Seinfeld*.

"No, Quilt Mistress," Eva answered, head still down on the table stifling a laugh. "Please, quilting is something that I cannot do without."

"That's the attitude, Eva, darling," Heidi said, Soup Nazi gone like he never existed.

"What's next for you, Jana?" Eva asked, only turning her head from its resting place on the table, hair tumbling around her face.

"Marilyn has room in her schedule to machine quilt on this top next week. For my next project, I'll embark on a Victorian crazy quilt. It should be an interesting addition to the parlor, don't you think?"

Heidi and Eva nodded in tandem agreement, knowing an embroidered crazy quilt would balance the decor of their Victorian home. The crazy quilt was a distinct art form created at the turn of the eighteenth century with blocks made from different geometric shapes and fabrics. Fabric selections included velvet, satin, and elaborate brocade in addition to the typical quilting cottons. After all the blocks were pieced and sewn into a crazy quilt top, a quilter embroidered over all the seams. The effect was wildly elaborate, a bit overdone, if you will, just like the décor of the Victorian Age.

As they meandered through the bolts of fabric, Heidi, lifting a particularly pretty Christmas fabric, called out to her friends, "What are you ladies up to this weekend?"

The overwhelming sound of silence made her stop and look behind her. Jana was eyeing Eva with a cocked head, and Eva had a slow rosy burn across her cheeks.

"Uh, huh, just as I suspected. Out with it, girl." Heidi, hands on hips, joined Jana in boring in on Eva. Looking at Jana, Heidi gave her the trademark *do you know something that I don't know* look. Jana shrugged.

"What? Why are you looking at me?" Eva quivered as her face slowly recovered from the unusually reddish glow. If they only knew the odd string of events—her first coming to terms regarding the end of her relationship with Seaton on the highway, then the phone call from Steve that same night. Whoa. If one believed in karma, this definitely was a great example.

"You tell us, honey." Heidi said, enjoying this table turning on the usually calm and collected Eva. "Shall I try some of my best novice coach moves on you, or will you just tell us what in the world has gotten over you to bring on that blush?"

Suddenly with a girlish charm, Eva raised her shoulders and held her breath for a second, letting air out, albeit quietly. "Steve and I are having coffee tomorrow morning at Grizzly Tracks."

"Go on," Jana said, engaged but uncharacteristically quiet, unable to hide an incredulous expression as she crossed her arms, directing full concentration on Eva. It was about time she had a date.

"Isn't that enough?" Letting a sufficient amount of silence pass, the mark of a trained coach, Eva grinned openly. "You got me. I have the worst case of the butterflies. Can't hide anything from you two under a guise of nonchalance and sophistication."

"Honey, I haven't seen any nonchalance or sophistication since I returned to Bear," Heidi deadpanned.

"Don't interrupt," Jana said without a trace of irony. Coming from Jana, this was a rather novel concept, one not lost on the other women who exchanged a glance.

"Steve called me and asked if I'd be walking Dash and Scout on Saturday morning. If so, would I be up to meeting him at Grizzly for a mid-walk warm up." Looking from Heidi to Jana, Eva added giddily, "So, I was able to form a few words and said *sure, that sounds nice.*"

"And?" Heidi added, drawing out the word.

"And, that's all. We really didn't talk much, just detailed our plans, and that was that." Flustered, Eva admitted, "I feel like a high schooler."

"You look like a high schooler," Heidi mused aloud. Eva looked the part in more ways than one. She was beaming coyly at the prospect of this first date with Steve at the safe and unassuming coffee shop. In addition, she had the slim, toned figure of a young girl and was dressed in a casual pink chenille turtleneck and low-slung whitewashed blue jeans, the kind she used to wear in high school that were now once again in fashion. Most eighteen year olds might not be wearing black silk long underwear beneath the jeans, but that secret was out of view.

18

Eva stood awkwardly in front of Grizzly Tracks with Dash and Scout. She shook involuntarily. Was it the frigid air or memories? The temperature was cold with the sun hidden beneath a covering of clouds.

A second later, before her skeletons rattled and demons settled in, Steve barreled around the corner in the Green Hornet, gave her a salute, and proceeded to execute a perfect and rather difficult parallel parking maneuver. Eva's heart jumped as relief swept over her.

Steve took a deep breath. He'd been off-balance about this casual cup of coffee since dawn. This woman was a knock out. Mature and worldly in her experience and smarts yet, from what he could tell, she seemed vulnerable, gullible even, despite her outward zest for life. Steady, boy. It was time to learn more about this lady. Such a lady to land in Bear.

"Hey, Eva. Good morning. Cold enough?" He naturally put his hand on her back and gently steered her into the coffee shop.

"Hi, Steve. Yes, definitely." Definitely? Nice, Eva. Suave opening.

"Hope you weren't waiting long," he said, taking the leashes as he opened the door. "Are these dogs warm enough?"

"So far no paws are freezing." With worry written on her face, she looked up at Steve and quietly added, "What should I do? I didn't think to ask when we spoke on the phone. I can't leave them outside in this weather."

Smiling a million-watt smile, Steve responded to her concerned question in kind, "Ah, your dogs. I have that handled. Heidi said the dogs aren't a problem and offered up Sander to watch them if necessary."

"Sander?" Eva considered making a comment about the young man but let it drop.

"Yes, Sander. Remember him from Thanksgiving?"

"Yes, yes, I remember him." Sander was hard to forget, and she was intrigued by him.

"I saw him the next day while I was plowing snow out of the alley for Grace and Lois. He was walking through town. We got to talking, and he needed a side job to help make ends meet. His freelance writing for magazines seems to have dried up. Well, I thought of Heidi and Grizzly, and Sander took it from there."

Eva took in the comment and they entered Grizzly, dogs and all. From behind the counter Sander and three other baristas were kibitzing and serving up coffees. The scene was classic coffee shop. Sander and his two cohorts looked the part of New Age coffee servers. They were tall and wiry, had cropped dark hair regardless of sex. Sander and one young man sported freshly barbered goatees, the other a soul patch. The girl was willowy, wearing a white shirt, white apron, and silver earrings pierced up and around one ear but only a cartilage cuff in the other.

If Eva were a betting gal, she'd wager there were at least four tattoos among them, and would raise the ante on eight or more. Wyoming was subtly changing with the times. Residents hoped the Equality State would remain untouched by the normal societal trends and keep its out-West ambience. Seems there was room for both.

"It smells good in here," Eva said. Dash and Scout were spinning around like tops, her legs tangled in leather leashes.

"Yes it does," Steve replied, biting back a comment about the leashes, avoiding the whole fiasco.

"Coffee is perfect for today." What a dork! Another lame comment, best just stop talking.

"Absolutely. What would you like?" Steve said. He proceeded to unwind Eva from the leashes in his hands, brushing her arms and legs in the process.

Who said it was cold? "Umm," Eva managed, struggling for her equilibrium.

"The offerings are plentiful," Steve said as he handed back the leashes pulled taught, dogs sitting at attention as he eyed her intently.

"Thanks," she whispered, grasping the leather loops. Steve leaned in close to her, signaling up at the brightly lettered chalkboard menu. He had that musky *man* smell, not cologne, just that man smell. Nice. Regaining composure, she contemplated the options. Eva looked up to the young man waiting patiently, then glanced over at Steve. "The other day with Charlie I had a sugar-free vanilla cappuccino with skim milk that was to-die-for good. I'll have that."

Without missing a beat, Steve said to the young man with "Chad" on his name badge, "Chad, one of what the lady said, and for me, café mocha with double espresso, please." Steve lasered in on the display of delectable desserts. "Would you like one of those to go with your skim milk, sugar-free concoction?" He asked, biting back a broad grin.

Eva felt her face blush. She was taken under Steve's spell and they hadn't even sat down with their coffee. In fact, she had barely spoken fifty words to him. The lemon drop shortbread with a thumbprint of lemon icing looked especially good. Steve caught her lusting after the treat and spoke to Chad, "Add two of those lemon cookies. Please."

"Come on, let's have a seat." Again, he gently put his hand on the small of her back to guide her across the room. Steve steered her to a round table near the window. He pulled out her chair and automatically extended his hand to take the leashes so she could take off her coat and sit. Within moments, Chad brought over their coffee. Eva found herself speechless, sitting across from Steve, both of them holding warm mugs of coffee. All the while, Dash and Scout, due to the miracle of the corner radiator, had lain down without a ruckus.

Was it her imagination, or was the pressure from his hand still resident on the small of her back?

"How's the coffee?" Steve spoke up, breaking the silence. Eva nodded, mid-sip cappuccino. "Good." He went on. "So, tell me, what causes a young woman such as yourself to pick up and move to a place where you don't know anyone? Granted, it's been two years. Just call me curious."

Eva scrunched her shoulders in contentment as she prepared to answer. She'd had this question before, so she wasn't just making up the answer. "Mountains. Big blue skies. Access to see moose, deer, eagles. Really good hiking." She stopped, amazed at her calm response and gazed purposefully at Steve, face aglow.

Steve pursed his lips, eyes twinkling, and voice serious. "Can't argue with that assessment. You sure came to the right place. Keep going."

"I decided to follow my dream. I realized that if I didn't like it out here or was lonely, I could always move back. You know? It doesn't have to be permanent." *Spontaneous*, she wanted to shout. A miracle, really. It sounded so mature, so obvious. If only he knew.

Her gut-level response touched him. It captured the essence of what brought Eva to Wyoming. Raising his eyebrows, Steve shifted in his chair, picked up a cookie, and before taking a bite, asked her a follow-up question to keep her talking, "Well, has it been what you expected?"

Quiet. Thinking. "It's more, Steve."

"Such as?"

"This place is surreal. Every day I wake up and can't believe what I see through the window."

"Wyoming has that effect."

"I love my log home. Working as a coach. This town has been welcoming, and Jana and Heidi are the best."

"They're two in a million." Progress, he noticed Eva was warming up.

"Even the dogs are fun." Glancing over at her charges, she shook her head and added, "Despite the fact they have the uncanny ability to make a mess out of any free-standing item."

Chuckling, Steve pushed the cookie plate her direction. "Pets and mess, they go together. That's what my Mom used to say."

"Do you have any pets?"

"Not exactly. Pet sitter under duress is more like it." Changing the topic, Steve continued. "Well, I must say, this place is one that's hard to leave once you land. Believe me, I've tried."

"Really? Now your turn to tell me more. You don't seem like the type to leave Bear." Eva picked up the cookie and bit in. The rich shortbread melted in her mouth. She unconsciously closed her eyes to absorb the taste. The tart, fresh lemon flavor, butter, and sugar frosting erupted in her mouth. Yum. When Eva opened her eyes, Steve was staring at her, mildly amused, head cocked.

"It's delicious," Eva sputtered, embarrassed. Aargh, caught in the act of culinary pleasure.

Smiling broadly, Steve ignored the cookie escapade and continued, "My parents, as you may have heard from Heidi, are highly educated wanderers. Their studies and research gained them the privilege of invitations to speak around the world."

"Impressive."

"They're of amiable character, so they get along in most circles in and out of Bear."

"Did you ever travel with them?" Eva asked, picking up the buttery crumbs with her fingers.

"Yes, some, as a kid."

"No longer?"

"I haven't for a long time. Plus, there was a time that I wanted to move out of Bear to strike it out on my own. Now that I think about it, I think my aim was to be *Steve Mason, regular guy*, instead of *Steve Mason, son of the illustrious Tom and Maggie*."

Eva nodded, picking up her warm drink. "What kept you here?"

"Let's see, how can I put it?" Suspending his words for effect, Steve gazed into Eva's eyes, squinting as if trying to read them, then continued, "Mountains, blue skies, moose, eagles, and deer. Trout, mountain streams, and did I say trout?" A giant smile came across Steve's face that had Eva blushing again. Not missing the moment, Steve leaned forward and brushed Eva's cheek with a tender fist as he whispered quietly for her ears only, "Seems like, lovely lady, we have a few things in common. That is, of course, if you'll accept the trout and streams as additions to your list."

"It's a good list," Eva said, unsure if he could hear her voice over the sound of her beating heart.

Steve continued bantering about local facts. "I hear you're a sewer, too. You'll have to meet Grace. She produces miracles from fabric and, I might add, is a saint at mending my clothes." The casual, intimate conversation absorbed Steve and Eva. An hour passed like minutes. Openly hesitant, Steve glanced at his watch and locked his baby blues onto Eva's eyes. "Eva, unfortunately duty calls. We must continue this another time." Thinking about an opportunity, Steve startled with an idea. "Can I have the honor of taking you to the opening of The Sicilian Ball? Our new friends are working like black ants to make their opening date, and I'd hate to disappoint them if the restaurant weren't filled." In a tone of mock seriousness, he added, "We should do our part."

Eva, entranced by Steve's eyes, signaled a yes just before it came out of her mouth. "Okay. Sure." She wanted to respond demurely, but the two simple words emerged instead. They were enough for Steve.

"I'll call with specifics." Without premise, Steve impulsively picked up Eva's hand, engulfing it with his own strong, calloused hand. Lifting her hand to his lips, he brushed a kiss on the inside of her palm and gave her a wink. He stood up to assist her out of her chair while she was still reeling inside from the wink. She felt off balance as he helped her with her coat. He went over to gather the dogs as if he'd being doing it for years and patiently waited, handing her the leashes once she was properly bundled for Bear. Seaton never entered her mind.

19

The Sicilian Ball shimmered with candlelight from the tables and fireplace mantel, and from the crystal bulbs hanging down like stars the length of the wooden bar. Marlo admired the room, pure Tuscany, ready for celebration after the grape harvest. Humming to herself, Marlo put the matches in a hidden compartment she found in the hostess stand. She ran her hands over the first page of the reservation book. Life was good.

Rearranging everything while moving nothing, satisfied, Marlo reached behind her back to untie the white apron. Her black silk blouse hung loosely over a flowing skirt made up of rings of gold, purple, and olive fabric, colors that mirrored the mural on the restaurant walls. She swiveled her hips to swirl the skirt; there was time to wear the apron later. Marlo had made the simple skirt and had been amazed to find the perfect mixture of colors in the wrinkled remnants of her stash.

Surveying the room, she raked her hands through unruly curls. She sucked in breath to calm herself and blinked her eyes for moisture. The candles provided a reddish glow to the end of her curls as she nearly floated toward the bar. Chad, daytime barista–cum–nighttime bartender, was arranging glasses behind the bar and watching Marlo's excitement. "Marlo, you look great. Nice skirt."

"Thank you." Marlo nodded coyly and looked up at him, happy for the affirmation. "I made it myself."

"Sweet. It suits you. This place looks terrific." He put down one glass and picked up another to polish. "You've done a bella job in decorating and preparing the dining area."

Marlo curtsied to accept the compliments. "Can you believe it?" The question was rhetorical.

Chad raised his eyebrows.

"Our grand opening is only minutes away. I'm going to find Gianni and see if he needs any Prozac!" She laughed and was off. Watching Marlo dance her way to the back of the restaurant, Chad, caught in Marlo's wake, uncharacteristically started to hum.

Enrique and Gianni labored like skilled mercenaries in the kitchen. They were decisive in their movements. Marlo hated to break their concentration but needed to tell them the time. Pots of all sizes were on the stoves, vegetables lay chopped on the counters, varieties of olive oils and vinegars arranged on countertops. The smell was heavenly. The aroma of garlic, basil, and onion permeated the room. A pot of water was simmering for a future order of pasta, with a bowl of clarified butter and olive oil standing close by. The crusty baked bread offered such an aroma that Marlo could almost taste the fleshy Italian bread soaked in a mixture of balsamic vinaigrette, crushed garlic, extra virgin olive oil, and freshly grated aged Parmesan and Asiago cheese.

"Uh, hello," Marlo said, suddenly shy, not wanting to disrupt the living art taking place in front of her eyes. In unison, Gianni and Enrique turned to Marlo. To her surprise, they offered smiles full of white teeth against their darker skin.

"Marlo, bella, tell us, what's going on up front?" Gianni's voice was calm, professional, treating her as an equal. Touched at the warm greeting at this intense time, she ran over and gave the two of them bear hugs, first Enrique, then Gianni. She bubbled, "Oh, the front is inspiring, Gianni, only to be upstaged by the miracles happening in this kitchen. The waitress and busboy are poised and ready. We just need some guests." She closed her eyes in bliss, adding, "It smells heavenly!"

"But of course, my dear, *this is* the place for these types of smells." Gianni beamed as he stood straight and looked at Marlo. In an instant, Marlo could see that Gianni wasn't anxious; he was excited, like a child on Christmas Eve anticipating a visit from Santa Claus. It was the energy that exudes from people when they're in that zone, doing what they love.

"You be the chef, chief," Marlo said, hugging her own shoulders. *This must be what Eva calls fulfillment when she talks about her clients living a life on purpose. I get it.*

"Did you see that bread on the counter?" Enrique pointed with his chin. "That, our Marlo, is Italian boule, round bread. We found a baker in Wilton willing to try our recipe. Italian boule is a classic."

"It smells glorious," Marlo said, her mouth watering.

"It has both a crisp crust and a wonderfully soft tender dough inside, chewy, a bit like French baguette, with a mild flavor and sweet aroma," Enrique enthused, closing his eyes as he imagined eating the bread. "They used our white starter with organic grapes that Gianni has been carrying around, similar to that of sourdough—the results: magnifico."

"Enrique, I'm salivating." Hands on her stomach, rolling her eyes with pleasure, Marlo added, "Now that you gave me a run-down on the bread, my taste buds are impatient."

"Perfect," Gianni said. "Marlo, as you take orders, use that savory vision to explain dishes to our guests." Turning to wink at Enrique, he went on, "If you do a good job, we'll throw you some bread crumbs later on."

"Hey!" Marlo yelled. Gianni, laughing, put up both his hands to keep away the madly swinging Marlo as she flung herself at him. Marlo found herself airborne, slung over Gianni's back, her feet wagging.

The two sucked in their breath, laughing, and ended up in a heap on the spotless floor. Hugging her for real, Gianni took her in his arms affectionately, then pushed her up to stand; she turned and reached out a hand. "You!—don't you know by now not to keep food away from a woman?"

"Si, yes, I see that," Gianni said, standing, wiping his hands on his apron.

"Real women have voracious appetites, even more than most men, I'd say," Marlo added.

"Moreover, you can rumble like one, too."

"Exactly. Survival when among you buffoons," she said with a wink.

"It is good, si. We need that love of food if you girls from Wichita want to work in an Italian restaurant," Gianni said, eyeing Enrique, whose knife kept up a steady beat through the whole ordeal, chopping sweet red onions.

"So, you were saying about the activities in the front?" Enrique interjected, ponytail bobbing in a hair net as he nodded toward the door.

Marlo clasped her hands together and spun around, skirt swaying in her wake. "It … is … ready," she replied, drawing out each word. "The place shimmers with Italian romance. Chad is shining up the bar as if he's waiting to have a regular crowd come in for drinks. Devine!"

"What are you saying, Marlo?" Enrique balanced the knife point on the cutting board, held it by the handle, his dark eyes gleaming.

"Let's open! It's time. Both of you, up front. You know, turn over the 'Open' sign and pull up the shades. It wouldn't be wise for me to do it alone." Her serious cadence caused the men to put down their tools. The three walked down the short corridor into the dining area. Chad, standing behind the bar with a wine glass and white towel in hand, froze watching the goings on. A somber Marlo stepped aside for Gianni to lead. Understanding her ceremony, he slowly and deliberately raised the shades in the front windows and turned the sign to "Open." He switched over the dead bolt, and it made a resounding click.

After the ritualistic proceeding, he gave a small bow toward Marlo and Enrique, saluted toward Chad. Then, out of character from what his workmates knew of Gianni, the typically reserved man did a tight double heel spin, landing with his arms outstretched, and quipped, "Showtime!"

The four yelped and Enrique burst into a popular rap refrain about partying like it's your birthday. They joined in dancing together through four iterations, stopping in a pant, flushed.

"Without you three, this moment wouldn't be possible," Gianni said as he cleared his throat of a small catch.

"Gianni, you're the master," Chad spoke up, caught in the mood as they were huddled in a circle, arms around each other's necks.

"I'm so grateful for you." Gianni beamed. "This restaurant, The Sicilian Ball, is officially open, in honor of you three, and of course, my great grandfather Dario."

Grace Johnson Cartwright was dressed to the nines. Her striking plum suit was decorated with pewter filigree buttons. On her delicate feet she wore black dancer's shoes with a small strap. No one but her knew the shoes were more than sixty years old. Grace arranged a matching pressed wool hat atop her silver hair, pulled up in a chignon, carefully ensuring that the hat's lace didn't distort her vision. Looking in the mirror, she closed her eyes and a bittersweet memory flooded her mind as if it were yesterday. The memory brought on a tinge of sadness.

"Auntie Grace, you're beautiful." Lois had to swallow the lump in her throat. Her aunt was breathtaking, looking young and vibrant.

"Oh, my dear, thank you. I'm a bit over the hill, as they say nowadays. However, you, Lois, look pretty. Let's see, give me a twirl." Grace took in her niece as she spun a circle, her dress swirled easily with layers of fluttering fabric.

"Is it okay?" Lois asked softly.

"That dress is stunning on you, child.

"You think so?" She was still tentative.

"Dear Lois, your slight figure is all the rage. The deep bias cut of that gored skirt is beautiful. The cream lace offsets your face against the navy velvet." Among other vocations, Grace had at one time been a dressmaker for the society ladies in St. Louis, and her years as owner of the Now and Then Dress Shop had firmly established her reputation as a fashion authority in Bear. Her comments on clothing were explicit and identified the specific sewing technique that was used to create "the piece," as she called tailored clothing.

Grace hadn't sewn the dress Lois wore but had kept it in her carefully tended stash of vintage clothing. She encouraged her niece to wear the clothes. The styles looked stunning on the young woman's svelte, almost too-thin figure. As an ancillary benefit, the vintage fashion suited Lois's personality without having to spend a dime on newer, less brilliant attire.

Blushing because she felt so feminine and liked it, Lois hugged her aunt gently, taking care with Grace's powder-soft, translucent skin. "Thank you, Auntie, I love it. Sometimes I wish I lived back in time when this dress was new. What a tale this dress could tell."

"Pshaw. Honey, do take care of your wishes." Grace knew all too well that the good old days weren't necessarily good. Besides, she wasn't sure she wanted her niece to hear the stories that dress could tell. "Let's go see this new restaurant. An Italian place in Bear—I never thought I'd see the day." Lois held out Grace's coat and handed her a scarf. "I'm up for the short walk, so don't be worrying your pretty head that it's too far." Bundled and ready to go, they ambled the two blocks to The Sicilian Ball.

The restaurant was buzzing. It wasn't often a new venue opened up in Bear. People were awash with curiosity, and Gianni received support from his adopted town. The holidays were coming, the new restaurant was opening up, and the snow hadn't covered their streets from impasse yet this season. Most tables were filled, and eight of the ten bar stools were taken. Truly, this was a time for celebration in Bear, Wyoming.

Heidi, Sander, Jana, and Dale made it off to dine at the restaurant on opening night. The four friends arrived at the restaurant bearing gifts for their hosts. Heidi brought a bouquet of long-stem white roses with lacey foliage and baby's breath. Sander provided a bottle of champagne from Reims, France. Dale had built a wooden picture frame for the restaurant's first dollar bill, hand painted in a Tuscany plum color, and Jana had whipped up three white aprons with the names Gianni, Enrique, and Chad embroidered on the top left.

When Heidi invited Steve, he explained that he had plans, and that "two's company, and a half-dozen is a crowd." *Well, aren't you the stealthy planner, Heidi had teased. Too good for the group now, eh?*—knowing full well of his surreptitious romance.

Charlie Cunningham, complete with bow tie and smart suit, sat at a small table with an unknown distinguished woman. Lois and Grace had a seat up front by the windows. Heidi and friends sat positioned at a middle table without a clear view of Eva and Steve, who were comfortable in the back corner. Most diners were from Bear, with the exception of one of the larger tables that hosted a group from Jackson. A few single men were propped up on the bar chairs joined by couples happily waiting for tables. Everyone was sampling the Italian Chianti that flowed freely on opening night.

Marlo zipped in and around the tables like a hummingbird. She was cosmopolitan in her colored skirt, her dark curls a perfect accent to the Italian décor. Her self-esteem soared as she capably worked the room, instinctively aware that Sander watched her every move.

"A little starstruck, Sander?" Dale chided Sander so only he could hear. "She's looking rather beautiful if I do say so myself."

"Uh, no thanks, I have enough," Sander replied to a question not asked.

"Okay then," Dale said, amused, watching the young man fix his gaze on the moving Marlo.

"I'm having veal scaloppini," Sander replied, startled by Dale's voice and completely missing his comments. Laughing, Dale agreed, indicating that the veal would be a good choice, sparing Sander any embarrassment.

"Our watiress should be coming soon, yes? Are you all ready to order? This bread is soo-o delicious." Jana was oblivious to her rush of unanswered queries and missed the raised eyebrows Heidi gave Dale as Jana waxed on with excitement. "Don't you love the olive oil on the table?" Just then Marlo appeared at their table with a tray of water glasses, not too much ice, and a broad, beautiful smile.

"Welcome to The Sicilian Ball. Thank you for celebrating with us on our opening night. Please enjoy the festivities." Marlo paused for effect, gave a short curtsey, and caught her breath. "So, what do you think?"

"Incredible, Marlo. This place is really hopping." Heidi was sincerely amazed at the success. "Opening at Grizzly Tracks wasn't quite so, well, dramatic," she deadpanned.

"You guys really have it going on here," Dale agreed. "The customers are happy. A great sign for a new place. How's Gianni holding up?"

"Gianni is amazing. He and Enrique are pounding out these beautiful plates like they belong on the cover of *Saveur* magazine. Oh, that's a cooking magazine," Marlo added. Quietly she leaned into her table of friends and offered, "Did you see Eva and Steve over in the corner? They're so cute. Both shy and polite, just like a prom date."

"So we noticed. Yup, old Steve stood us up, saying he already had a dinner companion," Heidi replied. "Guess it's good for the two of them to have human companionship."

"Totally," Jana added. "Eva's getting a little too used to living with dogs, and with Steve watching his parents' cat and all." She signaled the need for a toast with her almost-empty glass in hand.

The group picked up their Chianti glasses just as the waitress arrived to take dinner selections. As Marlo settled next to Sander, he momentarily lost composure before giving his dinner order, mesmerized by his stunning girlfriend. Twice in one night the typically guarded Sander lost himself. The thin mountain air had a mellowing effect.

Back in the kitchen, Enrique and Gianni took unspoken cues from one another, norming into their roles. Enrique appeared with a sprig of parsley, a completed sauce, or a bulb of baked garlic before Gianni breathed his need. Enrique was in charge of antipasto, insalate, and garnish. Additionally he shared the dessert preparation with Gianni, most of which was done earlier in the day. Gianni was a master in his element, creating the night's specials, pastas, meats, fish, and crisp vegetables, and directing cream sauces, garlic butters, and freshly made marinara. The commercial ovens and gas stoves performed excellently. The counters were orderly yet filled.

"Gianni, Enrique," Marlo called, breathless as she came rushing into the kitchen. "All of our friends are here. You need to come out for a minute and see. It's enchanting." Both men looked up, then at each other.

"Marlo, great idea. But we're cooking. How can we go out and socialize?" muttered a focused Gianni, slowly whisking cream into the pot of alfredo sauce.

"Si, Marlo is right, Gianni. My grandfather used to say that a chef must stay in touch with his clients," Enrique added, placing fresh basil on a split chicken breast over homemade marinara.

"Ah," Gianna said, lowering the heat under the alfredo.

"Aren't you curious?" Enrique asked, rubbing his hands on a sauce-streaked apron.

"There are people, I can tell by all these orders." Gianni motioned around the kitchen.

"Gianni!" Marlo crooned.

"Nothing will go wrong. We can escape for a few minutes," Enrique said, pushing his friend from behind the counters.

Moments later the two chefs walked the few steps from kitchen to dining room, followed by Marlo, a déjà vu of hours earlier when they paraded for the grand opening ritual. Gianni stopped short and turned back to face Marlo, tears streaming down his face.

"Keep going," she insisted.

"Momma mia." Gianni mouthed the words, crossed himself, and moved toward the dining room.

"This is it, what we've been working for," managed Enrique, using his fingers to blot the tears trying to escape from the corners of his eyes.

The restaurant bustled and smelled delicious. It was busy, but not packed. He recognized almost half the faces. Chad was at the bar laughing with a customer, shaking an apple martini in a chrome drink mixer. The tables were intimate but festive, and the light was romantic but not dark. Marlo gently wiped Gianni's tears, and gave him a gentle push.

"Go see Jana and Heidi right there in the middle, then visit one table of someone you don't know. That's all you need to do right now, Gianni. Now go." Marlo could hear him take a couple deep breaths before moving.

Gianni took in the room. People were laughing and eating, the clink of forks on dinner platters a symphony to his ears. His eyes locked in on Jana. She was talking with a glass of wine in her hand and almost dumped it all over Dale. Gianni felt calm. A familiarity. Food, people, noise. This is *him*. Jana gets this, he thought. Her zest for life is a spice for the room. Smiling, Gianni remembered ten years ago when he and Jana had burnt the white sauce and dumped the whole pot in the garbage before anyone found out. What might they do now?

Eva noticed Gianni coming into the dining area and motioned to Steve.

"Look at him," Eva said, sipping her Chianti.

Steve turned to watch Gianni. "He's in his element. It's a feat to pull this off in Bear. I don't remember such an opening, especially one by a nonlocal."

"I love seeing this whole place come to life," Eva said, her mouth watering as she watched plates go past. "Everyone seems to be celebrating."

"Old Bear needed some new excitement."

Eva eyed a familiar face across the room. "My new client, Charlie, is here. What a handsome couple he makes with his lady friend."

Steve followed her gaze. "Cunningham is a good guy. In high school he dated Heidi's mom, my Aunt Mary." Steve paused at the memory of his deceased aunt. "Quite the winning lawyer, Charlie."

"I agree with that," Eva responded, careful not to use reveal any personal information gathered during coaching. "So, do you know everyone in this place, except the group from Jackson?"

"What do you mean? I divulged some explicit details about those folks." Steve winked at her as he took a sip of wine. Earlier, Steve had Eva laughing so hard her eyes watered at an imaginary description of the secret lives of the people from Jackson sitting at the large table. The hilarious stories about a make-believe plastic surgeon, clandestine art dealer, and African hunter had her completely out of control with giggles. The pretend conversation kept them talking and diffused the new-dating jitters.

"Yeah, lots of these people are familiar," Steve said as he glanced around him. "Grace and Lois are here—I must introduce you later. Judge Jerry is here with his wife, Marta. Two of Bear's finest police officers are at the bar. Those other guys shooting whiskey I don't recognize.

Before Eva could drill for more information, their server appeared with platters of piping hot food. "Bon appétit," Eva said, smiling over at Steve. "This looks great." Then, going back to her question, Eva went on. "I'm intrigued by Judge Jerry and his wife," she said, swirling pasta in her spoon for the perfect bite. "She looks to be fifteen years younger than he is."

Steve nodded his head, taking a sip of the deep red wine, "Yes, it was scandalous for Bear. They hooked up and married within a couple of months. He met her when he was on some trip overseas—Italy, maybe—and came back smitten and jovial. Seems they were both divorced and hit it off."

"Life goes on. I guess that's a good thing," Eva noted. Still, they seemed an unlikely couple, even after a vacation romance.

"What about you, Ms. Karlsen? Is there a man waiting for you in some far-off land?" Steve asked, his voice low, for only her ears.

Eva swallowed hard for composure to answer his question; his voice and his blue eyes had an effect on her. "Actually, no," Eva managed, her heart pounding. Steve waited, watching her intently. "There was, but not now. It's me and the dogs."

"There was …" Steve said, mirroring her words. His eyes narrowed, watching her for more information.

"Was," Eva confirmed, thoughts trapped in her brain but no more words coming out of her mouth. She picked up her wine for support and took a long, slow sip to steady herself.

"So the dogs are my current competition?" Steve asked rhetorically, then continued, "Are you sure there are no other humans involved?" Eva managed a smile and shook her head. Her vulnerability was palpable. Leaning back in his chair, Steve let out a long sigh. "Dogs are rather tough competition. And I've seen you with yours."

Laughing in spite of herself, Eva pushed back old memories. "I'm on a clean slate right now in Bear. A start over," she offered, deciding to pull herself together. She liked this guy.

"So, can we, ah, start?" Steve asked, setting down his fork, wiping his mouth with the napkin from his lap.

He was such a vision of male energy wrapped up with tenderness that Eva thought she might swoon. Was this really happening?

"Starting would be nice. I'd like to start slow, like this," Eva said, gesturing to the tranquil environment they established at their table.

"I can do slow," Steve answered. "Tell me, how did you come about those dogs?" As they continued their meal, Steve and Eva traipsed down winding paths of conversation. Eva wondered what had taken her so long to get out and relax with a man. She stamped out the murmur of caution that tried to steal the stage.

After dinner, Steve drove Eva around Bear, pointing out the Christmas lights that she'd never find on her normal routes through the town. They talked about holiday traditions and swapped stories about how they learned the truth about Santa Claus. Eva found she was sharing stories from her youth that she hadn't thought of in ages. And Steve was interested. She loved that. Steve was full of anecdotes and history of Bear that comforted her like a blanket. When they finally got back to her cabin, he walked her to the porch. Before saying good night, he lifted her chin with his hand and stroked her cheek, then gave her an ever-so-light kiss good night.

21

Stretched back in the chair, body arched, Steve clasped his hands over head. Ah, what a relief. He quickly sat forward in front of his Mac, causing the iron screw at the base of the old desk chair to grind in complaint. The chair was a respectable companion to the large rolltop maple desk. He loved the cubbyholes, drawers, and slots to store papers, desk supplies, and mementos. How could he possibly work at any other type of desk? The desk was upgraded to the twenty-first century once he installed a computer keyboard drawer. This effective little tip had been shared by Dale at their Thanksgiving fire-lighting discussion. Steve had it installed by the next Monday.

File saved, Steve closed the document and moved into email. He perused the list of new messages, scanning down the sender names. Smiling, he opened the one that just recently came in from his mother, themags@email.com.

Dearest Steven,
Your Father and I are fine, enjoying the journey, as they say. He is just playing this part of American Academic to the hilt. It's hilarious, and I love him for it. In Istanbul we had a cocktail hour at the American Embassy, quite a lovely place. Tom—your Father, I should say—wore wire-framed glasses, a pocket watch, and a tweed blazer, and he embraced his role. He had swarms of young intellectuals flocking at his feet. What was that movie that made it big when you were growing up, the one with Kevin Costner playing a professor and archeologist? Anyway, it was great. I was able to talk to the Bahrain ambassador, an oil Sheik (who had met Michael Jackson), and steal away to the kitchen to understand exactly what they had been feeding us that night.

How was your holiday? Did Heidi feed you well for Thanksgiving?
Lois wrote that there is a new restaurant in town, Italian? Now that I like.
Well, it's time for me to go. This next week is our university circuit talks,

and I must get my beauty sleep. Give Snowball a kiss for me, dear.
Love, Mummy

Typical. Maggie's messages were as eclectic and interesting as his mother herself. He could tell she was getting into the foreign nature of a trip when she signed her name as *Mummy* instead of Mom, Truly-Your-Mother, or Mommy-the-Mags. Sending a reply, Steve imagined the phone ringing in seconds if he mentioned any word of Eva, which he hadn't, not yet.

Eva, who laughed until tears at his made-up stories about the people from Jackson. Eva, who ate her plate of Italian food with gusto, saving *just* enough so she could savor the flavor at lunch the next day. Eva, who sparkled at The Sicilian Ball wearing emerald cashmere and that short black shirt. Not that he minded the length. What a lady. And that soft, brief kiss. He shook himself back to the present and the duties at hand.

Enlisting focused thought, Steve opened a new message, wrote a few short lines, zipped the newly completed document, attached the file, and sent it off. Done. One more task marked off the list. If it were up to him, the Gros Ventre mountain range would be as popular as the Rockies and the Grand Tetons. His article about them was a start. Plus, it helped with the publishing requirements needed to maintain certain academic status with his doctorate.

Steve walked into the kitchen and saw the charcoal cat perched in her favorite spot. The animal's prized location, a nook below the countertop, was built into the cabinetry for storing cooking paraphernalia. Steve never filled the space, preferring to look up for his kitchen tools, and not down. Snowball took an immediate liking to the spot, and that was that. Stopping, Steve leaned down and tenderly pulled the animal out of the cubby with two hands. He stroked her soft dark fur and kissed the top of her head. Gently, as he had taken her out, he put the animal back in her comfort area. The cat shook her head, swatted out with her tail, curling back up in a ball to continue her nap. If he was anything, Steve was good to his word. This included requests from his mother.

Continuing on his mission, Steve rinsed out his coffee mug, filled it with black roast, and went back to the desk. It was time to organize his fishing life. There were more emails to be answered, files to be edited, and letters to be written than he cared to consider. Steve had two work passions, the study of Wyoming history and trout fishing, in no particular order. Spring, summer, and early fall lent themselves to wonderful trout fishing in the Jackson Hole area. Steve was one of—if not the—best-respected guides around.

Many of his clients were themselves indigenous to the area, male and female, young and old. This was an accolade to Steve, as locals took pride in knowing the areas' best fishing holes and typically kept them private. However, there was something about Steve Mason. His fishing holes, his technique, and his knowledge equaled an outdoor experience one seldom forgot or could replicate.

As he worked through the afternoon, the fruits of his labor, as it were, watched over him. Steve was flanked by pictures stuck in the cork surface of the wall around the desk, photos of speckle-belly trout, brown trout, and rainbow trout. Most of them featured happy clients squinting against the sun, grasping a fish, with a Christmas greeting printed to the right. Barely holding on to its stickiness, a small, square yellow paper clung to the edge of the rolltop. Earlier that day, Steve scribbled a hardly legible note: *After guide work, call Eva*, as if he needing reminding. It was encouragement to finish work, and calling Eva his reward.

Across town, Marlo prepared the dining room of The Sicilian Ball for the evening's guests. Tables were set, napkins folded ornately and properly posed on bread plates, olive oil carafes filled and ready. Everything was in order. Only ten minutes until they opened and time to light the table candles. Marlo went to the hostess stand for her trusty matches. The secret compartment where she stored them was empty. Puzzled, Marlo, in her quirky fashion, closed the drawer and opened it again. Still gone. She looked on the top of the stand and underneath on the shelves. Nothing. No matches. *That's odd*, she thought, and she let the mystery leave her mind as she made way to the bar to borrow matches from Chad.

22

Anthony Joseph Sanderson crept out of bed so as not to rouse Marlo. She was curled in a fetal position, innocent as a child, her back nestled close to where he once lay. Leaning over to examine her face, he stroked a random curl off her forehead, never touching her skin. *My beauty. My marvel. God, what will happen when you know the truth about me and my made-up circumstances? That's my fear. This damn job. Trapped in this cycle of secrets. One day, Marlo, one day.*

Swallowing his aggravation, Sander snuck out of the small bedroom and donned a fleece. The trailer was mostly airtight, but no metal structure could keep the plummeting temperatures of a Wyoming winter at bay. Soundlessly, with trained adeptness, he went to the office at the back of the trailer and pulled out a black canvas briefcase from the tiny closet. It was dirty, worn, and heavy. In seconds, Sander had set up a technical array of laptop computer, wireless modem, and a small printer. Disengaging the audio capability, he typed in a series of codes and passwords at breakneck speed, fingers fluttering over the keyboard.

His eyes scanned the messages with panicked urgency. Last time he felt this was the Machu Picchu leg of this job. The ancient energy from the mountains of Peru unnerved him. There the norm *was* the abnormal. Rounded, green primordial mountains, ancient stone fences, and crumbling structures set the tone. Add in the swirling mist and primitive languages, and the intensity skyrocketed. The prehistoric gods laughed for eternity nestled in stone crevasses. It gave him the creeps.

Machu Picchu is where things got perplexing. The operation had no unplanned media leaks or unintended casualties. That was good. The problem was, there was nothing in Peru at all. No leads, no messages, no adversary. All those dead ends sent Sander to Bear. Except for the magnificence of the natural venue, South America was a bust. The job was unfinished.

Hooking up with Marlo was such an uncanny coincidence that it was, well, too weird. Compared to Peru, at least Bear had a semblance of normality. He still wasn't accustomed to the general dullness of the town or the lack of ambulance bleating. Yet the peace of the place made his work seem less undercover. Either that or it was his wishful thinking.

Marlo changed everything. He didn't plan on Marlo. She had become his blessing and his curse. While in Machu Picchu, her dark, dazzling beauty caught the attention of his male desires. The moment he laid eyes on her, he knew he had to compartmentalize his attraction, put it in the bottom drawer, so to speak, and focus on the job. Then it happened. He overheard her conversation with another hiker about moving from Wichita, Kansas, to Bear, Wyoming. All his training kicked in, his radar up for any clue. Was she a plant? Her presence had him off kilter, unprofessional. Only the night before he overheard Marlo, Sid had instructed him that, to complete the job, he must visit a "small town called Bear nestled in the Gros Ventres." Sid had a way of making assignments sound regular and carefree, like the mundane process of financial accounting.

Finance. Damn! Why didn't he just stick to it and be content with finance? He had a promising career at a global Fortune 200 conglomerate. The powers that be liked his Ivy League schooling, his bilingual skills, and numerical savvy. Now he was living in a second-rate trailer, for God's sake. Living in a trailer with a beautiful woman. He would never have met Marlo on his New York, London, and Tokyo circuit.

She thinks I'm someone else, for the most part. What will she think of me? What must she think of me right now, believing what she does about me? Some kind of loser who chucked his degrees and now works in a coffee shop. Barely a dime to his name? But she's still here. Curious. She's becoming a native in this town. She works at the new restaurant with unabashed passion. That passion. Mmm, yes that. Sander closed his eyes, rubbing the throbbing tension from the bridge of his nose. Time was of the essence, and he needed details. There was more at stake than ever before.

This job was a bigger game than Sander anted up for, a gamble he now had to win. Seconds after passwords allowed access to a secret network, three messages appeared on his screen. In an unconscious habit, Sander scanned the room, checked his back, ensuring solitude. Suddenly the chill was gone from the room. Beads of sweat formed on his brow. He read the messages three times and memorized their contents, details confirming that the Barratino family is connected to someone in Bear—but who? When done, he deleted the messages.

Distractingly, a green flashing icon in the shape of a komodo dragon appeared on his screen. Sander smiled in spite of himself as he opened the window and entered yet another password. Sid was online. The man never slept. He was up and messaging Sander at all times of the night, wherever he might be in the world. In typical fashion, Sid offered his pseudoparental support and boss's prerogative, giving Sander loose directions peppered with choice words such as "ruthless," "labyrinth," "puzzling mosaic," and "be careful." *Perfect.*

23

Dash fixated on Eva. One paw wrapped around her arm, his gaze penetrated into hers. As she leaned over to pet Scout's head with her free hand, the wiry pooch slid down on the floor turning on her side so Eva could rub her belly. Dash, intent on stealing more attention, put a second paw around Eva's arm. He was now balanced on his furry derriere, both paws wrapped around her.

"Why the pestering? We had a good walk, the sun is shining, and I'm just meeting Marlo for coffee." Luxuriating in the dogs, Eva unwound from Dash. She knelt on the floor and pulled the soft animals close, wrapped one arm around each dog's neck, and hugged them gently.

"Oh, I love you babies. Now, you'll be fine. Don't make me feel guilty. Come on, *kennel*." At this Dash romped across the floor to the mudroom where two identical blue kennels sat side by side. Scout, however, immediately flattened her body against the floor, not moving, pressing her head low between her outstretched paws.

"Scouty, come on. *Kennel*," Eva said in a stern voice as she held back a grin. The canine wasn't keen to go into her kennel. She liked to play the game "I'm not going to listen" several times a week. After a moderate power play, Scout cavorted around like a roadrunner, circling the kitchen island twice before running right into her kennel.

Within twenty minutes, Eva was settled across from Marlo in a booth at Grizzly Tracks. She shimmied off her coat, tucked her hat in a coat sleeve, and pulled sunglasses atop her head.

"Hi. Sorry I'm late. Encountered some minor domestic animal problems, then the ol' International started begrudgingly."

"No worries." Marlo was cuddled in the corner of the booth. "Glad you made it. By the way, I've only been here long enough to order this latte." She lifted the cup in a toast and took a sip.

"Good. So, Marlo, how is life treating you?" Eva winked at Marlo as they watched an androgynous teen stealthily set down a latte on the table in front of her.

"Eva, life is good," Marlo responded, glowing radiantly.

"Tell me, what's good?" Eva asked, warming her hands on the gourmet drink.

"I love the restaurant and working with the guys. You know, Gianni, Enrique, and Chad. We're a team and I'm an accepted and key player. A team where I was not the last pick, you know?"

"Ah, yes." Eva sighed, welcoming Marlo's sweet honesty.

"They make me feel talented and appreciate my contribution. I like it. I feel worthwhile."

"You're not kidding. Marlo, you make that place sing. The restaurant lights up because of your magnetic charm."

"Really?" she said tentatively. "You think so?" Marlo's cheeks had a tinge of blush as she giggled, unconsciously playing with a tightly wound auburn curl.

"It doesn't take a rocket scientist to figure out you have those three men wrapped around your little finger."

"Well, that wasn't my intention, but it's not a bad thing," Marlo said playfully. "I want to be part of the reason The Sicilian Ball becomes a colossal success."

"You're heading in that direction," Eva encouraged.

"For the first time in a long while I'm doing something that I love and am good at. I've worked at jobs or studies that I could do but didn't like or could only do in a mediocre fashion."

"Mediocre? That wouldn't be a word I would use in the same sentence as the name Marlo." Marlo looked shyly down, and a soft blush rose in her cheeks. Eva continued, letting the young woman sit with the pleasant sentiment. "There's something special over at that restaurant. I couldn't be more thrilled for Gianni and all of you, as well as for the town of Bear, which, by the way, thrives on having a new destination."

"Um, ah, thanks."

As if on cue, a dashing Chad walked up to the booth. "Ladies, top of the morning to you. Compliments of the proprietor." Chad set down a plate of treats that had the potential to cause hardening of the arteries by just looking at them.

"Yum," the women said in tandem.

"Surely," said Chad, wiping his hands on his apron.

"Ooh. Thank you. Tell Ms. Daniels her generosity is appreciated."

Bowing in acknowledgement, Chad turned and left. For a mesmerizing second, they watched the handsome man saunter back to the counter, his long-sleeved flannel shirt and apron unable to disguise his muscular build.

Eyes sparkling wickedly, Marlo changed her attentions and scooped up one of the delectable treats in front of her, flavors erupting on her taste buds. The sweets were giant-sized seven-layer bars of Midwest fame: butter, graham cracker crumbs, semi-sweet chocolate chips, butterscotch chips, walnuts, coconut, and condensed milk, built in that order and baked to perfection.

"Desserts don't get any better than this," Marlo mumbled as she captured a falling crumb of coconut and chocolate, her appetite in contrast to her slight frame. "These are so good. My Nana used to bake these when she would visit us in Wichita from Lawrence." Chocolate smudged next to her lips.

"My mom used to make them, too. It's one treat you don't outgrow," Eva said, sipping latte to clear her palate.

"I wonder if I should try to make these at home, you know, to give the trailer some nice smells."

"Baked goods do the trick."

"Not sure if health-nut Sander would eat all this fat. The man is a machine."

Eva saw an opening to delve into Marlo's relationship with the strange man. "Marlo, I'm curious about you and Sander. How did you two meet, if you don't mind my asking?"

"That's a long story. The short story is we met in Machu Picchu and decided to come together and live in Bear. A bit spontaneous, I know, but it seemed to be the right thing to do at the time."

"I'd say that was spontaneous," Eva said, knowing her life could use some unplanned action.

"Everything and nothing makes sense at Machu Picchu." For a moment Marlo was in a trance, her eyes staring off on nothing in particular, remembering the details of Peru.

"Okay, go on," Eva prompted after several seconds, slightly amused. She examined and then took the perfect bite out of her confection.

"To take you back a bit, remember when I told you at the Junior Women's Club that bad love brought me to Bear? It wasn't some fabulous love affair gone wrong or discovery of an 'other woman.' For me it was my father. Or more accurately, I should say, my mother's husband. Stepfather, I suppose."

Eva nodded in reply.

"See, it was my mother who had an affair and got pregnant just before she met and married Ralph some twenty-odd years ago. So, for me, the only father figure I ever knew was Ralph. He's the one I call my father or dad, married to my mother, but not my real father. Confused yet?"

"Simple as pie, I can tell. Are you sure you want to go into the details and dig up this story right now?" Eva wasn't sure what this would bring up for Marlo.

"It's fine. Without the heartache between Ralph and me, heck, I'd still be back in Wichita waiting tables on the wrong side of town. I might have never made it to Machu Picchu and to this little piece of heaven."

"I'm certainly glad you're here, Marlo."

"See, growing up we didn't spend much time together because he was always working and traveling. The problem was, I was a continuous reminder to him of what he couldn't have with my mother. Ralph is sterile. I'm an only child for my mother, and Ralph could never accept the fact that he would never be a biological father."

"Ouch, touchy issue," Eva said.

Marlo sipped her coffee and continued. "Well, on a positive note, he never held it against my mom. To his credit, he fell in love and married her when she was young and pregnant with someone else's baby. Not too many guys would take that path. He still adores her and treats her like a queen. Wedded bliss, really, except for me. I think if they had children together, things would be much different between Ralph and me."

"Whoa, Marlo, even I'm at a loss for comment on that tale."

Marlo paused, drank some more coffee, and quickly took another bite. "The tension with Ralph is why I left Wichita. It's best for my mom, too. She loves me, but her life is with him. The bad love between Ralph and me was spreading, and it was time to move on."

"That's bittersweet, Marlo. I admire Ralph for nurturing your mother when she needed it most, but it doesn't make sense that he didn't do the same for you. Seems like a conflict of character. I'm sorry." Eva was heartbroken and knew no other words of empathy to share with Marlo. Family was a precious commodity.

Marlo shrugged and gave Eva a vampy grin. "Don't be too sorry for me. I have my share of baggage that's best left back in Wichita. Starting a new life has lots of advantages."

"Ah, true again. Moving is a way we get to make things up on how we want our life to be," Eva said, comfortable sharing her thoughts with Marlo.

"Making it up. I like that," Marlo said, lips pursed as she contemplated the idea.

"When I ask my clients to make things up, they get tons of energy. Making things up removes barriers and gets the juices flowing," Eva said, finishing the last of her cookie, picking up a chocolate chip that had fallen onto the plate.

"I like that," Marlo said again, then, "Enter Sander. Sander, you asked about Sander." Once more came that momentary lapse from the present, the faraway look whenever Marlo thought of Sander.

"I sure did. Sander is definitely not the normal guy we see in Bear," Eva said, sounding like a local.

"There's really nothing normal about him," Marlo said in a soft lilt. "Sander and I met quite unexpectedly in Peru. He was traveling solo, researching for a magazine article, and hooked up with my tour group." Marlo started to describe her adventure to Eva, reminiscing with dreamy eyes about her chance acquaintance with Sander and what brought them to Bear.

24

The abandoned ruins of Machu Picchu held a paranormal energy. Prehistoric mountains turned into structures the higher you climbed, and mysticism held court on top of the world in the Andes. Two thousand feet above the Urubamba River, three thousand steps and the intricate terracing system motivated weary climbers, their eyes full of wonder. After the early morning mist burned off, the sun revealed vibrant green grass, aqua blue sky, and golden shimmering rocks.

Despite her fatigue from the long hike and high altitude, Marlo was struck by the power of the place. The smooth natural stone and jutting rocks renewed her stamina. Charillo, the Peruvian guide for the group of nine travelers, had few words for his assorted charges. It was hard to determine if this was because he spoke little English or because few words could increase the wonder of their experience. His knowing eyes and slow, distinct gestures provided enough direction.

Once on top of the summit, Marlo explored solo. She found herself a smooth rock to practice her favorite standing asanas. She started with the mountain pose, then the eagle pose, and ended in the sun salutation. The warm rays were like a beacon to Marlo, creating the appearance of an apparition. Unbeknownst to her, she was a vision to behold, becoming one with her environment.

This snapshot in the universe wasn't lost on the socially distant young man who joined the group. Sander tagged along with the hikers the day before down in the mountain village. Fluent in Spanish, he had convinced Charillo to take him along by bartering two packets of Big Red chewing gum and a partially drank fifth of Jack Daniels.

Marlo mesmerized Sander. Her zeal. Her beauty. Her youth. He watched, his mouth agape and head comically tilted as she practiced yoga. Charillo materialized beside Sander, gently kicking a small stone to garner his attention. Eye contact and negligible head motion communicated volumes. A semblance of a smile appeared on Charillo's typically barren face, one of knowing and wisdom, as he guided Sander to another location on the site to allow the woman her privacy.

From then on, Sander found himself near Marlo, observing her mannerisms, casually listening in on her conversations with others. The elation that naturally oozed out of Marlo was a stark contrast to the sinister work and serious personalities he'd been entrenched in for thirty-six months. She gave him hope. She stirred his safely buried sentiments. Careful.

They connected on the descent. Marlo was in front of Sander and slipped on loose stones, teetering to almost fall. Sander, trained in quick reflexes, caught her before her potential spill. He held her several seconds longer than necessary for her to catch her balance, his sinewy arms circling her slight waist. Speaking softly into her ear, he whispered, "Careful, fair maiden. You might fall." Gently positioning her upright, wiry muscles taught, his eyes locked on hers. Those were the first words he had spoken in her presence, words she had not expected from the private man.

In a rare moment, Marlo was speechless. The quiet stranger had saved her from an embarrassing tumble, and he cast a similar spell on her that she had done to him earlier in the day. His piercing brown-black eyes, slick hair, and olive skin were at home on the mountain. He had an aura of danger around him, and Marlo was attracted to the peculiar risk of him. A shiver spiked through her limbs.

After tripping over words, Marlo gathered her composure and a mighty grin to mumble, "Thanks, quiet guy, I needed that." From that point on, the two were companions, Marlo talking and laughing with the group, pointing out sites, and Sander close by observing, scanning the scenery, and communicating without words.

Following dinner at the campsite outside the village, when group members giddily shared the next steps of their individual journeys, the blood drained from Sander's face. Marlo told her new friends she was "starting over in a town called Bear, near Jackson Hole, Wyoming." It was Sander who blinked to maintain his composure this time. Did he hear right? The coincidence was too bizarre even for Sid to dream up. He calculated the implications. Was she the unsub? Naw, couldn't be. Could she?

The final night fireside chats were a litany of future adventures. When asked by the group as to his plans, Sander nonchalantly shrugged and muttered he would "sort details out tomorrow." Later, in the wee hours of the morning as they sat together watching shooting stars, Marlo spontaneously and unexpectedly asked Sander if he too would like to start over with her in Bear.

"Could we make a go of it?" she wondered, white teeth shining in the moonlight. For Sander, it was as if the stars and planets aligned for a miracle befitting the location. Marlo received an answer to her bold question in the form of quiet, heated passion that neither would soon forget.

25

"As I hear you, Martin, you aren't crazy about having this conversation with your wife," Eva offered, sensing something different today in the way Martin referred to his wife, Rita. Leaning back in her chair, Eva glanced up and out to the vast Gros Ventres. The peaks were sparkling white sequins reflecting the winter sun. She closed her eyes to be present in the coaching call with Martin, momentarily separated from her breathtaking environment.

"That's true, you're right," Martin acquiesced. This was a typical response from Martin when he agreed with a comment from Eva, saying that she was "right." At first it bothered Eva because as a coach, she didn't want to be right, per se, but provide input and intuition to provoke deeper learning and self-awareness for him. However, as in all relationships, including coaching, you accept certain nuances to keep the peace. Eva knew when Martin referred to something as "right," it translated to mean that whatever was just said between them resonated positively.

"Tell me more, Martin, about this dilemma you're facing with Rita."

Across the country, the large bulk of Martin strained the metal braces of the office chair as he changed position in angst. Over the phone came an audible exhale and a barely perceptible clearing of the throat. "I want to take Rita and the boys to Prague, my Praha, to visit the Czech Republic. Rita says it's too expensive."

Eva heard his discord, his struggle for composure. She was glad to be coaching over the phone. The phone allowed her to concentrate on coaching Martin. Being in the physical presence of Martin could turn their calls into regular conversation, safe, comfortable distractions. Not being able to see a client was actually a benefit to her coaching. *I need to make sure I stay in the dance with Martin,* she thought. Martin needed her as a coach, someone to encourage him to find his own answers and allow him to be human.

"How do you feel about her response?" she probed.

"Angry. If we couldn't afford it, I wouldn't suggest it!" Martin's voice burst as he stood and slammed his hand on the desk, unable to maintain the calm poise any longer.

"What else?" Eva winced at his outburst and was unsure where to direct. She opted to let him vent.

"I can't believe she would be so stubborn on this topic. Rita knows what a trip like this means to me, to show her and the kids Praha and the countryside. She's not being fair to me." Martin frowned, stretching the palm of his hand, sore from the earlier abuse.

"She's not being fair?"

"No."

"What's not fair, Martin?"

"Rita."

"Because ..." Eva stated, holding the space on the phone.

"She has no right to take away my dream. She betrayed me."

Now we're getting somewhere, Eva thought. "Betrayed you."

"Yes."

"Martin, take a minute to close your eyes and take a deep breath. Just breathe for a minute, and let's talk this through. You mentioned a dilemma. Is it a dilemma you're trying to figure out, or are you having a fight with Rita?"

Silence came over the phone for several seconds.

"Eva, Rita doesn't know how I really feel. When she responded like she did, I completely dropped the topic. I've let it fester in me, and she's oblivious to my feelings."

"This sounds like a difficult conversation that you should have with Rita."

"Humph." Martin sounded like a wounded child.

"Would you rather let it fester or take the plunge and talk to her about it?"

Mustering a laugh, Martin acquiesced, "I must do a little swimming with Rita and dive in on this topic, somehow. The trouble is, I'm not sure I can talk to her about it without us both losing our tempers. When that happens, we both lose."

"What do you say we practice?"

"Practice?" Martin's voice signaled interest but confusion.

"I have a little technique that might do the trick. Here's how it works. First, you explain the difficult situation to me. So that part is already done."

"Right."

"Second, if you agree, you will play the part of Rita and we'll talk about this situation based on what I know already and what you know about Rita."

"I know she's against it."

"Martin, trust me here. For our practice, you need to respond to my questions in a way that you think Rita would respond. Make up what you think she'd say. Be Rita."

"I'm listening," came a perplexed tone over the phone, Eva could almost see Martin with a ruffled brow and forehead creased in concentration.

"Third, we will switch roles. Don't worry. We'll go step by step."

Martin was quiet on the phone, absorbing the directions. He contemplated the role-play, knowing he could accept or not. "Eva, I'll try your game. I have nothing to lose."

"Great. Let's begin. First, stand up and reposition yourself in some way, even if you stand up and sit down again. The movement will symbolize a change of view for you to respond like Rita. I'll do the same."

"Ready." Martin had moved to a couch across his office.

"Rita, I'd like to ask you if we could talk without arguing over the possibility of a trip to Prague," Eva spoke as Martin. "We both can have the opportunity to share our thoughts."

Clearing his throat, Martin-as-Rita answered, "Yes, I can talk to you."

"Thank you. Rita, from our last conversation I know you're not interested in our family taking a trip to Prague," Eva said, becoming the persona of Martin to the best of her ability.

"That's right. I don't think it's a good idea," Martin-as-Rita offered.

"I'd like to understand your feelings on this topic. Is now a good time?" Even as Martin, Eva asked permission to pursue a topic. She noticed if she asked permission, it diffused tension, setting up for better dialogue.

"Yes, I can talk now." Martin's stressed bulk relaxed on the other end of the phone, melting into the couch.

"Are you concerned about taking the children to Prague?" Eva-as-Martin probed.

"It's not that I'm concerned about taking them to Prague. That would be wonderful for them. It costs too much," Martin-as-Rita let out what he knew to be her current roadblock to the potential trip.

"Tell me more about your concerns regarding the cost, Rita." Silence. Eva heard Martin's mind whirling to see what the issue behind the issue might be. "There are other more pressing priorities. I don't want to run out of money for them."

Eva appreciated the attempt by Martin, but it was broad. "I see. What are the financial priorities on your list?"

"Well," Martin continued in a low, humbled voice, "we need to install a new furnace."

"I see. What else?"

"Our house needs an update that paint would solve. To travel to Prague, we need to board the dogs and buy suitcases."

"Okay. So priorities are the furnace, painting, boarding the dogs, and suitcases. Is that right, Rita?" Inwardly grinning, Eva was proud of Martin for identifying Rita's needs.

"Yes," Martin-as-Rita answered. He knew she managed the household within a budget, but she didn't have a complete picture of the finances. He handled the savings and available cash.

"Rita, what else is on your mind?"

"These things matter. If we go to Prague, the furnace and the paint will never get done." Stalling at first, then Martin-as-Rita added, "Or that's what I think. It has been a year since we talked about installing a new furnace and updating the home with paint." Martin's voice was full of anguish at his beloved wife's pain and perspective on this topic. It hit him between the eyes. Thick headed. He saw his own procrastination.

"I sense you're disappointed that I've not fixed the furnace or attended to the painting," Eva-as-Martin proposed confidentially.

"Yes," was the confession-like response that came from Martin-as-Rita.

"Rita, what if I commit to you to start both efforts before we plan our trip?"

Letting out a short breath, Martin offered after a pause, "I would consider it."

"What can I do to get you from considering a trip and to making an agreement?"

There was a brief hesitation on the phone and a pensive Martin-as-Rita continued, "I like the idea for us to start the process for the paint and furnace. I also need to understand our complete financial situation."

"I'm happy to do that. You'll see that we have enough money set aside for the trip." Eva guessed a bit here, but she had known Martin for a while now and thought she might be close.

"That would be good."

"Rita, do you want to go to Prague?"

"I'd love to go to Prague. But I cannot think about the trip until our home is in order and I understand more the finances." Martin's demeanor changed. His energy was renewed. His passion for his wife ignited like a switch when he looked at life through her eyes.

Sensing a breakthrough, Eva stopped the difficult role-play. "Martin, please stand and move to where you were before the role-play to complete this portion of the exercise." Eva was pumped. She held her breath, waiting until he transitioned back to himself.

"Okay, I'm back," Martin rasped wearily.

"What was that experience like for you?" Eva asked, now standing, wanting to be fully available as a coach for Martin. She glanced out the window just in time to see a hawk fly past with a trout held tight in its talons.

"Mmm, this is pretty good, I think," Martin answered, drinking from a glass of water. He was across the country, yet completely connected to Eva.

"You think?" she asked, recognizing a call of a hawk from across the lake.

"Until I put myself in Rita's shoes, I didn't remember we had talked about updating the paint and the furnace."

"They're important to her," Eva added, stating the obvious.

"Yes. She also needs clarification of financial matters before any major purchase. This is a trend for her. I forgot."

"Often all we need is another perspective."

"Euuf. All these things crashed our trip." Martin's remorse was palpable.

"What else?"

"I didn't consider my Rita. I've been self-centered," He picked up the empty water glass and set it down again, frustrated with his own realization.

"Martin, what can you do with the results of this practice conversation?" Eva ignored his self-criticism, which she knew wouldn't help. She resisted the urge to give him a script and an order to go talk to Rita. Years of corporate decisiveness reared its head; Eva held it at bay.

"How could I be so blind?" Martin's voice came barely audible.

"You aren't exactly blind, Martin. Just a bit forgetful and excited about the trip."

"Humph."

"Would you like to proceed with the exercise and switch roles?"

"Honestly, no." Silence. Then, "But, Eva, this practice I will do because I don't want to trip her triggers as, uh, Americans say."

"Deal." And the two proceeded to change characters. Across the country the coachee and coach slugged through another difficult role-play, smoothing out the weak spots, deepening awareness for Martin. The coaching game prepared Martin for real conversation with his wife. He was ready to have a caring dialogue to reach out to the love of his life.

Later that afternoon Eva's legs treaded air as she sat perched atop a kitchen barstool. She doodled on what intended to be a Christmas to-do list. The sinking sky was a palette of grays. Heavy clouds covered the sun and dropped snowflakes the size of the clementine she was peeling. Eva hadn't made progress on her list, her mind blank, mesmerized by the white orbs vanishing into the lake. A loud blast of *Mission Impossible* disrupted her reverie, exploding from her cell phone. Startled, Eva picked up the intruding device.

Eva glanced at the unfamiliar number on display. "This is Eva," she said hesitantly.

"Eva, darling, this is Heidi."

"Heidi, hi. I didn't recognize the number," Eva said, popping the last segment of the juicy clementine into her mouth.

"Were you sleeping?"

"No, just daydreaming. But I'm back among the coherent, thanks to my obnoxious ringer."

"What's going on?"

"I was trying to make a list of what I need to do for Christmas and was in a trance watching the snowflakes falling into the lake." Eva said nothing about the word "Steve" that appeared in her doodling.

"Tsk, tsk." Heidi continued, "Not being completely productive? Now there's a welcome change."

"I'm not that bad! What's up?" Eva sensed a purpose behind the banter.

"Dearest, do I need a reason to call?" Heidi mocked defensively.

"No, but I can just tell there's a reason behind this call. The strange number, for starters. Where are you?"

"I'm at the library. Jana's fault. She's setting up the special events room with holiday books from around the world. I, of course, generously lent duplicates from my history class to supplement her tiny collection."

"Your charity never ceases," Eva teased, knowing full well Heidi had a heart of gold behind her glib façade.

"Right. It boggles my mind how many books I have about the history of the holidays. Christmas, Kwanza, Hanukkah, you name it. If it's a holiday, we have elaborate stories about it."

"You got that right. Is Jana sponsoring the 'Twelve Reading Days of the Holiday Season'?" Eva remembered that she read *The First Christmas Tree* for the event last year.

"That she is. And you'll soon get her solicitation to fill in one of the spots, so keep your calendar handy. On to the real reason for my call."

"What might that be, Heidi?"

"You're staying in Bear for the holiday, right?"

"Yeah …" Where else would she go? She wasn't remorseful. Eva smiled in memory of how her dad had sheepishly asked permission to take a dream trip to China that overlapped the holiday season. She had no issue with his decision and was glad he continued to find adventure and fun in his life—not having to depend on her to plan his holidays. They had a healthy, adult, parent–child relationship that had grown comfortable in the ten years since her mother's death.

"It's a date." Heidi continued, "Remember Thanksgiving? We—Jana and I— want to assemble our new group for a progressive dinner on Christmas Eve."

"Really." Eva dragged out the word for effect. "That sounds intriguing. Tell me more."

"We were wondering if you'd host one of the courses. You know, we'll have three or four houses, probably three. Four is complicated. So the options would be hors d'oeuvres, main course, and dessert."

"Huh, could be fun. I'm available. No plans, unless Dash and Scout committed to some invitation I don't know about." Eva's mind swirled with the possibility. Even before she settled into her home in Bear, Eva had a holiday fantasy about serving hot buttered rum in rustic pottery mugs while baking cookies with a crowd in the kitchen, the entire scene taking place with the 1940s Fred Astaire and Bing Crosby movie *Holiday Inn* playing in the background. Idyllic.

"So, is that a yes?"

"Yes ma'am."

"You have that amazing kitchen, and if we manage to actually get people out of the kitchen, your family room is big with that, well, incredible view."

Beaming at the depiction of her still-new-but-already-cherished home, Eva cheerily responded, "How can I resist *that* request?"

"One must know how to procure favors." Heidi said.

Eva imagined Heidi, rapidly tapping her long red nails atop the readers' service desk at the library and sporting a plunging neckline just short of tasteless. "You're the queen." Pausing, Eva asked, "Could I host dessert?" Eva suddenly flushed with excitement at such a proposition for the holidays.

"Mademoiselle, cherie, you can definitely host dessert," Heidi expressed in a haughty French accent. "Before committing, consider that dessert is the last course and we'll be at your home for a while, depending on how the group is getting along. And of course, the weather."

"Not a problem. This will be fun."

"Thank you, Eva. Remember, expectations for epicurean delicacies are high during the holidays. Ta-taa!" Typical.

A Christmas party at my house. Suddenly her list had renewed potential. To a non–list maker, lists appear banal and rigid. Eva saw this as an oversight. When it's your own list, there is a carnal satisfaction in crossing things off. One step closer to the prize. She wrote with fury across her steno tablet, smearing blue ink on the side of her palm.

Christmas
1. Hot buttered rum recipe
2. Write a holiday letter & Christmas cards, by Dec. 15
3. Buy a gift for Steve????
4. Bandanas for Dash and Scout
5. Find Christmas quilts; hang one on front porch rail / rest inside
6. Set up nutcracker collection
7. Book for Twelve Days at the library
8. Tree
9. Firewood
10. Cookies: sugar, butter almond bars, rum balls, Mom's fudge
11. Quilt-related gifts for Jana, Heidi, anyone else? Marlo?
12. Rich, delish dessert for progressive dinner
13. Load iPod with Christmas songs
14. Order DVD of *Holiday Inn* to replace video
15. Holiday outfit?

After completing her list, Eva moved to her computer for some Internet shopping. Much later, Visa card smoking, Eva let out a long breath as she glanced past the sleeping dogs and out the window at the snow covering the banks of the lake. She had a thriving coaching practice, actual *girlfriends*, and a dreamy new man in her life. Now she was part of a holiday party. Was this for real?

A few years ago she lived a different existence. By many standards, her life then was considered ideal. No one knew about the heartache or the deception of Seaton. Most people considered a corporate job a gold mine, and traveling the world glamorous.

She closed her eyes, clutching her shoulders and rocking gently in the chair. Corporate life can be fine. Except she lost her equilibrium after Seaton. She needed to be successful. Break that glass ceiling. Earn those frequent flier miles. Show her sense of importance with an irrational sense of urgency. Her actions crashed with her values. Her ego wouldn't step aside. The internal conflict suffocated.

She was trapped in a box whose lid slowly closed out all the light, all the life. She didn't recognize herself but kept on playing the part. All those years. Those useless years. For what? To find out you were in love with someone's husband? To have your trusted boss leave for a new job? To see stock options dwindle to nothing? To have urgent midnight oil projects never see the light of day?

"Thank you, God. You saved me." Eva surprised herself at the spontaneous interaction with spirituality. Natural. Not even scary. Wrapped in a blanket of peace, Eva started the mission to complete the tasks on her Christmas list. She made a choice to look forward to *what might be* this Christmas season and blocked out past regrets and mistakes.

27

"Merry Christmas, Grace." Steve saw the tears swelling in her eyes as he kissed her on each cheek. He handed her a bulky gift, wrapped in green and red foil. *Good stock*, Grace used to tell him when he was growing up, *just like your Papa*. He warmed at the memory.

"Why, do tell, Son, what is this you brought?" Grace said gaily. Dressed in holiday finery, Grace was divine in a vintage dark green velvet suit, faux cream fur around the collar, mother of pearl buttons, and a long, graceful skirt flowing off her still-shapely legs. The fitted jacket was elaborate with details that would make any modern dressmaker envious. A velvet hat sat on the side of her head, set off by silver close-cropped hair.

"That is for you to open."

"Why, my word." Grace held the package to her chest.

"I suggest you open it now." Steve cocked his head with a lazy grin as he folded his arms across his muscular chest. Grace shook her head and obliged the younger man.

Unwrapping the gift, she let out a small gasp. "Why, it's fresh trout! Steven Winston Mason, a gift to an old woman doesn't get any better than this!" She motioned for him to step in for a hug and a seat.

"It's local, of course."

"Child, it better be local," she teased.

"Only the best."

"That it is. That it is. Thank you!" She paused, proud of the man she had watched grow from the time he was a baby.

"You're most welcome, Grace." Steve was as excited to give her the gift as she was in receiving it, maybe even more so. He took pleasure in her surprise. When he had found a stream still ripe with trout in season, well, he'd been a man with a mission.

"Good for the heart, this trout," Grace said, shaking her head.

"Enjoy them. You can either freeze or cook them."

"Mmm."

"You know the culinary secrets, Grace. Whatever you do to those fish will make a mean meal. Oh, yeah, I'm hungry now."

Grace gently folded the crisp white butcher paper back over the fish. Steve knew there was enough for at least three meals for her and Lois, and even James if he was around.

Wide eyed, she looked again up to Steve and uncharacteristically blurted, "Steve, did you know Lois and I are going to visit James?"

"Really?" he said, eyes flashing. "Tell me the scoop." Steve had heard this from James in a recent phone call, but he wanted to indulge Grace a story about her James, knowing it was a harmless ruse.

"Why, he sent Lois and me plane tickets. A taxi is coming to get us shortly, so I must freeze this beautiful fish. Yes, dear James has us flying down to Southern California for a visit. Can you imagine that? Christmas in California without any snow!"

"That explains your fancy get-up. If you go near Hollywood, they'll discover you to star in the next blockbuster."

"Ach, hardly me in this old body. It's our budding Lois who we have to watch out for, yes sir." Grace's face grew pensive as she considered her niece. "So, what are your plans for the holidays?"

"I'll be here in Bear holding down the fort."

"Someone has to, I suppose."

"With you gone, my parents away, I'll do some guide planning, finish a couple of papers, and visit with, uh, friends for Christmas." He noticed Grace narrow her eyes. Busted. He thought he hid his excitement about the holidays. True to her name, Grace let her intuition be silent.

"You sound happy. That's good." Grace held out her hand for him to help her up. Once standing, she put an arm around Steve and embraced him. He was solid in every sense of the word. "Have a Merry Christmas. We'll miss you all the way from California." She said, pulling back and patting him on the back.

"And I you. So then, I'll check on the house. Now that you live up here above Bear Claw Quilts, it makes for a little less worry." Steve said, sincerely caring for her like a beloved aunt.

"Appreciated, as always."

"Give my love to Lois. And a good thump on the head to James. Keeps him straight." Steve kissed her cheek and went on his way.

28

"Oh my gosh, can you believe what we just did?" Jana asked, linking her arm into Eva's with a licentious smile as they stepped onto the sidewalk, holiday music coming from Jackson's town square.

"Completely," snickered Eva with a companion devious grin. "We're officially vixens of the West." The two giggled with such fervent relish that they captured gazes of fellow shoppers, envious regarding the possibility of their secret.

"'Riveting Rouge' and 'Bodacious Black,' names worthy of our prized purchases." Jana gleefully added.

"Makes me not want to cut off the tags," Eva said.

"And me, a librarian. Maybe we should start writing an anonymous advice column for the *Bearly News*. These new garments will give us an entirely different perspective!"

Eva laughed. "'Garments' is stretching it a bit."

"Stretchy, yes. Talk about perspective."

"Oh, Jana, how can we possibly wear these and keep a straight face? Heidi will be so proud!" Eva flushed.

"Heidi is the lingerie queen," Jana confirmed. "She'll completely approve and, let me tell you, she'll be back here and purchasing that 'Passionate Purple' before you can say 'color wheel'!"

"For sure. Naming lingerie is sort of like naming quilt squares. What do you think?"

"Eva, even we quilters have to realize that talk about quilting somehow puts a wet blanket, if you will, on a lingerie discussion."

"Names, Jana, I'm talking about names of things."

"So, tell me about some exotic quilt blocks."

Eva considered. "Well, maybe it's not so easy. 'Drunken Path,' 'Nine Patch,' and 'King's Highway.'"

"There's 'Wild Goose Chase,'" Jana suggested.

"Hey, we could work with that 'King's Highway.' It has lingerie potential."

Jana eyed her friend, brow arched, and playfully hit her in the stomach as they walked. "Eva, why, *I'm surprised!*"

Eva grinned, pleased with her innuendo and the irreverent shopping. "I have a client who's opening herself up for more possibilities in life. She would just love this outing."

"Can you elaborate?" Jana's interest sharpened.

"It is energizing, what she's doing. She's making changes in the small stuff that defines her. Like updating her wardrobe, getting a personal trainer, and not being a doormat to her family. Don't get me wrong, she's not being selfish or less of a wife and mother, but she's being more of herself. The small stuff is adding up to be the big stuff."

Jana pursed her lips in concentration, ruffled her brow, and signaled to Eva. "Go on."

Glancing over, Eva wondered if there was more to Jana's inquiry than just topical interest. Her friends and associates over the past years since she started coaching had developed an interest regarding the content of coaching calls. Eva never shared anything that would break confidentiality, but she would share the impact of a call if it touched her. "Well, this wonderful woman is stepping into herself."

"Stepping into herself?"

"She's doing the things she reads about in magazines that other women do. She's claiming her own life. Taking some chances, spending money on herself, and being direct about her needs."

"Really?" Jana said, intrigued.

"She's embracing life. In fact, this woman is living out a childhood dream of going to Paris with her best friend and their husbands. Imagine. What a thrill." Eva continued, pulling her scarf tighter around her neck, "In a way, Jana, we're doing that today."

"Ha! Jackson is nice, but it's not Paris," Jana chided, pointing just in time to the Kentucky Fried Chicken franchise down a side street off the square.

"Ah, funny. What I mean is, here we are buying expensive lingerie in Jackson just because we want to. It's frivolous and outside our budget if we did it a lot, but for today, no worries. It's not hurting anyone or taking anything away from another person. It's just fun. For us."

"Fun," Jana said aloud, but to herself.

"Simple. See, there are many people—especially women, Jana—who don't embrace small opportunities for their own enjoyment," Eva said, shaking her bag of lingerie to prove her point.

"So, are you saying the more we pamper ourselves, the more fun we are to be around?"

"Sort of. I think there's truth in that statement. To contrast, have you ever been around someone who is *sooo* happy in their misery? And they definitely want to tell you all the gory details?"

"That I can relate to." Jana went on, "Tell me, Eva, how did your client get to a point where she started living her life instead of imagining it?"

"Great question. Actually, a friend of hers is also one of my clients. He saw her vanishing from her own life and gave her coaching as a gift. He believes in coaching and wanted her to experience something that was only for her."

"That's a pretty astute friend," Jana said, deep in thought. She tucked a wayward strand of wavy hair behind her ear. "Eva, how did this client of yours actually start changing?"

Realizing Jana was serious, Eva slid into professional mode, her excitement to talk about coaching the best defense to the cold weather. "It's a process, Jana. In coaching, we start with a known thing someone wants to change. For example, to lose weight, be a better leader, change careers, you know, something typical that draws people to coaching. Lots of time I ask them if they just made it up, what would they do different—more of, or less of—to achieve the change they want in their life. No reality needed."

"Making it up leads to change?" Jana asked, side-stepping a piece of ice on the sidewalk.

"This concept of 'made up' gets the creative ideas to percolate," Eva answered. She slipped on the same ice Jana missed and held tighter to Jana's arm for support, not missing a beat. "Once my clients reach their goal in one area, the coaching blossoms into other areas. I've experienced if they can see past the boundaries they set for themselves, like making it up, possibility and opportunities open up."

"I see." Jana said.

"Sad to say, people don't share their aspirations with those they love. Some people feel listened to for who they are as a person for the very first time when they have a personal coach."

"Why do you think that is, Eva?"

"Careful, Jana. Don't let me go too far on my 'why coaching is so great' soapbox." Glancing at Jana, Eva linked arms and indulged herself to talk about her passion. "First, coaching is a safe place, completely confidential. No judgments. Second, as a coach, we use techniques to push people toward their goals, fears and all. Then a coach can mirror back to a client so they notice when they do—or don't—live their life in ways that will reach their goals. At the end of the day, it creates the ability to make conscious choices in line with their values. It's thrilling."

They walked a half block in silence as Jana absorbed Eva's words. After taking a short break to admire an especially beautiful pair of turquoise and black western boots, Jana broke the quiet. "Huh. So, with this lady you mentioned who received coaching as a gift. What was it that helped her change?"

"As a coach I am unbiased and can let her see possibilities. I'm not part of her daily routine and don't focus on what others might call obstacles. One tool I used for her is a choice list." Eva glanced at Jana, who was still engaged, so she continued, "I had her list seven things in her life she didn't like. Then we turned those negative things into positive choices."

"So she would see the positive thing that could replace a negative?" Jana said, a bit puzzled. Then with a breakthrough expression, she went on. "Wait, so it would be like adding brown sugar to a dish that has too much chili pepper?"

"Exactly. Instead of waiting to smell cookies burning in the oven, you set a kitchen timer."

"Deciding up front."

"Choice," Eva affirmed.

"Choice," Jana added slowly.

"See, one negative she had was that her dog slept in her bedroom, and she hated it. Long conversation short, what she chose instead of the dog in the bed was a room that was her special place. She didn't like the dog and kids taking it over like every other room in the house. What she wanted was a boudoir for her and her husband. Her choice list ended up something like 'I choose to have my bedroom be my sanctuary.' That all started from her not liking the dog in the bedroom."

"Pretty interesting, Eva. I'm starting to get coaching." Gesturing to herself with her hands, Jana went on. "See, me, having a profession as a librarian or sometimes chef, it's easy to understand what I do. In two words people know my vocation." Nodding, Eva understood the haze that the term "life coach" could muster.

The two stopped at a store window decked out with white lights, mannequins wearing brightly colored winter western wear, elaborate bling belts, silver necklaces, and long crinkle skirts. Looking at one another without words, they pushed open the lavish door using the massive elk horn handles to start the next leg of their shopping journey, stamping the snow off their boots as they entered the shop.

Chad watched Marlo go through all the right motions to open the restaurant. That was the problem. Marlo's not someone who went through the motions. "Marlo, tell me, what is it?" He didn't mince his words. It wasn't necessary, as he spoke so few of them.

She froze, then turned to face him. "How do you know, Chad?" It was all Marlo could marshal up, her eyes clouding over.

"It's obvious. You aren't dancing, singing, and prancing around here like its homecoming. Something's up."

"Oh." Marlo said.

"You're acting like a regular bored hostess setting up the place."

Forcing a smile at the comment, Marlo closed her eyes. When she opened them, she looked at Chad, quietly speaking her thoughts. "Sander is acting weird. Have you noticed anything at the coffee shop?"

Frowning, and pressing his lips together, Chad did a playback through the last couple of times that he worked with Sander over at Grizzly. "He looks tired. Which, by the way, isn't new. Sander's not exactly warm and friendly."

"At home he paces around, getting up at night, strained temper. I'm not sure if he's tired of me or what's going on." Marlo's face wilted as she spoke.

"Marlo, Sander is kind of different. Did you ever consider asking him?" Chad bit back the temptation to ask if Sander had been abusing her in any way.

"What if it's another woman?" Marlo said, her voice cracked.

"Coming from a guy, if you're thinking that, just ask. Sander is private. If you ask him something, he'll either answer you or tell you it's none of your business. You can figure it out from there." Chad ruffed her hair, giving her a hug before making his way back to the bar.

Watching him, Marlo spoke up, "Hey, Chad, thanks." Turning to her, he gave a pursed lip smile and a bow. Bowing had become contagious among the restaurant men.

In the kitchen of The Sicilian Ball, Gianni and Enrique were planning for the dinner crowd. They had the specials organized and the sauces sautéing, and they spoke in controlled whispers to contain their excitement. Tonight, they had been told by a local reporter, a food editor from *Haute Cuisine*, their favorite food magazine, might be dining in their restaurant.

Later in the evening, after gnocchi soup was garnished and eaten, Chianti was poured, and tiramisu was savored, the small restaurant team huddled in the kitchen to debrief the night. Flushed, Gianni spieled in half-Italian, half-English. Marlo, Chad, and Enrique stood around Gianni, befuddled. Then he paused unexpectedly, tears streaming from his eyes. It was Enrique who broke the spell. "Gianni, please, we're not working from the same recipe here. What is it you're trying to tell us?"

Trance broken, Gianni realized he'd slipped into Italian, his instincts engaged with the thrill of the moment. Wide eyed, he took his colleagues in his arms, reminiscent of the restaurant opening.

"We're going to be featured in the magazine. The food magazine, *Haute Cuisine*. Not just a feature and recipe, which, si, would be good, of course, but the cover story." He paused, looking at each of them. He could see they were weary at this late hour, but they slowly understood the magnitude of the honor.

Marlo let out a whoop and danced around the kitchen. Chad, relieved to see typical Marlo behavior, pursed his lips in a smile of acknowledgment. Enrique pointed to Gianni, then to himself and to the restaurant in general, shook his fists overhead as he arched backward. They reveled in their success as they cleaned the restaurant and prepared for the next day.

Gianni, before leaving for the night, emailed his family in Sicily, sharing the news. His joy couldn't be truly celebrated until he linked it to the source. His family. They believed in him. They pushed Gianni to reach confidently for his dreams, even if it meant his leaving home.

Enrique dropped Marlo off at the trailer, watched her walk inside, and drove off after she flicked the porch light twice.

"Sander, I'm home. Wait 'til you hear." Marlo was breathless with excitement.

No reply. Silence.

"Sander?" *Where is he?*

Her enthusiasm dwindled with each step. Marlo walked from room to room. There was no sign of recent activity. The breakfast cereal bowls were still in the sink. Marlo shivered with a growing fear. Looking out the front window, a pickup truck drove slowly by, not too unusual for the town or this time of night in a trailer park.

Whispering an oath under his breath, Sander rubbed his head after crashing into an icicle protruding from the eave of a building. Just what he needed, distraction to lose the trail. Hearing the sound of an engine, Sander jumped back against the side of a dark alley entrance. A pickup truck drove by, standard issue for this part of Wyoming. Curious as to where the truck was headed this late, Sander stretched to see where the vehicle turned. No such luck.

Damn. If only Sid were here. I really need a partner. He knew, however, they could materialize if he just gave the signal. Enlisting discipline and leaning into his training, Sander stepped gingerly across the ice to exit the alley and reach the sidewalk. The streetlights were on, albeit dimly, thanks to the environmentalists, and the snow was falling steadily, both situations outside his control and potentially perilous.

Sander meticulously parsed each detail sent in from Sid. He tentatively outlined a theory to answer the puzzle. This latest clue sent Sander to a place that scared him. The hairs bristled on the back of his neck. Not for his safety but for what could happen. The Sicilian Ball. Where Marlo works. Just thinking of her caused Sander to press his eyelids closed with worry. This quest and Marlo existed at polar opposites in his mind. Goddamn, this was a mess. Work. Women. *Marlo.* He needed focus to complete this job. He gave his word.

Sander cautiously moved down the street. The night was shrouded in a veil of snow, which left footprints, his own and others. Vulnerable, Sander restrained himself and moved without a sound while walking naturally. If he was seen, he could pass for a nighttime walker, but if stealth movements were recognized by police or his enemy, their suspicions would be raised and his cover blown.

As he approached the restaurant, his heart raced, thudding in his ears. This was the night for the order, and the destination was brutally clear. Was he being taken for a ride? Was the clue too obvious? Trust Sid. He had to trust Sid; it was the only way. Two days earlier Sid forwarded a message oddly worded in Italian: "L'isola italiana ha un bambino giocattolo ed è ospitato da un animale imbottito in Wyoming. Otto giorni prima metà inverno celebrazione." Translated into English, the clue read, "Italian island has a child's toy and is hosted by a stuffed animal in Wyoming. Eight days before mid-winter celebration."

It took Sander four minutes to figure it out: The Sicilian Ball—Bear, Wyoming—eight days before Christmas. Thank God for his ninth grade English literature teacher who forced double meaning in every sentence and made him study imagery.

Sander spied a footprint on the sidewalk. Sloppy, he thought, but possibly unavoidable in this weather. Senses alert, he calmed his nerves with the mantra that he alone knew the clue. The snow buffered sound, a small—well, large—gift, and Sander moved along the opposite side of the alley from the streetlight to avoid casting a shadow. Creeping up to the back door of the restaurant, he was appalled but satisfied at a second piece of sloppy work. The back door was slightly ajar, which made his entrance sophomoric. Concern gripped him. Sander wondered if this was a setup, a trap. It wasn't like the Barratino family to execute with mediocrity.

Entering through the kitchen, Sander erased the picture of the place lit up with Marlo's energy. *Mio bella Marlo.* Thank the Lord that they didn't find out about him and Marlo. Crouching low, he crept through the restaurant. Where was the bastard? Or them? His body bristled like a wild cat, ready to pounce. Then he heard a rustling, a low muffled swear, and a big clunk, a solid sound like wood.

No conversation or noise from any other location around the restaurant. This could be good. Maybe there's only one. Sander's eyes adjusted to the darkness, and he moved toward the sound. A single ray of light came in through the windows from the street, just enough to make out large objects.

"Wha … ?" A thickly accented voice called into the dark room as Sander plunged toward the noise. Completely dependent on instinct and a murmur of a prayer, Sander, airborne, collided with unseen objects. He smashed into hard wood, human limbs, and ceramic tile.

"Umph," came out of Sander as his muscles accepted their beating upon impact with the hard tile. With surprise as an advantage, Sander immediately sprang at the thrashing foreign body, his prey. In seconds the perpetrator's head was in a lock, his right arm twisted behind him. Sander used his knees to force the intruder's legs apart and, with calculated precision, smashed the unseen face against the floor.

"Your vitals, pal, or your body will cease to function." The raspy words angrily seethed out of Sander as he tightened his rein on the prisoner. His heart raced and his mind spun as he attempted to anticipate the next move. The captive muttered obscenities that caused Sander to further enforce his upper hand. Squeezing the perp's neck, Sander felt the man's tension release in submission, signaling that breathing won over loyalty in this precarious situation.

"It's a farce. There's nothing. Let me go," came the response in battered English. Followed was a string of unique Italian expletives that would've impressed Sander given different circumstances.

"Cold day in hell." Sander smoldered out the words in a slow, low muttering. Enraged, Sander pulled tighter, letting actions speak volumes. "Which is where you're going. Talk." The sloppy footprint he'd seen in the snow indicated this was no pro.

"Goddamn broad. She gave it to me wrong." With this second admonition, Sander realized his intruder was working the job, at least at the restaurant, alone. That meant he was calculating his next move to freedom. This made things more tenuous for Sander, and he accelerated his movements. He felt the man's chest, waist, and legs for a packed gun or worse. Then Sander hit pay dirt: a Glock automatic and a sharpened steel eight-inch sheathed blade. He tossed them aside. Relief flooded his shoulders having found the lethal weapons. No such relief for the figure clothed in black. He flipped the man over, flat on the floor in break-neck speed. Knee in the back of the inert man, Sander cuffed his wrists in one stealth move, sweat spreading across his brow and back.

"Move a muscle, you're meat," Sander said as he tied the man's ankles with nylon cord.

"It's not me. That bitch."

"Yeah, what's that she had wrong?" Sander's voice cut the air like a knife.

"Bitch lied to me. *Goddamn* broad. She's going to cash in herself." Despite his predicament, the man's incredulous voice wouldn't let go of the fact that a female cohort pulled the wool over his eyes. He was so irate with the woman that he ignored his situation with Sander, calculating instead how to place blame for the job gone wrong.

"Cash in what and where? Better speak pretty fast if you want to walk in the next decade." Sander's eyes narrowed as he glared at the man through the dark-ness. He needed a clue.

"How do I know you won't fuck me over and use my information?" Exasperated, he swore another oath in Italian before addressing Sander. "I'm a dead man either way. Fuck," the man spat out. He was wearing down. It had been a damn long night.

"Just answer the question. I'm getting bored." Sander didn't let on to the man that he was baffled by, one, the news of a woman in this job, and two, the second time the same case surfaced nothing. Sander held his aura of detachment and calm as his brain logically processed all known information. Eyes crazed, he emit-ted an eerie aura of unpredictability.

"Hell if I know. She makes no damn sense. Sits in that dump of a cabin all day smoking on the porch. She stares down at this cattle town and rocks endlessly in that fricking chair. That place gives me the creeps. So quiet you can hear a bat fart. Give me New York in the summer, and you can keep this natural shit. I need some civilization."

Rambling, that was another good thing.

"Shit. She mumbled something yesterday about there being a second suit in the trailer." His rambles continued, but Sander's mind stopped when he heard the words *trailer* and *second suit*. Goose bumps covered his arms. His blood turned to ice in his veins. Marlo.

Years of intense training kicked in. Sander reached in his pocket, pulled out sleeping salts, and covered his prisoner's face before the captive even knew what happened. Running through the restaurant and out the back, Sander flew through the streets of Bear. Not hiding tracks or troubling about noise, he ran, sprinting for more than his life. *Marlo. God no, not Marlo.*

A hundred yards down the street from the trailer, a pickup truck was parked just off the road. It was dark with an open bed and a few scrapes, typical for vehicles in Bear—just not a regular on this street. The truck had been stationed in an open area and not in front of any trailer home, left unwittingly yet a clue for a trained eye. Sander forced himself to calm his breathing. He silenced his movements as he approached the trailer. Their trailer. The home he shared with Marlo. His heart pounded against the muscles of his chest. Sweat crept uncomfortably down his back and brow in spite of the frigid temperatures.

Passion and emotion must go away, Sander, when you're feeling them the most, Sid's voice boomed in his memory. Sid conveyed this wisdom to Sander untold times during his training. It finally made sense. Sander couldn't bungle this job because of clouded judgment.

Marlo's involved. The object of all his passion and emotion. Dear, sweet Marlo. Overhead a large bird flew low, covert—probably an owl, and shook Sander out of his revelry into the present. All that's vital is what's happening right now. My moves, my actions, my thoughts.

Scoping out the trailer and recalling the internal floor plan, Sander moved in. Surprise would be on his side, again, but not for long. He couldn't predict what Marlo would do, or—God forbid—what might have already happened. This was a new adversary, a devil he didn't know.

Marlo was frozen with terror. Her captor, a woman-man, lounged on the couch. Her sinewy limbs were slung over the armrest, relaxed as she sipped a Diet Coke, having helped herself to the refrigerator. It wouldn't have been clear if the being were male or female if she hadn't made the reference herself.

"Well, well, well. It looks like this is up to us gals to figure out, eh?" Her voice was flat despite the attempt at dark wit in the humorless setting, eyes blank. Her minion had told her this trailer was the base of undercover operations in Bear, but somehow she wasn't convinced. It didn't add up; this girl was no agent.

Instinctively moving her arms, Marlo panted with fear, barely holding back hysteria. Rough twine cut into her wrists and ankles, the red burn swelling with each breath. *Where's Sander? What's happened?*

It had been a pitiful struggle, a trite maneuver for the androgynous being. When she had knocked, Marlo had answered cheerfully, expecting Sander. She had slugged Marlo across the neck, yelled obscenities to elicit panic, and tied her up. It was so simple, it was almost wrong. No challenge. One thing the woman they called Pete—née Petrokovina—liked was a challenge.

Shutting her eyes to ground herself, Marlo pulled up the vision of Machu Picchu. She imagined stretching on top of the world, feeling the warmth of the sun on her limbs. She luxuriated in the memory of how the rays renewed her body after the exertion from the demands of the hike and altitude.

"No thinking. You come back to me," Pete spat out, startling Marlo before she was anchored. Pete's gaze penetrated Marlo, who couldn't speak, a rag roughly jammed into her mouth. "You don't move. No sound. You can nod if I ask a question. That's what you can do. Capisce?" Standing, Pete looked down at Marlo, whose arms overlapped angularly across an exquisitely made black cashmere sweater.

Marlo nodded slowly, willing herself not to gag.

"Do you have them?" The words came soft, almost a purr as Pete walked around Marlo, examining her every inch. Not harsh this time.

Taken off guard, all Marlo could do was shake her head frantically. No. *Them? What was she talking about?*

"Does your colleague have them?"

All Marlo could think of when Pete mentioned "colleague" was Gianni and the restaurant. Have what? She wanted to scream. What are you talking about? Then the obvious hit her hard. Sander. She must be talking about Sander. Oh God. What is it? Sander has a mystery, but she had thought it was a torrid and painful event in his past that she would be able to change with love and laughter.

A crash thundered like a crack of lightning invading the still, snowy night. Both women pitched in alarm. Instantly Pete changed her stance to one of fight, a strange jagged position like something from an Asian foreign film. Hurtling through the door like Spiderman, Sander was a weapon on legs. Marlo couldn't keep her eyes off him. It was like watching a movie, no, like being *in* a movie. Sander ignored Marlo and sparred with Pete. They were matched with energy and motion. Marlo could feel Sander's pulse, could tell he was assessing the situation. Then it happened. Sander launched himself toward Pete. The collision was so precise that Pete's body moved unnaturally in the air before crashing to the floor. She let out a gasp, an almost female sound.

Sander, without reservation for Pete's gender, punched and kicked until her body contorted and lay suddenly still. Breathing heavy, he drew her arms behind her listless body. For the second time that night, he cuffed a perpetrator's hands and skillfully secured ankles. Staring at the inert figure, he collected his breath, chest heaving.

Sander silently turned to look at Marlo. His eyes were heavy, holding emotion. He shook and dropped his chin to his chest in a self-deprecating movement that had Marlo quizzically eyeing him. *Was she next?* Sander moved toward the chair that had become her cell. Was it minutes or hours? She didn't know whether to try to escape from him or not. Sander deftly cut the ropes that tied her hands and feet, gently took out the rag from her mouth and picked her up in his arms. He held her close. His gasping breath was joined by her soft sobs, pent up fear, and finally, relief.

"Marlo, Marlo, Marlo. Oh Marlo. I'm so sorry. You weren't part of the plan." Sander held her tight and carried her around the room. After several long minutes, he eased her down so she could stand on the floor, once again embracing her tightly to him. He trembled at what might have been.

"Sander?" It was all that Marlo could stammer. Her instinct was to let him rescue her. Was she right? Or was he coming for her next? Her energy banks were empty, and fleeing just wasn't going to work.

Hearing her say his name, Sander stroked her hair, pulling her close, like a child. Taking a deep breath and clearing his throat to get to his words, Sander loosened his grip on Marlo and locked on her eyes. "There are some things that I didn't tell you."

"I see," she said, barely audible. Marlo trusted something in his voice but at the same time willed him not to hurt her. She looked at her wrists, covering them each with opposite hands to hide the red marks.

He tenderly placed his hands over hers. "No lies."

Her eyes wild with curiosity, fear abated, were answer enough for him to continue.

"I, uh, I just avoided some critical facts."

"Facts?" Marlo asked, as she twisted to get a good view of his face. He looked older than he had that morning. There were deep ridges across his forehead.

"I hope someday you'll understand. Before I can explain there's one thing I have to do." He stepped back from her and deftly took out his cell phone. His eyes never left hers, his movements controlled.

Marlo thought she'd fall without his support. She stood suspended in awe at the state of affairs.

The recipient on the other end answered on the first ring: "Sid."

"Sid, Sander. Two losers, no bounty. There has to be more."

There was five seconds of silence on the other end of the phone. This change of events baffled the all-knowing Sid. Two people? he asked Sander. What now?

"We need to search both sites and get these two, ah, cleaned and into custody. My cover's blown. Alert Washington."

"I'll have someone there in two hours. Are they restrained?"

"Uh, yeah, they aren't moving too fast." Sanders voice had taken on a casual quip, combined with a friendly ease that was unusual for Marlo to hear. She continued to hold his eyes as the picture in hers changed from terror to bewilderment.

"As for the issue of cover, no problem," Sid continued. "Stick to the truth, keep it simple. The usual. Say you tracked down some dregs with a few clues, captured them, that's it. Feds will work with the local sheriff."

Sander nodded in agreement. "Got it." This tactic would work to keep things in the right perspective for Bear residents. "Sid, something doesn't feel right. We've got the unsub and it doesn't make sense."

"I'll call you back." The conversation over, Sid ended the call.

Frosty air blew through the hole in the front of the trailer, the odd clank from the broken door a clumsy contrast to the silence of the room. Sander caressed Marlo's shoulders, equalizing, thinking, then broke connection with Marlo to evaluate the carnage he made of the front door. Dumb luck. His split-decision assessment was right—it was flimsy and easy to break down. If he'd been wrong—he shivered at the thought—the outcome of this situation would've been tragically different.

Sander considered all that could have gone wrong. The surprise attack only worked given that Pete's guard was down while she devised how to torment the defenseless Marlo; Pete's evil reputation preceded her. Sander had never seen or met Pete face to face, but he knew she was a ruthless fighter, smitten with control. Her trademark was incorporating violent horror into interrogations. How did she get involved? How did Sid not know? Whoever the bumbler was over at The Sicilian Ball must've rubbed off on her. There is a God, Hail Mary. He hadn't expected Pete, even with the female references from the earlier fight.

Sander felt Marlo's eyes. He turned to her and exhaled, arms hanging at his sides. Thank God she wasn't hurt. Heaving out his breath again, Sander sat on their worn couch, pulled her onto his lap, and told her his unabridged tale.

31

The next morning, Marlo, Gianni, Sander, Dale, and Judge Jerry, acting in his role of chief of police of Bear, stood in the entrance of The Sicilian Ball. Dale, formerly an Air Force top gun and detective of high standing from the New York City Police Department, had offered his detective services to Jerry when he had moved to town five years earlier. He was surprised by Jerry's call late the night before, asking him for help with intruders at Sander and Marlo's place and at The Sicilian Ball, never imagining that something like this could happen in Bear.

Sander had privately confided to Jerry that he was a federal agent but that he needed to keep a low profile. Only few people could know his true identity—especially Marlo's new friends, who would have many questions about what had taken place—but it wasn't something that should appear in the *Bearly News*. Sander told Jerry the Feds would be in charge of the investigation, but covertly. Jerry agreed to front the operation. Earlier that morning the SWAT team had cleared the cabin of clues they shared only with headquarters, leaving Sander, Dale, and Jerry to find only clues that the recent inhabitants were chain smokers who drank Diet Coke.

Sander wiped his forehead with the back of his hand, adjusting his stance and studying Marlo's face as Jerry bragged to the group that Pete and her boy were detained and that local safety was restored. "All the clues and movement patterns point to this restaurant. The cabin was only a holding place. From our search, the cabin had nothing to do with the stolen goods at all. It was used by Pete and her pal as a base to stay and observe." Jerry spoke with authority about the case, keeping an eye on Sander for hints that he was saying the right things. Gosh darn if the young lanky agent didn't play along with him like a champ. Pretending to be in charge didn't hurt anyone, did it?

Dale decided on an obvious question to start. "Tell me, Gianni, Marlo, has there been anything unusual at all in the restaurant since it opened?"

Shaking his head, Gianni ruffled his brow. "Everything is unusual, Dale, because everything is still new. We're just learning the town, the restaurant, each other."

"I understand. Think minor. Like, misplaced olive oil or a package you never opened. Something little that maybe was out of order that you didn't process in your normal restaurant routine. We think this was a drop site." The group was silent for many seconds looking at one another and out over the restaurant, not quite sure what "drop site" really meant.

"Well, Jana brought us the olive bottle, which is cool and different," Marlo said, motioning in the direction of the glass jar. "Then we had this antique hostess stand that Gianni's grandfather sent from Sicily."

Sander walked over to the ornate piece, the same spot where the night prior he had restrained Pete's accomplice. Still thinking, Marlo added, "Once I went to get matches from that little hidden spot, and they were gone. Is that unusual?" She stopped and looked up at Dale.

Instantly Sander knelt on the floor, hands moving around the piece. His fingers found the holed compartment that Marlo referenced. It was empty. Intrigued, he continued his quest. He poked every crevice of the intricately carved wood with his hands, making short and purposeful movements. Gently, he turned the item on end to get a better look underneath and inside the stand. Something moved under his touch. He stopped, adjusted his knees, and turned the stand. Awkwardly set on the underside, another small compartment opened up, like a hidden drawer. Inside the tiny area Sander felt something that was out of place.

It was soft and thin against the rough wood. Satin cords. He grasped the material and gingerly tugged them out. A small gasp came from the group as Sander dangled a midnight blue velvet pouch of substantial weight with black satin cording.

"Bingo." It was all he managed to say as a smile spread across his stress-laden face. "This must be our bounty." He walked over to the bar, comrades in tow, small bag resting in his palm. Sander whistled as the sparkling contents tumbled out, softly landing on a padded maroon bar mat.

The gems were gorgeous. Intricately cut emeralds, rubies, and diamonds, they were large stones, the smallest more than a carat in size. The group was mesmerized. Sander noticed as Jerry nervously scratched the side of his head and took a step back from the priceless collection.

"Holy moley, that is some bounty," Dale managed. "Is there someone else out looking for this stuff?" he said, purposefully looking up at Sander. Dale was unsettled at the look he got from Sander. Something didn't add up. Why would this type of drop be in Bear?

Marlo was speechless, looking from the gems to her friends. Gianni shook his head in disbelief, a million thoughts going through his mind on the origination of the gems. How did they get in the stand? What about his grandfather? His family back in Sicily; were they in danger? There had been times when gem drops came from Morocco to carriers on the island. But his family was never involved.

Shifting with a new sense of unease now that he was out in the open and not cloaked with the comfort of disguise, Sander looked at the multifarious group, taking in each of them with his eyes. Judge Jerry spoke up, seeing the concern of his flock. "You don't need to worry. Those involved are now captive here at home and abroad." It was a partial truth, but his words were technically honest so far as he knew.

Gianni cleared his throat, uncertain as to his voice. What might this do to his new restaurant business and his reputation? As he opened his mouth to speak, Jerry put up a hand in understanding. "This job had mob beginnings but went awry through a wayward junior boss. Fairly complicated. Gianni, your family isn't associated. Just the hostess stand was involved," he said with a grin and a wink. "The stand has some historic significance, did you know?" Jerry said rhetorically. "It was a bit of a globe trot they had to sort this through, but it's over."

Scanning the gems, Sander picked out a magnificent square-cut, dark-colored emerald and turned to Marlo. "Marlo, many days will pass before the fear of seeing you tied up goes away." His voice was low, intimate. "Knowing your pain was my fault is more than I can bear. Please forgive me." Taking her hand, Sander pulled her close, oblivious to his public display of affection. "One day you'll have an emerald like this, from me, on your hand. It will be honest and gorgeous. Like you." Marlo was speechless; she clutched onto Sander, nestling her head into the crook of his neck. The others were captivated by the raw emotion coming from Sander and his eloquent words. Sander gently traced her chin with his fingers, sensuality sparking from his touch. Marlo remained silent, smitten.

"Like fresh basil to compliment beautiful scampi," Gianni mused to himself. "Bella." He focused on the loose gems, admiring their deep hues, muttering in Italian.

Judge Jerry leaned his healthy girth back on his heels and pursed his lips. His eyes were dark as he watched Sander, but his body language supported his love of a happy ending. Dale had a new sense of camaraderie with Sander and their similar experiences. Sander, it appeared, was on the up and up. This was a good day.

On the outskirts of Bear, news of the surreal event with its almost fatal ending reached Eva. She shivered, thinking of Marlo's experience. In a way, it paralleled her story with Seaton. They had not known who Sander really was either. Both men made up their life stories—Sander, purportedly for the greater good, and Seaton, for his own selfish desires. But wasn't this real life after all? People making up stuff. Thank God Marlo and Sander were safe and, she hoped, better off for sharing the unscripted adventure.

Eva admired the precocious risk Marlo had taken in asking Sander to Bear. He'd accepted. Marlo followed her heart and trusted the part of Sander she was attracted to, that part he chose to share with her. He wasn't entirely honest, to say the least. Yet somehow, someway, it worked out. Should everyone know all of the details of our past? Maybe not. Maybe we need to tell them what matters to the relationship at hand. Maybe we need to trust people for the part of them they're willing to share.

32

Charlie Cunningham, Esquire, preened like a peacock amidst the thirty-odd students aged fourteen to twenty-three cavorting around the old barn. They buzzed like bees in and of the stalls. The center of the building was large and open, a good fifty feet square. In neat piles at one end, utilizing some of the stalls, were stacks of supplies—wood planks, plywood sheets, nails, paint, plaster, and all the associated tools necessary to use with the appropriate medium.

Rapidly rubbing his hands together, Charlie was deep in dialogue with a young girl who was waving a paintbrush as she spoke. In one especially passionate gesture, she slung the brush up in the air, the still damp blue paint swiping part of Charlie's shoulder and the back of a boy diligently working nearby. All three were oblivious to the result of the motion, so intent was their conversation and toils at hand.

Rosalyn emerged from an old cow stall at the back of the barn. Her hair was tied up on top of her head with a large blue and white rag reminiscent of the "Rosie the Riveter" heroine from World War II. She carried a clipboard and had a pencil tucked behind her ear. Two rather burly young men were talking to her, and she walked, listened, and took notes all at once.

"Ralph, take the nails and give them to Tommy to complete the stage steps. And you, Ricky, go and see what Louise is carrying on about up in the loft." Seeing Charlie signal to her, she walked over to her esteemed leader and gave him her best Katherine Hepburn stance of womanly strength.

"Ros, the man from the *Bearly News* is here. I'd like you to be with me when we talk."

She crisply nodded in agreement, pursed lips, character intact.

Taking in the view around the barn, Charlie looked at her and added, "Dang it, woman, I'm right proud of the way you motivate these young folks." Words weren't necessary, and Ros turned in step with Charlie, side by side, as they crossed the expanse of the barn toward the waiting men. It was obvious who the newspaper people were; one had a large camera, the other a pad of paper and a briefcase, and they were standing forlorn and idle among the bustling activity.

"So, Mr. Cunningham, this all came up rather quickly." Ron Raymond, editor-in-chief, cleared his throat and glanced at his watch, which read four forty-five in the afternoon. After an exchange of niceties, the questions began. "What do you have going on here?"

Leaning back on his heels, thumbs linked in his suspenders, Charlie watched the scrambling in the barn. Gathering his thoughts, he sized up the young editor. Ron Raymond was a man of average build, brown hair, brown eyes, and decades Charlie's junior. He was certainly no adversary, only a young bloke doing his job. "Why, Mr. Raymond, we're embarking on a new fine arts theater for the students and residents of Bear." He flashed a winning smile and did a play with clearing his throat. "Isn't that obvious?" he said with a wink to Rosalyn as his arm made a huge swooping motion across the barn. At this cue, Roslyn subtly stood just a little taller, pulled back her shoulder blades, and eyed the momentarily mute editor.

"Sure, sir, of course, yes." A practical, traditional man, Ron felt uncharacteristically out of his element in the company of Charlie and Rosalyn and their band of students. "Can you, er, elaborate for me?"

"Why, Mr. Raymond, these fine young people of the village of Bear are building dreams. Yes, they are, building big dreams." His mind wandered back to his coaching conversation with Eva. Dreams, yes, dreams can come true if you define them. If you even make them up. The lady coach pulled a miracle out of an old codger. Yes indeed.

"Do you mean that the barn reconstruction is a dream?" Ron asked, trying to track with Charlie.

"Not the structure. See, this place is an open canvas for these young folks to experience, spread their wings, succeed, and—why, I suppose on occasion—fail."

"An open canvas, sir?"

"This environment we're creating is a place where there aren't lines, so to speak," Charlie answered, chin nodding.

"I see. Can you explain that for me, please?"

"What I mean is, there aren't lines that they have to stay inside or spaces to color the right way."

"Interesting," Ron said, feeling drawn in by the possibilities that Charlie was putting out to others.

"These young folks are creating. Being. Growing."

"Okay." Gaining momentum, Ron persevered, standing taller by association. Important things were going to happen here. "So, tell me more."

"These kids and young adults live in this beautiful place of Wyoming. I want them to understand that gift and use it to their betterment. To experiment with the fine arts, to act, dance, sing. See them all working?"

"Yes, quite impressive actually."

"This was an old dilapidated barn. With a little social positioning," Charlie paused, cleared his throat and leaned into Ron conspiratorially. "Er, or one might say *sucking up*—please don't print that—we've been able to procure all these supplies for next to no cost."

"Can you elaborate on those who donated?" Ron asked, interested now with the story hook of cash.

"Why, yes indeed. See, we had Judge Jerry down at the community buildings do us a fine speech. Yup. Then, of course, the local restaurants like Grizzly, the new Italian place, and Beat's Barbecue tossed in some coin and set up donation jars on their counters. But, truth be told, and put down that pen, young man. Truth be told, it was the Babcocks who went deep into those endless pockets of theirs. Yes. Real contributions."

"So it was word of mouth. Did they understand this 'being creative' thing?"

"Son, it's something that older folks get. Being young is about being young. Trying. Experimenting. Failing. And trying again. Maybe you're a dancer but don't figure that out until after you try horseback riding, painting, and some figure skating. See?"

"I'm seeing your vision," Ron said, seeing a good story, too.

"It's about figuring it out for yourself and not worrying about what you already tried. The key is you. Not your folks or the uncles, or big brothers. What you want to try. Get it?"

"Well I think I'm getting this point, Mr. Cunningham."

During the interview with Ron, a small group queued up about five feet away. They were waiting to talk to their leader.

"Ah, Charlie?" Ros interjected without delicacy. Coyly she looked Ron up and down in manner that meant it was time he move on his way.

In his almost ten years of being in the news business, Ron learned the second in command was usually the gatekeeper. "Anything else you want to add for today? I can see you're in high demand." Best keep a relationship ripe for the next story. He had this one.

"Why, I think there's one last thing for me to add." Beaming at his band of adolescents and twenty-somethings, there was no mistaking Charlie's delight in them and his approval of their jockeying for his counsel. "Wouldn't you say, Ros, that we should share the name of this new place?" Rosalynn took the pencil from out behind her ear as she wrote a note for a sixteen-year-old boy and stuck it atop the box of paint supplies he was lugging. Taking her time to accentuate the point, she looked from Charlie to Ron and shook her head affirmatively in one distinguished nod.

"That would be, Ron, the name of this place is Possibilities. Yes, that'd be the name."

33

Head down, Steve clutched his leather portfolio as it was pummeled by snowflakes the size of quarters. No mountains were visible as he jogged across the parking lot toward the library. The pending shelter shimmered with light streaming from every window.

Darn near freezing, Steve thought, but he reminded himself there was no place he'd rather live. God knows he tried. And what would people talk about without extreme weather? Despite distaste for real crowds, he thrived on the energy Bear residents brought to local events. Cripes, the whole lot hardly made a crowd.

The Bear Township Library was decorated like a stage set for *The Nutcracker Suite* ballet, swags of evergreens, pinecones, velvet ribbons, and gem-colored glass balls adorned the entranceway. A Christmas tree graced the center of the great room, surrounded by reading tables and stacks of books. Steve stopped to admire the dozen different sets of colorful Russian stacking dolls in all shapes and sizes around the tree. The dolls were gifts to the library from Grace. Every spring for as many decades as Steve had lived, Grace Cartwright would bring a box to the library stocked full of books from other countries and artisan crafts from around the world, the most memorable of which were the beautiful stacking dolls.

Hearing his name, Steve looked in the direction of the voice to see a waving Jana.

"Steve, isn't this great? Look at all the kids," Jana gasped as she embraced Steve in a hug. "So, come this way. Wait until you see the room this year." Steve cocked his eyebrow and followed her as she jingled with each step from the tiny bells attached to her neon red knit sweater. She looked like a living ornament.

"What, no 'Hello Steve, glad you made it out in the weather, thanks for coming to read when you should be home writing papers?'" he chided as he walked behind her.

Jana stopped, turned around, and looked him square in the eye, "Darling, as Heidi would say, ain't no better way to spend an evening than reading to children. She might read them history, however."

"Heidi wouldn't say 'ain't.'"

"Incorrigible."

"Just saying ..."

"Besides, I made your favorite cookies. Happy?"

"Well, if you put it that way, maybe." Steve decided to stop the teasing; cook he could do, but baking was a whole other course of study.

"Huh," Jana said in a haughty tone. She was sovereign when it came to baking Christmas cookies.

"Butter cookies?"

"Of course."

"Are they thin?"

Laughing, Jana shook her head and put her arm around his waist, "Yes, Steve, they're rolled thin, I used real butter, and they're not too brown. Satisfied?"

Eyes twinkling, Steve nodded using his chin as a guide. "See? Now you're talking. Yes, I'm happy there are proper Christmas butter cookies to be had. How many are you expecting?"

"Oh, enough. You don't need to worry about that. With tomorrow being the last day of school before the holiday break, you know that every parent in town is sending the kids here tonight to get them out of the house. Their loss. I love them being here." Steve accepted this statement. Kids and Christmas went together just like kids and candy. Now you put together kids, Christmas, candy, cookies, and stories, that was enough to get anyone's heart and priorities in order.

They walked into the reading room and were absorbed into red, green, and blue lights; wrapped presents with golden bows strategically arranged; and aromas that wafted unmercifully from the goodie table. The front of the room had a large fireplace with a round stone hearth that filled most of the wall. It was as perfect to sit on as it was for displaying wicker baskets of pinecones and hand-sawed wooden log reindeers.

On the wall next to the door hung an Advent calendar. The tree motif had three rows of pockets underneath, those labeled one through nineteen were empty. Their previous contents now adorned the stylized green tree as they counted down to Christmas Day. Each day one delighted child took an ornament out of a pocket and pinned it on the felt tree. Peeking out of the coveted pocket labeled '24,' for Christmas Eve, was a triangle point hinting of a gold sequined star.

The gaiety of the event was contagious, and Steve was eating crisp butter cookies before he knew what happened. Jana patted him on the back as she fluttered off to complete final details before the night's reading began. According to tradition, the twelve readers came to support fellow comrades as often as busy work and home schedules allowed. This was Steve's first night in, and his night to read but he hoped to join a future session or two.

What a week it had been for Bear! Just two days earlier a mob-initiated international jewelry heist was uncovered in the town. If that wasn't enough excitement, the strange new reclusive resident had become a hero among his close-knit group, in one night subduing both an intruder at The Sicilian Ball and a trained killer who had broken into his home and held Marlo hostage. A quick tug on his pant leg broke Steve out of his daydream. Looking down, Steve saw young Kyle O'Connor, grinning ear to ear with a big red punch mustache. "Mr. Steve, Mr. Steve, guess who came yesterday to the reading?"

Kneeling down to be eye level with the child, Steve grew serious to respond in kind. "Why? Who was here, Kyle? I had to miss it."

Puffing out his chest like a journalist who scored a major story, Kyle continued, "It was Mrs. Santa Claus herself." He paused for effect. "No kidding."

"No way! Mrs. Santa Claus? That's some serious Christmas visitor. Are you sure? Mrs. Santa Claus came all the way to little old Bear?"

"Yup. Yes, sir, Mr. Steve. I saw her with mine own eyes. She even read the story *Santa Claus's Workshop*. She winked and everything at the special Santa parts so we all knew she had the inside scoop. And she wore those little wire glasses— spectacles, my dad called them."

"I'm sorry I missed it," Steve replied, lightly rubbing Kyle's cheek with his fist. "Tonight is my turn. You give me a signal if I need to read slower or faster, okay?"

Nodding his head, Kyle gave Steve a serious look and was off. Steve noticed the boy transformed with confidence, probably racking his little brain to think up a special signal to give during the story.

From across the room Eva watched the whole interaction between Steve and Kyle. Her heart missed a beat when he lightly rubbed Kyle's cheek with his fist. *That's just what he did to me in the coffee shop, when he called me "lovely lady."* The ambience mesmerized Eva like the rest of the participants, but seeing Steve Mason made her heart pound and she lost her appetite for Christmas cookies. A tap on her shoulder pulled her out of her head.

"Hey, girlfriend." Heidi stood next to her beaming, sporting a knit hat similar to the one that Marlo frequently wore.

"Heidi, hello. Nice hat. Aren't you going to be warm in here with that thing on?" Eva motioned her eyes to the knit hat, not the typical Heidi-style haute couture.

Putting her hands to her head, Heidi rolled her eyes in exaggeration. "The things we do for kids. After last night's Mrs. Claus act, I need to be incognito lest some bright child see the resemblance. Clearly this hat and a classy Mrs. Claus have nothing in common."

"I'll give you that. You were amazing. The outfit, glasses, you really pulled it off. Handing out ceramic mugs with hot chocolate mix was a real nice touch. You're going to make the rest of us look bad."

"It was a blast," she said, emerald eyes dancing. "As far as the mugs, I convinced a Grizzly supplier to donate them if I would buy their hot chocolate packets to stuff inside. Told him it was good advertising. You know, Mrs. Claus hand-ing out hot chocolate, it must be the best brand, yada, yada, yada. He bought it."

"Only you, Heidi. My reading is the night after tomorrow," Eva added wist-fully, still mildly distracted with Steve in the same room. "I'm getting excited."

"Clearly. This is a feel-good-about-yourself event. I have to hand it to Jana, who got the support from the library. Her superior, the Frau Librarian, isn't usu-ally open to ideas that require effort."

"The woman talks?" Eva added conspiratorially.

"Ha, sometimes. She's just not interested in being around people."

Having had a personal run-in with the head librarian after she first moved to town, Eva giggled and jabbed Heidi lightly with her elbow, eyeing the object of their conversation across the room talking to Steve.

"Ah, yes, there she is now, honing in on my cuz, your potential territory." Heidi glanced sideways at Eva, who suddenly was at a loss for words. Now was Heidi's turn to jab Eva gently with an elbow.

"Touché," Eva muttered, willing the redness away from her neck and cheeks.

At the stroke of seven o'clock, Jana called order to the room. "Everyone, set-tle down and listen in here," she said into a microphone, sporting an Elf hat with a bell-laden pom-pom. As they came forward, Jana arranged children of all ages in a semicircle. "Welcome to all of you. Our reader tonight is Mr. Steve Mason. He's going to read you the all-time classic story, *Rudolf, the Red-Nosed Reindeer*. Now stay low and you'll all get to see the pictures." Jana handed the microphone to Steve, who declined its use.

Steve wasn't a stranger to the town children. They knew him from reading events and true stories about his fishing escapades. He sat on the center of the fireplace hearth and cleared his throat. Eva settled into a chair toward the back, thankful for the luxury to watch Steve from afar without having to be discreet. He wore a rich green sweater that had a rustic look to it, the thick wool yarn tinted with brown flecks. Homemade perhaps?

At first Eva was disappointed with the choice. She had been hoping to see if Steve would reveal something about himself by choosing a rare story, but she for-got about her wish the moment he started reading. His voice and character inter-pretation was captivating. Paying close attention, she noticed that the book he used was tattered, one he must have had for years. Eva comfortably put away the topic for future discussion. Up front, young Kyle O'Conner was so taken by the tale he forgot his task to signal.

After the festivities, Eva sensed a presence, then felt Steve gently clutch her elbow.

"Ms. Karlsen," he spoke just loud enough for her, filling the space with his scent. "How nice to see you this evening." Making intimate eye contact, he released his grip, never letting go of her eyes.

Eva, tongue-tied at the interaction, managed to gather some composure.

"Hey. Hi, Steve."

"Back at you. Glad you came."

"You were wonderful up there. They hung on your every word."

Grinning a million-watt smile, Steve took a minuscule bow. "Thank you. Coming from such an accomplished reader as yourself, I'll accept the compliment."

"Now, how would you know that?" She'd read *The First Christmas Tree* last year and was certain Steve wasn't in attendance.

"Your reputation precedes you. This is a small town, remember?"

"Well, I try. It was nothing like what you just did back there."

Seeing that she was ready to go, hat and gloves in place, Steve ignored her praise. "Might I escort you outside?"

At a loss, Eva tipped her head in agreement, squeaking out a soft, "Sure." They walked through the library and out the door in silence, but the quiet spoke volumes. Eva turned to look at Steve, who greeted her with a lopsided grin. *That face should be illegal.* Once again he gently guided her with his hand on her back and matched her gait. She loved that. Outside, it was Eva who broke the comfortable silence. "So what lies ahead for you over the holidays?"

Thinking for a second, after they stopped at the side of her snow-laden aqua International, Steve took in a breath to ward off the cold air. "Well, tomorrow night is time spent with you. I can't think beyond that just yet, lovely lady."

The husky tone of his voice had Eva's insides do a summersault, not trusting herself to speak. One thing she learned from coaching is that you didn't have to have a quick comment or comeback. As a human being, you were allowed to let there be quiet in a relationship, in conversation. Eva permitted the indulgence.

Never in a rush for words, Steve picked up her hand and brought it to his lips, locking eyes with Eva. "I'll see you tomorrow night." He opened the door, motioned for her to climb in. Deftly he pulled out the broom from the flat bed of the truck and brushed the snow from the windows. It only took one winter living in Bear for new residents to travel with brooms, shovels, and blankets. Local tradition had it that if you had a truck, you kept the broom and shovel in the back, for your use or communal assistance, as required.

Once his task was complete, Steve tossed the broom in the back, banged on the truck bed, and waved her farewell, a sincere display of gallantry.

34

Safely pulled into her garage, Eva put her forehead on the steering wheel. Steve Mason was under her skin. He was so—well, *so*. He puzzled her with his chivalry and patience. His education and background belied his simple living. And how could such a man be available, live in Bear, and quite clearly be interested in her?

This was indeed a dream, and she would be waking up any moment. There must be something wrong with him, a dark secret perhaps? Catching fish with his teeth? A penchant for collecting bat scat? A long, lone whine from Dash interrupted her thoughts before they grew grim. Eva hauled herself out of the truck and into the house at the beckoning of her canine charge. Unbeknownst to Eva, it appeared as though Dash had a sixth sense to save Eva from herself and her penchant for dark memories of Seaton.

Stomping the snow off his boots, Steve scooped up Snowball and rubbed her head. Setting down the animal, he went over to the bookcase and gingerly placed the storybook back on the shelf, tucking in the loose pages. Bittersweet memories. Standing in front of the shelf for many minutes, Steve carefully closed the old beveled glass door. His torment of what could have been, what he missed, thrashed in his mind. Memories of the past were awakened as expected from his reading of *Rudolf*. He allowed them to flow through his pores, sending a wave of anguish through his body, submitting to the sadness, then to peace, as he had for the past twenty years.

In spite of the sorrowful remembrance, Steve loved the bustle of the holidays—and, no, the holidays weren't just for women. The season was as much a thrill for him now as when he was eight years old. The shopping for gifts, dastardly snowfalls, shiny red and gold wrapping paper, ringing bells, homemade candies, long drawn-out dinners. He anticipated Santa through the eyes of young relatives and townfolk.

His thoughts turned to Eva, and his insides scrambled. Sharing the holidays with Eva. What might *that* be like? Eva, a woman who appears to be as shy as she is confident. Eva, with such a distinctive natural beauty that it took his breath away, to say nothing about what she did to his romantic imagination.

If he didn't know any better, he'd say that she approached this budding relationship with an honest openness. No games. Yet her attitude seemed tinged with caution. *I wonder what that's about.* Slow was good. The last thing he needed in his life was the distraction of whirlwind romance. He could focus on his research and guide business. *Or is Eva just what he needs?* He could imagine Grace saying those words as she knowingly clucked her tongue at their next monthly coffee.

35

"Sarah, you have relentless perseverance. What you've built in the last month for your business is mind-boggling."

"Thank you, Eva." Sarah said quietly, looking out her twenty-second-story window. The buildings, sky, and roads far below were all varying colors of gray.

"I'm proud of you," Eva said, as she scanned the manila file that stored the notes from coaching calls with Sarah, including an idea to raise with her today.

"That means a lot," Sarah responded, standing up to walk around her office, loving her wireless headset. "I'm trying to sort out my life."

"And with solid results. Sarah, there's an exercise that can potentially bring you even more awareness. Would you want to try it?"

"I'm game for anything today, Eva," Sarah said. "My agenda was to brainstorm the upcoming meetings and share my excitement without having to hold it back. And, well, we've already done that!" Eva felt Sarah's smile beaming through the phone lines.

"Great. So, Sarah, the first thing I want you to do is write down seven things that you have in your life right now that you don't like."

"Things I don't like?" Sarah volleyed back the question, stopping in her tracks.

Eva heard the tension at her request for negative thoughts. *Forge ahead, this will help Sarah.* "Things you don't like. No judgment, just write down situations you find yourself in—things that happen, things you do, whatever—that you would rather not have in your life."

"Okay," Sarah responded slowly, settling back into her chair behind her desk.

Knowing that Sarah wrote begrudgingly, Eva encouraged, "Minor things count. They don't have to be complex or gory."

After several minutes, Eva asked Sarah for a status and paused again after hearing the response. Her gaze found a sticky note she had placed on the wall above her desk one year ago. It held the words "awareness," "commitment," and "practice." Those three words defined coaching. Eva reminded herself of this simple truth.

"I should stop at seven, right? Once I got on a roll, I could keep going with this one." Sarah's energy had waned from earlier in the call. She felt almost as gray as the scenery.

Eva cringed, now doubting her timing for this exercise and hoping that it wouldn't spoil Sarah's celebration of her consulting business. She plunged ahead. "Seven is good. Read me one of them."

"Clutter. Everywhere in my house," was Sarah's first response.

"What is it about the clutter that bothers you?"

"It's a mess. It gets in the way. I can't find stuff."

"How does it make you feel?"

"Embarrassed. Also like I'm tied down and incapable," was a quick reply from Sarah.

"What would you choose to have instead of clutter?"

"Like a clean, organized house?"

"You tell me. Instead of clutter, would you choose to have an organized home, spacious and freeing?" Stillness came over the phone line. Spacious and freeing seemed to be the opposite of tied down and incapable.

"Yes, that sounds appealing."

"So, Sarah, if you could choose to have an organized home, spacious and freeing, would you take it?" Eva paused to see if her words resonated with Sarah.

"Yes," Sarah spoke with soft conviction.

"Great. Now say the whole sentence like you mean it."

"I choose to have an organized home, spacious and freeing."

"Great. Sarah, I want you to write that down on another sheet of paper. Make sure that you start with the words 'I choose.'" Giving her time to write down, Eva gained some confidence to take Sarah through the repetitive but worthwhile exercise.

"Are you game to work through a few more?" Sarah and Eva worked through her list of "don't likes" and changed them into grander, broader statements of things that, if she could, Sarah would choose instead. Eva skillfully steered Sarah clear of finding solutions. For today, the exercise was to transform the "don't likes" into positive life choices that she might be missing. After completing the seven statements, Eva started to wrap up the session.

"Take a minute now and read them to yourself, knowing you can wordsmith later. How do they sound to you?"

"Ooh, really good," was the warm reply over the phone from Sarah.

Phew. "Here's the deal. Trust me on this one. For the next week until we talk again, I want you to read this choice list at least once a day at a time you'll remember to do it. When you read each one aloud, take time to imagine seeing that choice in action. Touch it, see it, taste it, smell it. The whole task takes less than five minutes."

"Huh. But what about plans to make them happen?" Sarah said in a skeptical tone.

"Just be with the idea of it all. No work yet. Tell your subconscious that these are things you choose to have in your life." Eva was building up tension for Sarah. The more tangible the tension clients could create for what they want, the easier to get them committed to change their status quo.

"Mmm," Sarah said, responding with mild understanding.

"I'm not a psychiatrist, but what I've learned from my studies and experience is that our subconscious always answers 'yes' to what we think. So, if you get used to the ideas of these choices to be real in your subconscious, you're setting yourself up for 'yes' answers by your conscious."

Silence.

Choking back laughter, Eva continued. "Sarah, that explanation was heavy. I just ask you to give it a shot this week, and we can talk about it next session. Are you up for that?" What she really wanted to do was apologize for the intrusion of the exercise and withdraw the task list. Eva resisted the urge, remembering her instructors telling her to lean into the tools, that people know what's right for them. Coaches serve clients by opening the door to possibilities.

Hours later, Eva walked around her office stretching her arms and waist to release pent-up anxiety. She loved her profession. There were days when Eva worried she wasn't giving her clients enough value or a consistent dose of major league ah-ha's. It was then that Eva missed being part of a team to banter with about frustrations and accomplishments.

When she completed her coach certification training, her small class made an effort to stay together after the official training was over. It was tough to schedule, and Eva made forty percent of the sessions, yet each time she found value being part of the group. Maybe she should contact *them* for a change? It would only take an email to get things moving. After all, she preached about relationships. The more you nurture them, the more you are rewarded. Simple actions make such a big difference. You just have to do it—or rather, remember to do it.

Staring out at the lake for several minutes, Eva, shivered unconsciously, using the movement as a nudge for action. She went into the kitchen to review her Christmas list that was in dire need of progress. Back in her office again, she sat at the computer. Poor Dash followed her every step and landed in a solid clunk on the floor for the third time in ninety seconds. Wherever Eva went, he shadowed her and plunked down. In contrast, Scout never left her cozy spot over the heating duct. She watched Dash and Eva move about, ending up right where they started. Surely Scout wondered why they expended all that extra energy for no apparent reason.

Editing the Christmas letter, Eva concluded it worthy. The personal epistle fit on one page full of facts, fun, and sufficient endearment to friends and family living afar. Living afar. Who was it who really lived afar? Now there's a concept. She was home in Bear. Odd that, after only two years, she considered Bear home more than any other place she'd lived. Had she even called those other places home? Hard to remember. Previous addresses consisted of large apartment complexes where she crashed after flying home late from some city. Most mornings she was off to work before the sun crept above the horizon. Wasn't home about being content, fitting in?

Her old life on the corporate treadmill seemed so far away it exhausted her to construct the memory. She hardly could reconcile the life she had lived in those driven days. What was she driven toward? It appeared she had the wrong map. Thank God she realized it when she did. Sure, she missed a few friends and dependable acquaintances. She had fond reminiscences of their times together. Her life was in Bear now, and she never yearned for the past. She had an honest relationship with her dad; they talked when it felt right and made sure to visit once a year.

Are my roots too shallow? Jana, Heidi, and now Marlo were real friends. She relished the simple treasure of girlfriend banter and window-shopping. She took comfort in her new stomping grounds at the Grizzly, the library, Bear Claw, and walking by the school. This town was home. Eva felt grounded, and she hoped her roots would take hold. She had once only dreamt of the camaraderie she had now developed in two short years. Then there was the new addition of Steve Mason. Which reminded her, what should she wear on their date that evening?

Intruding on her thoughts, a slim, strong paw equipped with sharp claws landed with abrupt precision on Eva's lap, then slowly scraped down the jeans that were thankfully protecting the skin on her calf. Scout stood with vigor, held a red rubber play toy, and wagged her tail ferociously. When Scout wanted attention and play, there was no denying her intent. As soon as Eva pet the animal, Scout scooted both front paws into Eva's lap. The dog's long snout and toy moved back and forth, propelled by the force of her tail. This time from across the room, an aged-beyond-his-years Dash watched with sad brown eyes, unmoving from his laying position.

"Scout, no scratch. That hurts." Undeterred, the animal did it again until exasperated, Eva pushed back her chair and stood. "Okay, I'll play with you, but only for a few minutes." At these familiar words, Dash heaved his furry girth up and bounded over to join in the revelry. Both dogs were in a flurry of turning circles around and between Eva's legs.

Eva walked to the mudroom, deciding to give them the deluxe treatment since her work was complete. Dash immediately planted his curly bottom on the floor and stared at Eva with adoring eyes. Scout performed small vertical cat-like leaps, the complete opposite reaction. Shaking her head with the predictability of it all, Eva took down the Frisbee that hung on a nail high inside the closet. She slipped on winter boots and the threesome went outside.

Eva commanded Dash to sit and stay as she threw the Frisbee for Scout. The dog flew after the toy and vaulted into the air to catch the flying disc, oblivious to the snow cover. After several throws and catches, roles reversed and Dash had his turn. The animal frolicked across the snow to jump and catch Frisbee. Running back, he scampered with his front paws out together, then back, moving like a live rocking horse. Their unabashed enthusiasm for the sport endeared them to Eva and made up for the rampant fur balls that inhabited most corners in her home.

On the other side of town, a different scene played out. Steve flipped his cell phone closed with a sharpness that matched the pounding in his chest. What was that about? Why would she call after all this time? Sweet, seductive, alluring. *Typical.* Life could bring up bad news at the wrong time. There definitely wasn't any room for *her* in his life. Was there? Granted, there were some amusing aspects to the woman. She had been an interesting diversion. Diversion, shit; she was a hidden land mine waiting to explode. Dangerous.

Steve forced himself to change gears and took his frustration out by relentlessly pounding the computer keys. His eyes flashed across the screen as his fingers moved like pistons over the keyboard as he made final changes to his paper. Daily, he thanked his high school typing teacher, Miss Ruth, for *her* relentless teaching of touch-typing. He remembered the entire class sitting in front of old Royal typewriters at a time just before the computer age hit the local schools. Miss Ruth, all of four feet eleven inches, stood in front of the class, peering over bifocals and calling out strict commands with authority. *ASDF, pause, JKL semicolon. Again class.* Over and over again. For impact, she used a long wooden yardstick and struck the old green board as she articulated each key.

"Mr. Mason, do *not* look at your hands or you *will* type me a page from the dictionary after school." Punishment of that nature caused Steve and his buddies to sit tall and look at the board or their papers, never their hands. Detention meant missing sports practice or, even worse, missing a hike in the mountains, a horse ride through the valley, or, season permitting, some fishing down at that secret trout stream.

Saving the document, Steve rolled back in his chair, stretching hands overhead, pushing the metal spring to its limit. This paper on the Gros Ventre Indians was different. It challenged the reader to enter the Gros Ventres' system: the natural vegetation, love of the mountains, and their adept awareness of the river and stream networks. He took the reader from a factual reading experience to an experiential one, luring people into the perspective of the how these gentle souls respected their environment. The landscape was more to them than a nice view. It was their world. Their existence. The land was life giving and life taking. *The boys at the University of Wyoming may not appreciate this work. I can hear them now, saying it's a bit too soft for them. Ha, maybe I should send it to Berkeley or James down at USC.*

Content, Steve completed the process of printing and reviewing and decided there was no time like the present to email it to the department chair in Laramie for review. Done. Shackles removed! Checking his inbox, Steve scanned the list for anything worthwhile. Seeing notes from his mother, James Cartwright, and an old college friend, he took time to answer the messages. As he typed, Snowball leapt up and curled into a purring ball amid his ample lap.

Christmas Eve was in full swing. Morning snow had fallen on the streets of Bear but had stopped in time to allow snowplows and shovelers to ready the roadways and walkways for evening festivities. Lights glittered through the village. To keep with tradition, the residents of Bear went visiting, sharing plates of cookies, bottles of homemade Swedish glogg, chocolate pecan pies, and cranberry walnut breads. By midday, the streets were dotted with activity and goodwill. By late afternoon, the group of eight friends convened downtown to start their progressive dinner.

Participants at the First Annual Christmas Progressive Dinner picked up where they left off from their Thanksgiving extravaganza, with lots of hugging and teasing. The appetizer stop went without a hitch at Jana and Heidi's Victorian, and the group had walked together to Dale's home for the main course. Only a month had passed, but their relationships and interrelations had deepened.

Sander, still a man of few words, observed the crowd, arm slung over Marlo's shoulder. He held a calm reserve and never broke physical connection with Marlo unless necessary, a casual arm around her neck, pulling her into his lap, holding her hand, something, some touch. He acted as her subliminal safety blanket. Watching the whole interaction, an astute Heidi whispered to Eva, wondering if he was aware of his actions. Probably.

The success of the restaurant and the ordeal of the break-in had brought Marlo and Gianni closer. Gianni was careful not to let his protective nature for Marlo upstage the romance between Marlo and Sander in any way, real or perceived. Ironically, Sander approved of the protection Gianni had for Marlo. One night when she had shared with Sander that Gianni now called her his *bella piccola Marlo*, beautiful little Marlo, Sander had smiled knowingly, kissing her hair, muttering to Marlo that the man had exquisite taste.

Steve gently smoothed a loose strand of hair from Eva's forehead as he handed her some punch. There was a patient, shy approach they took to their relationship. It was strangely comforting. Dale wove through the group, eyeing Heidi for assistance. He rubbed his hands together to ward off the jitters. Taking the hint, Heidi gave him a sly wink and sounded out a loud, shrill whistle she'd once used to curb a New York City taxi.

"People, it's time to give your undivided attention to our esteemed host, Mr. Dale Sawyer. Without further introduction: Dale," Heidi said, immaculate red lips held smug.

"Right. Follow me," he said, leading the crowd down a short hallway from the living area to the dining room. The table was set with a charming simplicity. Dale made the arrangement his own, not one copied from his beloved Beth, lest her memory steal his mind from attending to his guests. He needed to be Dale now.

"Your menu consists of prime rib roast, oven-baked potatoes, caramelized carrots, and French bread." Dale audibly sighed after his announcement, which brought on taunting and teasing from his ruthless friends.

"Got three words for that type of grub, Dale. Bring it on!" quipped Steve.

"Meat, that's what I call dinner," added Sander.

Gianni couldn't resist a comment. "Il Signore ha misericordia. Lord have mercy, Dale, if you need a second job, let me know. My taste buds are dancing with expectation!"

The women were mesmerized by the man who announced he had prepared prime rib for Christmas Eve dinner. It was all so right and an unexpected delicacy. The group of singles didn't indulge in a home-cooked prime rib dinner very often.

Talking between bites, it was Jana who broke the silence of the eaters. "Dale, this is so good. What did you use in this pepper rub? I've got to have this recipe." She eyed him expectantly.

"Ah, well, see, I sort of made it up," Dale responded, uncharacteristically timid twice in one evening.

"Made it up? Good Lord, this is fantastic! Gianni, you best hope he doesn't open a steak house to rival your Italian place," Jana teased, impressed with the flavors, closing her eyes to wallow in the taste. Dale was not quite sure what to do with that comment and held his fork midway to his mouth. Gianni came to his rescue. "I say we'd welcome competition, would draw more eaters, yes?" He was happy to eat the food prepared by another.

The ensuing conversations were a myriad of shared cooking secrets, the simplicity of using real herbs, and an abundance of accolades for the chef. Dale was happy. The emotion caught him off guard. It was one he hadn't experienced in the three years since Beth died. As he went into the kitchen to replenish the horseradish sauce, he realized this new stage of life was *right*. His body bristled with an unexpected surge of goose bumps despite his warmth from nerves and cooking. Closing his eyes, he sensed a physical parting of his grief. A piece of him opened up. Air. Dale unconsciously moved with a lighter step, memories safe and cherished, making room for a future. He had a sense of peace and a new lease on living life.

Grabbing coats and purses and pulling on boots, the group packed up and caravanned across town to Eva's. Tending to the welcome committee led by Dash and Scout, they pitched in and made themselves at home. The holiday spirits were present on their flushed faces as they joked and partook in scrumptious sweets and libations.

Eva's home twinkled with Christmas lights and jovial conversation. Heidi took charge of the iPod to replay her favorite holiday song over and over again. They sang a hammed up rendition of the Dean Martin classic about snow outside until Jana and Gianni had tears streaming down their faces.

Dash padded over to the hearth where Steve sat chiming in with a deep tenor voice. The tasty hot buttered rum gave him a roaring voice. He absentmindedly set down his plate with remnants of pumpkin cake and one last bite of mincemeat pie. Dash, of course, thought the plate was fair game since it was close to the floor. Under Steve's radar, "the Dasher"—a holiday-appropriate nickname from Sander—swiped up the treats and plunked down in front of the fireplace with a satisfied thump. Marlo, the only human to witness the escapade, let it go unmentioned, opting that a happy Dash laying by a singing Steve was a good omen for the midwinter's fete.

"Ah, no can agree to that one, Eva. I think candy canes rule at Christmas time," choked out Marlo, eyeing her next bite of pumpkin cake.

"Marlo, Marlo, Marlo, candy canes are great, but in front of a chocolate Santa? A *milk* chocolate Santa? I can't see it!" pitched back Eva, adding her two cents on the number one Christmas candy.

"I have one for you ladies." It was Sander piping in this time. "I'd propose that homemade chocolate fudge with just a little bit of crushed fresh candy canes, not last year's from the tree, mind you, makes the ideal Christmas delicacy." Marlo watched her beau, crimson cheeks growing deeper as her affection for the man crept into view.

"My dear friends," Gianni spoke up. "While I'd like to preach about the glories of American holiday treat traditions, I must bid my farewell. Tomorrow is Christmas and I'm catering dinner for the Babcock family."

"On Christmas Day? Gianni, I didn't know you were working." It was Heidi who asked the question. She had decided to keep Grizzly tightly shuttered on Christmas Day, caffeine deprivation aside.

"Don't be sorry for me. This is a great opportunity. Tonight's party is celebration enough for me. Tomorrow is my first catered affair."

"Babcocks, eh? They're a discriminating crowd," Steve said, considering both the influence and old money the family yielded.

"What are you serving, Gianni?" Jana asked, unsettled by her internal sting at hearing he was working on Christmas. Jana had hoped to spend time with him on Christmas Day, although they had made no plans.

Gianni detailed his menu for quail stuffed with sage-apple dressing, winter chard flavored by onions, acorn squash whipped with butter and maple syrup. Other sides included fresh cranberry sauce with almonds, braided oat bread, and oyster pudding. Dessert was classic baked Alaska, the only request from the clients. The group of friends salivated at the menu, in spite of their bursting stomachs.

"Gianni, you'll nail it," said Sander. Marlo put her head on his shoulder, nodding in agreement toward her beloved Gianni, eyelids heavy. Checking out Marlo, Sander continued, brushing her forehead with a kiss. "It's also time this sugar plum fairy gets some sleep."

At this first departure, the group went into a lengthy process of giving hugs and well wishes. Eva handed out premade plates of treats as her friends put on their coats. The parting gift was a holiday tradition ground into the core of every Midwestern hostess. After Heidi walked out the front door, she winked at Eva and signaled an adieu to Steve. He watched Heidi walk through the light snow covering to her car.

"Care for some help putting that kitchen back to order?" Steve asked Eva.

Heart pounding, Eva answered with a shaky, "Sure."

Closing the door in a smooth motion, Steve turned to Eva. His right arm around her back, the left slowly came up to caress her arm, blue eyes locked on hers.

"Eva, this night was magic." Unable to find her voice, Eva snuggled next to him, engulfed in Steve's warmth.

"Thank you," she whispered. "That's how I wanted it described."

"Lovely lady, you done good." Steve backed up a tad, lifted her chin with his hand, and stroked the side of her cheek. "So," he said, not breaking the mood in pace or tone, "let's make small work of that kitchen." He let her go slowly and guided her into the kitchen, his hand burning into the small of her back.

The romantic interlude left Eva cradled in an envelope of soft velvet. It was a dream, this Christmas Eve night. *Pinch me.* Steve clattered naturally around the kitchen next to her, rinsing and putting plates and glasses into the dishwasher as if he belonged. "I appreciate the help, Steve. It's considerate." He turned to face her and his lopsided grin uncannily calmed her nerves as he held dirty wine glasses. Continuing, she spoke to Steve, almost muttering to herself, "A man who knows his way around cleaning a kitchen … ." They worked contentedly side by side, not worrying about the hour or the next steps.

"Steve, I have a question for you."

"Shoot," he answered, handing her a dried wine glass.

"At the library you read *Rudolph* with such emotion and, I don't know, there was something more there."

Setting down the towel, Steve turned to look at Eva, his eyes holding a sadness that had Eva suddenly confused. "Oh, Steve, I didn't mean to pry."

"No, Eva, no prying. It's fine. Actually, thanks for asking." Clearing his throat and casually crossing his arms, he leaned against the sink for balance.

Eva was still, patient.

"*Rudolph* was the favorite story of my friend, Billy. Lois and James's brother. Grace's other nephew. Billy died twenty years ago when he was only thirteen."

"I'm sorry." Eva closed her eyes, listening intently.

"Billy was hit on the road by a drunk driver. He never knew what happened. He didn't suffer, thank God." Steve went on. "Back then there wasn't so much talk about drinking and driving as there is nowadays, but it still happened. Billy was coming home from a trip to the candy store, which he loved, when a truck careened around a corner and struck him down. Poof. It was that fast." Billy had been ripped away. Boyhood dreams stolen. They had plans. At twelve, the two performed the blood brothers ritual at a site of an Indian burial ground, according to local lore.

Eva was tongue-tied. Steve paused in reflection and then continued.

"Being a tad older, I was his keeper when I wasn't working him over. It was a huge blow, a trauma to me, and Bear, to lose Billy. I guess that's no surprise. He was the kid with the red freckles and tussled hair. The remorseful kid who'd accidentally hit a baseball through the dress shop window, then came to the front door with his cap in hand shuffling his feet to apologize." Smiling with the memories, Steve unfolded his arms and rubbed his palms together. "I loved him. He loved Rudolph. We'd read it so much, we memorized it, but the pictures were too much fun not to have the book at hand."

"I, I don't know what to say."

"No words necessary, Eva. It was a long time ago. Some days it's fresh, others it's distant." He cleared his throat and placed the damp dishtowel across the side of the sink.

"Lois is the spitting image of Billy, their likeness uncanny."

"Oh."

"I suppose it's a heavy load to carry for an older brother she hardly knew or can remember." Steve paused again. "So, you figured me out pretty good. I think I like that."

Eva stepped next to him, "Steve, I'm sorry. I had no idea."

"It's part of my life, Eva. And I don't hide the fact that he died or that I miss him. To honor Billy is to celebrate his life, not to mourn him anymore. That doesn't help anything. We mourned and mourned. Once we started picking ourselves up to talk about him, and talk about him a lot, was when we started to heal and move forward."

"Is this part of the bond you have with Dale?"

"Yes, I suppose it is. We'd most likely hang out anyway, but the fact that we relate to this damned sadness doesn't hurt."

"Beth died the year before I moved to Bear." Eva regretted not to have known Billy or Beth.

"What I learned is don't be a hero or pretend nothing's wrong. Talk about them, and talk about them as much as seems right."

"So tell me another story about Billy." Eva hardly needed to prompt Steve. He smiled at her, picked up the towel, and continued his duty of drying the dishes.

Closer from sharing a heartache, they reminisced of past holidays. Outside, the snow fell softly, refreshing the trampled snow on the streets and sidewalks with a smooth white blanket. There was, for this moment in time, a peace on Earth in Bear.

37

Giddy with laughter, Heidi mimicked the accentuated heel–toe walk of a runway model, her eyes haughty, squared chin up, mouth set to form an expressionless face. She exaggeratedly crossed her feet one in front of the other in the standard catwalk sway before collapsing on the floor next to Jana and Eva. She was pretty convincing.

"Frau Heidi, would you like another chocolate? Maybe it'll fill in some of that space causing that protrusion of your distinctively model-like collarbones?" Jana offered up a gourmet holiday sweet, brightly wrapped in red and silver foil, prominently placed in the middle of her palm.

Gasping for air and wiping the tears from her face, Eva pouted with dismay at Jana's candy offer to Heidi. "Hey, what about me? Don't I have any bones that need more padding or—*what is it* you are trying to say?" In mock anguish, Jana offered Eva a treat with similar formality.

"Oh, my side hurts." Slowly gaining composure, Heidi rolled onto her back in front of the crackling fireplace as she carefully unwrapped the treat, examined it on all four sides before popping it into her mouth. "How do those women exist? I mean, really, life can't be much fun without indulging."

The house was still decked in Christmas finery of evergreens boughs, sap-laden pinecones, and a roaring fire. Aromas from a thick Pennsylvania Dutch vegetable beef sage stew, homemade pecan caramels, and a buttery Bavarian pastry were intermixed and wafting from the kitchen, all courtesy of Jana's skills with the help of her comrades in arms.

"Well," Jana offered, suppressing her laughter, "you know, people might say it's just as curious why the three of us, reasonably attractive—no, very attractive—very funny *and* chic, highly intelligent, available single women are spending a beautiful New Year's Eve like three teenagers at a slumber party."

"You forgot *gainfully employed, independent* single women," Eva spun around to lay on her side, scrutinizing Jana with a critical eye, her own narrowed and dancing, a smudge of dark chocolate hanging on to the side of her mouth.

"Jana, I never quite looked at it from that perspective. I was enjoying our own little party from my view only," Heidi added as she flung the candy wrapping in the general direction of the fireplace. Looking over at Jana, she set her red lips in feigned resentment. "Thanks for spoiling it."

"Okay, okay, no spoiling intended. Just an observation," Jana said, playfully acquiescing to the peer pressure.

Sliding onto her back and stretching out like a lioness, Eva groaned with comfort. "Let's face it, if we're honest, would we rather be here just the three of us? Or say, out on a date, at some New Year's Eve bash—if they even had those kinds of things in Bear—or here with maybe some, uh, male companions?"

Like in a sitcom, Jana and Heidi eyed one another then answered Eva in unison with a buoyant and unscripted, "Here, just the three of us." Eva responded in kind, her translucent blue eyes gone dreamy. "Although, I must admit spending time with Steve window-shopping in the snow after the shops were closed was way romantic." She uttered a small groan as she moved onto her stomach, adding, "And without near the calories provided at this soiree."

Heidi almost spoke but thought better of it and held her tongue. She evaluated the point that neither Eva nor Steve fooled anyone with their slow-moving romance. He didn't ask her out for New Year's, curious enough. Steering the subject, Heidi spoke up. "As you two know, I spend a lot of time with middle school girls. Were we ever really like these girls are today in the total 'drama queen' kind of way? I think it's a new phenomenon."

"Heidi, how did you get from Eva's romantic window-shopping escapade with Steve to middle school tween-age drama queens?" Jana said, exasperated with the switch of moods. Heidi squinted at Jana in a mock 'how dare you' gesture and positioned herself cross-legged in front of the fire.

"Leave her go with it, Jana. This could get interesting," Eva sat up, circling her ankles to regain circulation after being prone for so long. "Besides, I think we might have been drama queens, but we kept it inside or only told one person. Nowadays it seems that broadcasting emotion is all the rage."

"So, let's have at it. Us three. What's your buried drama queen story?" Jana and Eva moved their tired, well-fed bodies to upright positions, sitting cross-legged, like Heidi, to form a circle.

"I have one," Heidi said, suddenly serious. She looked from Eva to Jana, down at her hands and cleared her throat. "Truth be told, I was once the *other* woman." Keeping her courage, she went on, eyes still focused on her hands, not seeing the surprised yet nonjudgmental looks on Eva and Jana's faces. "While I was staying with my sister Helen in New York City, she introduced me to a guy named George who was one of the buyers for the art gallery that Helen managed in Soho."

"George? His name was George? Heidi, this better not be a joke," mocked

Jana as she tucked herself into the ornate Christmas quilt she finished earlier in the month.

"Oh, no. I almost wish it were. What a great scene this would be for a French accent." Heidi's effervescence fell just enough to trigger her friends' attention that this was both serious and difficult.

"Heidi, you don't have to give us the gory details if it's painful. What you already said is confession enough." Eva spoke the obvious for Heidi.

"It's fine. I completely fell for George. God, he was the epitome of tall, dark, and handsome: completely sexy, unavailable, and mysterious. I'm sure I wasn't his first indiscretion," Heidi murmured solemnly. "Somehow it would be less sorrowful for me if I was his one and only affair. You know, it could be something that he and I shared and could hold dear in our forbidden memory banks. But it wasn't. He's an entertainer. I was a song he sang. It's fini. Old Billboard. We're no longer on the charts."

The song metaphor hit Eva in the heart, "Heidi, I'm sorry you're sad. I can tell you liked him."

"Yeah, I did. I'm such a jerk. I knew he was married, but somehow I was drawn to him. It was wrong from the get-go. I guess I'm sorry it happened, but at the time it seemed right. Our relationship was a whirlwind of excitement. Here, now, looking back, it was only wrong. I'm the one who hurt. His wife had no idea, thank God."

"And George, where was his radar in all this?" asked Jana.

"George, as Eva would say, lived in the moment. He probably couldn't believe his good fortune. We dined, danced, had incredible sex, traveled to exotic locations on art buying trips, and at the end of the day, he went home to his devoted wife. He had me lock, stock, and barrel. I was the best time he ever had."

"You're not a 'time,' Heidi," said Eva.

"Don't be too hard on George," Heidi sighed. "It was the same for me, sort of. I could be an actress in real life and I was. Such a mistake. That's it, you know. I was acting. I was acting how he wanted me to be, and how I wanted to be if I wasn't really me. It was a surreal existence. Life just danced around us. It was perfectly not real. We had no responsibilities except to indulge one another. I played dress-up, acted like a vamp, ate in fancy restaurants, and stayed in four-star hotels. In some strange way, I think I thought it would go on forever, and the sense of emptiness at the end of a weekend or evening would eventually disappear. That living the secret lie wasn't so bad if we loved each other."

The log in the fire broke from the heat and tumbled in the grate, the red embers swishing and sending sparks up the chimney. Eva broke the ensuing silence. "Heidi, do you still love him?" Eva's empathy for Heidi was raw, her honest, loving friend, who carried such cutting pain from a foolish mistake. It was familiar. Too familiar.

"No, I don't love him. In fact, I loathe him, even though at one time I believe he thought he loved me, or rather, the idea of us, and our façade. We were misguided. How could it go so far? How could he cheat on his wife? And me, too, I guess, in a weird sort of way."

"Don't beat yourself up now, Heidi. It's over. One of those unfortunate 'learn and don't ever do again relationships,'" Jana said.

"Being the other woman isn't what I wanted. It was a false comfort, a trick of romance, and I regret it. I'm sorry for my actions. It wasn't how I wanted to be. When I left New York to come back to Bear and run Grizzly, I knew what a jerk I'd been. He used me. In fact, I left all the gifts, clothes, purses, jewelry, gorgeous shit he gave me in the hotel for the maids back at The Plaza." Heidi paused. "I'm sure they love those Prada bags and shoes," she sighed wistfully, wit still intact.

Jana pouted. "Dang, Heidi, you know I could use some updated accessories!" she said, gathering the briefest of smiles from Heidi, who nervously swept her silken black hair up and down into a ponytail, accentuating her widow's peak, before releasing it to fall into its untamed glory across her neck and back.

"An experienced vixen in our mix," Eva teased as she scooted on the floor and put her arms around both Heidi and Jana. "Heidi, we love you. We don't care about the past."

"I know. I really do. My deal is to move forward, past mistakes and guilt. I admit it, I want a man." Heidi leaned into her friends, her elegance not lost even in the downtrodden mood. Casually decked out in her 7 for All Mankind designer blue jeans, a long-sleeved violet V-neck cashmere sweater, and silver chandelier earrings, Heidi gave any professional model a run for their money. This gorgeous creature, probably avoided by many men because of her alarmingly good looks, was lonely and seeking forgiveness.

"Heidi, you aren't obliged to tell everyone everything you ever did. It's not necessary to purge out all your past errors to a potential mate," Eva said, defending Heidi again. "There's no life rule that mandates complete disclosure."

"That's easier to say than to do. I have this inbred sense that I have to be a complete open book." Heidi sighed, knowing that her friends might not come to this same conclusion about her.

Jana saw her cue. "Hey, I'm the librarian here, and no, you don't have to share the whole book. You're entitled to skip a few chapters and still get the gist of the story."

"Thanks for listening," Heidi said, soberly concluding her story.

The quiet that followed was anything but void. Standing for a stretch, Jana twisted her solid, athletic body side to side and bent over to touch her palms on the floor. "Oh, that feels good. Sitting on the floor is a killer." As she rolled up her spine, she noticed the clock. "Hey, it's 12:20. We missed New Years!"

"Be right back," Heidi said. Back to her antics, she extended both arms in the air, held a pose angling her wrists á la Cruella de Ville, turned, and ran into the kitchen. Seconds later, she emerged with a bottle of champagne. "Happy New

Year! This, compliments of Gianni, being business coffee partners between The Sicilian Ball and Grizzly. Santé!"

Settled into the comfort of overstuffed couches, the three sipped the cool bubbly in front of the warm fire. The long-stem glasses were heavy leaded crystal, cut with beautiful shapes from an old world Baccarat artisan. Next it was Eva who edged forward to share her tale.

"I once knew a guy named Seaton," she began. "He was the best and worst thing that ever happened to me." Eva told the story like it was yesterday. She hardly paused. It came out as a long soliloquy of contrast between hearty passion and caustic sarcasm. The allure of the man. Her unabashed love. The betrayal. Even the rainstorm. When she was done, Eva looked up at Jana and Heidi. Jana's mouth hung agape and Heidi was tongue-tied. "That's it. That's my drama queen tale. I've never told anyone."

Finding her voice, Jana asked, brown eyes quizzical, "Never? No one?"

Heidi was up like a jaguar and filled the champagne glasses in one fluid motion. Setting down the heavy bottle, she turned her attention to Eva, exposed by the emotional wound.

"Eva, you did nothing wrong." Speaking with the compassion of someone who had been in a similar situation, Heidi kept on. "Seaton is the one who left out those 'tiny details' of wife, house, dog, and kids. Slime ball. At least George was brutally honest about his history of indiscretion and marital status. I'm sorry, darling." Heidi plopped down on the couch next to Eva, as much as someone graceful and dignified as Heidi could plop, draping her long arms around Eva's neck.

"It helps with the puzzle of you, Eva. Your moving to Bear was a bit of an anomaly. It fits now. Your own business, the dogs, the fixer-upper cabin, even the old International." Jana paused, downing the champagne. "You built yourself a new life. Sort of like when a dog wants to lie down, it digs and digs at the rug and moves around and around in a circle before safely lying down with a satisfied thump."

Heidi squinted at Jana, taking in the commentary, then speaking with a British accent, "I think I agree with that assessment, Watson." Pausing, she continued in her normal voice. "It was a quandary to me that talk of men or boyfriends was never on your mind, or at least never ripe for conversation. You had a knack to keep that tap off whenever we tried to open it."

"Purely coincidental, believe me," Eva joked, knowing that she was deliberate to avoid conversation of relationships. That is, until recently with the entrance of Steve Mason.

"So how are you right now, Eva?" Jana asked sincerely.

"I've let Seaton go." She sighed audibly, physically relaxing deeper into the couch and comforted with the buzz of champagne. "Even recently, I let him intrude without realizing it—letting that bad experience taint relationships with men even before they started. I am moving on, as we say."

"Let's drink to that," Heidi said, filling the glasses again.

"Here, here," cheered Jana.

"You two are such great friends," Eva said happily, "Life's coming together right now. Steve is a welcome diversion from dogs and work."

"Yes, he's a diversion at that," Jana added slyly ribbing Eva. "Every available woman in Bear from eight to eighty-eight has her eyes on your diversion—except Heidi and me, of course."

"She speaks the truth, fair Eva," Heidi said, adding, "Steve is one hell of a guy." Pensively, she looked at Eva and smiled her knock-'em-dead full-lipped grin, emerald eyes sparkling. "Lucky for him that you're an awesome match all around the board, like Bogie and Bacall."

Scrunching her shoulders shyly, Eva cuddled farther into the couch. She loved the compliment and wished she had a better command of the old Hollywood movies, especially *Casablanca*, the immortalization of Humphrey Bogart and Lauren Bacall. Geesh, her mind was on an alcohol wander. "I like that things are slow. In fact, I don't even like to use that word, slow. We're doing what we want to do, getting to know each other." Eva contemplated her words. "Okay, this all sounds corny. We've both been single for a long time. Neither of us was out looking."

"Mmm. If more singles weren't on the prowl, they probably would be happier and find the right mate." Jana yawned absently. "Hey, we could start a group at the library. This topic might just bring in the masses."

"Yeah, the Non-Prowling Singles group," chirped Eva.

Heidi turned her head to size up Jana, and responded with mock vehemence, "Oh no. No more groups to compete with the Junior Women's Club. At least not until my tenure as chairperson is over."

After minor bickering, Eva brought them back to the topic of drama queen stories. "Jana, do you have a tale for us before sleep zaps our bodies?"

Curling her feet up and under her on the couch, Jana pulled the quilt close around her body. "Well, it might not be drama queen material for this crowd since it doesn't involve an illicit relationship, darn it all." At that, both Heidi and Eva threw holiday pillows in her direction. Holding up her hands for protection, Jana forged ahead with a knowing smile. "However, it was drama, nevertheless. See, when I was in cooking school ... ."

Jana told the tale of a gourmet dinner gone awry. Every spice combination botched and the soufflé tumbled. The dignitary guests were neither amused nor forgiving. The experience took away her cooking confidence and the respect of the arrogant but culinarily connected and industry political chef who was her mentor. It was so humiliating that Jana packed up her ambitions of being a big-city chef and leaned on her training as a librarian. She ended up in Bear, rooming with Heidi. In spite of her effervescent nature, she'd been empty and downtrodden. The story was as gut-wrenching as the tales of forbidden love shared by Heidi and Eva.

The New Year brought deeper unity for Eva, Jana, and Heidi. Their past, both shared and private, made them the unique women they had become, which they wouldn't be without having experiencing pain and regret.

38

Breathing heavily, faces flushed to crimson, Eva and Marlo were invigorated as they completed their early-morning cross-country skiing excursion. Dash and Scout fought like a couple of bounding bear cubs. Rotating balls of golden brown fur across the top of the powdery snow, they made a giant caterpillar shape in the snow, like a child making an angel. Once their bout of ruffian behavior was complete, the dogs shook off the snow, eyed each other up, and did it all over again.

"Phew, great skiing. Thanks for coming, Marlo." Eva poled right up to the edge of her porch. Dash and Scout lay in the snowbank in front of the porch and chewed to release the big pieces of snow wedged into their pads. Scout bit at her paw with a vengeance, white teeth bared as she snipped ferociously at the icy snow.

"Look at that dog. Geeze, wouldn't want her to get angry at me," Marlo said, fascinated by the commotion the animals made the entire skiing expedition. Changing focus, she answered Eva admirably, "Yes, thanks. This was a great workout. You really can go, girl!"

"How did those new skis work out?" Eva asked, wistfully lusting after Marlo's shiny new skis and quick-release ankle boots.

"Ah, these are heaven. They fit like kid gloves. So much nicer than the hand-me-downs that I found in the trailer closet. Sander did right by these." Marlo beamed as she jumped parallel a couple inches in the air to loosen the snow off the top of the long narrow skis. After the snow was off, she disengaged her boots from the bindings and lifted the skis up in her arms in one sweet motion.

"He's the man. What a great gift for your first winter season in Wyoming."

The giant smile on Marlo's face was response enough as she lovingly cradled her new skis and poles, trademark knit hat affixed atop her head.

"So, what's on your agenda for the rest of the day?" Eva inquired, finishing her minor struggle at removing her boots from her ten-plus-year-old ski apparatus.

"Tonight is the women's club meeting, as you know, and other than that, I'll be fixing up the trailer and doing some shopping. Sander is back from his trip late afternoon. The restaurant is closed today since its Monday, so I'm free," Marlo said as she clacked the skis on the walkway to dislodge the final pieces of snow.

"That sounds nice. For me, I have coaching calls and need to review my speech for tonight." Groaning aloud, she continued, "I hope I don't bore the group to death. Seems my stories are self-absorbed. I hate that, plus, it reminds me how I used to be."

"Eva, you're too critical. We love it. Me, even being new to Bear, I like to hear other people's pre-Bear stories and what brought them here or back here. It's encouraging."

"Well, I hope so," Eva said, unconvinced.

"Have fun with it, and you'll be great. Which reminds me, I have a yoga class later at that new studio in town."

"Yoga in Bear? Now that's progress."

"Totally. I'm psyched," Marlo enthused.

"I imagine," Eva said, wondering if the girl ever stopped moving.

"You should come with me some time," Marlo added, always up for a social event of any type.

"Uh huh." Eva smiled broadly, mildly shaking her head.

"It'd be fun."

"Hey, Marlo, thanks for driving this direction today. See you tonight." Eva set her skis on the porch in her prized cross-country ski holder and hugged Marlo through their layered clothing. Marlo was off in a heartbeat, pumping her ski poles in the air for a motion of farewell as she trudged toward Sander's truck. In tandem, Dash and Scout suspended chewing snow chunks as they watched Marlo march to the vehicle. They looked up at Eva and frolicked around her, knowing instinctively it was time to go inside, and there was a high probability that a peanut-shaped dog biscuit would come their way if they sat still throughout the paw-wiping ordeal of all eight paws.

Less than an hour later Eva was showered and reviewing the files for her next three clients. They came three in a row with no breathing room, so organization was key. Specific coaching dates changed based on the rhythms of their lives, so Eva needed to be alert on who was calling when.

Her third client was Debra, who continued to take charge of her life and live her dreams. *What a thrill*, thought Eva. *I wonder how her Paris vacation plans are progressing.* Within a minute of the hour, the phone rang.

"This is Eva."

"Eva, hi, Debra calling." The voice was so distant that at first Eva thought the phone connection was bad.

"Debra, hey, what's going on with you?" *Something was amiss.*

"It's ... " and then inconsolable sobbing crossed the line.

Eva held the space patiently, and after several minutes broke into the crying. "I'm here, Debra, when you're ready." She was braced for anything, mentally clothed with emotional shockproof armor.

"Roy is sick. They don't know what it is, and he's going in for testing today." Debra's voice was small, her vivacious energy drained.

Stunned despite trying to be shockproof, Eva felt the blanket of sadness covering her client. This was serious. "Debra, I'm so sorry." Eva paused, drew her eyes tight, fingers on the bridge of her nose. "Would you like to talk now or do this another time?"

"Let's talk." The sparkle was gone from her voice, Debra's new lease on life vanished. The bleakness gripped.

"Debra, can we talk about what's swirling around for you right now?" Eva purposefully shifted from what she might have wanted to ask, which was what's wrong with Roy, when did it start, doctors prognosis, etcetera. Eva could almost hear her coaching mantra: it's about my clients, not me, what they want to discover and do for themselves, their lives. Her curiosity was for their benefit, not hers.

"Stricken."

"Yeah, I hear you."

"I'm stricken with anguish," came Debra's heartbroken words.

"Where do you feel your anguish, Debra?"

Silence. Then boldly, she said, "In my gut, moving up toward my lungs." As Debra spoke, Eva imagined a tightly fisted hand in front of her abdomen, pulling it up slowly to rest just below her heart, settling on her chest. Her head bowed, chin hanging too low. Anguish.

"What color is it?"

"Red." Debra paused. "Black. Purple."

Bruised. "This anguish, it's dark and deep."

"It hurts. It's consuming me."

"Consuming you in what way?"

"It's a huge dark scary cloud swallowing me. But maybe it's like one of those storms in Hawaii that can blow right over. You know, one that lasts from two to three in the afternoon, then goes away."

Hope. "Debra, what do you want to say to this anguish and cloud?" Eva wasn't quite sure where to go with Debra. Her intuition told her to stay right with her, right where she was, no big moves necessary. Eva took a deep breath, ensuring it wasn't audible over the phone.

"I want to tell it to go away."

"Try that. Tell it to go away."

"Go away," Debra said loud and clear, then after several seconds: "Go away," she said again, slowly, softly. "Go away." Silence.

"How are you now?"

"I'm still breathing. I'm starting to get a grip on myself."

"Stay with that grip, Debra." After a brief interlude of quiet, Eva continued, "Breathe fully. Feel your entire body right now. From your toes to your head, to your arms and legs, even the place where the anguish settled before you told it to go away."

Quiet.

"Be with yourself, all of you. What do you feel in your gut now, Debra?"

"Less stricken. Not so dark. I'm even feeling strength return. Roy needs me to be strong. We're jumping to morbid conclusions."

"There's a big unknown out there. How can you, the strong and compassionate Debra, approach that unknown?"

"I don't know."

"What if you pretend, just for now, that you do know? What would it be?" Eva asked, comfortable in her coaching zone.

"A strong me would use what works in other areas of my life."

"Such as?"

"She would make a list." Debra said with a positive conviction.

Eva asked, "What type of list?" noticing that Dash was watching her every move, and Scout was licking her pads, tender from the earlier bout with snow.

"Two-sided list. One side of what I need to do right now to prepare for today and the next few days of waiting. This will keep me from imagining the worst. I want to be compassionate and loving for Roy, not a basket case."

"Would you like to make that list right now?

"Not really. I have a paper, and I'll write the title for now. I'll do the rest later."

"You mentioned a two-sided list. What's the other side, Debra?"

"The other side is the what-if side. What-if it's not a problem. What-if it's serious, what-if it's a routine situation."

"Comprehensive."

"I need to gather my thoughts without conclusions for a change." Debra studied chemistry as an undergrad and approached life like a scientific proof, facts versus hypothesis, to be her protective gear at this tenuous time.

"Debra, for each one of those lists, can I ask you to add something?"

"Any suggestions are welcome."

"Would you add to each list how you want to *be* in the what-if situations and how you're going to keep yourself grounded in each what-if situation?" After she was done speaking, Eva frowned. This didn't come out right.

"Can you say that again?"

"Yeah." Eva winced. "So, for example, let's say the 'what-if' is a serious situation. In addition to the actions on the list, what about adding how you want to mentally approach the situation?"

Space filled the line. "Well, I want to be strong for Roy. I want to understand fully the situation, the prognosis, the treatments, the lifestyle changes, and the biological issues. So I want to be well-read about the illness, smart. I want to keep my family moving forward."

Amazing.

"What do you need to do more of, or less of, as you just stated?"

"Mmm. Now I get it. Like, take care of me during the process?"

"Exactly."

"Like on the airplane when the flight attendants say administer the breathing equipment to yourself before helping others?" Debra chuckled in spite of the dismal situation.

Great analogy. "Yes, Debra, that's it."

"I don't want to tumble. I need to keep up my exercise routine and ensure the kids keep up with their responsibilities. Once I know full well what's ahead, then I can reevaluate the situation."

"Debra, this is a stressful, emotional time. Give yourself permission to be human."

"It's hard."

"Yeah, it's hard. Are there people you can reach out to for support?"

"Yes, I have some good friends and loyal neighbors." When she said this, Eva heard the relief in Debra's voice for this option.

"Can I give you an opinion?"

"Please." Debra was desperate for something to hang onto.

"Put your energy into what you can impact. Let go of those things you can't control."

"You mean don't worry too much."

"What do you think?"

"Worry won't do much for Roy. Or the kids."

"Or for you." Eva held the space with Debra for a long time.

After the call, Eva hung up the phone, and the softness of it resting in the cradle had a different sound that day. It was the hollow sound of melancholy, of potentially lost dreams, and of the unknown.

39

"Indeed, it's a welcomed dejá vu to speak to this illustrious crowd," Eva said, sweeping her hands in front of her. "Thank you all for being here. And thank you, Heidi, for having me again and for the kind introduction. In thinking about tonight, I was perplexed on how to start this phase-two speech. My life in Bear has settled even more since I spoke to you before the holidays. And because of that, pre-Bear experiences seem secondary. However, I know that isn't true. Anything that we forge ahead and do in our lives is to some degree a result of something in our past. Whether that's something that we liked and that worked out well, something that we regret, or something that we learned and can apply in new ways."

Eva settled her gaze on the Jackson Hole Area Junior Women's Club members, taking in the eager faces. They'd accepted a relative newcomer like herself, and the pure companionship that she felt with them was palpable. Odd, as she knew few of them by name.

"Last November I spoke about my youth and growing up. And relationships. Remember relationships? That's how we interact, how we treat others, and how we are treated by the other people we come across in our lives. Our interactions with people make us complete, like that last piece of a thousand-piece puzzle; or they can bomb, making a mess of everything." The audience rumbled a slow, cautious snicker. They knew full well they could easily be the coveted puzzle piece or the blasting bomb, depending on the situation.

Taking a sip of water, Eva looked around the familiar room. The Jackson Hole Area Junior Women's Club had come out in full force. It was an eclectic crowd, as one might expect. She adored this locale, these people. The guy with the brown national parks cap was there, and she spotted Marlo, knit hat adorning her locks, in her favorite back corner. The room looked fuller than in November, most likely a result of January weather. People had bulky jackets strewn across their laps and zippers loosened on Sorel snow boots. All the dead-of-winter clothing filled up the space more than the late fall outerwear.

To Eva's left, about two-thirds of the way back, sat Steve. He was next to a man she didn't recognize, right behind Jana. Eva cleared her throat to refocus her mind away from Steve and into her talk. It was harder for her to bare her soul now that she had deeper friendships—er, relationships—than before. It's peculiar that it's often easier to talk about personal issues to strangers than to friends and family, which may be one reason for the big success of Internet dating. Then it struck her, a good lead in for her message.

"You know, it's interesting that when we know people better, we have more to lose and more to prove. We become more vulnerable. Would you say that's true?" There was a snapshot of time where the group weighed this question, then Eva started to see small nods of recognition and agreement and some audible "sures" and "yeses."

"So here's the deal. Remember, I was an ambitious woman who achieved what I thought I wanted when in fact didn't *really* want it after all. I was fortunate enough to finally realize this key point. After some time, I came up with an idea to change my profession without radically changing my life. It was a relationship that empowered me to make a change." Eva continued to speak with passion about her past life, trials, and tough choices.

As she talked, Eva suddenly wondered why she was the one speaking. Shouldn't she be learning from this group? They're comfortable in their skin. Most of them have chosen a life of character over collecting a sense of security. Is that it? Is the one relationship I should examine the one I have with myself? What's missing in my life? I know it's something obvious, if I would just take the time to think about it.

Eva caught herself before she spiraled into a self-consumed abyss. Unbeknownst to Eva, she was communicating volumes with her tale. Her wide eyes were brilliant with vulnerability and a desire to share, to help. The shy way Eva fussed with the hair behind her ear when it was already in place gave her an adolescent air. She forged ahead, pulling herself back to the present.

Steve was captivated by Eva. To openly stare at her, watch her move, was a treat. He loved the women's club. Sliding back in his chair, arms loosely wrapped across his broad chest, Steve considered Eva. Getting to know her was an interesting process. She divulged flocks of information on her stance and her sentiments on some topics, but on others, nil, nothing at all. Eva talked on and on about work projects, travels, acclimating to Bear, her beloved dogs, and coaching. However, rarely—maybe never—did she speak of old friends or romantic relationships, and news of her family was offered only upon request. The lady was an interesting dichotomy.

Spotting Marlo in the audience, knit hat askew, Eva realized that she needed to keep it simple. "Have any of you ever felt like you needed to change the course of a relationship or someone was going to get hurt?" Murmurs permeated the room.

"Right. What brought me to Bear was the realization that I was staying in a dysfunctional relationship with my profession because it was comfortable. Once I decided to follow my heart, things fell into place. I let down my guard. Specifically, I didn't have to know it all." Eva stopped and leaned into the podium more for strength than effect. "That is my challenge to you. Be a learner. Give yourself permission to follow your dreams. It's worth all the bruises. Thank you."

Eva stepped down from the podium. Her head throbbed. *That was a disaster. I didn't share the right points. What a mess.* Eva absently picked up her purse, automatically putting herself in a position to exit the building while never hearing the applause as the meeting was adjourned.

"Eva, hey, wait up." Heidi tapped her shoulder. Curious about her distant behavior, Heidi scrutinized Eva before speaking. "That was a great speech."

Looking at Heidi, Eva swallowed without speaking.

"Eva?"

"That was a muddle, Heidi. I'm so embarrassed. The topic, I didn't cut it down enough and realized halfway through I was in over my head." Once again, Eva found herself fighting back the floodgates of emotions in a public setting.

Spotting the pool of tears welling up in Eva's eyes, Heidi took her arm and steered her away from the crowd to a rarely used unisex rest room at the other end of the hall. Once they were safely behind the wooden door, Heidi pulled tissues from a box of Puffs and handed them to Eva. "Eva, for whatever it's worth, you did good out there." What could get this confident woman in such a state? "Honey, darling, what's troubling you?"

"The veil between success and failure is so thin. You can be up one minute and down the next without really seeing the pin that popped your balloon. It can happen to me, Heidi, and I might never see it coming."

Eva was so distraught, Heidi was unsure of what to do. So she did nothing. Just stood there with her. "Eva, I'm not reading between these particular lines, honey. Was it something that happened today that you didn't see coming?"

"Not today. It's just always looming. The fear of failure and rejection, being exposed, then taken advantage of. I'm not equipped to handle it. I judge myself on my success, whatever that means."

"You are successful."

"Yeah, right."

"Gosh, Eva, you have a growing practice, a nice home, two dogs, even if they do produce massive amounts of hair balls." Heidi glanced at Eva and saw that the rib at her pampered canines didn't change her mood.

"But what about tomorrow? Or next week? What if I lose my clients and can't pay the mortgage? Then what do I do? What if the people who heard me tonight tell everyone they know what a loser I am, and boy, don't hire her. She's the one who needs a coach. No, make that therapy!"

Heidi had never seen Eva in such a state. This called for drastic action. "Eva, how many clients do you have?" Heidi turned on her own calm, cool, and collected New-York-City-art-buyer-air—a drastic action for a Wyoming native.

"Twenty-one," she replied rather curtly trying to find composure.

"How many months worth of salary do you have saved for ready cash?"

"Five."

"How many of your clients were in the room today?"

"One, Charlie."

Scratching her neck, never taking eyes off Eva, who wasn't looking at her, Heidi considered another question, her eyebrows up and arched. "Do you have medical insurance?" She felt proud turning the tables of self-awareness to the perfectionist Eva.

"Yes. A good sole proprietor policy that's actually affordable for some strange reason. So *what*?" she added with uncharacteristic spite.

Smiling to herself, Heidi knew she made progress. "Okay, sounds like you have your security in place: cash, house, clients, insurance." She paused for several seconds. "What about real friends?"

Eva responded by nodding her head, tears streaming.

"Eva, are you a good coach?" Heidi knew that sometimes a solid yes–no question was key.

Eva stopped her personal groveling and fidgeting with her hands, looked up at Heidi, eyes red, wet. Grimacing with sadness, she nodded and choked out a meager and not altogether confident, "Yes."

"Yes, *yes*, you are a good coach. Yes, your life is in order. Yes, nothing is ever certain. But, darling, you're in good shape right now. Positioned to take care of whatever could possibly happen." Heidi leaned down to kneel on the floor, eye level with Eva, who had moved to sit on the wooden-top commode. "Lord, Eva, the whole town of Bear combined probably doesn't have five months of salary in the bank."

"But it can change. Then what do I do?" She let out a long breath, touching her forehead on Heidi's. Neither woman moved. Then Eva whispered, "Seaton seemed real and secure. What if my life isn't how it seems?"

"First, Eva, Seaton lied and you can't work around that one anymore. Second, life is life. Stuff happens." Heidi told it like she saw it. Then she got it. "Eva, you are secure. You have security in Bear, you belong here."

No comment.

"So, you have a job you're the boss of and, since I'm not blind, a budding relationship with the most eligible guy in town, all my familial bias aside."

Eva almost had a twitch at her lips. "Relating my experience tonight brought back emotions I thought were gone. Oh God, what a basket case."

Heidi caught the signal of change and was glad for it.

Eva went on, "I'm so bent on security, it gets in the way of my life. Strange, because I've learned to take risks, but the security thing, or should I say chain, comes and locks me prisoner."

"We are what we are, Eva. Look at you. You have things in place to attend to your security needs. Yes?" Heidi held Eva's hands to gain balance to stand upright.

"Right again, Sage Daniels." Eva said to Heidi.

"Are you ready to go out there and greet your adoring public?" At this request Eva gave Heidi her best evil eye, then an accompanying heartfelt bear hug.

"Yes, I'm ready. Thank you, Heidi. All of a sudden I was scared. And I felt like I choked."

"Well, that's the past. You're fine now. All prepared. You even told me." Smugly, Heidi linked elbows with Eva, and they made their way back into the fray.

Flustered, Gianni mumbled in a mixture of Italian and English as he paced around his flat. "Sì, no—sì, no. Ah, merda!" Gianni sat down with heavy frustration, leaning over with both hands molded to the top of his dark brown head as if he could pull out the right answer from his brain. *I'm a businessman now. I have people depending on me for their livelihood. I must not introduce distraction into my life.*

Then, like a little black bird had chirped to wake him out of his revelry, he sat upright. Looking back and forth across the room as if he expected to see someone, Gianni froze. Exhaling in a loud puff, he spoke to the walls again. "Grande Nonna Giabaldi, your spirit lives on, and I feel you even in this humble place." He slowly walked around the room, picking up his heirloom marble mortar and pestle, remembering the day she pressed it in his hands.

The bowl and blunt oblong cooking utensil were used to pound seasonings into a powder or mix ingredients together to form a paste. Many a Saturday dinner pesto sauce was created using the piece. Traces of green pigment clung to the inside bottom of the bowl from the countless times fresh basil, grated parmesan cheese, pine nuts, and olive oil were blended together.

Per te, giovane Gianni. Cucinare come un artista. Amare come un bambino—"For you, young Gianni. Cook like an artist," she had said. "Love like a child." Her wrinkled skin was a contrast to her youthful soul. Her blue eyes, glittering like the sun off the Mediterranean the day she gave him the gift, were a contrast to her southern European heritage.

The bowl and pestle was a tool she had cherished. Reminiscing of his Grande Nonna was bittersweet—grief at missing her and enchantment in having loved such an honest and courageous soul. "You've blessed me with talent to work with spices and you shared recipes you swore not to tell anyone." Gianni chuckled out loud, pointing his finger to the air. "For that, I thank you. Yes, I'll act on your wishes." Then under his breath he added, muttering again, "Didn't I also learn English like a scholar, as you demanded?"

41

Pushing back from the table, Steve let out a mild sound of ecstasy after the especially fulfilling meal. "Grace and Lois, that was delicious. My stomach is bursting." He took the napkin from his lap and placed it in a pile by his plate.

"Thanks to you, Steve, we had such fish. My mouth has watered for weeks. Your fly-fishing skills do come in handy. Thank goodness for the benefit of freezers." Grace glanced over at Lois, who was pushing back her chair. "Lois, child, rest. Let's savor this meal that melted in our mouths."

Dale, a first-time dinner guest at the request of Grace, chimed in, "After that meal, *clearly* the cook paid her dues and dishes should be left to the eaters." Looking around the table, Dale went on, "Now that I think about it, I would say the task of clean-up belongs to me. Steve caught the fish, Grace anted up the recipes, and Lois pulled it all together." Dale was comfortable in his skin for the first time since Beth died. A freshness came from him; he looked light, ready. Sadness no longer prevailed.

"Dale, that's an admirable offer. In this house, we all chip in to clean up. Many hands make light work." Grace smiled as she smoothed her silver hair pulled into a loose bun under a rhinestone clip. "Then we can move to the sitting room to chat without you clunking around in the kitchen and taking too long," she said, winking at Dale.

"Fair enough," Dale responded, eyes narrowing as he examined Grace, "Next month it's dinner at my place."

Jumping right in, Steve blurted, "You ladies are in for a treat. At Christmas Dale cooked a mean prime rib that had everyone fighting for seconds. He's a whiz in the kitchen." Steve punched Dale in the arm, adding, "Don't let his pampered looks deceive."

"Might have to invite ladies *only*!" Dale volleyed back without missing a beat.

"Touché," Steve said. "But I'm not sure a greenhorn like you can catch any fish."

Dale let the barb go, turning to Lois and Grace. "So how do you like this flat?" He was familiar with the building; Bear Claw Quilts was housed on the first floor.

"Oh, I like it quite well," Lois responded, anxious to participate in the banter. "It has an interesting mix of activity and calmness. On occasion we hear a spattering of noise from the shoppers in Bear Claw, then at night, silence, just us up here." Lois noticed Grace's head bob in agreement. "And we have a spare room for James when he visits."

Dale watched Lois with admiration as she navigated her way into the conversation. She was uneasy at first, the signs subtle. The way she observed others talk and then fussed with kitchen preparations to keep busy weren't lost on Dale. This girl wanted to add value, to be valued.

"James, yes, do tell. How was your visit to California? I can't believe we made it through dinner gossiping about recipes and work and didn't get to your trip," Steve asked, leaning sideways in the old oak chair, stretching out his long legs and resting his elbow on the wooden arm. "I haven't spoken to him since before your visit."

"Our James is doing quite nicely," Grace spoke up, happy to talk about her nephew. She had a similar cadence and language as Lois; the two were clearly cast from the same mold. As Grace herself often said, the nut doesn't fall too far from the tree. "You should see the size of the university! The campus is so big I don't know how he finds his way. Best of all, he loves his studies and reported that his grades are good." Grace was as proud of James as if he were her own son.

Chiming in, Lois bubbled, remembering the trip, her shyness overpowered by exuberance. "One day after his exams were over, we went down to the boardwalk on the Pacific Ocean. The sun was shining so warm even in December and all. There were people selling fish and, oh, we had fresh crab right out of the shell. We ate it as we walked about."

She paused, gauging the assurance of her audience. Satisfied, Lois continued. "Then there were giant sea lions barking right over the side of the dock making a ruckus of noise. James just laughed and said that the fishmonger taught them to do that so we'd buy his sardines and throw them out for them to eat." When she was done, a slow burn of red came up Lois's thin, pale neck as she shared the story with sublime animation.

Steve watched her with gentleness. She was like a sister to him, and to see her partake in the wonders of the world outside the city limits of Bear gave him deep satisfaction. Grace took in Lois for several seconds, too, nodding in memory. "Our boy is doing just fine. I am so proud of him. You should have *seen* the way he took Lois here in his arms and swung her around. Brought tears to my eyes it did. The way that young man takes care of his sister is pure love in action, yes indeed. Lois, you go right ahead and blush and cry, child. There isn't anything better in the world than that."

"No indeed, there's not. I couldn't agree with you more, Grace," Dale said, taking the tension away from Lois who was struggling to maintain her composure. Dale swallowed hard and wasn't sure he'd be able to keep his emotions under wraps. The young woman had a fragile exterior yet was capable and brave. There was a similarity in their experiences; she lost her parents in her youth and he, his wife in his prime. Different, but the same.

Steve absorbed the talk around the table, not sharing the serious discussion he had with James regarding Lois. He swore to James he would watch out for her safety and guard her heart, if possible. Looking at Lois, Steve knew that the girl was a woman now and didn't need him as a pseudoguardian. She'd be humiliated if she knew of the pact. Grace's words gave a brilliant description of the relationship between Lois and James. The two siblings forged a deep bond through pain and growth as they recreated their life after their parents died, and it had been hard for James to leave.

"I have a sister and female cousins back East and would be proud if anyone characterized me like you just did James." Dale said. Then an idea drifted across his conscious. "Say, Lois, where are you working?"

"I clerk over at the Shop-N-Save."

"What's it like working there?"

"My hours are good. I work from nine to four so Grace and I can spend morning and evening together. Plus I have weekends off to do the necessary cleaning and errands," Lois answered with an unexpected professional polish.

"I see."

"Clerking isn't necessarily challenging, but it's nice to see the people shop, and I never grow lonely." At this, Dale raised his eyebrows and moved his chair closer to Lois to engage in deeper conversation, momentarily forgetting about Grace and Steve.

"Where did you go to school, Lois?" Dale probed.

"I attended junior college at Hoback Junction and earned an associate degree in business administration," she answered sitting up straight, hands folded calmly in her lap, the freckles on her face contrasting in an appealing way with the green tweed of her long-sleeved shift dress, circa 1960s, care of Grace. Her slim calves, locked together at the ankles, swung sideways under the chair.

"Would you ever want to do business administration work? Accounting, ordering, that type of thing?" Dale asked.

"Well, I'm not sure. I want to stay in Bear. I'm happy. My aspirations aren't such to fly the coop."

At this Steve was the one who sat up straight, overwhelmingly proud of Lois standing up for what she wanted. He glanced at Grace, who watched keenly with faintly squinted eyes, concentrating on the conversation.

"That's only good from my perspective, Lois. See, it just occurred to me that you and I could enter into a business arrangement." Dale shifted in his seat and slid his hands together, fingertips matching steeple-style.

"Really?" The word came out of Lois without a hesitation, and the combination of humor and confusion with which she annunciated the word was comical.

"Hear me out. See, Bear Claw Quilts needs a manager. Someone who can tend to the books, schedule, and manage the staff, order supplies, submit hours for payroll, spend time on the consumer floor, that type of thing."

Lois leveled her gaze at Dale, not moving her hands from her lap. "I'm not really a quilter, Dale. I help Grace stitch and sew on occasion, but my skills aren't creative."

"That's perfect. I'm not in need of a quilter. God willing there are enough of them around to keep the shop going. I'm in need of someone to manage the business side of Bear Claw Quilts. I'd be available at any time for consultation, plus provide training to get you started." The excitement built in Dale at the same pace the concern was seeping into Lois. Sensing her hesitation, he added in a conspiratorial tone, "The commute is terrific."

At this joke, Lois made a reticent smile, not in self-doubt but an emergence of confidence. She just might well accept the challenge. Shop-N-Save was a steady job and paid well enough for her exerted effort. The work was monotonous, and her wrists hurt at times.

Languishing in the turn of events, Grace took in the scene. Her eyes scanned Lois, then Dale and Steve, shining with something, yes, with unbridled pride. She locked into Steve, who gave her a beguiling wink.

"I don't quite know what to say. It's an intriguing offer." Lois trembled slightly, overwhelmed. This was almost too good to be true. Typically, when something feels that way, it's just that: too good to be true, and it ends in disappointment.

"Well, then, how about you come over to the shop and we discuss this further?" Dale made plans with Lois and jovially clunked the dishes in the kitchen, just as Grace predicted.

42

Torrential rain assaulted the roof like a jackhammer as Eva took off her headset. Her client, Sarah, had filed a restraining order against her ex-husband. Finally. His once-polished demeanor wore through to a cheap veneer. Sarah had taken the world by storm after graduation, moved up the corporate ladder, impressed the industry, and married her dashing boss. Now she was the focus of his jealous, cruel, egotistical rage. Here she was starting over for the second time in two years. Tough.

At least that jerk loser is finally on the police radar, Eva thought, head bent, eyes closed at imagining the trials the feisty young woman faced. Scout walked over and set a long snout on her lap, sensing Eva's need for companionship. *What is it about some women who attract such bastards?* Her question was rhetorical. Eva knew she considered her own past as much as Sarah's current reality.

Can I let Seaton and all that crap go in order to move ahead? Her mind reeled, torn with dreamy thoughts of Steve. He seemed to have such character, yet she didn't know his history. Maybe he was as yummy inside as he was outside. But if he was not? What if he was a dashing, clever guy who zipped in and out of her heart? Then what, history repeating itself? Was Steve made of solid oak, not veneer? Hadn't she thought that of Seaton?

The punishing rain pummeled the earth, creating a soggy mess from dirty snowdrifts. Hypnotized by the weather, Eva was glad the unseasonable rain wasn't more snow. Her shift from thoughts of romance to weather was safe territory for a Midwesterner moved to Wyoming

43

The waiter placed the entrees in front of Jana and Gianni as they held their breath in expectation, a habit they acquired in culinary school. Jana eyed Gianni and cocked her head, waiting for his response to the rather large and flamboyant meals that had been placed in front of them. It took judicious self-control for Jana not to speak out, fire questions, and plow into the plate of food. Gianni, winking at Jana, slowly leaned into his plate absorbing the aromas of the food and sat back slightly to look at the presentation. He turned the plate, and he, too, cocked his head as he examined the dish.

The caramelized onion mashed potatoes weren't touching the meat and thankfully not sponging up a pool of red juice coming from the medium-rare filet mignon. The crisp vegetable medley of yellow squash, zucchini, and red onions with a hint of fresh basil was sautéed in butter and dashed with white pepper. Their salad course had been one of blue cheese, walnuts, and raspberries atop a mixed green-leaf combination with baby Boston lettuce. Heaven. The warm bread served before the salad was delicious, with just the right mix of grains and moist goodness. The two chefs had to force themselves to stop eating the soft rolls with small tufts of wheat, which melted the whipped honey-butter to create a tasty and satisfying nosh. Content, Gianni lifted his wine glass with conviction, his hand massive against the gentle crystal stem.

"Jana, I do believe that this meal is of sufficient quality for you to indulge. I approve that by visual appeal and bouquet, it'll satisfy your palate and provide a good culinary experience. As you deserve. Appetito buono." Cherie. Gianni's dark features were accentuated in the pale light emanating from the candle on the table. Dining in other restaurants gave him great pleasure, and sharing a meal with Jana was, well, a much-anticipated treat.

"Thank goodness!" Jana exclaimed after listening intently to Gianni. "I don't know what I would do if you said I couldn't eat this. It looks wonderful." Jana clinked her wine glass with Gianni's, the wine coming dangerously close to the edge of her glass, took a sip, and without further ado, dug into her steak.

Nodding in approval, Gianni continued talking, not a hurry in the world. "I love you Americans and the way you go after food with gusto. I remember in culinary school how Mr. Sirrius would scold the Americans for jumping right in, but I must say, I rather find it refreshing."

Jana stopped her fork midway to her mouth, spying Gianni over her hand, not sure if she'd just been lambasted or complimented. Finishing the bite, she cleared her palate with some wine, a rather large gulp accidentally escaping from the base of her throat.

"Gianni, did you just accuse me of eating my food like a barbarian?" Jana asked, taking a fleeting look at Gianni, who looked dashing with his black hair slicked back, then she concentrated her efforts to cut off another mouthwatering morsel of beef.

"No, no, that wasn't my meaning. Il mio amico, Jana, my friend. See, it's gratifying as a chef to see people delight in food."

Chewing, Jana acknowledged his comment and pursed her lips, deciding she had better finish the bite before responding. This was a date, after all. He was paying for her meal but he didn't need to view it midway down.

"Americans tend to eat first and talk about it later, si?"

"Guilty as charged," Jana answered, thankful for the comfortable banter. She basked in the warmth Gianni carried around with him, to his restaurant, friends, food, and now, she realized, romance. *These Italian guys are everything they're cracked up to be!*

A corner fireplace was ablaze to ward off the chill of the January evening. On the wall three-dimensional objects of wooden gates, rolled barbed wire, old fly-fishing equipment, and straw cowboy hats reeked of Jackson. "See all this—what—paraphernalia on the walls?" Gianni spoke with a deep accent, heightened by the wine. "Marlo would indeed approve that it sets the right tone for the restaurant. Huh, she is right."

Holding her steak knife suspended in the air, balanced between her thumb and middle finger, Jana nodded in agreement, drawn into his brown eyes. She breathed in and went on, "So, Gianni, tell me, what's it like for a Sicilian-born and -bred man to move to America and open an Italian restaurant in the West? Isn't the culture shock debilitating? Don't you miss the ambiance of Sicily? Your big family?" Jana sang out questions, thinking aloud and bursting with energy.

Wiping his mouth, Gianni leaned back pleasurably in his chair, placing the napkin back in his lap as he took another sip of the full-bodied Cabernet. He was pleased with Jana's exuberance and effervescent stream of questions. *She hasn't changed that much. Maybe more beautiful. I know her lost dream, but she never speaks of it. Mio caro Jana, I admire your ability to forge ahead into new territory.*

"Let's see if I can remember that litany of questions." Gianni smiled devilishly. She was a vision to him. All excitement and life. Real. "Moving to America is still exciting. Everything is big in America. The land, the buildings, the people, the mortgages, and the dinner plates!" he added, chuckling at his own humor, tipping his head toward the food on their table.

"God bless America," Jana responded, watching Gianni as she ate.

"Sicily I will miss always. My Sicily will be the same. It doesn't change through the ages. Memories of Sicily cannot be stolen. She's all about the senses." Gianni smiled as he spoke.

"It must be gorgeous. Heck, I've never been east of Brooklyn."

Gianni wanted to say *Sicily is not as gorgeous as you look this evening with your wavy hair and luscious mouth.* This classmate of his had blossomed into a vibrant woman. Remembering her question, Gianni kept things light. "Ah, she is, she is. As a chef, Jana, you can relate to this, the salty smell of the blue ocean, often tranquil on the surface but ferocious underneath. Then there's the rusty odor from olive presses mixed with the heavy aroma of the fruit and the loud bantering from those reaping the harvest. Of course, there is always the bustle of the small family vineyards with the tannin scent and rustling leaves. Not to mention the unmistakable human odor from an honest day work. Now, I'm carrying on too much. Surely you must stop my ramble."

This heartfelt sentiment had Jana spellbound, taken by it like the ending of a cherished book and wanting to read it over and over again to prolong the experience. *Am I smitten by this guy or by his romantic soliloquy of the old country?* Swallowing her silent revelry, Jana found her voice. It wasn't easy; his lips looked as tasty as the wine they drank. "Wow, well, your life across the old Atlantic is steeped in tradition. It's one that embraces the environment. You know?"

"Mm, I suppose it is," he said rather dreamily transporting himself to the place. Gianni flashed on a conversation he had with Sander earlier in the week. Sander was asking about his family and Sicilian acquaintances. Everyone seemed curious about them these days.

"What about your family? Do you hear from them much? How do you handle not seeing them?"

Gianni raised his eyebrows in concentration, considering her question. "Jana, remember the coincidence of you procuring the olive bottle for me from the docks in New York City?"

She grinned. "Yes, that was a total score, if I must say so myself."

"Which I adore, by the way, as you know. Well, it's a bit like my family. See, I love them and I make sure that the relationships don't break, but I don't have to have them handy. Just like I cherish the olive bottle and want it safe, but I don't need to use it in the kitchen. See, it's an extravagance that completes the restaurant just by being there. Capisca? Make sense?"

Jana's mind rattled to decipher what Gianni was communicating.

Taking the silence for comment, Gianni clarified his point. "See, I don't have to have them, my family, here," he said, opening his hands in front of him, palms up, then making a gentle fist, "to have them here," he said, placing his fists crossed over his heart. The rest of dinner couldn't have been sweeter.

44

"How did we ever agree to this? Marlo could be my daughter if I were a child bride," Heidi quipped. "Since when do the *younger* tell the older what to do?"

"Older, Heidi, really?" was all that Jana offered in response, rolling her eyes and trying not to laugh. "Besides, my, ah, not-quite-svelte bod could use some yoga with all the dining we've been doing. We must devise new ways to entertain instead of eating and drinking. Not that I mind it, I'm afraid."

"Are you two sure you're not siblings?" Eva commented to their jousting. "I think this is a fun idea. I've never attended any type of body-conscious class with girlfriends. Isn't this what we're supposed to do?"

"I can see us doing something useful like learning the tango, but honestly, Eva, downward facing dog wasn't a life skill I had in mind," Heidi said, executing a perfect example of the pose.

Eva stood holding her right foot behind her back to stretch her quadriceps, suddenly got the giggles, and toppled over. Heidi made no comment, moving to sit spread-eagled on the floor, graceful limbs in a full stretch, arm high overhead and then touching the opposite knee akin to a ballet maneuver. Jana, toes in hand, gently stretching her torso down as low across her legs as possible, mumbled just loud enough so Eva and Heidi could hear her. "This might be a long hour. Aren't we too old for this?"

Marlo bounded into the studio looking chic, young, and vibrant in a body-conscious outfit of low-slung capris and a cropped tank top embellished with an evergreen "ohm" symbol. She was the vision of health accentuated by brazen dark auburn curls and a dazzling white smile. Life was good.

"Hey, guys, you made it! You're going to love Crystal. She's amazing."

The surreptitious eye contact between Heidi, Jana, and Eva at the name "Crystal" was worth the price of the course. The only communication from the trio to Marlo was the exaggerated heightening of Heidi's left eyebrow. They were still mute from her effervescent entrance.

"Oh, yes, you will like her," Marlo added, catching their reaction and choosing to ignore. "She's awesome. And brutal. I can do my headstand, which I could never seem to manage in other classes." The bubbling Marlo was as much in her element in the yoga studio as she was at The Sicilian Ball. "Here she comes now."

In came a woman of about thirty with a reasonable figure and stature and carrying a rolled mat and bottle of water. She had short, cropped hair that twisted in dirty blonde curls and black spectacles balanced on her nose. She looked normal and, darn it all, they liked her just by her *real* appearance and congenial nature. There were no Amazon features, nor any aura of Palm Springs arrogance, Boulder naturalist, or New York City high fashion about her. Zero clichés. Bummer.

"Ladies and gentleman," she said without accent, "I'm Crystal. Today we practice Iyengar yoga poses. You can follow along by watching me. I'll help position you if you need help." She glanced around the room, taking charge of the space. "Remember, when one does yoga, it's called 'yoga practice,' as we're always striving to be better, thus practice. In yoga, an 'asana' means a pose, 'pranayama' means breathe, and Ivengar is a particular yoga discipline. Any questions?"

No one spoke. The class of twelve women and one man watched in awe and nodded obediently. "Okay, then we'll get started. Make yourself comfortable. The rest rooms are down the hall and the water fountain likewise. This is my second course session at this new studio, and I'm open to all your questions and suggestions." Professional, pragmatic, and personal. Refreshing.

At the end of the class, the energy in the room was outwardly calm. Inwardly, the participants had pushed their muscles and psyches to become the asanas, the poses constructed of their own human mass. After Crystal finished the instruction, she stood, fluffed her crumpled curls, and pressed her palms together in front of her chest with a short bow, saying aloud, "Namaste." She addressed her students. "For those of you new to yoga, this is a traditional ending and beginning to a class. We all bow to one another. 'Namaste' is often translated as 'I bow to the divinity within you from the divinity within me.' That's it. Great class. See you next time."

After quietly collecting their mats and water bottles and pulling on coats and hats against the January chill, the group left the studio. Their serenity was suddenly confronted by a stream of honking cars that trailed after a limousine pulling cans tied to the bumper with strings and sporting windows covered with "Just Married" written in white shoe polish. Despite the cold air, a gleeful Sandy and Nick were standing inside the limo, waving from the sunroof. The hood of the cape covering Sandy's elaborate gown was barely atop her upswept hair. Their enthusiasm in sharing their excitement with the town confirmed they made the right decision to wed after all. A happy start to a hopefully happy life.

"That just makes me feel older yet," commented Heidi, squinting after the car in the bright sun. "Those kids look like they just won the lottery." They stood, speechless, and watched the parade of cars pass.

Migrating over to Grizzly, the four women herded to a round window table, holding their preferred hot beverage in hand, yoga mats tossed haphazardly on the floor. From behind the counter, Eva spotted Chad watching them with intense curiosity, a highly amused expression on his face at their unusually serious demeanors and solemn entrance.

Marlo broke the spell. "So, what'd you think of class?"

"I liked it. Once we improve our poses, it'll be more invigorating. It's slow moving since I don't know what to do," Eva said, entranced with the fact she'd finished a yoga class with girlfriends, real friends—three of them no less.

"Easy for you to say, Eva. Those animals of yours keep you limber," Jana added, rotating a kink out of her neck. "Marlo, this is a great idea. Thanks for pushing us into it."

"Did I really push you? Oh." Marlo added, suddenly awkward with her still new friends.

Heidi piped in, warm café mocha in hand and a change of heart, "Darling yoginis—especially you, Marlo—I think this is quite the cosmopolitan extracurricular for Bear. It keeps us hooked into the pulse of the rest of the world. If I were still in New York, I'd imagine doing such a thing over lunch."

Jana listened while contemplating the class participants. "Say, who was the lone male? I wonder what it's like to be the only guy in class." The women shrugged, the man a complete unknown to the group.

"I have something on my mind," Eva offered in a precarious voice. "It has to do with the 'namaste' and bowing at the end. It's not that I mind the ritual. It's just that it made me feel, well, empty. Does that make sense to you?" The others were quiet, watching Eva and presumably reflecting on her comment.

Marlo twisted a curl and took a long drink of cappuccino with extra espresso. "Mmm, not to me, Eva. It actually made me feel more complete."

"How can I say this?" Eva said aloud, struggling for words. "I think the 'namaste' bow is a fun way to end class, you know, closure for yoga and onto our next endeavors. What I mean is, it gave me a sense that something is missing in my life. I just don't know what it is." Just as Marlo was going to add something to Eva's thought, Dale Sawyer came up to the table, unwittingly interrupting the conversation.

"Hi, ladies. How's it going?" Dale was flushed from the cold, a yellow scarf hanging loose around his neck, his brown leather bomber jacket unzipped, and a hot cup of java enveloped in his hand, black. Heidi gave him a slow once-over head to toe and offered an approving smile accompanied by a coffee-in-hand wave. They were on to new topics, new interactions, Eva's *something missing* temporarily forgotten.

45

That evening Eva curled up on the couch in her office, wrapped in a violet chenille robe, silk long underwear, and sheared booties, pampering herself as she sipped mint hot chocolate. Ah, Thursday nights were divine. Friday was technically her day off unless she had a workshop or a complimentary coaching session. Tomorrow was a free day. A gift. To make things even better, she planned to complete a couple quilt projects, get in some cross-country skiing, and deal with the looming stack of correspondence. Setting the mug down on the end table, Eva turned on her back, stretching like a lioness, the soft texture of the cushions absorbing her weight.

"Ahhh, this is so nice!" Eva said aloud, arms and legs extended. Dash stood and arched his back, blinking from a nap. Scout stretched her limbs in opposite directions, then relaxed like Eva. She looked like a child's picture of a dog recumbent on the carpet.

The clink of the ceramic mug was the clue their mistress was in motion. Dash migrated over by Eva, large velvet head parked on her chest at she lay on the couch. She hugged him close, lavishing in his fur while Dash stood still, taking it all in.

What was it? What was this nagging feeling?

It started again yesterday after yoga class. She worked hard all morning, had fun with the girls, and was generally loving life, then swoosh, like a visit from a stealth scavenger, her feeling of fulfillment was stolen. Throwing her head back hard against the coach, startling young Dash, Eva closed her eyes. She rubbed him with the tops of her fingers as he arranged his furry bulk on the carpet. Eva focused in on her life.

Let's see. The house made it through its second winter. No leaks this year, and just one heater blip. Dogs are healthy, no gashes from the fence since last spring. Business is in the black, not gangbusters. I like my clients. I'm healthy; holding my weight pretty reasonable despite chocolate indulgences. Social calendar is improving, thanks to Steve Mason.

Yummy. Great girlfriends like Heidi, Jana, Marlo; I'm getting to know Lois and Grace. What else could there possibly be? Lying supine for several more minutes, Eva's eyes flashed open. Standing, she went over to her computer and brought up her coaching tools folder from her hard drive.

How could I not think of this? It's so obvious! Opening a file, Eva leaned back in the chair, arms crossed, her legs outstretched as she considered the colorful pie chart on the screen. In her coaching, Eva employed a tool called "Life's a Pie." If a client was stuck, the pie tool zeroed in on areas to explore for action. Envision a pie, she would tell her clients, each piece of the pie is assigned a part of life. Eva used health, career, finances, relationship, recreation, friends, personal growth, and spirituality. Frowning at the screen, Eva took out a sheet of blank paper from the printer and drew a circle with eight pie segments.

Starting with "health," she was satisfied with the current state. She made a line across the end of the segment close to the outer circle. She had a similar reaction to the segments for "career," "finances," "recreation," and "friends." Tapping the pencil gently atop the pink eraser, Eva contemplated "personal growth." What had she done to push herself lately? She shook her head in an immediate recall, yoga fit the bill to satisfy personal growth. Eva had been savvy about mastering complex tax nomenclature, too. With these both considered, personal growth received a solid mark.

Two segments stared back at her. "Relationship" and "spirituality." Eva groaned. Tackling those doozies would require supreme honesty. Hearing her moan, Dash lumbered over to her and flopped an ample paw on her lap with solemn determination. Eva absently pet his head. Relationship was on the upward turn, but tenuous. Steve and Eva had something going, whatever "something" might be. At least there was someone in the picture. *Mmm, yes, and he's definitely a someone! Coach Trina would approve.*

Speaking, Eva scratched her shadow dog, "Not that you're not enough, Dashy Baby," and she leaned to kiss his head. On her sheet, Eva gave "relationship" a middle-pie mark without reservation. It was improving, and that, indeed, was progress.

"Spirituality" leered from the chart. *What is spirituality anyway? Being a good person? Helping others? Letting people be who they want to be and worship what they want? Or does it cause the goose bumps she gets when praying on her walks? Maybe the joy she used to feel singing hymns in church? What is it?*

Recalling her yoga class, Eva wondered at her odd, empty feeling after the namaste bow. *Was that it? Was she noticing spiritually missing from her life?* Uncomfortable, she drew a line connecting the marks, creating a lopsided circle. Relationship and spirituality created a wheel with a bumpy ride.

When coaching, Eva asked clients, "What do you think of the results?" Based on their answer, she would follow up with a simple, "Would you like to talk about what's going on or not in the *x* piece?"—*x* being the shortest piece in the pie.

Often the short piece was not the immediate problem. To achieve certain goals in life, people often knew things were purposely off balance for valid reasons.

Eva once worked with a budding executive who had nonexistent pie pieces for fun and friends. When he considered this, he was satisfied that—for that time in his life—he made the choice to sacrifice fun and friends while he focused on career aspirations. Similarly, a young stay-at-home mom had no desire for more money or pursuing a vocation outside the home. Bumpy isn't bad unless it causes dissatisfaction.

After her session of self-coaching, Eva brooded. She wanted something different regarding spirituality, but *what*? She paced by the bookshelves, the library ladder, and the sleeping Scout, ending next to the massive window. Holding an elbow in each hand, she cradled herself and took in the mountain and lake view amid rapidly ensuing dusk. *There's so much outside of my control. What's the solace in uncovering this thing called spirituality? Is it missing? Maybe. Maybe not. I believe in God, but what does it mean to be spiritual?*

Tilting her head to lean against the cold glass, Eva took in her unanswered questions. Clive Cody, the coach she had during her certification, would definitely have told her to *be* with the aggravating emotion. Not to *do* or *think* or *act* on it right now, but just be with it and see what came up. Eva considered this perspective and concluded she would in fact *be* with her discomfort around spirituality, whatever that meant.

Jana sat across from her therapist in Wilson. She wasn't thrilled about being back on the couch, but she longed for closure. Or was it a green light she wanted? The magical steak dinner with Gianni was a huge flashing neon sign to move ahead. *Do not look back. Advance to new relationship. Collect healed heart. Take a chance on life, love.* Like picking a "chance" card in a game of Monopoly. What was holding her back?

"What's holding you back, Jana?" Aaron asked after an unusually long quiet space. Dr. Aaron Sackman had a youthful, spirited voice that belied his middle-aged years and expansive girth.

Silence. Jana wasn't sure. What was holding her back? Aaron, seeming to have all the time in the world, glanced at his pocketwatch and tucked it in his vest pocket in a calming fashion; it fit perfectly in the custom Brooks Brothers pin-striped suit. He was the epitome of patience.

"Seems to me, from your tongue-tied muteness, that nothing of importance is holding you back, Jana Eberly. I say you go forward." Aaron had known Jana on and off for two years and had diagnosed her completely healed psychologically, brought right back to a healthy ground zero. It was Jana, however, who needed to own that feeling.

Jana peered at Aaron. This wasn't the dictum she expected from him. He was typically ambiguous, almost psychobabble-ish versus directive in his therapy. Catching her eye, he added pensively, "You don't need me anymore, Jana, even though I'll miss you."

"Geesh. Okay, I get it. You want me out of here, right?"

"Exactly," Aaron responded with a characteristic gummy grin.

Where *were* his teeth anyway? "Hey, let me ask you something, Dr. Sackman. Have you heard of life coaching?" Jana turned toward him, head resting on her hand, sprawled sideways on the formula black leather couch.

"Yes, of course," he responded with pursed lips and reflective nod.

"What's the difference between life coaching and therapy?" Jana asked.

Aaron tilted his head toward the window, an odd movement since he didn't have a neck; he looked like a large rotating ball. He reflected for fifteen seconds, then abruptly sighed loudly, startling Jana, who watched his every move. His sharp clothes were a contrast to his disheveled hair and long salt and pepper beard. Rumor had it he was one of the original flower children to descend on San Francisco from his native Queens. Another New Yorker who made the Jackson Hole area his home.

"In a sentence, my answer to that question is life coaching empowers someone to achieve the next higher level of their desires, while therapy heals an ailment to get you to the breakeven point so you can function at a normal emotional level."

Jana absorbed this comment. Taking her gaze from Aaron and scanning the bookshelves, her librarian eye landed on an antique copy of *Madame Bovary* nestled in the academic collection. "Huh." Then, continuing her questions: "So, does someone do therapy, then go to coaching?"

"Could be so," Aaron nodded. His head bobbed like an apple in a bucket.

"So, what you're saying is coaching helps a person reach their dreams while therapy heals a person."

"One could say that," Aaron replied, curious as to her line of questioning. However, this was her dime, not his. Life coaching had taken on quite a bit of interest over the recent years, his included. It was a force to be reckoned with, one that could have positive and collaborative impact with therapy.

"Are you saying I'm emotionally healed, Dr. Sackman? And not a proverbial fruitcake incapable of romantic relationship?"

"If you want me to repeat myself, I will," Aaron said, gently clearing his throat for impact.

"Brother, and I pay for this abuse!" Jana added lightheartedly, gesturing boldly with her arms as she turned to lie on her back. Jana rolled off the couch and extended her hand with sincerity. "Thanks, Doc."

Rocking himself to dislodge his mass from the chair, Aaron accepted her hand and held it softly in his pillowy, slightly clammy palm. "Jana, don't be a stranger." Considering for a second, still holding her hand, he went on, "One never knows, maybe I could gander over to that hamlet of Bear and look around. I heard there's a new rather excellent restaurant."

At the mention of the restaurant, Jana blanched and blushed at the same time. This wasn't lost on the good doctor, almost as if he knew the association. Jana gained her composure, turned and waved her hand in the air as she walked out of the office, grabbing her quilted bag off the ground. In traditional Jana style, if somewhat learned from Heidi, she offered a loud "ciao" over her shoulder and was off.

Aaron stood for several minutes watching the door after Jana and her energy left his pristine, now unnervingly calm office. Wistfully, he lumbered over to check his next appointment.

47

Sander had his arms wrapped around Marlo so tightly they looked attached at the forehead. Reluctantly, Sander released Marlo from his grasp and watched as she floated through the oval beveled glass door of Bear Claw Quilts. After a two-count, he gathered his senses, turned, and meandered toward the library to work, laptop under his arm.

Marlo waltzed in, flush from her interlude with Sander. "Hey all, how's it going?"

Heidi, Eva, and Jana were arguing over the nuances of whether to choose fabric with a cream on white background or a white on cream background. The trio turned in unison toward the voice, immediately acknowledging Marlo. "Well, what brings you to these parts?" Heidi asked, taking in the young woman's happy gait. Shaking her head, Heidi wondered if she would ever in her life exude the "I'm in love and loved" aura that dripped off Marlo and Sander.

"You all are coming to yoga with me, the least I can do is check out this shop that steals all your free time." Marlo looked awkward in the country setting of the quilt shop.

It was Heidi again who spoke up, "Lois, this is our friend Marlo. Marlo, this is Lois. She's the manager of Bear Claw."

"Hi, Lois. We've seen each other at the Shop-N-Save. Great to meet you." Taking in the variety of products and the sunny, comfortable décor, she added, "This is a nice shop."

"Thank you. I've just started working here," Lois offered. "And I love your restaurant," she added, not quite an afterthought. Lois and Marlo were close in age yet had drastically different backgrounds, looks, and experiences. Their interaction was cautious and polite, like the daughter of a divorcé being introduced to her father's new young girlfriend.

"Oh, thanks. Me too. It's not really mine, you know." Marlo answered, proud of her association with the popular jaunt.

"Let me know if you have any questions," Lois smiled.

"Don't let me keep you from your work. I know all about distractions." Marlo made her way to stand next to Eva, examining the fabric. "What are you making?"

Eva sighed and set down the bolts in her hands. "Oh, I don't know anymore. I started this appliqué quilt before the holidays, but it just doesn't work for me. Too much detail."

"I see," Marlo said, not readily grasping the quilt dilemma but seeing something else in Eva.

Eva forged on, still in her own head. "I hate not to finish it, but it's making me crazy. My frustration with this darn appliqué project is in the way of any creative juices for another one."

"Ah, so you're a perfectionist, are you?" Marlo blurted harmlessly, focused on the quality cotton fabric lying on the table, rubbing it between her fingers.

Eva's mouth dropped. Jana looked at Eva, then at Marlo and let out a low, hearty laugh. "Now that's a good one, the pot calling the kettle black—and by the looks of Eva, you nailed it right on the nose." Heidi went to sit on a stool, propped with her long legs crossed, relishing the dynamics.

"Why, I, I ..." Eva stuttered.

"Ha," Jana said. "Exactly," her eyes mischievous and dancing.

Then Marlo looked at Jana, catching on to the interplay. "You think I'm a perfectionist?" she said in complete shock, pointing to herself.

At this revelation, Heidi's brows arched like Elvira from the *Adams Family*. Lois moved surreptitiously from her stool to a neutral and secure post behind the checkout counter, her subconscious guiding her escape.

Under her breath Heidi exclaimed, "This has the makings to be more entertaining than a Broadway play. And people say that life is dull outside of New York."

Eva linked her arm with Marlo's and made a point to stand up straight and tall, catching her breath from her earlier stutter. She turned her head ever so slightly and lifted her chin to the side. "Marlo, I say that we embrace and take pride in our perfectionist natures. But it's about time I let mine down, if I feel like it, and quite frankly, when it comes to this quilt, I feel like it."

Stunned by the whole interplay, Marlo realized she had stumbled on a hot button of Eva's that was ragingly obvious with her other girlfriends. Without missing a beat, she tugged off her trademark hat and fluffed her hair. Elbows still linked, she turned to Eva and asked, "What are you going to make instead?"

"Not sure," Eva said. She felt unexpectedly free. It wasn't so much the quilt, although the project had become too much work and no fun; it was more than that. Eva had a knack for living her life in a way that took the fun *out* of fun by making sure she *did it right*. Doing things right can be an admirable quality. The trouble was her penchant for taking this philosophy to the extreme.

Years earlier, for a coaching session, she drew a picture of what she called her perfectionist-productivity gremlin. Yuck. Even the name was weighty. It was a big, ugly, fat, gnarly creature with pointed ears coming out the side of its head and a triple chin. Wound around its body and over its shoulder was a heavy iron chain with links as large around as the pipes under her sink. Sir Gnarly continuously built a wall out of cement blocks that he never finished. The blocks bore expressions such as: "Do it right!" "Don't mess up!" "Keep going," "Better not fail!" "Get your work done!" "Finish it up fast!" "No need to change," and the like.

Eva knew this gremlin had served her well in many areas of her life—work ethic, study habits, exercise—but, taken to extremes, it negatively impacted spontaneity and fun. How do you do fun *right*? After nudging from Trina, Eva put the picture of Sir Gnarly in her bottom desk drawer. This was done both figuratively and physically. Sir Gnarly reeked of her perfectionism. She could take him out and use him or not, her choice. The point was she could make the decision to act consciously with perfectionism in her life.

Eva came out of her memories with a novel idea. "Hey, Lois, does Grace still sew?" Eva winked at Marlo, letting her know she'd get back to her question regarding a new quilt project. Lois caught her breath before she spoke, startled she'd been included so naturally in the conversation. "Oh, yes, of course."

"Do you think she'd be up to barter of some sort for her hand-sewing services on this quilt?" Eva glowed in her new freedom.

Heidi, unusually quiet through the goings on, coiled her body lazily around the chair, like a snake resting in the sun. Propping her chin on her hands, she observed Eva's metamorphosis.

"Why, you'll have to ask her. I couldn't answer for Auntie Grace. She's out this afternoon getting her hair done and should be back within the hour."

"Fair enough. Thanks, Lois." Turning, Eva gave her best cat-that-got-the-canary grin at her three comrades. "So, I think that might solve the, ah, situation with this quilt. Marlo, come with me, I'll give you a fabric walk."

The two women left the main shop area, starting their tour in one of the smaller back rooms. Seconds later, there was a large ruckus on the front porch. Standing to peer out the window, Lois eyed the perpetrators and shook her head. The door banged open and in barged Steve, Dale, and Gianni, talking over each other. They were bundled for the weather and had dropped packs and other accoutrements in a pile on the porch.

"It was so!" Dale boomed, laughing and shaking his head with conviction.

"Please, Dale, surely you're delirious," Steve said, dripping with mock condescension and tapping his head in a "what could you possibly be thinking" gesture.

"You're both crazy. Mine, that got away, I could have used for a whole night of family specials," Gianni added, not one to be left out of male rivalry.

The women made eye contact, not sure what was causing the boisterous behavior. Jana and Heidi rolled their eyes in unison.

"Eh, em," Heidi interjected, clearing her throat with exaggeration. The guys stopped dead in their tracks. Until that moment they were in self-absorbed in their revelry. Dale froze and turned toward Heidi, as did Steve. Gianni, his mouth dropping open at seeing Jana, stood up straight. A red hue spread over the base of Dale's neck, lost on everyone except Lois, who observed the clash of the sexes from her post behind the counter.

"Dear cousin Heidi, how goes it?" Steve piped up, adjusting to the room of females. "I see you're sharpening your domestic skills, eh?" he teased, waving across to the bolts of fabric. He gave a short wave to Jana and a quick wink toward Lois.

"Steve, darling," Heidi said, pausing as she recrossed shapely, long legs with attitude. "What brings you to the quilt shop, and what's the, ah, reason for the abrupt intrusion?"

"Intrusion? It's just all of us," Steve said, waving his hand toward the familiar faces, now trying their best to act adult.

"Why, if we had been rich lady quilters who'd come from far and wide, you might have startled our hearts," Heidi purred.

"Mm, that might have been some good luck for us fellows." Steve guffawed.

"Charming," Heidi retorted back smugly. "So, pray tell, what caused this commotion?"

"Just trying to give these boys here some advice on the nuances of ice-fishing in the Hole." Steve tipped back ever so slightly on his heels.

"Hey, who caught that big brown?" Dale asked, poking an elbow in Steve's rib.

"Who told you where to drop the line?" was Steve's retort.

"Humph."

"And we're here because Dale needs our brawn for moving stuff in the basement." Steve exaggerated a weightlifter's pose.

"Yeah, right. I'd say us nonlocals here schooled the old boy today." Dale chided, knowing full well that wasn't exactly how it went down. "But more on that *after* he helps bring up boxes from the basement."

Gianni, surprised to see Jana in the shop, was noticeably dumbstruck, which wasn't lost on Jana, pleased that she caused his sudden befuddled behavior. His candor and compliments came so eloquently when they were out to dinner, just the two of them. His public shyness was sweet.

"Lois, how's the shop?" Dale asked, brash demeanor put away as he moved over to the counter, setting down a bank deposit bag. She automatically took it and placed the bag behind the counter in proper position.

"I have the inventory done and the schedule for the next couple of weeks. Also … " They were lost in quiet dialogue about shop talk, leaving the others to fend for themselves as they disappeared into the small office.

"So, where's the other member of your threesome?" Steve asked Jana and Heidi, knowing if he didn't ask, it'd be more obvious. He casually fingered the fabric on the table as Marlo had done minutes earlier.

"Funny you should ask, Mr. Mason. She's here," Jana answered in rapid fashion. "She trapped Marlo and took her on a fabric tour. Should be back any minute. Why do you ask? Any fish parts for her dogs?" Jana added mischievously, knowing the idea of fish parts would horrify Eva.

The camaraderie between Jana and Steve calmed Gianni's nerves. "Marlo is here?" Gianni inquired, "I knew she sewed, but didn't peg her as a quilter," he said as he looked at the bolts of material bursting from the shelves as if Marlo would materialize from within them.

"She's not—yet. We hope to convert her, what with her creative mind. Truth is, since we're schlepping our mats to yoga class, Marlo felt obligated to come and see what the fuss was about here at Bear Claw," Jana answered, calmly watching Gianni, insides reeling.

Gianni nodded, tongue unemployed. This random meeting with Jana after their intimate date had him out of sorts. Steve took a long, slow look over to Heidi, still perched on the chair taking in the scene. "Yoga? Well, well. Tell me more." He liked the idea of all that female stretching. The damsel Heidi wasn't taking the bait.

Folding his arms across his chest, Steve went on, "Now, I'd like to visit you ladies at the yoga studio instead of here at the quilt shop—no offense to Dale and Lois, of course." Pausing, he furrowed his brows, thinking. His words slipped out aloud accidentally as he considered how much he still didn't know about Eva and her life. "When did that start?"

"Last week. In fact, we saw Dale at Grizzly after our first class. He must have been too engrossed in fishing to pass on that little morsel of gossip." Heidi unwound her limbs to stand, stretching her elegant neck, and considered her last interaction with Dale. That man was a hard nut to crack. "And no, you're not invited," she snapped with mock vehemence at Steve. He gave her an alarmed expression and brought both hands up, resting one on his heart as if shot. "Exactly," Heidi concluded.

Surveying the room for any sight of Eva, Steve yielded to the fact that she was still out. "Duty calls. Come on, Gianni, let's get this done." Gianni made eye contact with Jana. He was shaken up at his inability to engage her in flirtatious banter. As a last courageous attempt, Gianni held her eyes, gave her a purposeful wink and the universal "I'll phone you sign" with his hand. This was sufficient attention for Jana, who smugly raised her eyebrows to Heidi after he left the room.

Moments later, Marlo appeared solo, oblivious to the men's appearance and subsequent disappearance. "What?" she said as Heidi and Jana diligently watched her don her hat. "I need to run an errand and get ready for work."

"What did you do with Eva?" Jana asked.

"She ran into Grace coming in the back door. They went upstairs to discuss bartering arrangements. Grace offered tea, Eva accepted, but I must be on my way. So it was good to see you all in this apex of creativity. Ciao." Patting her hat in place, Marlo was off on her own mission. Scampering out, she almost plowed down an unsuspecting customer.

48

Steve leaned on the doorframe as Scout sauntered across the dining room to lie down. Her aloofness was a result of Eva's clothes. Dogs have a sense about human clothes, a knowledge of what their masters are going to do based on clothing style and footwear. Dash and Scout were no different. Flimsy fabric signaled "leaving without you and stay *down*." Rich, soft textiles meant "home time and lounging." Sturdy outerwear with plastic grocery bags in the pocket meant "you get to go with," and bulky pajamas indicate "nighttime, relax and chill."

Steve held back a smile as he waited patiently in the entranceway, observing Eva engrossed in caring for her male dog. He recollected a comment from a fly-fishing client from Maine who had noted with a haughty accent that "as a symptom of their singularity, the unmarried couldn't see their unusual private habits for what they are, unusual." Clearing his throat for effect, sapphire eyes dancing, Steve startled Eva, who squatted down to wipe and pet Dash. "Well, uh, if you'd like some *alone time* with Dash, I could wait in the other room." His attempt to hold back laughter failed, as muffled chuckles slipped out.

Blushing, Eva pulled the animal close. "Har-de-har," she said, sparing. "Yes, well, we would rather like that. Huh, Dash?" Leaning back on her heels with an audible sigh, she took in Steve's presence, instantly thankful for the diversion of the dogs to provide a topic for conversation. His presence took her breath away. Steve Mason filled the room with a fearless smile, bulky clothes that covered defined muscles and his undeniable masculine smell. *What was that called? Pheromones. Yum, he definitely had them.* Steve overwhelmed the entranceway. Her entranceway. Now it was Eva who cleared her throat to attend to the conversation at hand. "I know. I'm *too* attached. I love them. What can I say? It's the penalty I pay for owning dogs."

"Lucky dogs, I'd say." Steve said, offering a hand. In one motion he pulled Eva up for a hug, not too long, not too short, just enough to get the dog off her mind and have her consider him. Slowly releasing his grasp, he took in the soft scent of her hair and safely changed the topic so he wouldn't lose himself in her embrace. He was entranced by her feminine charms, the smell of lily of the valley soap, and the tickle of her flyaway strands of hair. "So, lovely lady, what seems to be the problem with the fireplace?"

Momentarily mute after Steve's embrace, Eva stared blankly, then recollected the question. "Yes, the fireplace. No, it won't light."

"Yes and no. Typical female indecision, I see," Steve said, as he ruffled her hair and slung an amiable arm around her neck. "Now, Eva, I didn't expect that from you." Eva gave him her best glare and led him into the living room, grasping his hand that hung loosely down from around her shoulders, wondering if he could feel the rapid beat of her heart.

Steve knelt on the hearth and wrenched his bulk into the opening of the recently swept fireplace. After some grunting and rattling, Steve pulled himself out of the small space. "When was the last time you had a fire?"

"Our Christmas party," Eva said, interlacing her fingers, concerned over the fireplace. The home represented her personal liberation. She took care to give it the same meticulous attention as she did Dash, Scout, and her coaching clients.

"That recently? Okay, the flue was stuck but I got it to open. The draw is working. I'll have to come back in the morning to check it out from the roof just in case. It's too dark right now." He paused, watching her face sink over concern regarding the ailment that had fallen upon her beloved home. "Not to worry, we'll figure it out." He paused briefly, then went on. "I'm not too sorry, Ms. Karlsen. This means returning to oblige you for coffee in the morning."

Eva thought she would melt right there, like snow into the carpet. "Oh, sure. Yes. I can manage coffee."

His eyes shone and he was contented that he would *have* to return to help his damsel in distress. "You made it easy on me, see? When I was in high school, I'd leave a scarf or hat or glove at a date's home to make sure I had a reason to come back. This way I won't catch cold. Nor wait too long to see you." At this, Eva gave him a playful slap on the arm as he took the opportunity to fold her close into him.

Thirty minutes later they settled into a cozy table at The Sicilian Ball. "This place is jumping. I love the aura." Eva gazed around the restaurant, the aroma of fresh garlic with a hint of tarragon coming from the kitchen. "It's intimate, neighborly, and exotic all at the same time. Not to mention the fabulous food," she said, pointing to the warmed bread in the basket that begged to be eaten—after, of course, being drenched in basil-infused olive oil garnished with Asiago cheese.

"After hearing Gianni talk about his new recipes when we were ice fishing I knew we needed another jolt of this place." Reaching for her hand, he brought her palm to his lips, eyes burning into hers with sincerity and desire. "Thank you for accepting my dinner invitation at short notice. And not pretending to be busy."

"I must work on my alluring femme fatale skills." Eva said, surprising herself with the coy comment. Then bit her lip to hold back a smile as she continued. "You'd think I'd catch on, spending so much time with both Scout and Heidi."

Caught off guard by her response, Steve almost spit out his Chianti. "I'm telling Heidi." He gloated. "She's not one to take kindly being grouped with a dog regarding female charms."

Eva put her palm to her forehead, holding in her laughter, "You're so right. That's not what I meant."

"Uh huh. Sure. You might be able buy my silence if you share your tiramisu later." He gave her an uninhibited wink before examining his menu.

Thank goodness I'm sitting down, Eva thought, admiring her companion.

As they set down their menus, a waitress appeared out of thin air to take their order. She sang the praises of Gianni's specials and tempted them to indulge in her favorite appetizer of stuffed mushrooms with diced prosciutto, mozzarella cheese, pine nuts, fresh tarragon, and a secret ingredient known only to Enrique. She was off as quickly as she appeared, delighted at the appetizer order. Enrique was making a name for himself with his requested appetizers and desserts. He'd been pushing his creative juices to the limit, using the kitchen after hours for, as he called them, epicurean experiments. Hard work paying off, a fine thing indeed.

Drenching a bite of crusty bread in the freshly prepared dipping concoction, Eva looked up to see Steve watching her every move over the top of his wine glass. Feeling like a paramecium on a slide prepared for a science student, Eva steered the conversation before he could get the lead. An idea came to her suddenly. "Tell me about fly-fishing. What makes it so different from regular fishing?"

"Excuse me?" It was all Steve could utter, not a question he expected.

"Fly-fishing. What's up with that?"

Leaning back in his chair, completely relaxing into the moment, Steve lifted his chin to consider her question, unable to suppress a large lazy smile as it emerged across his face. "Have you ever seen the movie *A River Runs through It*?"

Eva thought for a second, recollecting the film. "You mean the one with Brad Pitt?"

"Yes, that would be the one."

"Oh yeah," she said, sipping her wine and drawing out the "yeah" with a throaty seductive tone. "I saw that one." Steve raised his eyebrows at her female admission to male attraction, something that until now hadn't surfaced. "Did you realize there was actually fly-fishing involved in the movie, or did you just fast forward to watch Brad Pitt scenes?"

Ignoring his jab, Eva took a sip of wine before responding. "Yes, I know it included fly-fishing. Brad Pitt was the younger brother who stayed home. The artist, as I recall."

"Exactly. He was indeed an artist. Big brother came back from college out east to see his little brother, Brad, out there in the streams. Casting the line with precision and grace, ah, dropping that fly just so, where the rainbow trout would surely see it and *snap*." Steve's psyche went to the movie and stream. As he told his short tale, he twitched as if it were him who cast a line across the sun glittering water.

This interplay mesmerized Eva. She realized at that moment that he, without a doubt, was an artist. Catching the moment, she moved in. "Tell me what you love about fly-fishing."

Steve took the bait without hesitation. "Mm. I love the fresh air. The movement of the rapid stream. The selection of just the right fly. The challenge of the hunt. The execution of the cast. The play of the wind. The thrill of the fight. The feel of the cool water around my waders." Pausing, he added with a mischievous grin, "Did I say the smell and taste of the bounty?"

Eva tingled watching this man talk about something he clearly loved. She ignored his rhetorical question and asked, "Is that what kept you in Bear, fly-fishing?"

"Mmm. You could say that was a big part of it."

"It's part of who you are, isn't it? The stream, the fish, the challenge?"

Steve reflected on her observation and indulged in more wine before responding. "You could say that. Fly-fishing doesn't complete me, per se. That would be too philosophical. Fly-fishing is something that makes me feel complete." He set down the glass, gesturing as he continued. "It's the whole package, as you say, the stream, the fish, the challenge, the air. I'd go further and say it's sharing it with others. That's what keeps me going with my bloody guide business."

"*Bloody* guide business?" Eva curiously mirrored back.

"Aye, bloody business," Steve answered in his best Scottish brogue, which became him, causing Eva's heart to skip a beat. "You'd be surprised how many clients of mine come from the British Isles, England, Scotland, Wales, places that have their own great fishing." He nodded with a bit of internal disbelief regarding the actions of his clients. He'd love to fish across the Atlantic. "It's the most frustrating, fun thing I've ever done. And to top it off, I get paid for it."

Feeling a bond, Eva murmured to herself, but it came out aloud. "Like coaching, I presume. Tell me about your clients."

Steve shared stories about his many clients. There was the Wisconsin deer hunter who couldn't get the hang of casting, threw his fancy fishing rod into the stream, and stalked off. Days later Steve found the rod washed up on the bank in pristine condition. Then there was the delicate young red-haired princess from Albania who was a natural at threading the rod and placing the fly exactly as instructed. She had a knack for staying with a fish and would only catch and release, never harvesting her catch. The good old boys from Texas were consistent, reliable clients, and after Steve humored them with their "country of Texas" jokes, they weren't so annoying after all.

Was he extra interested in that princess? Eva sensed a brewing angst of jealously looming within her as he spoke of her. As he paused, Eva needed him to talk more. "So what's frustrating about it?" She blurted the question, breaking into his memories.

"You mean *other* than the clients?" he teased. "Well, the paperwork, advertising, follow-up letters to book trips, that type of thing. I guess the business side of the business is the frustrating piece."

"I can relate to that. You'd think being your own boss would eliminate bureaucracy. But tax laws, paperwork, billing, lining up clients, cripes, it adds up."

Steve threaded his hair with his hands, thinking about the chore of it all. "Tell me, Eva, is this what you do all day? Get people to talk about themselves and feel wonderful?" Steve's voice was husky, directed only at her.

Her thoughts meandered, her heart stuck on his husky voice. "Ah, I, well, that would be nice," she said, knowing it wasn't always wonderful.

Steve reached across the table, took her hand, softly kissed her palm, and gently set it down, keeping her hand in his grasp. In an attempt to speak, she opened her mouth and closed it again, no words able to escape. At that moment, as if on cue to save a star-struck Eva, Marlo sashayed over with dinner artfully arranged on beautiful blue and yellow Italian crockery.

Marlo hummed to herself as she whirled around the table, filling glasses of Chianti for both Steve and Eva. Love was in the air! How she loved the restaurant. Here she was working in a beautiful place, serving happy customers, seeing her Sander perched on a chair conversing with Jana, and delivering wine to Steve and Eva who were clearly starstruck. Such fun. Sander caught her eye and gave her an intimate toast by barely lifting his glass as she danced by.

Almost two months had passed since her surreal clash with Sander's other world. That fateful evening was like a bad B movie, and when the fear gripped her, she shook her head to erase the memory. It could have been the end of something, of everything; instead, it was the start of something great. Marlo and Sander. An "us." We. A fresh shared life *without* secrets, old baggage completely opened—well, the baggage that mattered anyway. How often does that happen?

Looking down at her striking emerald ring, a gift from Sander, Marlo had a fleeting feeling of regret. Neither had any family close by. No relatives or parents to drop in or to invite over for dinner. No family to see *their* place, the kitschy trailer that they loved. Marlo wondered, was it less pressure *not* to have them nearby? Was their life more natural and unrestricted since they could be exactly who they wanted to be as a couple without familial expectations or influences? Maybe. Maybe not. Huh—she'd ask Sander what he thinks. When he wasn't lost in thought of his own, he'd been generous in conversation.

Sitting at the bar, Sander and Jana tormented one another with different points of view. The unlikely twosome struck a fond friendship proclaiming themselves restaurant widows per the eclectic hours their significant—or *hope* of significant—others put in. Since the stolen gem escapade, Sander was clear about his title of "significant other" with Marlo. Jana, on the other hand, swore Sander to secrecy—a talent he'd honed over the years—when she used the label with Gianni. She didn't want to jinx her budding romance by prematurely calling Gianni her significant other.

Of all places, Jana and Sander's friendship blossomed at the library. Sander was a voracious reader and constantly ran into Jana at her place of employment, which he also used as a pseudo office. *My tax dollars at work*, his favorite line to Jana as he checked out books or reserved his favorite reads. After a series of polite interactions, Jana realized Sander read everything he could muster from Jeffrey Deaver with the Lincoln Rhyme character, so they were bound for life. Jana fired up the local library networks' lending program to bring in all the author's titles and others in the crime investigation genre.

The two chattered about the mysteries and forensics until they had to attend to their "duty calls." Jana absorbed the parallels to Sander's real-life experiences that made his comments mesmerizing. For Sander, the new friendship was satisfying. He started to open up to a life in Bear that included activities other than work. Friends were becoming as natural to him as hopping on a plane to fly to exotic locations.

Later in the evening Marlo watched Steve and Eva leave the restaurant. Eva, too, had no family around. Or none that she ever spoke of, for that matter. Mmm, she'd chalk that topic up for their next visit to Grizzly.

The icicles slowly dripped under the overhang like a parody of children playing a glockenspiel in elementary school music class. Hypnotized by their rhythm, Eva was startled when Scout swiped her leg with a spindly paw. "Hey, you, it's not time yet, Scouty girl." Eva purposely didn't use the words "out," "play," "walk," or "eat," knowing these words would trigger the animals to double-team her in a relentless fray until she addressed their whims. It wasn't time for dogs. Scout persistently pushed her nose into Eva's lap, a worn tennis ball in her mouth. "Scout, you're a pest. You need to wait. No."

Lying on the other side of Eva, Dash watched the interplay with a serious face. His wet nose didn't move from the floor, yet his big brown eyes were active and worried, waiting for a word or mannerism to come from Eva acknowledging that Scout had broken her reserve for both their benefit.

"Uh," Eva said aloud, with a sense of unrest. It was hard to figure. Life was going well. Her home was in solid repair. Steve removed a nest built by a pair of yellow hawks the previous mating season. The melting snow from the rain caused it to shift and wedge into the top of the chimney. He had kept his promise to investigate "operation chimney" in broad daylight. Eva knew having the chimney job lined up took away the end-of-date-tension the night before.

So why the unrest? After his successful roof mission, they indulged in mint-flavored hot chocolate while watching strays from the National Elk Refuge find their way to high country. It was so natural to be in his company. *I wonder where he had to go so early?*

Ruminating on Steve, Eva closed her eyes. In seconds, Scout, tennis ball in mouth, plopped the damp toy in her lap. "Young Scout, I must not worry. Enjoy, right? Be in the moment with this relationship."

Then, like a sharp kick, she was stuck by the "Life's a Pie" exercise. What was it she agreed to? Oh yes, a self-induced Coach Clive *be with* spirituality challenge. He would ask what she had discovered so far. Truthfully, she hadn't given the challenge attention other than *wanting* to give it attention. Real consideration took effort. "Aargh."

Maybe it was time to raise the topics. What might her friends think? The group would have an opinion. Strange, faith and spirituality were the vortex of most world wars, yet they were topics rarely spoken among her friends. Gianni was the only one who referenced faith and did so in his own theatrical, Italian Catholic fashion. Faith. It was personal, not private. What did it mean? She walked toward the window contemplating her question.

50

Eva's eyes teared from the frigid air that whipped her face, breath lodged in her throat from an abrupt inhale. The scene in front of her couldn't be real. The woman's red leather pants and matching cropped jacket seemed spray-painted on her exquisite Victoria's Secret body. Black hair tumbled around her face like raw silk, matching her black stiletto Jimmy Choos. Her perfect nose turned up, and her pouty lips glistened. The green from her eyes exploded with color. Expertly applied makeup made her look plucked from a fashion magazine. The goddess's arms were wrapped around Steve Mason like a vice. Even worse, Eva recognized that face: The woman didn't just resemble a Victoria's Secret model. She *was* a Victoria's Secret model.

Every reality of honing a new relationship drained out of Eva. All of the memories of her comfortable banter over coffee with Steve earlier that morning were blown away with the freezing gale. She should have known! She blinked in an attempt to change the scene in front of her, but it stayed the same. Except the scene was from a nightmare, not a movie. Just when she thought things were different—bam!—out of the blue, another woman. This couldn't happen again, yet there she was barely ten feet away. Oh, this is why he had to leave her. He had it all planned. No. How could he?

Dizzy, Eva started to weave. She needed to sit. Be someplace else. Wake up. Eva shook her head to make it go away. It didn't. The truth was clenched in an embrace right in front of her. *Escape.* How could she flee without being seen?

Eva had recognized Steve's broad shoulders and unmistakable gait from behind, but the second before she opened her mouth to call out his name, the phantom Ms. X had floated out of the shop, enveloping Steve with all her sexual glory. *Steve had been waiting for this woman. Did he send her in on a shopping mission? Oh God.* Just months ago it was Eva and Jana who exited this exact shop with their bags of seductive for-their-eyes-only lingerie. Eva ducked into a doorway, queasy. Her legs shook with disbelief. Steve was a womanizer. Pulling her in like one of his fish.

She thought he was honest, different. But it wasn't true. Uncontrollable tears of betrayal streamed down her face. Her heart was severed and bleeding out of her eyes. She felt the fool. Illusion; her confidence in their relationship was just that, only an illusion.

Driving on autopilot, Eva pulled the International into the garage. How did she get home? Inside, she uncharacteristically flipped open the dogs' crates without greeting them, threw the car keys on the table, and paced around her kitchen, trapped like a wild cougar in a glass cage. She didn't know what to do or where to turn. Should she call Jana or Heidi? No. This was *her* problem. Was she being irrational?

No, no. No. Their relationship, a courtship, really, was mellow and slow. That's what she thought made it so wonderful. She needed fresh air and exercise. Out the door, leaving it ajar, and up a path behind her home, Eva hiked at a furious pace. Singleminded, Eva marched up the trail, considerably off her normal route. She was wounded.

How long had she been hiking?

The woods were still, full of snow, and they took on a foreign aura—that "this trail isn't traveled much" feel one can get when hiking alone. Eva didn't notice. Her throat was sore and dry. Had she eaten today? What brought her to Jackson? Was it for errands and a treat from the Swedish bakery, then she forgot both? Steve and the lady in red. Oh, sure, he probably calls her the "lady in red" just like he called her "lovely lady." She loved that nickname. It had always landed on her as so tender, so kind.

Oh God, oh God, oh God. Are you there? Please help me. I don't know what to do. I'm scared and sad and tired and mad. I'm mainly sad, Lord. Betrayed. Stupid. Again.

Eva hiked over the increasing number of rocks, ducking under barren branches overarching the snowy trail. She'd assumed. Assumed! Her Dad had been right. *Never assume anything, Eva Marie. If you do, you know what they say—makes an ass out of you and me. Get it? Ass-u-me?* He'd always thought it was so clever. She'd roll her eyes to humor him. Now it wasn't so funny. It was true. She'd assumed that she and Steve were building something special.

A relationship. Didn't they talk about why they both loved Wyoming while on their first Grizzly coffee date? That seems rather intimate, like a real relationship. Sharing thoughts. Wasn't that what relationships were about? Steve was the guy who passionately read the story of Rudolf to the kids at the library.

Will the real Steve please raise your hand?

Tears streamed down her crestfallen face as she considered the positives of Steve. It didn't add up. Maybe she didn't want it to. Stopping in her tracks, Eva caught her breath. She looked over the trail edge and couldn't see the valley with her house and lake. Whatever.

A thought hit her suddenly. When someone says something is too good to be true, it usually is too good to be true, so it's not true, right? Does that hold for the opposite logic? If something is too bad to be true, is it too bad to be true?

Fudge. Eva slowed down. Maybe there was another angle to consider. Maybe? If she were coaching someone, she'd invite consideration of other perspectives.

Eva, give up the mother, apple pie, coaching crap already. You got screwed again.

Before Eva could toss around her idea, an obstruction appeared on the trail. It sparked an eerie something-is-out-there-watching-me shudder. Right in the center of the trail was a giant nest of moose hair. Piles of coarse brown, gold, and black hair created a perfect circle five feet in diameter. In the center of the hair nest was a huge clavicle bone, white and tissue free. Smooth. A sick shrine. To the right of the path was even worse. Four feet away lay a whole, sans the clavicle, moose skeleton, completely stripped clean. No flesh, no blood. The skeleton was all that remained. It was positioned on its side as if it were sleeping. Head out in front, four legs hanging down, with spine and skull intact. Nausea overtook Eva. Her head spun. The world went black.

Dash and Scout were agitated. Scout sniffed the edge of the open door between the mudroom and garage. Dash had gone into the kitchen and gingerly placed his paws up on the counter, smelling the keys Eva haphazardly tossed. The dog walked into Eva's office, her phone ringing, and went to stand in front of the glass window.

The answering machine sang out her voice, "This is Eva. I'm currently on the phone or away from my desk. Please leave your name and number and I'll get back to you as soon as possible." At the noise, Scout appeared in the doorway eyeing Eva's desk and the source of her voice. Dash lay down with a whine and thud. Scout left the office entranceway and went back into the mudroom. She picked up a hat of Eva's that was carelessly tossed on the floor. As she took Eva's hat in her snout, Dash appeared. Staring at one another, the animals left the house through the open garage door.

"Hallo," Gianni answered his phone absentmindedly, disrupting his concentration on a new menu. "Who?"

Disbelief.

"Ah, si. Well, I'll be damn. How's life?" Moments later, after placing a second unanswered phone call, Gianni grabbed his cell phone, coat, and keys and left. Using his natural sense of direction, since he had only been there once on a rather festive, dark Christmas Eve, he miraculously arrived at Eva's, smiling and relaxing when he saw her unmistakable aqua International in the garage. Parking behind her vehicle, Gianni went up to the front, stomping his feet knock off the snow. He rang the bell. No answer. No dog noises, either. Strange. Not one to enjoy the cold, Gianni walked around into the garage.

"Eva, it's me, Gianni. Are you in there?"

No answer. Seeing the open door into the house, he walked inside with a growing sense of concern.

"Bella Eva! Beautiful single women who live alone shouldn't leave their doors open," he said loudly with a tinge of teasing. No reply again. Getting bolder, Gianni went inside and instantly felt the void. He spied keys and crossed himself. L'aiuto di dio lei. God help her. After searching the house, he made another phone call.

In town, Dale paced on the sidewalk outside his home as Sander ran up, hardly out of breath, thanks to a professional physical fitness mandate.

"Did you contact Steve?" Sander asked, shifting the backpack on his shoulder.

"Yes and no. I left him a message on his cell phone," Dale replied.

"Let's go." They were off. Both men were trained for emergencies, to stay level-headed. Gianni, on the other hand, was not.

"Gianni's shaken up. I give him credit for calling. It might be nothing. But then again, it might be something." Dale said, focused on the road and thinking through options.

"Not to be dramatic, but I have a thermal blanket, water, beef jerky, and a compass. I trust Gianni's instincts," Sander added, placing a small pack on the floor between his feet.

Sighing heavily, Dale nodded. They drove in silence the short distance to Eva's place. Gianni was out front pacing in the driveway. The men jumped out of the truck and took in Gianni's animated details.

"She's gone. No dogs. Open door. Car keys on the counter. Mama mia. What should we do?"

Sander walked away from them and circled the house. He whistled. Dale and Gianni appeared in the back. Sander pointed to the ground, wet and muddy with snow. Tracks. Dog and human.

"The tracks are fresh. You two up for a hike?" Sander asked, tilting his head up beyond the lake into the mountain.

"One of us should stay here. We need a contact point," Dale logically offered. They all looked at each other, and Gianni pointed to his chest. "I'll stay. Call me often." Gianni crossed himself again.

"Will do. Hey, Gianni." Dale stopped and turned. "Call Judge Jerry and tell him what's going on. No alarms at this point, but let's get the local authorities in on the situation. This is their territory. They might have ideas." Gianni nodded, and the three men tended to the business at hand.

Following the tracks of Eva and the dogs wasn't mentally challenging, thanks to the damp ground and freshly made tracks. The path was a game trail that wound straight up the mountain. The hard part was physical. "Geeshe, you need to be a mountain goat to transverse this terrain. I haven't experienced this type of climb except at Machu Picchu," Sander commented, heartbeat increasing from anxiety and exertion.

"Tell me about it. What would she be doing up here alone? Leaving the house open doesn't paint a pretty picture."

"There's only one set of tracks. That mean something?"

"Maybe. Maybe not," was all Sander replied, not wanting to consider the worst. His eyes searched the woods and path in a slow, methodical sweep, always moving, always watchful. Could Eva's disappearance be at the hand of the Barratino family? What the mob family would want with Eva, Sander didn't know, but he knew from a call with Sid that they were close to discovering the family's connection in Bear. After an hour climb, Sander put out his hand. The men stopped silently on the trail. Ahead one hundred yards was an obstruction. Fighting the urge to run, they approached cautiously. On the trail was a large covering of moose hair. In the middle was Eva, lying unconscious on the ground. To one side Dash had his full body length against hers, his head resting on her tilted shoulder. Scout was on the other side, spooned in close next to Eva, Scout's head up and alert, a clavicle bone behind her. As the men advanced, the animals remained motionless, vigilant.

51

"No one would believe this," was all Sander could mutter. At the voice, Dash gave out a low whine—a plea for help? "Eva's dogs are quite the trackers." Despite his bravado, Sander was overwhelmed with relief. Ever since the narrow escape with Marlo, he had a renewed respect for danger for those who weren't trained. This wasn't a movie.

Dale knelt by the trio. Dash wagged a long tail, not otherwise moving. Scout moved a paw, stretching to the man but not leaving Eva. As Dale picked up Eva's hand to check her pulse, he heard someone yell his name. Steve appeared on the path, winded and shaken. Rushing up to the huddled group, Steve leaned over to catch his breath, hands on his knees.

"Take it easy, mountain man. One trauma victim is all we can handle right now," Sander said, patting Steve on the back. "We just got here. Dale's checking her out. She's unconscious. Not sure why. Possibly hypothermia or dehydration from the physical exertion."

Emergency situations were out of Steve's bailiwick. He felt useless and at a loss for words. The dogs still didn't move.

"Let's get her home. She's not dressed properly. If it weren't for these dogs, she could've gotten frostbite, or worse. Eva," Dale whispered in her ear, then, "She's really pale. We need to get her warm." The men extricated the dogs from Eva, petting them and applauding their effort. Instinct told the canines that these men were okay. They stood, not moving far from Eva.

"Eva, wake up," Dale said, louder, gently shaking her shoulders.

"Mmm." She moved, startled, opening her eyes and closing them again, her vision blurry. Weak, she felt woozy. Her body shook. Much better to close her eyes. Sleep.

"Eva, it's me, Dale. Steve and Sander are here, too."

"Oh, who?" Then she was out again, oblivious. There was a sweet breeze, soft and fluid like a spring day. No, she decided not to get up and go with the breeze. It was way more comfortable lying cozy in the grass. The call of the breeze was persistent and a bit annoying. She needed to change positions so it wouldn't interrupt her sleep. It felt so good to sleep. She was so tired.

"Let's go," Dale urged. "We're losing her. I'll carry her. Steve, get those dogs moving so they don't trip on us." His military training coming out, Dale gave directions, his mind whirling on how to get Eva home without further peril. He picked up Eva, who was as limp as a rag doll. "Come on, honey, let's get you home. You're just a slip of a thing. Rather handy right now."

"Dale, she's dehydrated. Give her some water." Sander handed him a water bottle. "Trust me on this one. Delusional, tired, pale, and in shock."

The trip down the mountain was slow, cold, and long. Dash and Scout led the way, stopping as they went to let the humans catch up. The men took turns carrying Eva, Steve refusing to give her up until he himself was close to exhaustion. When they entered the clearing behind Eva's home, they saw Gianni waiting and pacing. Jana, Heidi, and Marlo flanked him, worried. Thank goodness for mobile phones and the new cell tower in Jackson.

Spotting the group, Heidi dialed 1-800-HOME DOC, the new house-call doctor that had recently opened in Bear. She was slightly impressed with herself that she'd remembered seeing the flyer posted at the Shop-N-Save.

Safely tucked into her bed, warm, and watered, Eva's head spun. Nightmare did not even begin to describe the situation. She was embarrassed by her flight and rescue, and was raw with emotions of betrayal. A soft knock disrupted her thoughts.

Heidi, who held vigil, motioned for Steve to come in. "Shh, she's coming to. There's got to be some story about what sent her up the mountain. It's not like her." Heidi was more concerned about her mental health than her physical health. With the prognosis from Stan Noble, MD, she knew Eva would recover physically. Dr. Noble was at her door in fifteen minutes flat, negating the need for the hospital or ambulance. "Food, water, and rest until she gets her strength back. The quickness of her friends—and, uh, dogs—is what kept her from real harm," the doctor had said. Heidi couldn't wait to tell Eva that the new doctor in town was the lone man from yoga class. She'd cringe. Best to wait until she was fully coherent. The coincidence made Heidi smile.

Steve's eyes never left the prone, vulnerable Eva. He heard Heidi's comment but was locked in on the forlorn figure of Eva.

"Can she breathe under all those quilts?" Steve asked, feeling powerless.

"She can breathe. Here, you take over. I need some coffee." Heidi, in a rare display of maternal instinct, put her hand on Eva's forehead, bringing it down to cup the side of her face, paused, then left the room.

Standing awkwardly, Steve watched Eva, then settled into the chair next to her bed, pulling it close to the mattress. "Eva, it's me, Steve. Can you hear me?" Eva heard a voice. She opened her eyes and took several seconds to clear her vision. Struggling to sit up, she didn't have the strength to speak.

"Hey, take it slow, lovely lady. Easy." He said it with so much care and affection. Eva was confused. "What are you doing here? What about Jackson?" Raspy whispers crept from her throat, her mind groggy.

"Shh, be still. It's okay." Steve gently stroked her cheek, growing more concerned by her confusion and questions.

"No, the lady in red," she spoke, then was down again, eyes closed.

Steve watched Eva, distressed. *Maybe something more is wrong than just exposure and fatigue. She's talking foolish, dreaming.* He sat by her side, gazing at her for what seemed like hours. Eva slept like a corpse. He didn't like it.

Much later, to purposefully disrupt his vigil, Heidi crept in by his side and lovingly pulled her cousin to standing, hugged him, then gave him a gentle push to leave the room. Heidi was sipping hot chocolate and flipping through a *Western Lifestyle* magazine when Eva stirred. Setting down the magazine, Heidi leaned over to put her hand on Eva's arm. "Eva, it's me, Heidi."

"Heidi? What's going on?" Eva shook her head on the pillow, trying to clear her mind, her body uncharacteristically limp.

"Eva, look at me," Heidi said sternly, worried.

Turning her head to Heidi, Eva opened her eyes wide, like a deer.

"What do you remember last, Eva?"

Closing her eyes in concentration and with a spent breath, Eva spoke softly, sadly, "Heidi, I fled. I thought it was real. I'm such a jerk."

Inwardly, Heidi smiled. This sounded more like Eva, lucid and speaking with conviction, albeit puzzling. She looked weak and thin but on the mend and no longer in any health risk.

"Darling, this is me, Heidi. Honey, what are you talking about?" Again Eva shut her eyes. This time she turned to her side and tucked into a fetal position. Instinctively Heidi tucked quilts around her friend and again pushed the hair off her pale face.

"I'm cold. And hungry," Eva said, not answering the question.

"That I can handle. Why did you go up the mountain alone without any supplies?"

"Ohh, Heidi." Tears tumbled down her face.

"Eva." Heidi gently brushed away the tears, allowing them to flow, not telling her it was *all okay* because it wasn't, that much was clear. She hated when people would tell her things were okay when they clearly weren't.

"In one short second, all that I hoped for and thought was real disappeared. I was in Jackson. Steve was there. I was just going to call out to him. Then, then there she was. A gorgeous woman all over him. Right in the street."

"Eva, let me get you some food. You aren't making sense here." As Heidi made a move to get up, Eva grabbed her arm.

"Heidi, it was Steve in Jackson. I saw him with another woman. She was a model. I've seen her in the Victoria's Secret catalogue."

"What?" Now it was Heidi's turn to be befuddled. She knew her cousin. She knew the status of his love life *most* of the time. And if she knew anything, she knew that he was falling hook, line, and sinker for her crazy Midwestern friend.

"When I got home, I panicked. My life was crumbling. I'd been so happy, and, poof, it was all gone. Smoke and mirrors. I needed to get away." She lay her head back down on the pillow, "Uh, I'm so stupid. Again."

"Wait, so you saw Steve with a woman in Jackson, drove home, and then you decided to take a little jog up the mountain?"

Eva's eyes flashed open again. Looking at Heidi, stricken as the reality of what she did sank in, she coyly nodded her head.

A hint of appreciation moved across Heidi's face. "Huh. I'm rather proud of the drama queen move. That's pushing your range, girl." Heidi playfully nudged Eva and then went on. "Eva, you could have been hurt. Or worse. This is Wyoming you live in now, remember?"

"I told you I was stupid."

"You're not stupid. Just misled, Darling. You stay right where you are while I get you some food."

"Thanks," Eva said in a thin, almost pathetic reply.

"I'm sure there's an explanation for this weird state of affairs." Heidi left the room, muttering to herself.

Minutes later it was Steve who came back in, a plate in hand that contained all the food groups, compliments of Gianni and Jana.

Eva eyed Steve, distressed that Heidi had sent him. She watched as he came across the room to sit down. What else could she do? Trapped.

"Eva, we need to talk. But first, eat. You're pale. You've got me, all of us, worried."

His voice was so honest, so clear and calm, that Eva automatically listened to him. She nudged herself up in the bed, took the plate, and started to devour the food, not making eye contact. If it wasn't so sad to see her weak and forlorn in bed, it would've made Steve laugh to see Eva eat with the abandon of Jana. They sat in silence. Eva felt nervous, humiliated. She was so hungry her stomach was still growling as she ate the rather large array of food on the plate. How did they prepare this tasty food from *her* kitchen?

Steve offered a hand when Eva finished, and she handed over the empty dish. Looking up at his penetrating eyes made Eva weepy. She gulped back her tears, not wanting his sympathy but too distraught to be brave. She was wounded. It was plain to see her frailness and pain.

"Eva, Heidi told me what you saw. I know what it must have looked like, but please, hear me out."

Eva riveted her eyes on him, then down again, studying the quilt covering her lap, fidgeting with the small stitches. Clearing his throat, he continued. Eva did not move. He noticed her body was still, tense, and she stared straight ahead at the quilt. "Her name is Veronica Lodge. We used to date a few years back. Every year or so she passes through Jackson and will give me a call. Her parents have land in the area and she visits to ski and shop. Mostly shop." Eva had no words. She glanced up at Steve and he turned to look at her. Their eyes connected and once again Eva diverted from his gaze. Veronica Lodge? She was confused.

"Eva, I was as surprised as you were in seeing her. She practically tackled me on the street. This, I'm afraid, tends to be her style."

"What?" It was all she could manage to speak.

"I'm not seeing Veronica, Eva. She spied me walking down the street. I was making my way to the Fly Shoppe. See, I had an appointment with a distributor who wanted my opinion on some flies, and Veronica busted out onto the sidewalk. She doesn't do anything with discernment. For all she would have cared, you could have been holding on to my arm. She only has one agenda, her own, and she's oblivious to the havoc she leaves in her wake."

Eva loosened her grip of tension at that last sentence. Steve had veiled disgust in his voice, somewhat atypical for him. It was like angelic singing to Eva, a tone she had never heard from him. And it was directed to the lady in red. Alleluia. Minor triumph. No, *major* triumph.

"Oh," was all Eva could murmur. If she was embarrassed before, now she was mortified. She'd made a complete fool of herself. Put herself, her friends, and dogs in danger. Oh, no, she did create a drama queen scene this time.

"I'm sorry, Eva. I'm sorry that you would have even thought that I was interested in someone else. We haven't spoken of it, Eva, but right now, if you'll still accept it, I'd like you to know that you fill all my thoughts of romance." He tenuously reached out for her hand. She let him hold it. "Seeing you lying prone next to those dogs, pale as the snow, my heart stopped." Pausing, he added with a slight laugh in spite of himself, "Despite the beating it took with that little jaunt up the mountain."

Cringing at what she put her friends through, Eva fought for a solid voice. "If that gorgeous woman was Veronica Lodge, that must leave me to be Betty," Eva said quietly, feeling the room spin from the trials of the day and from Steve's declaration. Betty once again.

He looked at her quizzically. Eva clarified, "You know, from the Archie comic books? Veronica Lodge and Betty Cooper? Veronica always had it going on, lots of money, clothes, boys, and Betty was just not quite up to snuff."

A thread of recollection came across Steve's eyes, then that Hollywood smile. "Ah, now I know what you mean. I do recall, and yes, the *live* Veronica Lodge used to soak up that parallel, now that you bring it up. She's pretty, Eva, but you, you're beautiful."

Eva couldn't stop her tears. Twice in one day. She let out the tension. This amazing, strong, smart man was here for her. Because he cared about her. That thought alone was overwhelming.

Later that evening the small group of friends sat around Eva's living room. Gianni prepared a simple pasta before leaving for the restaurant, Dale cracked open the wine, and Sander fed and tended to the dogs, duly impressed by their tracking abilities. All the while Steve, Jana, and Heidi pampered Eva beyond her embarrassment. She now acquiesced to the situation caused by her misinterpretation of events.

"So tell me again, how did Gianni know to call you, Dale?" Eva said, trying to sort out the sequence that led to her discovery. She felt safe and cared for, letting her foolhardy actions go. Now she was plain curious.

Dale sat casually over the arm of her plush couch, eyeing the fire, then focusing back on Eva. "Your coaching client, Martin, called Gianni. From what I can tell, this Martin character had a sixth sense that something was wrong with you when you didn't answer your phone."

"Martin?" Her beloved actuary coachee from Schenectady. Ugh, could this get any more mortifying?

"He knew Gianni from when they were in New York studying for their citizenship. See, Martin remembered that Gianni had moved to Bear, and he knew that's where you live. So on a whim, Martin called Gianni. The coincidence is amazing."

"Martin never mentioned knowing Gianni." Eva curled tighter on the couch. She created a lot of worry from her flight of fancy. *Dumb.*

"You know what they say about we're all six degrees from one another? Well, I see and believe it more and more the older I get." Dale paused, taking a drink of the robust red Chianti, and gazed into Eva's eyes. His glance held Eva. His eyes were void of any ridicule or condemnation, no sign of "what were you thinking?" It was just pure, simple friendship, full of care and acceptance.

Gaining the strength to divert her look from Dale, Eva slowly closed her eyes with recollection. "Martin." Eva groaned in angst as she put her head in her hands. "I missed our coaching call. It moved to a new day. I completely forgot when I came home from Jackson. I was in such a tizzy," she spoke to herself, whispering as if she was alone in the room.

Watching her intently, Dale felt a new compassion for Eva. One moment she was complex, like doctorate-level regression analysis, hard to figure, yet the next minute she was as easy to read as a Dick and Jane primer. "Well, Eva, it's a good thing this Martin didn't forget. He called Gianni, who, of course, enlisted the cavalry to ensure you were found safe and sound," Dale added, winking at Eva to help her relax. He could only imagine her discomfort at this public display of emotion that started from her feelings toward Steve.

Sander watched the scene and the open friendships. He couldn't let them know he thought she might have been kidnapped for ransom by a Sicilian mob family. He needed to slow down and return to being methodical. His bones told him he was close. Romance must be rattling his brain.

Dale stood and walked over to Eva. "Hey, you gave us a scare, and there are no words to explain the relief to see you up and around. Take it easy tonight. I've got to go." He leaned over and kissed her cheek.

"Thanks, Dale," Eva managed weakly. "And I appreciate the lesson about the winter kill. I thought that moose skeleton was some cult shrine. Here it was just a winter kill, licked clean of flesh and blood, and only the bones and hair left for the mountain."

"Here to help," Dale offered, waving to the rest of the group as he left.

As if on cue, Sander, Heidi, and Jana shifted positions and made way to exit. Heidi pointed to Eva to stay put and turned to Steve, sitting in the chair opposite Eva on the couch. "Dear cousin, make sure Ms. Karlsen is properly cared for and that she doesn't lift a finger." She stopped and turned around again. "And give those two mutts a little extra pasta. They deserve it." She walked back to Eva, hugged her, whispered in her ear, and left the room.

Long minutes passed after the cars cleared the drive. Eva and Steve silently faced one another. Steve went to stand in front of Eva. "Can I sit down?" he asked, motioning to the space next to her. Eva nodded. With the human movement, Dash stood, arched his back, and frolicked over to Steve, tail wagging and moaning a whiny pet-me-now noise. Scout had been sleeping at Eva's feet and now turned to look at Dash, annoyed at his typical display for affection, and settled back to sleep. The predictable dogs eased the tension.

"This is more than a little awkward. I feel foolish for my ridiculous display of juvenile behavior," Eva said.

Putting his arm around her on the couch, Steve pulled her near. He felt her heart beat faster at his touch and his own muscles twitch in restraint. "Eva, it was not foolish. It was endearing. And sweet. And I only wish that I had seen you in Jackson. Damn." Steve let out a loud sigh. Shaking his head, he pulled her closer. Eva relaxed in his grip. "God, I don't know what I would have done if something happened to you," he said aloud, more to himself than to Eva.

"I owe you an apology," Eva said, looking down in her lap, folding her hands.

Steve was about to speak and Eva put up her hand, "Let me explain. Marlo told me that when that terrible situation happened to her in the trailer, she knew in her heart that Sander would never hurt her. Marlo trusted him completely because of what he was willing to share with her, not the parts that he chose not to share." The guilt was creeping in; she hadn't shared anything of her romantic past with Steve, which she knew was the reason for her irrational behavior.

"Okay," Steve said, moderately confused, shifting on the couch to face Eva.

Eva took some water, needing to sort out how to tell the story. "When that happened to Marlo and Sander, that made me realize we don't have to tell everyone everything, and that our pasts don't have to be revealed for new relationships to work, but I guess I forgot about that when I saw you in Jackson." Seeing Steve nodding at her, tenderness in his eyes, she went on. "But there is a past story that

I need to tell you, because it matters and I should have told you." Eva settled in and told Steve the story of Seaton, how she met him at the conference, their panel discussion, and the subsequent whirlwind romance. Then she detailed her surprise visit to his home in Arlington, which led to her aversion to relationships and mistrust of men. It was foolish—she knew better than to judge or stereotype. She thought she had gotten over the experience until she saw Veronica throw herself at him in Jackson. The betrayal washed over her and she reacted by running away, up the mountain.

Taken by her story and her honesty, Steve kissed her head and pulled her close, letting this sign of protection and acceptance be his response. Words were not always needed. The two sat together into the evening with just the sound of the fire as it burned down. Dash snored, and Scout put her paw on the larger animal's back. Steve and Eva, both exhausted and content, let the silence speak volumes. They followed the dog's example to be comfortable in one another's presence. Such a peculiar course of events to deepen their budding relationship. Or was it past a bud, developing into a blossom?

52

The stillness on the phone was a good sign. Interesting how you can have energy in quiet—like when you're driving in a car with another person and neither of you are talking, yet the aura of the vehicle is warm and comfortable, or not, depending on the circumstances. You can feel the emotive root of the silence.

The exercise Eva had under way with Sarah was an imaginary trip to twenty years into the future. She did this with most clients. Once Eva got them to the future, she had them explore their prospective home and surroundings that entered their vision. They go up to the door and knock, and it's them—their future self—who answers. They ask questions of themselves about lessons learned and valued experiences of those twenty years. As part of the experience, Eva has her clients give a name to the essence they have of them self in the future. She uses this reference, this name, in other coaching calls and homework assignments. The memory of the guided vision becomes a resource for clients to find deeper answers and to further their personal growth.

Nevertheless, Eva—even after all her years of coaching—was shy when starting this exercise with a client. The story used for the guided meditation was strange, and her "look good" gremlins got in her way. Thankfully, she battled the gremlin away and forged ahead on behalf of Sarah. Sarah! She was making such strides in her life and in her new business. The entrepreneurial role fit her like a glove. Sarah had become a woman standing up to violence and not apologizing for it. This spirit made Sarah a role model. It was her turn, her time to shine.

"Do you need more time?" Eva asked quietly.

"I'm almost done," was Sarah's response. Several seconds later, "Okay, I'm good now."

"Great. First, how was this exercise for you?"

"Really interesting. Inspiring."

"Yes, it can be. Tell me more."

A deep breath came over the phone and Sarah cleared her throat. "I don't think I've ever consciously thought about what my future might be like, or what I might be like."

"Yes …"

"I was, I was, well, wonderful and wise." Sarah paused. "Even calm, loving."

"Did you come up with a name for yourself?"

"Yes, I did," Sarah answered timidly. "It sort of floated by in my mind after you asked the question." Quiet.

Eva practiced patience, permitting Sarah all the time she required.

"Her name is Gracious. That's it. Just Gracious."

"Mmm, that says it all, Sarah, doesn't it? Gracious."

"Somehow, Eva, it does. I wouldn't have thought. Thank you. This was really great."

"Compassionate, tender, loving. All that comes up when I hear you say 'Gracious.'"

"Yeah," Sarah agreed softly.

Sensing a lot of emotion in Sarah, Eva didn't want to push things too much and take her away from this new place of learning. "So, Sarah, while all of this is fresh, write down a few questions that you can answer from the viewpoint of Gracious. Ready?"

"Sure."

"What would Gracious want you, Sarah, to have more of today? What would she want you to start doing? Stop doing? And last, what would Gracious do in your situation with the business?" Four questions seemed sufficient. She paused as Sarah wrote. "If you accept, I'd like you to think about these questions today after we hang up, then consider them each day over the next week. Will you do that?"

"Yes, I'll do that. This is most interesting."

"Sarah, you seem like a rosebud ready to bloom beautifully, petal by petal, day by day." No words came over the phone, but Eva felt the smile as they ended their call. Rebirth. Eva leaned back in her chair and looked at the Gros Ventres; she never tired of their beauty and now had deepened respect for their danger. Blowing out her breath, she was still in disbelief at her new life. Her rebirth. It was four years ago that she experienced this same future-self exercise with her coach, Trina. She imagined this place of Bear through the person she still had not yet become. Visioning had prompted her to act and change her life for the better. Could she pass that gift to her clients?

53

The hummingbirds buzzed back and forth with such fury that Eva was momentarily frightened until she realized they were not interested in her. From inside, Steve watched Eva flinch as the early-spring hummingbirds dive-bombed for sugar water. "Careful, they bite," Steve jested as he joined her on the porch armed with a stocked backpack and fresh coffees. He was anxious for Eva to find the homemade blueberry muffins. They were her favorite, and he had Jana to thank for the foolproof recipe.

Eva puckered her lips, agitated that she was startled by the birds and Steve. "Thanks for the warning." She paused, scrutinizing the small creatures, turning with her eyes twinkling at Steve, "They're really fighters."

"Kamikaze pilots, more like it," Steve agreed as he moved his head slightly back to avoid a potential collision with the apparently alpha male bird.

"How long have you had your feeder out? Isn't it still too cold?" Eva asked, taking the cup of coffee he offered and strategically stepping out of the line of flight from a raging hummingbird.

"Right after the first thaw, I put out sugar water," Steve said, Eva still watching the tenacious fliers. Late April was cold in the Wyoming mountains, but a good time to start feeding the hummingbirds. If you didn't get your feeders out early, the territorial, entertaining birds would find another place to eat, and one could miss their flying escapades all season.

"This particular crowd doesn't seem to get along," Eva said, contemplating the pecking order. "That one with the copper and yellow chest is a real bully." Eva squinted at the culpable bird, then turned toward Steve. Catching him watching her, she tingled inside. This man was moving into her heart, despite of all her caution.

"Very observant." Steve walked up next to Eva on the porch, setting down his pack and coffee. He nestled snuggly behind her, crossing his arms around her waist. "Your Copper thinks it's his personal feeder. Watch what he does." They stood in comfortable silence observing the hummingbird dance.

"He doesn't seem to eat."

"Well, he does, but only when he's ready. He isn't happy just having enough to eat. He wants to be the *only* one eating."

"Oh, I see it. He sits in that pine tree and monitors the action. If some other bird comes to the feeder, he chases it away with a vengeance."

"Exactly." As they watched, seven other hummingbirds flew over to the feeder, wings moving like engine blades, all frenetic for the sweet nectar. Before they could get a solid hold on the yellow plastic flowers to suck out some nutrition, Mr. Copper came zooming across from his perch in the tree like a fighter pilot. It was a sight to see them buzzing to and fro with a loud intimidating whir.

"Mmm, good coffee, Steve. Thank you." Eva leaned back against Steve's chest, relishing the warmth of his body enveloping her. The morning air was brisk, and most of the snow was gone. However, the early days of spring weren't predictable; the crystal blue sky could be deceiving.

Weeks had passed since her ludicrous abandon up the mountain, time healing her personal embarrassment. The mountain debacle endeared her to Steve more than she imagined, yet they both took their time, savoring the freshness of discovering one another.

Kissing the top of her head and pulling her close, Steve cradled Eva, slowly turning her around. "Well, lovely lady, if we're to make the journey we planned, it's time to leave."

"Mmm, yes, drill sergeant," Eva said, comfortable beyond belief in his arms.

Steve leaned back slightly and lifted Eva's chin gently. Winking, he murmured, "Please know that it takes real determination to unwind from you." Eva was breathless, lost in the pool of his blue eyes, the dark, riveting pupils boring into hers. Whispering wickedly, he continued, "Besides, Mrs. Beasley is getting a good show. I see the cherries on her kitchen curtains swaying. She was probably on the phone sending gossip all over town as soon as your International pulled in the drive." Still the new girl in town, Eva's escapades didn't go unnoticed with her telltale truck and dogs, and some locals liked the idea of a love story involving their own Steve Mason.

As Eva and Steve stepped off the porch arm in arm, a black-and-white woodpecker flew up to settle on the trunk of an aspen. His long, tight beak hammered methodically against the white, hard bark of the tree. The sun reflected off the soft, reddish-brown feathers on his head as he paused to look around for bugs while surveying the hummingbirds. As he turned his head, the red feathers underneath the bird's beak glowed. Aggravated by the hummingbird commotion, the woodpecker flew off to a higher perch in a large quiet pine.

Ninety minutes later, Steve pulled the Green Hornet off a roughly graveled road and parked. Pulling the brake, Steve turned toward Eva and pointed out the window. "This is a good place for us to start our exploring. See, look over there to the west. That's the direction of Jackson. To our east is the Wind Range mountains that nestle up to the Saw Tooth that are part of the Gros Ventres, your favorites, those you see from your house."

"This is beautiful," Eva said, unloading herself from the truck. From this vantage point, the land was infinite. In Bear, the environment was intimate. You were in the mountains at a high elevation without seeing the vast expanse of grazing lands and vistas available within miles of town.

"Look over there." Steve's excitement to share the land was palpable. "That's the pass the early homesteaders foraged. See the ridge that comes over and has a natural descent down the mountain?" Mesmerized with the beauty of the landscape, Eva absorbed the view and pulled her pack over her green parka. She saw the path. In his element, Steve shared knowledge, both real and mythical, about the area. "That direction is where the Shoshone Indians settled after being pushed from their lands by both the whites and the Sioux. And if you imagine a rushing creek the other side of that butte, about seventy years ago you could see cowboys tending cattle this time of year through October."

"I love it." Eva shuffled the gear in her pack to get comfortable and pulled on warm gloves. "What adventure do you have planned for today?"

"Well, I propose, out of the three exploration options—cowboys, homesteaders, and Indians—that we pursue the homesteaders. The cowboys and Indians were in more wild areas and some higher grounds. I think we can find the old Hayley cabin. Could be fun."

"I like that idea," Eva said, patting her gloved hands, ready to go.

They settled into a quiet trek, zigzagging up the mountain infused with the coffee they had finished on the ride from Bear. The grand pine trees were straight and stately. Minutes into their hike, Steve turned to Eva, index finger to his lips. He pointed across the woods. Standing like generals were two large buck elk. Behind them were four smaller elk of different age and gender, running up to higher ground. After they all leaped away, Steve softly broke the silence. "The elk are making their way back up to high country from the National Elk Refuge in Jackson. They travel for miles to get to their principle mountain home locations and start their feeding and mating rituals."

"It's incredible that they know where to go."

"Instinct. They live by it."

Eva reflected on his comment. "I'm working to trust my instinct more. Yesterday one of my clients was in such a quandary. As her coach, I was almost going in a direction to fix things for her, which is a total no-no, when my intuition—instinct, if you will—kicked in."

"What did you do?" Steve asked, curious about her coaching. He'd seen a transformation, albeit subtle, in his friend Charlie Cunningham, one of Eva's clients.

Shaking her head and smiling, Eva looked to Steve and replied, "I asked her what she wanted to do. Simple."

"And?"

"And, well, she paused for a moment on the phone, then went into a small rant on what she *wanted* to be doing, not what she needed to do."

"The old wants and needs; are they so different?"

"More than you might think. It depends if a person is living her life how she *wants* to be living or if she is living how she *thinks others* want her to live. The later was the case with my client."

Steve rubbed the back of his neck as he considered this. "Huh. So what happened?"

"She erupted with ideas for actions in line with her values. I helped her through some prioritization, and she moved in the direction of her dreams." *Eek, that was a bit heady*, Eva thought.

Steve could tell Eva loved her work. It was peculiar to him, yet he was starting to learn how this life coaching business opened up opportunities for people to live more fully. If anyone knew the importance of that, it was Steve.

Shyly looking at Steve, Eva knew people didn't really understand life coaching. It was one of those things you have to experience to appreciate. "It's tough work, Steve," she grinned, "and someone's got to do it."

As they climbed, they dropped into casual conversation about migrating elk and the passionate history around the different views on the National Elk Refuge. Within an hour they found the old Hayley cabin. The cabin was built in the late 1880s. It had timber logs and dirt construction with remnants of tar shingles nailed to the wood plank roof. Nestled into the side of a hill, the cabin had a view overlooking a huge mountain plain and distant buttes. The cabin was one room measuring twelve by fourteen feet and too low for Steve, six foot one, to stand straight.

"Look at this place." Eva gasped, thrilled. "It's almost like someone left yesterday with all the furniture in place." The winter snowfall and snowmelt had cleaned up the dirt, wiping the inside clean. There was a rusted bed frame in the center of the room, sans cushioning, and a rickety wooden log table in the corner. Against the left wall stood a small three-burner iron stove with a smokestack running up through the roof. On the back wall was a wooden strip from an old fruit crate with the words "San Jose Apricots and Plums" nailed to the wall. Hanging from below the wooden strip were pieces of fiber, remnants of a homemade calendar fashioned out of old flour sacks.

Steve watched as Eva reverently examined the articles in the cabin. She touched them as if they were glass, careful not to put weight on the wood.

"This floor, the planks are so straight. How did they get these?"

"Typically there would be a few men to start the cabin. They might haul up planks from the nearby towns, or more likely, bring up a two-man saw and take their time sawing planks from a large straight pine."

"Ah, got it. How many of these vacant cabins are around?"

"Hard to say. They get crushed by snow through the years or burn down from unattended fires. Or, of course, some hikers vandalize them."

"Have any been found recently?"

"No, my little explorer. Would you like to find one?" He smiled at her as he shared his bottle of water with her.

"Completely. That would be way cool."

Nodding in agreement, Steve downed the water. "This is the area where there could be settlements. The land is ripe grazing land and could've been used for ranching. The mountains have wild mushrooms and blueberries, too. Deer, elk, and trout were good eating."

"You're just a font of knowledge, aren't you?" Eva teased as she gazed at Steve. He was the complete package. Steve's looks, well, it would take a blind person not to gawk the first time you met him, with those masculine features, chiseled face, and defined physique. She considered his education, variety of friends, and the unwavering devotion he extended to Grace, Lois, and James. He had a calm nature, but Eva wondered if it shaded sizzling emotions when the right buttons were pushed.

As if reading her mind, Steve interrupted Eva's thoughts with a husky voice. "And you, you're as gorgeous as those first leaves that sprout on an Aspen." He pulled her close, holding her through the bulk of her coat, touching his nose to hers and connecting foreheads. "Those leaves match the color of your eyes, that alluring combination of green and gold. How do you do that?" Loosening his grip, Steve's hands came up to cradle her face. His mouth covered hers in a deep kiss.

Just as the pounding of their hearts beating together blocked out reality, a branch cracked, breaking the magic of their embrace. Looking in the direction of the noise, they spied the telltale sign of a fluffy white tail bouncing up and off into the woods.

"Darn longhorn, can't ever seem to get you to myself," he murmured into her ear. Reluctantly stepping back, blue eyes smoky with passion, Steve unconsciously shook his head to clear his mind and change modes. "Come on, lovely lady, let's find you a cabin."

Catching her breath from the kiss and thankful for his talkative state, Eva watched the longhorn for several seconds after it left, unsure if her voice would be steady. She took Steve's cue and walked in front of him on a winding game path beaten down by the migrating elk. Minutes passed in easy silence as they climbed. The ground was partially covered with snow, and the reflection from the sun created a blinding array of white glitter.

With sincere interest, not just practical, safe conversation, Eva blurted her random thought to Steve. "How did the Gros Ventre Indians dress? Didn't they live in these parts?"

Surprised by the topic, local history his intellectual obsession, Steve answered, keeping step with her hiking pace. "They sure did. They inhabited this entire range on and off for decades, picking up and moving based on weather and food, local disputes, and proximity of the whites. The Gros Ventres are typical Native Americans—that is, from a white man's stereotype."

"And that is what, Professor Mason?" Eva asked.

Ignoring her joke, Steve continued in an academic tone. "In the Gros Ventres' culture, the tribal men dressed in deerskin pieces with shirts tied with cords, decorated with dyed porcupine quills. The top clothing could be ornate works of art. They would also wear basic deerskin leggings and moccasins to protect their feet."

"And the women?"

"The women. The women wore one long piece of deerskin that covered them from their ankles to their elbows. Underneath they wore leggings and deerskin moccasins."

"Ah. So, as kids, when we cut neck and arm holes in brown paper grocery bags and decorated it with crayons for Thanksgiving, we weren't far off the mark?"

Laughing, Steve acquiesced, "I guess not. They even sheltered themselves in traditional teepees made from buffalo skins and long pine tree poles, just like you'd think."

"Mmm. So they were big buffalo hunters?"

"Yes again. I suppose that isn't saying too much as most Plains tribes depended on the buffalo. Incidentally, the Gros Ventres would go on collective buffalo hunts. If a brave would ride out in front or against orders to frighten off a herd of buffalo, his punishment was, ah, severe and not one we'd care to discuss."

"No rogue hunters allowed, eh?"

"Correct. Scaring off a herd of buffalo reduced the tribe food supply. Depending on the time of year, this could be fatal because of the need to prep and store the meat, furs, etcetera."

They continued on their hike using game trails as guides to mark their direction, chatting about real and surmised tribal traditions. A hawk flew low and smooth in front of them, its stealth voyage startling the pair. Curving around a grove of aspens, it was hard to tell who was more surprised, Steve or Eva, when in a small clearing stood a rather large cabin. Still unsettled from the hawk, the two glanced at each other with a sense of wariness. The structure looked stable, livable. Clandestine.

Not speaking, Steve instinctively tugged the sleeve of Eva's coat and gave her the quiet signal. The hair on her neck bristled with fear. Placing Eva off the trail and behind a clump of trees, Steve cautiously approached the cabin. A mountain lion or black bear could find solace inside such a structure—or worse, a disgruntled human. He crept around the back to check for signs of recent inhabitants. There was no garbage, woodpile, or tracks to be found, just the upward slope of the mountain and a layer of long pine needles that had nestled into the top of the crusty snow.

After several minutes of silent investigation, Steve, looking back at Eva, transformed into a twelve year-old boy. His eyes gleamed with excitement, and he leapt up and let out a whooping yell. "Eva, we found you a cabin! I can't believe it!" Running up to her, he lifted her like a rag doll and swung her around. "Come on, let's go inside."

Eva's heart beat like crazy. This was some day. "Really, this is a cabin that *we* found?" Guarding his enthusiasm, Steve took in the cabin, scratching his head in complete disbelief. He hung his arm casually around Eva's shoulders in camaraderie, scrutinizing the site. "I've never heard of this one before. There's no sign of modern life. And remarkably, it appears that animals haven't destroyed the contents." Hugging her close, he added, "What's strange is that it's not far off the trail."

One side of the cabin butted against the rock of the mountain. At the northeast corner there was a fence built two-thirds the cabin height. The other side of the cabin was nestled against a row of pine trees that appeared to be planted in a line for protection against the elements. The entire site was old but not decrepit.

Steve carefully opened the door with a minor push from his hip to loosen particles of ice. Not skipping a beat, Steve turned to Eva, swept her off her feet and into his arms. "Eva, this is the threshold of your cabin, courtesy of the State of Wyoming. Squatters rights."

Giggling, she hung on to his neck and took in the site. "I'm speechless. Steve, I can't believe I'm speechless at a time like this. It hardly looks touched." Pausing, still in his arms, she gave him a pensive glare. "Are you sure you didn't know about this place?" Tears welled in her eyes.

Setting her down gently, he arranged her hat properly on her head. "Completely. Really. This is new for me. Do you think I set you up?" Her line of thinking just came to him. He shook his head. "No, this is a real find." Then looking over at her, he smiled that million-watt smile. "But if I were smart enough to think of it, staging the whole deal would've made for a great hike." He swooped out of range as Eva leaned over to swat him with her gloves.

Like kids at Christmas, the two examined the cabin, sharing and pointing to objects. "This is surreal, Steve. It's like they just up and left, leaving things in place."

"I agree. This is an unusual find. It was common for a structure and bed frames or tables to be left, but the contents of this place are almost like a museum. Dishes, chests, remnants of bedding; Eva, this cabin still has all the necessities for frontier living," Steve said, blown away by the historic find. Eva swelled with pride at seeing his reverence for something she knew matched his years of study.

Walking gingerly, Eva examined the wood planks of the bed frame that were rotten and fallen into disarray onto the floor, dishes and tools scattered around. Inside one of the bed frame corners a wooden box protruded from the rotten wood. Eva walked around to take a closer look.

"Steve, look at this, under the planks." Eva nudged the bed slats aside, wood fibers that melted with her touch. "It looks like a box or something." Kneeling next to her, Steve carefully pulled the wooden box closer to the edge, brushing off years of debris. He lifted it over the edge of the frame and set it in front of Eva. Solid. His heart was beating at the thrill of it all. His whole life he had dreamed about discovering an historical find. To share this with Eva brought him a deep satisfaction.

"Okay, lady, here you go. Let's have a look inside." The crate was twelve inches high by twenty-four inches in both length and depth. "It's an odd shape, like it was made to go under the bed or in the flat space of a wagon. Fairly sturdy."

Eva eyed Steve and softly touched the top of the container. It had a fitted lid, no locks or hinges, made of just wooden planks and nails. Pulling off the lid, to her disappointment, all Eva saw was a stack of old cloth feed sacks. It made sense; people living in this harsh area would covet them for a variety of uses. Eva lifted out the top sack, colored with black, yellow, and red lettering. Digging deeper, she saw it. Her breath caught. It was a beautiful, hand-sewn quilt in the double wedding ring design. "Steve, look at this quilt. It's a treasure. An heirloom."

Happy for Eva but let down in the contents, Steve cleared his throat. "Whoever lived here wanted to keep this quilt safe, wrapping it up like that."

"Wait, look here. It isn't very big. It's not finished. I thought it was filling up the crate." Lifting a side of the quilt, Eva exposed more contents. Shifting on his haunches, Steve leaned in closer. Whispering, she went on, "Steve, what is that? It looks like a small chest of some sort. Wait, there's more."

Steve moved around the crate and saw that the partially finished quilt had been used as packing material for other objects. "Eva, let's take this back to the truck and check out the contents of this properly. I have contacts in Laramie who'll support this venture." Training overcame instinct. He knew he had to do the right thing.

Disappointed but understanding the rationale, Eva helped Steve reposition the contents, and they slowly gazed around the cabin as they moved toward the door. Before leaving the site, Steve walked around the cabin perimeter methodically. Memorizing the setup, style, and size of the outbuilding structures, fence, woodpile, and lean-to, he stopped next to Eva. "The box is an awkward size, but stable. I think we can carry it back to the truck if we take it slow and deliberate."

"Are you kidding? I'm so excited, slow and deliberate is my middle name."

After a plodding and tumultuous hike back to the truck, a sweaty and tired Steve and Eva fastidiously moved the seats and arranged miscellany for a stable platform to place the wooden box on the floor of the back seat, wrapped with Steve's travel blanket. The ride back to town was quick. They were both lost in their own thoughts and anxious to open the contents of the crate.

Once they reached cell phone range, Steve called his old colleague, Brian

Schumacher, at the state university. After a series of questions, Brian gave Steve the go-ahead to keep and explore the chest, indicating that it had been found on common grounds and he had full right to do so. The great State of Wyoming would appreciate any of the contents with historical significance; however, it was his full right to keep the crate in good conscience.

"Thanks Brian. I'll call you later with what we found." He paused. "Yes, you can come over to look, and we'll take you to the site." Clicking the phone shut, Steve looked over at Eva and gave out another whoop as he slapped his palm on the steering wheel. "Oh, yeah, it's ours. This is a thrill." Eva observed Steve, absorbed in his element. All she could do was scrunch up her shoulders, fold her hands in front of her, and smile, pointing to the road so that Steve might stay on it until they reached Bear.

54

Staring at the wooden box that sat on a white sheet over the kitchen table, Eva motioned to Steve to unveil the contents. He took out the quilt and laid it carefully on the sheet. The fabric fibers had been protected from mold and pressure inside the wood and under the burlap feed sacks, but the quilt was old and would require special, professional care. Nestled under where the quilt had been were three different styles of boxes. Between the boxes was a bundle of three shiny sticks with metal ends. Steve picked up the sticks and examined them carefully.

"Look at this. These ebony sections have metal threads on the end. If we were to screw them together, it makes a walking stick. A cane. See that one? The top is an ornate crest of some type, and this appears to be the bottom one, an oblong point to balance on the ground."

Eva took the role of student, watching Steve as he spoke and studied the pieces. "Curious, this doesn't look like anything from around here. Or even American from the last century. Look at the design. It clearly has an old-world artisan influence. Unusual for these parts. Most people didn't have anything of value."

Placing the cane sections next to the quilt, he continued, catching Eva's eye and winking at her as he lifted out the largest and most decorated of the three boxes. He nodded to her to proceed and open the box. The box was made of ebony, like the walking stick, and carved with round swirls and leaves. Eva opened the round lid of the small chest, the latch free of any lock. She gasped, seeing the contents.

"Whoa," was a low mutter from Steve. "Go on," he prompted.

Eva carefully lifted out another, smaller, gold gilded box. Underneath the box was a velvet bag, the size that the gold box itself could fit in for protection—another curiosity, that the carefully stored gold box wasn't inside the velvet bag. As she opened the second lid, Eva couldn't believe what she saw. A Fabergé egg. The egg was set with precious stones of rubies, emeralds, and pearls. The gold was carved with animals and flowers. It was the most beautiful thing she'd ever seen.

"Open it." Steve held his breath. The egg. The stories. He couldn't speak his thoughts until he knew for sure.

"It's a ring. It looks like a blue sapphire set in white gold with diamonds. Steve, this is a fortune." Eva looked at Steve, his face was completely white. He stood and walked to the sink. He placed his hands on the edge before getting a drink. There were tears in his eyes.

"Steve?" Eva stepped toward him. He put up his hand and she gave him space. After a few long, quiet minutes he came back to the table. Nuzzling Eva's head, he held her close, not sure of his emotions if he spoke. Letting her loose, Steve picked up another of the small boxes.

It was a sturdy box, not ornate or carved like the one holding the golden egg. It contained several personal items: a decorative comb for a woman's hair, a man's razor, a boot hook, a shoehorn, dressmaker scissors, a kit of sewing needles, and two pairs of white leather gloves, one each for a man and a woman. A small black velvet pouch contained two thin pristine gold bands with the initials AMC carved on the inside of the smaller and HAC on the larger band.

Eva noticed the color had come back into Steve's face, yet he appeared to be in another dimension. A trance. His mind was racing, she could tell, but he was not speaking aloud. The third box was almost like two lids tied together with a piece of leather. The leather was no longer pliable, so Steve slipped it off, careful not to break the brittle cord. This third box contained letters. It was a large bulky stack of letters in long yellow envelopes. Picking up the letters, Steve smiled, and the grin on that man was like nothing Eva had ever seen. It was peace and joy and happiness and relief. Unable to contain her patience and quiet any longer, Eva whispered, "Steve, can you tell me what this is. What is going on here?"

As if her words broke a silent revelry, Steve took in a deep breath and cleared his throat, again ridding himself of emotion that was hard to contain. "This—this, all of this is for Grace," he said, pointing to the table and raising the letter bundle in the air. "These are her parents' things. Her past. No one believed her. The egg, the gold box, the letters, the ring. All these are things she used to talk about, and no one believed her. Her whole life in Bear, people—her peers—mocked her for making up stories about wealth and royalty. Grace always held her head up and ignored them, no matter the taunting," he paused, clearing his throat. "For whatever reason, they never let it drop, she was the perfect target. I have to call James."

55

Later that evening Eva and Steve sat quietly in the upstairs sitting room of the flat above Bear Claw Quilts rented by Grace and Lois. Eva watched the scene unfold. Steve sat Grace down and explained their hike. As he spoke of their finding the cabin, she was curious about the story. When he detailed the discovery of the wooden box, the quilt, and other contents, she nodded as tears began to fall.

Grace sat frozen, grasping the velvet pouch that held the rings. Tears streamed down her face. Next to her, Lois had taken the partially completed wedding ring quilt and set it on the ottoman next to Grace. Lois concentrated on putting together the walking cane. She'd risen to the occasion. She was never an ugly duckling, but the parallel between her blooming into a beautiful swan this moment was appropriate. Lois waltzed about the room alternately speaking to Grace and talking on the phone to James. A heavy chain had been released from her chest. The young woman was taller, lighter, glowing.

Kneeling in front of her Aunt Grace, Lois took both her hands. "Auntie Grace, this is the most wonderful day of all. It's all like you said. These are your family's treasures. Oh, I'm so happy." She laid her head on the older woman's lap, unable to hold back her tears of joy. Gently caressing Lois' hair, Grace pursed her lips, the emotions pouring out of her. "Child, you and James are my treasures." Looking over the top of her cherished grandniece, she caught Steve's eye, then over to Eva's. Once she could find her voice, she said in barely more than a whisper, "If I could trust my legs, I'd hug the stuffing right out of you two."

Grace Marie Johnson Cartwright was orphaned for the second time just before she turned nineteen. The death of her tiny but mighty Babushka Polina, the last of the elderly grandparents who had raised Grace after her parents' deaths when she was a baby, left young Grace without family.

Grace's grandparents, Ivan and Antonia Kozlov and Alexander and Polina Fedorov, had been lifelong friends. They escaped Leningrad before the 1917 Russian Revolution and immigrated to the United States, arriving in New York City. There, two other families, one Swedish and the other British, aided the young Russian families. They taught them key English phrases and gave them advice for opening a shop and starting a new life in America. They also provided them work and honest pay in return for their detailed and expert tailored patterns and clothing designs for men and women, a trade learned from their inclusion in Russian high society. As the young Russians became independent with new dreams of their own, they took the last names Johnson and Cartwright from their "American parents" and traveled to start a shop of their own in the thriving town of St. Louis, the growing city and gateway to the western frontier.

Grace's grandfather, Dedushka Ivan Johnson (nee Kozlov), was of some wealth and distinction in Russia and had miraculously transported a few hidden treasures on his long journey. When she was a child, Dedushka Ivan would tell her tales late at night of the Russian court of Nicholas II and Alexandra, mysteries of soothsayers, and exciting stories of wolf hunts in forests. Grace hung on every word, in awe of the faraway wonders. She imagined the treasures that Dedushka had given her parents before they left for Wyoming, treasures that were now lost. Grace had heard the story again and again of her parents' love and how her grandparents had toasted with vodka when their youngsters, Anna and Henry, pronounced their love and desire for marriage. Their joy was to be short-lived.

The young couple had inherited the adventurous spirit of their parents. They, too, planned to travel westward, this time to the expansive meadows and towering mountains of Wyoming. Baby Grace stayed with her grandparents in St.

Louis while her parents headed west to make a home for the three of them. But soon after Anna and Henry arrived and made their home in a small cabin in the mountains outside of Jackson, tragedy struck. One fateful day in May 1927, an earthen dam at Lower Slide Lake gave way and flooded the canyon, washing their truck along with the torrent; they were drowned.

The young couple had only been in the area a short time and was unknown to most of the local people. No one knew much about them except their names and that they had built a small cabin in mountains—exactly where, no one was sure, and it was presumed that the cabin had also been washed away in the flood.

When Grace's Babuska Polina died in 1944, Grace made good on the vow she had made to herself when she was just a young girl. She had always wanted to go to Wyoming to find her parent's cabin, but her grandparents wouldn't hear of it— after all, they had lost both of their children in what they presumed was a very wild, very dangerous place. Grace was not permitted to speak of it. Now she set out to find what she could about her parents—perhaps to find the family heir-looms her grandfather had given her parents before they left St. Louis.

She came to Bear with detailed stories of her parents and of tales of her ances-tral Leningrad. If that wasn't enough, the petite orphan girl's claims of a golden egg and a sapphire ring brought her ridicule and ostracism from jealous peers in the growing town of Bear. She had no evidence, nothing to prove her claims.

There was one man, the postmaster at the time, who took an interest in the poor young girl. There was something about her. It was a style, yes, *grace*, that set her apart. He didn't think she was crazy, and he saw through the brave exterior to her broken heart. Ironically, the man's name was Ian Cartwright, the same sur-name that her grandparents had adopted all those years ago. Two decades earlier, Ian had met a young man, Henry Cartwright, who was a giant of a man with hon-est eyes and arms of steel. His features were dark, ethnic, and chiseled, which belied his British surname of Cartwright. When they met at the post office, Henry had been sending a letter to his parents back in St. Louis. Henry shared with Ian his excitement to send word to his kin about his trip to return and bring his baby daughter to the wild Jackson Hole with its grand mountains and deep snow.

There was something about this forlorn girl that reminded him of the man. Yes, maybe she was telling the truth. Was it the intensity in her eyes? And who was he not to believe a young lady—a child, really—in need? May God strike him down! Ian and his wife, Simona, took in Grace as if she was their daughter. They loved her in tandem with their own child, Margaret, five years Grace's junior. Three weeks later, the three huge trunks that Grace had shipped before she departed St. Louis arrived in Bear. Their contents included a minor fortune in her grandmother's couture clothes and accessories of all colors and for all seasons. Most were designed by Grace and her grandparents. They had taught Grace to sew at an early age, and she had a steady hand and an eye for intricate detail that most seamstresses preferred not to bother with.

Grace and Margaret proudly wore the clothes through the years, ignoring snide comments from the townfolk. She lived a peaceful life, cherishing Margaret as a sister. As time passed, she loved Margaret's daughter and, subsequently, Margaret's grandchildren, James, Billy, and Lois. Grace's life was solitary but not lonely. She might have been scorned by those blinded to life's possibilities; however, she was adored by her adopted family.

The *Bearly News* ran a front-page story about the historical find that substantiated the honest claims of Grace Marie Johnson Cartwright who moved to Bear, Wyoming, from St. Louis. The Jackson Hole Area Historical Society asked to display her dress collection, and the Sewing Guild in Weber requested her to speak on the Russian-influenced styles of her grandparents and differences between the styles of the urban Midwest and the rugged West of her younger years.

Grace didn't want her memories to be a flavor-of-the-month for the news and special interest groups. True to her character, she accepted only one of the invitations and worked with the reporter Ron Raymond, from the *Bearly News*. The real pleasure of it all came in knowing that her beloved Lois, James, and yes, the Mason family, knew her stories were true. Their trust and belief in her was substantiated and real. Grace felt a tinge of remorse that her adoptive parents, Ian and Simona Cartwright from Bear, Wyoming, weren't still alive to celebrate the uncovering of the truth.

Dale Sawyer asked Grace if she'd like her unfinished heirloom quilt to be mounted into a frame and displayed at Bear Claw Quilts, his treat. She was honored. The gorgeous piece adorned the front hallway of the store where all who visited—foremost among them, Grace—could see it on a daily basis. At first it was bittersweet to see the incomplete wedding quilt that Anna had been making for Henry adorning the large wall, a reminder of their incomplete life together. Grace agreed to the wall hanging for the comfort it seemed to bring to others. She still longed to know her parents, just as she had dreamed of them as she worked in her grandparents' dress shop all those years ago. Time does not heal all wounds. It was consoling to know that her loved ones knew her story without a doubt, yet that did not change the private love she had harbored for decades.

57

Recent events had Eva's head spinning. *Who would have thought, in a quiet little town like Bear?* She put her coffee down to pet Dash and glimpsed the Gros Ventres out her kitchen window in a whole new light, imagining Grace's parents making up a new life for their family in those amazing mountains. Scout roused from a curled state and came next to Dash, vying for the same, or more, attention.

"You dogs," Eva spoke aloud, botching an attempt to be stern. "If I had *already* taken you for a walk, I wouldn't be getting all this affection. I know where I rate, personal walker, feeder, groomer, that's it." Doing her best to give the animals equal petting, Eva knelt between them, putting an arm around each one, holding them close, all three of their heads in a line. "Oh, I love you." Emotion swept over her as she thought of her irresponsible flight up the mountain. These amazing dogs tracked her, kept her warm.

"Why couldn't it have been a *real* drama?" Eva went on, still holding the animals. "Like escaping a mountain lion, doing something exotic? How embarrassing. Tromping willy-nilly up the mountain like a jealous school girl." Shaking her head at the irreverence of it all, Eva pushed herself to stand.

"Well, it was what it was," she sighed. "And you know what, dogs? I think I'm learning not to run away from relationships, whether they're good or bad. Profound, huh?" She paused and shook her head. "I earned myself more than a heavy dose of humble pie." The pets sat anxiously, hoping to hear "outside," "walk," or "go." They watched her every action to identify a slight movement in the direction of the laundry room and their leashes to coax her into a walk.

Understanding the dog signals, Eva put her hands on her waist for authority. "Not right now. Eva has to work, then later I'll take you." She was careful not to use a word that would give the animals a false hope. "Go lie down." Four brown eyes bore into her as Eva walked across the kitchen to her office and settled into her desk.

Dash slid down on the hardwood floor, pushing his front paws forward to allow a slippery descent into a sphinx-like pose. Scout wandered over to a carpet and curled up in a ball, lying in a ray of sunshine.

This call was going to be tough. Lauren had been a client for ten months, a good amount for a coaching relationship. After an intense start, Lauren put on the brakes and wasn't taking action in her life. From Eva's perspective, the calls had become forced and Lauren, lazy. She complained and placed fault for her troubles and missed goals on everyone else. The phone rang right on time; Lauren, like most of her clients, was prompt.

"This is Eva."

"Hey, Eva, Lauren here," came the voice from Phoenix, Arizona.

"Lauren, hello. Good to hear you. What's on your agenda for today?" No small talk, Eva wanted Lauren to ante up an agenda for the call.

"Nothing much. Same old thing," Lauren replied, her tone lethargic.

"Same old thing?" Eva mirrored. "What do you mean by that exactly?"

"Oh, you know, just going through the motions. Not much ever changes."

"Mmm, is that what you want right now, Lauren?" Eva decided she better ask. Sometimes the same old thing might be just fine. To each his own.

"No. All I ever do is work, home, errands; that's about it." This from a woman who told Eva she had dreams to reach. She lived in a beautiful climate and had much to add to the world. Something had changed.

"Lauren, if you don't have ideas for an agenda, there are a couple things I'd like to suggest. Is that okay?" Eva asked permission when she took control of the agenda.

"Sure, that's fine. Like I said, not much is going on here."

Taking a deep breath, Eva foraged ahead. "Lauren, I sense that our coaching calls are no longer doing much for you. You don't come prepared with an agenda, and lately you don't act on your commitments. Does this ring true to you?" Silence. A rather tense silence. Bingo, rang true.

Clearing her throat, Lauren responded, "It's just that I'm too busy to change and don't have time for anything."

After a longer than normal pause, Eva spoke her truth, "Lauren, we've been down this path of 'not enough time' before. I'm not seeing that you *want* to change anything. If you don't want to change, there's nothing that I can do as your coach to help you move forward in your life."

"What can I do? There are only so many hours in a day!" Lauren's voice leaned toward whiny, cracking her attempt to be calm, cool, and collected.

"Lauren, we all have the same number of hours in a day. It's up to you how you decide to use them. Your priorities."

"Right, like I have any control over what happens in my life," came Lauren's caustic reply.

"Lauren, you came up with great ways to take more control in your life. You aren't even attempting those actions, Lauren. You're wasting your time and money on these calls."

Quiet again.

Eva continued, not expecting a response. "Here's what I propose. First, if there's something you haven't told me, like a personal trauma that's in the way of your actions, I advise you to seek professional help from a therapist."

"No, that's not it. It's just that everyone else always …" Lauren was defensive.

"Lauren, please hear me out," Eva interrupted firmly. "I want you to do something."

"What?"

"Take out a sheet of paper and split it into two columns. On one side, write down what you have in your life that you love. Not just like but really *love*. The trivial and the triumphant."

"Hmph—like there's anything to write in that column."

"There might be, Lauren."

"Pff."

"Then, in the other column, list what you have in your life that you don't like, again, the little and the big."

"That one will be easy."

Eva ignored the remark. "Here's the deal. You do it today. Then attach it to your fridge and read it every time you pass it or go in for food. I mean really *read* it. No skipping lines. Just deal with it every time you pass by. Will you do it?"

"Puh," came over the phone.

Eva almost blurted out *Really, Lauren, how old are you?* Instead she said, "Is that a yes or a no?"

"Yes," Lauren sarcastically answered.

Eva almost heard Lauren rolling her eyes. "Okay then. At this point, I need to terminate our coaching relationship. Live with that list. If there's something you want to change and you want a life coach to help, let me know and I'll give you some good recommendations. I'm not in a position to be your coach if you're not in a position to take ownership for your life. It's not right for either of us and goes against our original contract."

Perplexed, Lauren responded, "Did you just fire me as a client?"

Shaking her head in her own disbelief, Eva said, "Yes, Lauren, I just did."

"Oh."

"Lauren, you're a capable, vibrant woman. Only you can live your life. My hope for you is that you do that, live your life."

"Oh."

"Bye, Lauren. I wish you all the best."

"Yeah, thanks. Um, bye."

Dial tone.

Staring at the phone, Eva felt oddly energized. *That wasn't so hard, and freeing somehow. Deal with the problem and take a stand. Gosh, that's just what I did, and in my heart, I hope it's just what Lauren needed.*

Three coaching calls later, professional work done, Eva was anxious to change and drive into town. Today was yoga. Jana, Eva, Heidi, and Marlo had become apostles of Crystal's calm, challenging teaching style. There definitely was something to the whole yoga movement. If she was honest, she liked the post-yoga visit to the Grizzly for coffee as much or better than she did the class. Catching up on the latest news—er, gossip—was one of her favorite things. How could she have gone for so long without girlfriends? They were such fun.

Giving farewells to the dogs, Eva paused on the porch, catching a hummingbird buzz away in her peripheral vision, and her recent life events rolled like a film. What a year, and it wasn't even half over. Personal speeches, jewel thieves, new friends, a holiday party, a romance, *and* a historic discovery. Wow.

Eva thought life would slow down once she left Corporate America. She had that one wrong. She was busy. Even her yard bustled with life; a dark turkey vulture flew low to the land, a pronghorn, white tail extended, loped across the edge of the road as Eva sat down on the step. Sun rays streamed into a golden fan through the clouds in that "God is there" fashion that sent a shiver through Eva.

Gorgeous. And real.

Sounds of the hummingbirds were rampant. Eva had hung an oblong red and yellow hummingbird feeder on the porch, the kind with a clear receptacle and red plastic molded flowers. She loved their buzzing and whirling. The noise placed her at the day her and Steve found the old cabin and the treasures for Grace's life. She would never forget being on his porch with the buzzing of the bees and the spying Mrs. Beasley.

What a gift it was to free Grace from the local gossips and give her tangible proof of her memories. Grace hadn't outwardly changed her behavior with the news, yet Eva noticed Grace's face glow brighter. It was the same Grace but with a contented peace emanating from inside her soul.

Grace had become her anchor. Eva was thankful for the companionship of the older woman in a way that words couldn't describe. During their quilting barter, the two had grown close so quickly. Grace was a role model, an elegant paradox of contrasts, dependent and independent, pensive and convicted, youthful yet aging in body. She loved firmly and completely, never wavering in her devotion or personal truths.

Eva and Grace met almost weekly since Grace agreed to complete her almost-train-wreck appliqué quilt project. Grace's tiny stitches and her artistic eye transformed the quilt into a masterpiece. Eva had plans for the finished product, and she couldn't wait to make the surprise.

Taking a final minute to breathe in the fresh mountain air, Eva heard the wind whisper through the silver aspen leaves. Did they sound like the rolling of the ocean today or was it the soft chimes of a bell?

58

"Where is he?" whispered Heidi, a bit too loud, curious about the obvious absence of the sole male classmate, the house-call doctor she now knew on a professional level.

"Geesh, Heidi, can't you let it go already? The poor man probably had enough of your gawking at him," punched back a lively Jana, dressed to the nines in her new Ohm yoga suit, clearly influenced by the chic Marlo.

"Ladies, please, I'm *trying* to perfect my downward facing dog and need complete focus." Eva giggled each time she identified the asana. She was secretly glad that Dr. Noble was absent, still embarrassed by her actions.

"Jana, you just think you're a fashionista in your new suit," Heidi said haughtily, grinning broadly.

"That's right. I don't just think it, I *know* it," Jana said, sticking out her chest, hands on her curvy hips to the delight of her roommate.

"Okay, class, relax, and back to child's pose." Crystal's voice was instructional, and she was back in the front after her stroll around the room to adjust student body parts. "Now, breathe, and if you're comfortable, close your eyes. That's right. Gently position yourself to lie flat on your mat. Slowly. Good."

A colossal groan escaped from Jana's lips. Eva eyed her, admiring Jana's absorption into the practice.

"Press your spine to the floor, all the way from the top of your head through to your tailbone. Gently. Good. Now completely relax." Pause. "When the music is done, you may pick up your mats." The students obeyed and formed a circle to execute their namaste and bow, followed by clapping and camaraderie.

"Phew, you know, the longer you do this yoga *practice*, the harder it gets. Does that make sense?" Eva asked, pulling her hooded sweatshirt over her head, static hair flying straight up.

"Tell me about it. I think it might be age," Heidi said back to Eva, who cringed in angst at the possibility.

"Nothing that Grizzly can't fix," offered Jana. "By the way, where was Marlo today?"

Heidi shrugged. "I know how much she loves this class."

"She's meeting Sander for a lunch date before he goes on a trip someplace," Eva said casually, pushing down the end of her rolled mat to even it out, remembering what Marlo had told her the last time they had class.

"That guy seems to travel a lot," Heidi said, reflecting on how often she had to revise the barista schedule at Grizzly to accommodate Sander's trips. Seems he was just in D.C., of all places, and somehow she didn't think he was taking in the Smithsonian.

"Hey, Crystal," Jana said as they walked toward the door. "Nice class once again. Would you care to join us over at Grizzly for some coffee libations?"

"Oh, why, thank you. Unfortunately, I can't. I'm headed out to Jackson for some training. I'm working on my certification in Pilates mat work. Maybe next time?" She grinned broadly, barely containing her excitement.

"Really?" was all that Jana could muster, blanching at the possibility of having to learn the infamous tummy-tough Pilates teaser position. Crystal shrugged in a hurried *yes* reply, waved, and was off, mat and boom box swinging in her wake. The three friends watched her exit the studio, their silence speaking volumes.

Heidi broke the quiet and deadpanned, "Let's just hope Marlo doesn't catch wind of that Pilates offering."

The trio made its way to Grizzly and settled into a round table near the front window. "When did you install that?" Eva asked, pointing to an iMac mounted on the counter, overlooking a view of Main Street.

"Do you like it?" Heidi asked. "We put it in last week. I want to update without going too mainstream. It was Chad's idea. It even gets a wireless signal from the new cell tower over by Jackson."

"Well, I must say it's unexpected. My first inclination is to say I don't like it, but then, I guess it's a good idea," Jana answered, slinging her workout bag onto the floor by her chair.

Heidi explained, "People without an iPhone can look up things or connect with friends without making this place a technological haven." Eva sipped her skinny latte, taking in the hardware addition, "It's considerate, Heidi, I do like it."

"You could call it *Connected in Grizzly*. What do you think?" Jana said, addressing Heidi, who predictably rolled emerald eyes. Getting up from her chair, Jana walked over to the machine and, with some pomp and circumstance, sat on the wooden backed stool. Accessing the Yahoo home page, Jana started reading, suddenly becoming engrossed and unusually quiet. Heidi and Eva looked at each other, then dismissed Jana's sudden interest in browsing the Net, absorbing themselves into the trials of self-employment. Seconds later, Jana piped up again, "Hey, come over here," not taking her eyes away from the screen.

Eva and Heidi, with skinny lattes in hand, a must for after yoga, made their way over to flank Jana, watching the screen. "Eva, didn't you say the name of your betraying womanizer was Seaton? Seaton Andrew Rushmore III?"—not a name one forgets easily.

Silence. Then, "That's right," Eva answered quietly, paling with the mention of his name. Unable to disguise her delight, Jana swiveled in the chair and pointed to the screen. "Might that be the distinguished gentleman?"

Eva gasped. "Oh. My. God. That *is* him." She leaned into the screen for a closer look. "He looks horrible."

"I was about to say the same thing, but didn't want to hurt your feelings, darling, as you were once smitten by the balding, pot-bellied slug," offered Heidi, folding her arms in front of her, pursing her lips to hold back a smug smile. "One thing I always say, you got to love it when a shithead, pardon my French, like Seaton, ages poorly."

Clearing her voice with vitality, Jana read out loud. "Seaton Andrew Rushmore III, of Arlington, Virginia, has been indicted on four cases of embezzlement. In addition to Rushmore's business failings, his wife, Sue-Ellen Haughton Rushmore, has filed for divorce and full custody of their three children based on several counts of infidelity and misuse of their joint bank accounts." At this reading of current events, both Heidi and Jana turned to look at Eva. Eva stood frozen, mouth agape.

Letting the reality of the situation sink in, she found her voice. "Why, it's like a sitcom episode. It's so unbelievable, it rings true. I never considered that Seaton would break the law for personal gain. He was filthy rich, worked for fun, really."

"Oh, brother. I hate that," Jana egged.

"And I never thought that he would lose his good looks. He was—how should I say it?—a drop-dead gorgeous womanizer. Now he's a sorry excuse for an almost middle-aged guy who appears to be headed for prison." She stopped, awestruck by the comedic reality of it all. "There *is* justice in this life."

"Justice indeed," Heidi added as she licked the foam off the side of her cup with nonchalance, "or rather fate." Her eyes sparkled at the news that the new iMac brought to Eva. Fate indeed.

"Wow." Then Eva added, "What's abnormal is that I'm not an emotional basket case at hearing this news." No one knew the depth of the grip her experience with him had on her heart. "Seaton was such a bad weed in my life; I've tried to eradicate him from my brain."

"And has that fine specimen of a man Steve Mason been helping?" Jana queried mischievously.

Eva ignored the comment, but the undeniable clue of creeping red covered her cheeks. Her mind reeled from the shocking news. "In fact, over the last year, I've become ambivalent about Seaton. I hardly care what happens to him. Not that I wished him ill. I didn't, and I find it rather fitting that he screwed up his life all on his own."

"Darn straight," agreed Jana, swiveling in the stool back to the monitor. "So, Heidi, we definitely approve of this new Mac in the shop." Changing subjects to follow Eva's lead and keep Seaton in the past, Jana posed a question to Heidi. "What's been going on with you over at the old schoolyard these days?"

Squinting in recollection, Heidi laughed a hearty smile. "I love middle schoolers. Yesterday I was on bus duty, and they were pseudo-lined up waiting for the buses. This one kid, Rocko, points to the oncoming bus, jumping up and down cartoon-like shouting, 'Here comes the big yellow Twinkie! The big yellow Twinkie!' Then the rest of the line proceeded to chant 'We want Twinkies. We want Twinkies.' So, that's my news. It just struck me as dreadfully amusing."

Jana and Eva just stared at Heidi. Heidi talking about Twinkies? It just didn't seem to fit. Change is good. Then Heidi continued, "Oh, I know. In my art history class last week, the kids all had ants in their pants. So I tried a little trick I learned to get them focused. They had to pair up, and then get a paper and pencil. When I said go, they had to make eye contact without breaking it, and one of them had to draw the other person without looking at the paper, you know, by feel. When time was up, they had to switch, repeat, and then share their drawings."

"And?" Jana asked, awestruck. Heidi always was the observer into their world. Hearing about her world was rare indeed.

"It was a success. It gave them a chance to do something different, have some fun, and connect with a classmate—you know, get some of that twelve-year-old energy out of their brains so they could put something new into it." Finishing her story, Heidi looked at her friends. "What?" she asked, squinting with suspicion.

"Nothing," Eva said, settling back into her chair at the round table, displaying a rather Heidi-esque mannerism. "I just don't hear you talk about school much. I like it. What else?"

"Well, the interesting part of this drawing experience came this week. Cindy McCoy stayed after class one day to do Internet research for a project. We started chatting and she asked if she could share something with me. Of course I was intrigued. She blushed a bit, then told me that Drew Cook asked her to be his partner for the drawing exercise because he wanted to draw her." Heidi paused to take a sip of coffee, softly nodding in fond memory of the situation. Mini Michelangelos.

"And?" Jana piped in, wanting to know the workings of the child's mind.

Licking milk foam from her lips, Heidi went on. "Cindy said they gazed into each others' eyes so naturally that they weren't embarrassed, and she felt warm inside. She said it was a romantic experience. Her first romantic experience. Simple, nice, easy."

"Aw," Eva clutched folded hands over her heart, "From the mouth of babes, yes?"

"Yes, from the mouth of babes."

The three friends sat in comfortable silence for several minutes, each deep in her own thoughts, enjoying the quiet camaraderie. Eva held her mug close to her chest and sighed audibly, a gesture, unbeknownst to her, that was a signal to her perceptive friends she had something on her mind she wanted to share.

Jana eyed Heidi with a sly wink, and Heidi focused on Eva with an amusingly arched eyebrow in expectation. Eva took the bait.

"Do you ever shovel snow?" she asked.

"Excuse me?" asked Heidi, dumbfounded. This wasn't even close to the question she thought would come from Eva.

Jana guffawed. Typical of Eva to raise an out-of-the-blue question. "Eva, honey, unless you forgot, we live in western Wyoming. You know the answer is yes. Was that a rhetorical question?

"What I mean is this. You know when you shovel snow, you try to start when it isn't too deep so it's not so hard, right?"

"Yes, darling, that's the preferred way if one has the time but no snowblower," Heidi drawled.

"Or a snowplowing friend," offered in Jana.

Ignoring them, Eva continued in her thoughts. "Well, there are those days when you're out there shoveling, and shoveling every two or three hours to stay ahead of the snow. It's like, here I go again. Same old, same old." Looking at Jana and Heidi, she realized she might not have wanted to embark on this discussion. But she couldn't get it off her mind. Closing her eyes for some self-encouragement, she forged ahead.

"Do you think that's how we look in God's eyes? You know, like, here we go again. Doing the same old sin, trying to be better today and never managing to make any improvements. Do you think he is up there in heaven thinking, *Geesh, can't you people manage to make a change and stick to it for even one afternoon?*"

Heidi laughed, emerald eyes twinkling. "Darling, why? Are we going to talk about God?" adding her own rhetorical question. "How wonderful."

Eva's mouth dropped for a fleeting second in amazement. Encouraged, she continued. "Yes. I need to talk about God. It seems that I'm missing something and don't quite know what to do."

"Elaborate, please," goaded Heidi in a pleasant way, not wanting to break her friend's train of thought.

"As you both know, I love it here in Bear, my home and dogs, my growing practice, you guys, and now this thing with Steve. I should feel completely full. But I don't." Eva then went into some detail about her personal coaching session using the Life's a Pie exercise and uncovering, to her surprise, that spirituality wasn't where she wanted it to be in her life. They were silent, absorbed. "I'm still a bit empty somehow. It's subtle and doesn't crop up that often, but it's there, lurking."

"Well, Eva, you're quite right. We haven't spent much time on our spirituality these days," Heidi agreed, a cosmopolitan vixen open to the realms of faith. "Yoga aside," she said as an afterthought.

"What about Christmas Eve and singing the carols?" piped in Jana, antsy with the topic, sort of reticent. Heidi shot Jana a "please darling" look at her reference to spirituality being wine-laden friends singing carols. Jana noticed, let down her guard, and gave a sheepish shrug.

"Spirituality? I just don't know how to approach it. Growing up, we did the church and Sunday School thing and a few years in the summer vacation bible school." Eva felt sudden kin with Heidi and Jana. She added, "But what about God?"

Pointing to her chest, Heidi said, "Guilty as charged. Gosh, how many frog crafts did we make out of painted cardboard egg cartons at VBS?"

Jana fidgeted, opening and closing her mouth without words. After a deep breath, she managed a shaky voice. "My Grandfather Eberly read from the German Bible. Gosh, I loved to hear him speak the guttural German, but I had absolutely no idea what he was reading. All I knew was the Bible meant a lot to him, and it was imperative that we grandkids sat and listened. More than half of the time, giant tears rolled down his cheeks after he was finished reading. We would sit there mesmerized by his bulk and authority in contrast to the tears. He never seemed to fight them nor was he embarrassed. When he finished, he'd slowly close the huge leather book and pat it with the same gentleness he used to console us after a spill on our bikes." Heidi and Eva were caught in the story, knowing how much her deceased grandfather had meant to Jana.

"So, what do we do now that we're theoretically grown up and want the effects of Sunday School?" Heidi prompted, not having the answers or ideas but wanting them. The three just looked at each other back and forth, minds peculiarly blank.

Comically lifting her hands, Eva sighed. "You have no idea how much better I feel. Just sharing that this is something I yearn for makes a big difference. Thanks."

"Eva, you're on to something here," Heidi exclaimed, rapidly knocking a blood-red fingernail on the tabletop. "The three of us, and quite frankly, Bear in general, lack in the spirituality department."

"What about Marlo? She would have reams of ideas on this topic, I'm sure."

"Let's not keep it from the youngster," Jana mused. "However, we might want to let the topic settle in our souls before Marlo wears us out with ideas and awakenings. No secrets, of course." Heidi and Eva murmured agreement to the approach.

"There are lots of books in the library on the topic. And the children's section is chock-full of stories of religion in other countries," Jana added, suddenly needing to contribute to the discussion. The image of her grandfather was stuck in her mind. It must be something that had touched him so deeply. Was it something she, too, was missing?

"I have an idea," Eva said. "The last couple weeks, I was trying an experiment to *be* with this topic of spirituality. I suppose, maybe, that led to this discussion. So, what do you say that we continue the quest, but it'll be thrice as effective with the three of us involved?"

Jana and Heidi were accustomed to Eva's use of the words "be" versus "do," so they let the comment go without questioning.

"Thrice it is, darling. Jana, are you in?" Heidi asked, eyes dancing, amused at the use of the word "thrice."

"Yes, I'll give it a go. This is untraveled territory for me, I admit. Having said that, I know Gianni would be hooting and hollering something in Italian if he knew we were talking about religion. Or spirituality, if they're different. He definitely has some deep-seated spirituality and religion," Jana said.

"Girls, we are tiptoeing around this issue, yes?" said Heidi. Both Eva and Jana looked at her, puzzled. "What? You know it's true."

"Meaning?" Asked Eva, not getting the point.

"Meaning, we should get our cute arses into a church and see what's been going on lately. What do you say?"

A rush of warmth blanketed Eva at a deepened comfort with Heidi and Jana. Goose bumps. Like the sensation she got when she prayed while walking the dogs. It engulfed her entire being. Spirituality? A relationship of a grand magnitude, an eternal relationship waiting for acceptance. Mmm, maybe.

The low, rocky rumble wasn't heard in town. The animals fled as the ground buckled. Several trees were askew, and the shape of the path was changed. Large hollowed thumps followed cracking noises as branches fell to the earth. The Gros Ventres absorbed the noise in the damp ground and the towering pines. Close to the trail, the movement uncovered another more purposeful path. Beneath the debris were large gray flint and pink sandstones winding into the woods. Nature had hidden what man had created, and now nature uncovered what it had hid. Let it sit for a while and see what happens next. Patience.

59

Dale heaved the box with a thud onto the counter, his cat-that-ate-the-canary grin unconcealable. The antic wasn't lost on Lois, who was bolder and more confident in her job with every week that went by. She pushed herself away from the computer, swiveled the chair, crossing her arms behind her head and openly scrutinizing her employer.

"What?" Dale asked mirthfully, eyes dancing.

"Exactly the question I was going to ask you, Mister Dale. You're peppier than normal today."

"Peppy? Ah, Lois, in my day I'd been called 'preppy,' but never 'peppy.'" He relished the interplay of barbs with Lois, embracing life after the abyss of losing his wife. The void had seemed too great to overcome, but he had learned that love lost doesn't mean life over. A simple concept, moving on; it was one Dale had found of utmost difficulty to manage in the real world. But possible.

"Dale. Out with it, or I'll tell the ladies that you're teaching the next class on how to make mitered corners when binding a quilt."

Dale blanched, knowing the elder lady customers admired his tenacity and the energy he put into maintaining the shop. God forbid if he were trapped in the classroom with them.

"That over-sixty set that comes in on Thursday mornings thinks you're kind of cute," Lois added mischievously.

"Miss Lois, you told me we had gaggles of young customers." Dale's weak attempt to change the topic wasn't lost on Lois.

"True. However, daytime courses are mainly older women who are empty-nesters or retired," added Lois with professional inflection to her reply. "And they, ah, like you younger folk."

"Mmm, hard to imagine me being categorized as 'younger folk.' Especially being around the likes of you."

"Such is life in Bear, Dale Sawyer." After her answer, the quiet between them was a fight of wills as loud as cymbals crashing. Dale broke down first—his excitement contagious. "It's here. It's the fabric that you found for Grace."

"Already? Let's look," Lois uttered in a whisper, arms shivering with goose bumps in anticipation of her aunt's gift.

Dale cautioned her. "We best be careful. I want it to be a surprise at the party, like we planned. Let's not chance her coming in the door or down the stairs. I'm not sure where she is right now."

Sighing with anguish, Lois pursed her lips seriously. "Me neither. I guess we need to hide this box and take a peek when we know she's out." With a curt nod in agreement, Dale whisked the box off the table and thundered down the stairs to the basement storage. Lois cringed at his noisy descent and made her way back to logging inventory on the computer.

The front door of Bear Claw Quilts rang the hanging bell seconds after Dale left the room. In waltzed Grace and Eva in sprightly moods chatting in singsong voices. Lois's mouth dropped, aware of the almost-divulged secret, her heart pounding at the almost-lost surprise. She cleared a lump from her throat. "Hello. What brings you two in here laughing and carrying on?"

"Hello, child," Grace said, never able to get over the fact Lois had grown into a beautiful woman. "Why, Eva and I here had a good trip to Jackson. One part of the payment plan she concocted for that appliqué quilt she was so thumbs about."

"Hey!" started Eva, attempting to be offended at the ribbing. Then, in a consenting tone, she went on. "Grace's right. I was going to botch the whole thing if it weren't for her magic."

"Do tell about Jackson." Even with her newfound assurance from the job at the quilt shop, Lois tended to live vicariously through whomever she came across, especially if it meant venturing outside Bear city limits. Walking across to sit at a nearby table, Grace sat and put her purse protectively in front of her. It was Eva's turn to have a Cheshire grin that was obvious to all, even Dale, as he surfaced from the basement.

"How to start. Oh, pshaw. You know I tailored suits and dresses growing up, and that I had the trunk of clothes that had belonged to my grandmothers. You know, they arrived after I so unceremoniously landed in Bear those decades ago." Grace stopped, looked to Eva for encouragement. Eva nodded, hands interlocked in a ying–yang position below her chest, her body in a slight sway.

"See there's a dressmaker over in Jackson who specializes in making patterns. Yes, well, I've asked him—it is *a him*—to look at a few of my outfits to see if we can make patterns from them." Grace paused, pursed her lips, opening them with a cluck. "See, child, you aren't the only one to start a new career."

Dumbstruck, Lois ran from behind the counter and engulfed her aunt in a bear hug. "Oh, how wonderful. Auntie Grace, this is completely amazing news. Why, why I had no idea."

"That was exactly the plan," Grace said proudly. "See, I wanted to give this a go myself. Eva here nudged me with what I can only imagine are her newfangled life coaching techniques, and by gosh, I did it." Eva stood to the side of Grace and attempted to wipe away the flow of tears too many to stop, her elation for the woman absolute.

"I'll be damned—I mean, darned," said a baffled Dale. "If this isn't the most annoying, unpredictable town. Strange strokes of fate happen daily."

Gushing, Grace continued. "See, once Eva got me to convince *myself* it could be done, we, let's see, we brainstormed, that's it, brainstormed ideas on what to do with the patterns. Our ideas were everything from sewing them ourselves to hiring a seamstress, to making patterns and selling them in shops, like the Now and Then Dress Shop, or even on the Internet. You know, the Internet is like a giant phone network that reaches around the world and people can use their computers to communicate on it." Stopping, Grace smiled as Dale placed a glass of water without ice in front of her. The older woman had charmed him as much as her grandniece, his protégé, had.

"Well, go on," Lois said, wringing her hands in her lap.

"See, we decided to take it one step at a time. First step is to get the patterns. Then we can see what seems right to do. Maybe we can give them a go ourselves. You girls being quilters surely could make a dress." Grace nodded toward Eva, whose jaw dropped at the incredulous assumption.

"Grace, I'm not sure that would be best for your business," Eva gibed in a self-deprecating manner. "You might have better luck with the home economics class at the high school."

Dale interjected, outlining possibilities from his entrepreneurial perspective. "That's not a half-bad idea. The girls could make and model the dresses. We could showcase them in Jackson, videotape it, and place clips on the Internet. You know, the options are endless."

Putting her hands up in mock frustration, Grace concluded, "You all have young brains and great ideas. Let's see what type of patterns this Aaron can come up with over in Jackson. He's a psychiatrist, so he's doing this pattern-making in his spare time. An odd bloke, he is. But I like him." Grace smiled to herself at the memory of the amusing man. His rotund shape and austere profession belied his artistic flair.

"Yes indeed, Auntie Grace, yes indeed." Lois burst with pride for her aunt and reached for the phone to call James.

Eva watched the sunrise paint the Gros Ventres with multiple shades of gold and pink. Her neighbor, this mountain, made waking up a thrill as she caught a flash of a lone pronghorn cavorting across the steep of the mountain. Her extra-strong vanilla biscotti cream swilled over the rim of her mug as Eva rushed to her spy scope.

The animal was far enough away that she couldn't see details with her naked eye, but the undeniable shape and movement identified the animal with its robust body and grand, round horns. She loved her spy scope. It brought nature right into her home. Eva could identify with comments from people who would say they needed to visit their cabin in the mountains or spend time by the ocean to rejuvenate. Nature had a way of grounding you, confirming you were part of life, part of the big plan.

The phone rang with a start. In a split second, Eva clicked the button on her headset. "Hello, this is Eva."

"Eva, hello. Debra," came her soft, guarded voice.

Alarms pounded in Eva's mind. Debra's husband, Roy, wasn't responding to the cancer treatments and hospice was on the horizon. There was no option for progressive treatments to create an optimistic prognosis.

"Hello, Debra."

Pause.

"What would best serve you today, Debra?" The question came out lame to Eva, but she wanted to focus on Debra, she needed to. Sure, as a curious human she wanted to center the conversation on Roy and talk about his illness, etcetera, then tell Debra how sorry she was for this unfair, awful situation, the undeniable truth of Roy's pending death. Yet, as a coach, she needed to do something different.

"Oh, Eva."

"Yes?"

"I didn't think of me."

Ah, it's time you did. "Where is your mind, Debra?"

"My Roy is dying, Eva, and there's not a thing I can do about it." She choked at the words, sending instant tears up to Eva's eyes.

"I'm here, Debra." This was hard. Really hard. "How do you want to be with him right now, as his wife?"

"I want him to know I love him. Know that I'm not mad at him for getting sick. Know that he can go in peace. Yes, that's it. He can go, Eva. I love him. He's the love of my life. That old cliché works. You know? If you love something, let it go. I need to let him die guilt-free. Release him from the pain."

This wasn't what Eva expected. People are amazing. "Debra, that's generous. What does that mean for you?"

Unable to hold back her anguish, Debra's voice was choppy with tears and sorrow. "I need to tell him. Tell him all of that. Then, Eva, then I have to live with what happens next. Have to accept it."

"It sounds like true love, Debra."

"It is true love, Eva. And it wasn't supposed to end this way. I was going to get senile, and Roy would die suddenly. Wouldn't that be easier?"

Eva struggled to keep her voice. "Loving him has been a great part of your life, Debra. What can you carry forward because of that love?" This caused a small sigh and almost a hint of happiness, if Eva wasn't mistaken.

"That's easy. I'll carry him in my soul. He was the calm one. The agreeable one. Roy's the one who'd raise his eyebrows and make that pursed frown thing with his lips. Then he'd say, 'Well, why don't you think about it from that other perspective?' God, I used to hate that! Made me love him."

"Carry that love in your soul. I hear it there already."

"I suppose it is. I guess I'll try to be the wife, the person he always thought I was. I'm not near as nice or good or smart as he thinks I am. That's it. I'll try to be that woman for him after he's gone. God, I failed while he was healthy."

Whispering, Eva mirrored her impression to Debra, "Debra, stay with me here for a moment. Look at your marriage. Your life together. Was failure any part of it?"

After some time, she answered, "No."

"I didn't think so. What was your life together?"

"Real life. Love. Fun. Kids. Frenzy. Dried-out chicken. Housework. Puking cats. Unexpected raises. Love."

"Love."

"I'm going to let Roy go, Eva."

"What does that feel like to let him go?"

"Dreadfully sad. Anguish. But I need to let him die without worry."

"What else? I sense there's something on your mind."

"I'm going to mourn him right and proper. No questions asked. He's my all, my everything. Then, Eva, when I'm ready, I'm going to make sure my girls learn that people live, love, experience death, and move forward. Death isn't final, either, I know that. It's just those of us stooges left here on Earth who hate death so. And, damn it, I'm going to talk about Roy every day. And talk *to* him! No side-stepping the issue that he's my love. My husband. I'm not going to be all droopy and full of self-pity."

Eva wasn't sure she could add to that soliloquy. Fortunately, Debra went on.

"Eva, this has been a clarifying session. Thank you. I know what to do and how to be. For Roy. For my precious girls. I guess, even for me."

After Eva hung up, she sat in silence for a long time, amazed at the miracle of Debra and the love she shared with Roy. This was one of those coaching calls where Eva didn't feel like she coached much, yet somehow the process worked wonders. Debra's own fruition moved her forward in the worst of situations. Then there was the comment Debra made about "those of us left here on Earth," that one—that one Eva needed to contemplate a bit more for herself.

61

Her client's gut-wrenching profession of love put Eva into a disturbing whirl-wind. *Moving forward*. Everyone around her was doing it, while she felt stuck in a one step forward, two step back dance. Sure, she delivered a brave Academy Award–winning performance at Grizzly upon hearing the news of Seaton's indiscretions. Fact was, it still hurt. Seaton seemed so right, charming, and attentive; how could she be so blind? No, stupid. Shaking her head, Eva knew Seaton was a con man. He tricked her. He tricked others, he *betrayed* his family, not just her. Ultimately, he got his just reward, incarceration. You don't go around deceiving people without consequences. Yup, Seaton's demise proved there was justice in this world.

Eva walked over to the window and watched the pair of moose, *her* moose, lumber across the edge of the lake, making their way into the shelter of the brush. Shaking to release Seaton from her thoughts, she settled on Debra and Roy. Now, they were at the other end of the spectrum. The depth of their love story unfolded over the course of the coaching relationship Eva had with Debra. Talk about someone having strength, *that* was Debra.

Could she ever be in a relationship where, with such pure simple, unselfish devotion, she could tenderly tell her mate that he could die peacefully without guilt? That she would uphold his memory and their love? That it was right and well for him to die *now* to end his pain, and he would dwell in her heart forever? Pure agony. Wouldn't she want him to hold on, to keep *her* from loneliness and pain? Debra and Roy were the epitome of what a relationship should be, or maybe better, what one could be.

Two people drenched in the acting out of love, cherishing any nuggets that might come back to them; not expecting any in return. They gave of themselves in both life and death, despite individual cost. It's the giving that begets the receiving. The more you give, the more you receive. Ah, this simple rule of life. It rings true every time.

The telltale sound of crunching wheels on the long gravel driveway summoned Eva from thoughts of storybook love. She was misty and anxious with the delusion of her prior relationships. But those tires were evidence of a real thing, the thrill of her present relationship.

Magically Steve's signature double rap on the door caused her heart to skip as she hastily indulged in one last primp in the hall mirror. Opening the solid maple door, Eva melted at the sight of him, catching her breath in her throat. *Masculine.* Covering the large expanse of his muscular chest was a green and blue flannel shirt with a cream buttoned Henley peeking out from underneath—mmm, appealing.

"Top of the morning to you, Eva," Steve said, one arm propped against the doorframe, the other behind his back, his voice deep as her name rolled off his tongue. A husky crooked smile lit his face as his blue eyes penetrated like beacons into hers as she stood motionless at the door. Momentarily transfixed, Eva collected herself, noticing a twitch of humor on his face.

"Well, hello, Mr. Mason," she managed, her mouth quivering. He was like a knight visiting the twenty-first century. She willed herself not to gawk at him in that irresistible pose. *Oh, thank you, God. He's at my door!*

Shifting his stance, Steve pulled his hand off the wooden frame and enveloped her in a one-armed grasp, holding her tight and close. She smelled fresh, feminine. Lilacs?

"I've missed you this week, my lovely lady, after all of our, ah, adventures," he said, murmuring in her ear. She felt right nestled next to him, a woman both soft and strong. He brought his arm from behind his back and pulled her tighter to him, shifting with minimal rustling what was now hidden behind her back. Was that her heart he felt? Nice. His lips found hers. The kiss morphed from polite "hello" into deliberate passion. A slight moan escaped her lips. Oh yeah, nice.

Eva automatically snuggled to get closer to him, searching his mouth with equal desire, immediately needing more than she realized. Minutes passed before they reluctantly parted. Eva pulled back ever so slightly.

Not speaking, Steve looked into Eva's eyes and kissed her cheeks and that sensitive place just below her jaw, pulling her again closer, making a loud exhale. He released her again only enough to see her face. Clearing his throat, he extracted one arm from behind her back.

He presented Eva with the largest bunch of tulips she'd ever seen. "Are those for me?" Eva whispered, heady from the kiss. The long stems were as vibrant a green as the petals were shocking yellow—two dozen of the most gorgeous pieces of flora imaginable.

"For you, Ms. Karlsen," he said, giving her a wink and an imperceptible bow as he drew out the "Ms." with a distinction all his own. "And ..." He paused, boring into her eyes. "If you can muster up another kiss like that, I'll find more where those came from."

Eva took the flowers, her mouth slightly agape as she composed herself. "They're beautiful, Steve, thank you," she said sincerely.

"A match for the woman," he said. They stood there in the doorway not moving, hearts thumping.

It was Dash and Scout that broke their mesmerizing force. Something had changed. Something was different today. Tension had deepened, the air, thick. "Please, come in," she managed, unsure of her voice, while Dash and Scout greeted Steve with glee.

Scratching his temple, a bit off center himself, Steve walked inside, gently closing the door. "So it takes a couple of mutts to invite a suitor inside, eh?" he quipped to Eva, watching her cheeks grow red as she held the tulips to her chest, outwardly touched by his gesture. They suited her.

Feeling feminine, armed by the flowers, she coyly tilted her head, speaking of the proverbial elephant in the room. "That's not fair play, Mr. Mason. You're not supposed to kiss me like that in broad daylight!" Eva said, rocking the flowers, then added, eyes cast down, "And you—you look illegally handsome today."

Not missing a beat, Steve glowed, enjoying her honesty, her shyness, and continued the banter, "And you most beautiful, Lady Karlsen."

"Sir," she said, with a slight curtsy.

"There's no Mrs. Beasley here at your place to spy on us. It feels dangerous to kiss you on your porch. Never know if someone is watching or not? Eh?" He walked over and unwrapped her arms from around the flowers, setting them on the counter. The dogs, sensing they weren't going to get attention from Steve or Eva, clunked down on the floor amidst their feet.

Steve leisurely cradled Eva's face, her skin soft against his rough palms. He moved his fingers up around the back of her head and behind her ears, his fingers laced in her hair. In a slight motion and effortless hoist, she was off her feet and quite literally swept up in his arms, their lips never separating. He carried her into the den, Eva's arms wrapped around his shoulders, feeling the rippling of his ample muscles as he walked with her in his arms. Through the expansive windows the Gros Ventres were tall sentries guarding the lake. The sun was just past high, illuminating the sky, casting shadows from the roof that stretched across the room.

"Such a view," Steve managed, clearing his voice, knowing he needed to speak.

"Yes, it is," Eva said, suddenly holding back the giggles.

Steve looked at her, let out a sigh, in agreement. "So."

"So, thank you for the flowers. I love them," Eva said, turning to him, smiling to let him know she appreciated his discretion.

"Mmm. Good," he said, hugging her shoulder as she sat next to him. He got it. "Did you come up with a plan?"

"Did you make a picnic?" He said, stone-faced.

"I did."

"Okay then, I have a plan. Put on some good hikers." The basket Eva prepared that morning sat on the kitchen counter, packed and ready. They would picnic on a fresh French baguette, three types of cheese, purple grapes, salami, four bottles of water, homemade brownies, two yogurts, and gourmet chocolate-covered almonds. Sufficient for a pleasant lunch out on the trail.

"My bella, Marlo, what are you hurting that pretty head about now?" Gianni walked up behind her, first wiping his hands on a white chef apron, then rubbing them together rapidly before stretching his tired fingers after a lengthy stint at the cutting board. He'd been chopping peppers of every color, yellow, green, red, orange, and a new plum variety. "Spring dishes," he said earlier to Enrique that morning, "must be filled of color from foods that come from the earth."

Startled out of her private thoughts, Marlo looked up at Gianni, groaned loudly, and placed her head of unruly auburn curls on the table in a display of irrational frustration. "It's Grace's party," came her muffled reply as her voice vibrated against the white linen tablecloth. "I'm not inspired."

At this response Gianni let out a hearty laugh, once again rubbing his hands together. "Ah, bella, that's all?" He paused. "Good. Well, I thought it might be something of import. Very well. See you later. I'm taking my fine Jana for a stroll around the block on her lunch hour." That was it. He whistled as he left the dining room, the door gently closing behind him.

Marlo, aghast, lifted her head to watch him leave, mouth open in disbelief, the restaurant now void of an uncaring Gianni. "Why, how could he …" was all she mustered in an attempt at self-pity. Just then the door catapulted open and in burst Enrique with two brown paper bags overflowing with groceries. Still hunched over the table, Marlo placed her chin on her hands as she peered at Enrique.

"Marlo, ciao," greeted Enrique, invigorated by his walk to the Shop-N-Save and the precious fresh cargo nestled snuggly in the bags. He coaxed the door closed with his toe.

"Ciao yourself."

Cocking an eyebrow, Enrique stopped, intrigued by his atypical disgruntled co-worker. "So what's the trouble with our Marlo?"

"'Our Marlo?' 'My Marlo.' Well, I guess it's nice to be owned," she snipped.

"Yes, I suppose that would be true," Enrique added, grinning to himself at the inherent benefits. "So?" he asked, setting the groceries down on an empty table and sitting next to her. "Tell Uncle Enrique."

"Grrr, you're so maddening. I want to be angry. And if it's not Gianni ignoring my concern, it's you coming in here like the big chef Wolfgang Puck with a bag of groceries."

"Two bags," he corrected in a polite tone, pointing to the bags with his index finger and holding up two fingers. "And it's mostly fresh produce."

"Two bags, la-tee-da," Marlo again shot back in a high-pitched voice dripping in sarcasm. They sat in silence for several seconds that seemed like hours. "Fine," Marlo quipped, "you just sit there all happy and satisfied, ready to create some amazing gastronomic creation and leave me here with the weight of the town on my shoulders."

"Mmm, the weight of the town, that's a lot. Exactly where does this weight come from?"

Letting out a deep sigh, akin to the yoga pranayamas she loved so well, Marlo frowned, ruffled her eyebrows, and answered seriously, "Grace's party."

"Grace's party," Enrique said, pursing his lips and nodding in recognition.

"Geesh Enrique, is there an echo in this room?"

"Is there an echo? Maybe it's Wolfgang Puck," he responded, looking around the room, then quickly putting up his arms to ward off the onslaught of Marlo's swinging arms. They playfully battled with her arms swinging until he took her wrists down and put his free hand on her shoulder, still securing her wrists. Laughing, he tilted his head toward hers and acquiesced. "Sorry, but you walked right into that one."

"Arrgh. Enrique, what am I going to do?"

"What you always do. Make magic. Why makes you ask?" Ignoring the English faux pas that she would typically correct, Marlo abruptly stood and started pacing around the tables, arms waving. "Grace's party! Don't you see? This needs to be the best, most awesome event ever. She should've had a lifetime of parties, and well, she didn't. Don't you see?"

Resisting the urge to echo, Enrique crossed his arms, knowing her question was rhetorical. "I see," he said after several seconds.

Marlo stopped in her tracks, rapidly twisting around to look at Enrique. "You do?"

He nodded, not sure where this was going.

"I knew someone would understand!" She hurled herself at Enrique and engulfed him in a hug with tangled curls and swirling skirt. "Oh, yes, well, we have so many details to work out. I must start my list. Thanks for your help."

"But of course. Any time." Giving her a short bow, Enrique picked up his groceries and went into the kitchen, amused by Marlo once again and the quirk of fate that in some way he had been her understanding muse.

Covering Jana's hand linked over his opposite arm, Gianni beamed. The two chatted incessantly about their mornings. The library apparently was a regular Wisteria Lane, full of intrigue and inappropriate rendezvous.

"Oh, gosh, Gianni, you should have seen it. A scorned wife from Jackson barged in on her husband in the reserved study room and found more activity than a little Internet browsing," Jana gushed.

"You mean, like, uh, what is it you say, hanky panky?"

"Gianni, yes, and let's just say sex."

"Sex. Sex can be good."

"Well, in this case, the wife picked up the pointy black shoes from the floor and chucked them down the history aisle and marched out. The *other* woman, a rather buxom brunette, fumbled with the buttons on her blouse. The culpable husband just stood there mute."

"Culpable, Jana?"

"Guilty, blameworthy."

"Ah."

"Life is better than fiction." Jana, like any good librarian, laughed as she told him that the whole incident took place by the stacks classified with the Dewey Decimal 900s, history. Some things never change with time.

"So then, Jana, shall we check out the biology aisle when we return?" Gianni tried to leer, then blushed at his little joke, which earned him a jab in the side and a head-thrown-back laugh. They stopped in front of the library after a brisk clip around downtown.

"Thank you, Gianni. This was a *perfecto* diversion from my normal lunchtime errands."

Picking up her hand in his traditional gesture, he kissed her cheek, adding, "The pleasure, dear Jana, is all mine." Twice in an hour, Gianni turned and was off whistling while a fine woman watched his retreat.

The early morning beauty was happenstance to Steve and Sander as they drove into the foothills to collect rocks for their project. They clipped by an old, manicured terraced graveyard built into the mountainside where ground creatures ran atop the stone fences. Once they reached their destination, they walked along with only the clicking of the flying grasshoppers to break the silence, their mission to find and quarry stones.

The men exchanged few words all morning, companions comfortable in their labor. Sander took a short exploration when they were done collecting rocks, running up a slope to check out a path that was visible from where they were working. Steve opted to return some calls and felt strangely satisfied that Sander had become curious with the local history on settlers and early homesteads. From a distance the path looked like an old road, but you could see fallen trees and debris. It could have even been a game trail from the clearing into the protection of the woods. Sander returned and, typical of his nature, nodded wordlessly to Steve. They finished loading the truck in silence.

On the drive back down to the project site in Bear, Steve spied a young moose peering at them through the protection of the willow bushes. In front of the rising sun, the animal's outline was completely dark—a priceless silhouette.

"Check it out," Steve said, breaking the quiet.

"The thing looks like Snoopy as the Great Pumpkin," Sander noted. Sander was right. The young moose had pointed ears and a long snout just like Snoopy. Huh. Steve did a double take at Sander as he drove. The comparison to a cartoon wouldn't have been what he expected from the ex-agent. Or was he an ex? Steve knew Sander was still involved in the gem heist case in some capacity, but he was not completely sure to what extent. The guy was so good at being present in the situation at hand; it was hard to place him in any other context, especially work of a covert nature.

Hours later, wiping the sweat off his brow, Steve smiled at Sander in easy camaraderie, blowing his breath out sharply as he took a break. "Seems the Feds drove home the concept of working out. Damn, you're in pretty good shape," he said, shaking his head at Sander, who hardly broke a sweat. They'd been building a stone bridge, carrying and digging in the hard dirt all morning. "Er, darn."

"Damn straight they did, darn it," added Sander with a bit of dry humor, catching Steve's eye, not missing a beat with his shovel.

"Ha. Funny," replied Steve, holding in a grin at the other man's chiding comment. "I bet a lot of those bad boys wouldn't know how to build a stone bridge."

"You got them there, Mason." Sander stretched his back and neck and slowly took in the morning's accomplishments.

"It's not too shabby, if I must say so myself," Steve said, admiring their handiwork as they put the finishing touches on their beautiful bridge; Grace's bridge.

It was the political pull of Judge Jerry Griffin who easily annexed a small plot across the street from the town square for the monument. Dale, Sander, and Steve barely finished their request weeks earlier when Jerry sat firmly in his leather chair to sign a permit for their request to use public lands.

"It's a fine tribute to Grace and her adopted family's history and their contribution to the growth and betterment of Bear," Jerry said, writing out the document, flair and pomp oozing out of his pores, fountain pen scratching across the paper. "Truth be told, it really is for Grace. Her work to start up the Now and Then Dress Shop. All those years she toiled so that those who fell into unfortunate circumstances had food, clothes, and shelter during their hard times. Whether their parents died, husbands left, or sickness came, they were the focus of her life's work—in addition to watching over Lois and James after their parents had died. Even with the personal animosity dumped on her, Grace never wavered in giving to this town."

"Sir," was all the trio could muster at the ease with which political power was motioned in the small town. *Different than in New York*, Sander mouthed to Dale, who'd been a bit awestruck and wondered if this action was in fact legal. Steve tipped back on his heels, nodding in agreement.

Maybe even more, the monument was a physical "I told you so" from the four men to Grace's naysayers. Several families in town donated stones used to construct the bridge, augmented by the stone hunting from Steve and Sander. The result was a beautiful arch made of smooth local stones fashioned with a solid hardwood walkway. A plaque would be installed halfway across the bridge that would read:

> *In Honor and Memory of the*
> *Johnsons and Cartwrights.*
> *A sincere thanksgiving for the*
> *Grace and devotion they gave to*
> *Our town of Bear.*
> *From your fellow citizens.*
> *2011.*

It was Dale who pushed for the use of the word "grace," and Sander who insisted it be first on one of the lines so it would be capitalized. Steve ensured that the right stakeholders in town were clued in for support. No need to start up any new feuds.

A garden was also planned. As input to the Bear Beautification Committee, Heidi asked her middle schoolers what plants came to mind when they thought of their town of Bear. The replies included sage, daffodils, Christmas trees, and, of course, the Wyoming State Flower, Indian paintbrush.

It was unanimous. The plot of ground would include the natural flora suggested by the children in addition to a small area for seasonal annuals and a stone bench to match the bridge. It was Sander who had suggested the gesture of the annual garden, knowing full well Lois would want to nurture the piece of earth dedicated to her ancestors, and mostly her Auntie Grace.

Steve enjoyed working with Sander and getting to know a new, formerly hidden side of him that was emerging. Indeed, the town was growing on Sander, and the town of Bear was steadily growing from the random acts he sowed.

Grace shook her head wearily as she sat down on the grand porch outside of Bear Claw Quilts. She arrived home from the hairdresser with a new coif, a birthday gift compliments of Lois. A half block away, Eva was walking the dogs and noticed the older woman leaning over with her hand to her forehead. Concerned, Eva jogged up to Grace, shushing the dogs with a stern reprimand to "be easy and gentle" before she transcended the steps.

"Hello, Grace," Eva said quietly, not wanting to startle her.

"Why, hello Eva, and your dears. How are you all today?" Grace looked tired; her words were full of genuine interest, but the older woman's eyes were sad.

"Oh, these babies are fine, spoiled and happy, as always," Eva answered as she looped the leashes over the porch rail to keep the dogs at bay. The two animals stood adoringly wagging their tails in Grace's direction while she doggie-talked to them from her perch on the bench. As Eva sat next to Grace, Dash pushed his rump out to gently slide down on his haunches, and Scout watched intently before nestling into a round ball, her back next to Dash facing the opposite direction. If it wasn't going to be all about her, well, it was their loss.

"How are you, Grace?" Eva asked, placing her hat and gloves in her lap, the Wyoming spring air still crisp.

Taking her time to answer, Grace looked at Eva, the resting dogs, then out onto the street she so loved to observe. "Well, since you asked, I thought I saw James today, riding by in a truck." She paused, not looking to Eva for an answer. "I'm afraid I might be getting senile."

Eva closed her eyes to hide her reaction. Of course! James had come in for the party. Poor Grace. She thinks she's seeing things. Deciding to go the innocent route, Eva forged ahead, knowing in this case that less is definitely more. "What makes you think it was James?"

"Eva, I've loved James as my own. Nephews matter, don't get me wrong, but that boy is a son to me. Especially since Margaret died."

Eva nodded, also knowing that James loved Grace like a mother.

"The man in the truck was a double for that child."

"Mmm. Could he be here in Bear, Grace, maybe on a break of some sort?"

Folding her hands in her lap, sitting straight and proper, Grace's face was serious in thought. "I spoke to him just two days ago. He was bursting with news about his classes. He's doing so well you know. Such a smart, good boy. Yes, well, he didn't say anything about being in Bear, and if he were planning a trip he would tell me he was coming."

Overcome with guilt but knowing she had to keep the secret, Eva gave it one more shot. "Grace, I think you're too hard on yourself. There's lots of burly guys in this town, and it's hard to know who's who sometimes with the glare and all on the windows." Eva knew it was a lame explanation. "Take Chad from Grizzly. He's a cute guy, maturing by the day."

Before Grace could answer, a black shiny BMW coupe sped around the corner and stopped on a dime in front of Bear Claw Quilts, engine roaring. Both women suspended talking and watched the vehicle. It was sparkling new, not the normal vehicle one saw in Bear and one that clearly could only be driven a few months a year in these mountains. Seconds later, the driver's door opened and to their amusement and surprise, Aaron emerged. Dr. Aaron. The short, dark, overweight man looked the part of a psychiatrist. However, the fact that he was also a gifted dress designer was incredible.

Waving papers, Aaron trundled up the steps, huffing as he stopped next to Eva and Grace. His excitement overthrew his manners and he interrupted their conversation—which, for Eva, was a blessing in disguise.

"Ladies, ladies, look here what we have." At their blank stares, he went on, "It's a letter! A letter from Vogue patterns. This is a big deal. Figuratively and literally."

Grace just stared at him, drawing the blue silk and wool pashmina tighter to her chest.

Aaron scanned the porch, located a single cane chair and dragged it in front of the bench. "See, here," he said, and he gave the letter to Grace. After a few seconds she looked back at Aaron with squinting eyes, twisting her head in confusion.

Aaron took in a deep breath. "Grace, Vogue's interested in your work."

"Vogue, Aaron?" Grace cleared her throat, "*The* Vogue patterns?"

"The very one," he said, tapping the papers nervously on his knee. "They would help us produce the patterns, market them, and, as it says here, give us an opportunity to oversee them being made by their experts. They have a whole series of ideas to promote the patterns, dresses, and your story. It's almost too good to be true. Even in their magazine. We need to have Dale look at this note from a business perspective and Charlie from a legal one."

At the news, Eva uncharacteristically nipped her thumbnail. She knew this was a dream in the making—a vision created from within a community using memories, and created because of relationships.

"Sander!" Judge Jerry jovially waved Sander in from where he stood in the office doorway. Jerry set down his sandwich, a bit of lettuce hanging off his mouth. Not engaging in small talk, Sander moved into the office.

"Judge, I need to make your introduction." On cue, Sid followed Sander into the office, and two other men stepped into view in the hall. "Judge Jerry, I'd like you to meet Sid Cameron, my superior."

"Fine man you have here, Sid. Good to meet you," Jerry said, standing up and moving to shake Sid's hand.

"Judge Jerry." Sid acknowledged, giving a curt nod to Sander and ignoring the lettuce piece that fell to the desk as Jerry shook his hand. He picked up a framed photo from Jerry's desk and studied it briefly. Casually setting the photo aside, Sid commented, "Sicily is a beautiful place. Your wife's family is from there, right? Marta Barratino—isn't that your wife in the photo?"

Jerry felt the heat come into his chest and was sure everyone in the room could hear his heart pounding when the man said Marta's name. No one in Bear knew she was a Barratino. But they knew. He sat down slowly. Sander took his lead and sat across from Jerry. "You had me guessing," Sander said, leaning back in the chair. "Tell me, why?" There was no pleasure from busting this case. A sense of emptiness and deep loss fell over Jerry. His life became vacant at the sound of those three words, tell me why. Closing his eyes to calm his mind, Jerry shook his head for a long moment. The clocked ticked from the bureau behind him; it had a bronze plate identifying his twenty-five years of dedicated service to the community of Bear. Which he loved.

"Don't know," Jerry said, quietly. Then with a breath, he went on. "It was a game. Like I'd be part of something big." He looked up at Sander, then across to Sid. "Sort of like the two of you. Trouble is I played on the wrong side. I thought the experience would make me better somehow. I had it made up in my mind that I wasn't hurting anyone, so it would be okay. I've always been the big fish in a little pond. But I had a dream of swimming in the ocean. Damn stupid." Jerry paused. "Funny thing, I love Bear and would never want to be anyplace else."

"Once you taste the dark side, Jerry, it is a trap like no other," Sander said. "I've seen more good men and women drop for a cheap thrill and a short stack of cash. But you—you knew better."

Sander watched Sid. This was tough. He liked the guy. Despite making that damn stupid choice, Jerry was loyal to his constituents. "I found your hiding place. Interestingly, I wouldn't have if it weren't for your good nature to give the plot of land for the community dedication. Steve Mason and I were in the vicinity getting rocks for the bridge when I saw the broken branches. The pattern indicated they were broken on purpose. I went to check it out."

Jerry looked at Sander, tears welling in his eyes. "That was the site of a church building. It never was finished, as you saw. Too far out. Not sure why my ancestors thought that was a good location to begin with." Jerry's voice trailed off. "I broke those branches so I could find it fast and in the dark. Didn't think anyone went up there anymore. Guess I was wrong."

"What's curious to me," Sander went on, "was why didn't you cover the cases of stolen gems. I assumed you planned to hide the loot with those large pink sandstones and gray flint stones. They were laying there like you wanted them to be out it the open. It was a mess. But easy."

Jerry wiped the tears from his face, uncaring about his sensitive state. "God only knows. It's this country, all it takes is rocks from up high to fall down, shifting things around when they land. The sandy soil moves easy. The geological shifts are unforgiving."

"Which is why you chose that place to begin with," Sander added.

Jerry looked at Sander, "Yeah," he said painfully, then, "Now what happens?"

"You are under arrest for the participation in the international brokering of stolen goods," Sid said, stepping forward, "Come with me."

"Eva, my God, I can't believe it is you!" Trina gushed, wrapping an orange and purple tie-died pareo around her full hips, positioning the headset over her hair, still wet from the ocean.

"I know. You've been on my mind. I'm so thrilled to talk to you," Eva said, swirling the hot chocolate in the bottom of her mug, pacing as she looked out over the lake.

"Girl, it has been so long since I've heard from you. Tell me, how is your life?"

How is your life. Right to the core of it. Trina had a way of knocking Eva from the trivial to the important. Taking in air to relax, Eva responded to her mentor coach. "My life, Trina, is real. That's it right now. Real."

"Yummy, Eva. What has made it real for you?" Trina asked, smiling to herself as she held back a teasing *finally* remark. She loved Eva and wanted to make sure she held her whole and powerful.

"Let's see. First, I actually fired a client," Eva giggled.

"That sounds like my business lady," Trina said, brushing sand off a log before sitting down. "What happened?"

"She was exhausting. I dreaded the calls, even though I know she's a great person. She always had excuses and wouldn't take anything seriously to improve her life," Eva said, reflecting on her calls with Lauren, pulling her sweater close more for comfort than for warmth. "I felt like our coaching had gotten to the level of complacency and just conversation. Nothing was happening between the coaching calls to further any personal learning or her taking action."

"Trusting your gut is always the way to go. You probably did your best coaching with her by ending the relationship," Trina said, knowing that once coaching got stale, it was hard, hard work.

"That's one way to look at it," Eva responded, getting in a groove of thinking about the joys of her life. "Let's see, you'll love this, I've taken up yoga with some of my girlfriends in Bear."

"And how is that for you?" Trina asked, pushing her toes into the sand. She stayed away from comments that elicited judgment, like saying "good." She told

Eva countless times during their mentoring, be careful not to judge your client. You don't know all their circumstances, so hold them true to their values and push them to the big lives they deserve. No labeling them as "good" or "bad." Now if they asked, you could contribute perspective, and if they begged, an outright judgment was fair game, Trina would add with a deep throaty laugh.

"Yoga has been so much more than becoming flexible!" Eva said, excited to talk about yoga, which she rarely did outside of class. "We meet at the studio once a week, work hard. Yeah, it's way harder than I thought. Then afterwards we kibitz and go out for coffee."

"Kibitz?" Trina mirrored Eva's word, herself having finished a hot yoga session that very morning.

"You know, talking, gossiping, and having fun. That's it Trina, I'm having fun. With girlfriends. Doing stuff that's in the women's magazines. Going out for coffee, practicing yoga, planning progressive dinners. It's my new real life."

"And what type of girlfriend are you?"

Eva breathed in the question, not expecting it or the flood of emotion it brought. Trina held the space, in no hurry to fill with words. "Trina, I have seen from these remarkable women the true value of friendship. And watching them, being part of them, has let me give of myself. Maybe I can't define that with words right now. But I feel it. I know what it is."

"It sounds like you have some very fortunate friends," Trina acknowledged, letting in a piece of judgment for a noble purpose.

Eva felt the acknowledgment. "I sure hope so. Because that's how I feel, fortunate," Eva set down her mug, spoon clanking inside. The sound brought Dash and Scout scampering into the room in search of a handout. Both animals came over by her, offering a furry head and paw, respectively, to gain some attention, albeit initiated by appetite.

"And what about male companionship?" Trina knew from Eva's message that there was love in the air. She was curious about this after the turmoil caused by her relationship with Seaton.

Eva laughed, "It's my turn to say 'yummy!'" At the recognized word, Dash cocked his head knowing the potential of getting a treat, then slowly relaxed, realizing no food was currently in store.

"Tell me you're not making him up," Trina teased.

"His name is Steve. He's a local. And we get along well." Eva paused for breath. She was excited to speak to Trina and share about Steve. "He likes me. He's normal in an 'unnormal' sense. What I mean is, I trust him, and he's funny, smart. Gorgeous."

"He likes you," Trina mirrored again. Coaching didn't have to be hard.

"He does. Can you believe it? We had a rough spot, my fault, and it's going good." Eva briefly explained the drama queen adventure in the mountain and their getting to know each other with the group of friends. And the adventure with the cabin and finding Grace's things. After some time, Eva knew she needed to let Trina get back to other responsibilities.

"Trina, I want to thank you for what you've done to help me create my life. The one I wanted. And I don't think I would have a thriving practice without your example. You need to know the influence you've had on me."

Trina let the words take hold over the phone. Before responding, she sipped iced pomegranate juice, sand gathered at the base of the glass. "Eva, it's the respect we give each other. You make the choices for action in your life. It hasn't been me. I'm here with you. But it's all you, girl."

Losing her voice, Eva closed her eyes and nodded, knowing that Trina understood the response without seeing or hearing it. After another pause, Eva said, "Trina, let's stay in touch."

Nervous, Eva's heart pounded as if she were a high school senior in expectation of a prom date. Not that she'd know. She hadn't gone to prom, and this was way better. Checking her look in the mirror, she fussed with her hair, wrapping a random strand around her finger in an attempt to accentuate some curly *umph*.

Scout interpreted Eva's actions, then rolled down onto her side in a play of boredom, eyes closed, fur ruffled under thin haunches. Dash was curled up on the hallway rug, seriously regarding Eva, knowing her primping meant she'd be leaving the premises. Without him.

Hearing the telltale sound of gravel crunching in the distance, Eva jumped, dabbing her lipstick one last time. Was her anxiety because Grace was finally getting what she deserved or because Steve Mason, *the famous* Steve Mason of Bear, was her date for the party of the century? After their picnic hike the other day, Steve and Eva sat for a playful hour at Grizzly sipping coffee, eyes locked as they collaborated on naming combinations for quilt squares and fly-fishing flies. Drunken Tarantula, Kings Flyway, and Tsetse-in-a-Corner were a few of the combinations that had them laughing to tears. She had felt special when he called her a few days ago to share what he had learned about the unbelievable story of Judge Jerry's dual life. It was a confirmation for Eva. Having had several dates, and an adventure, they could easily sit down for coffee and cavort like real friends.

"Hey there." Eva gushed, opening the door for Steve before he could knock. He stood close to the doorframe again, his face barely twelve inches from hers as she opened the door. Eva shrugged with childish glee.

The effervescent reaction wasn't lost on Steve. From behind his back he produced a single long-stemmed rose; a perfect beauty. In a fluid motion he took her hand and gently grazed the pink rose along her cheek.

"Lovely Eva, a rose for you," he said, noticing the blush in her cheeks. She was a woman-child, an anomaly in a complicated world. Complex, yet simple. Intelligent, but eager to learn. What a package. Without any words he took her in his arms, inhaling the fresh lilac scent in her hair. "Mmm, if you aren't careful you'll show up the lady of honor."

Soaking in his warmth, Eva turned to search his eyes. "Oh, Steve, that won't happen. I'm so excited for Grace and Lois that I can hardly stand it." Her glowing face was an open book.

"Mmm, and I can't stand this close to you without a kiss." The words came out low and husky. "You are breathtaking tonight."

Eva was a smart woman. She pulled him tight, their lips locked. Slowly pulling away from each other without words, Steve shook his head at her and nodded to the door. Eva obediently picked up her purse and a small package wrapped almost too pretty to open, and she led the way out the door. Duty called, and they both knew it.

From the street, The Sicilian Ball was decked out with distinctive Italian charm. Small white lights glittered, the wrought-iron bench ready for a patron, and the front window cast shadows from the merriment inside. Lois and Grace sat patiently in the car. Aaron had insisted they wait while he pulled his bulk out of the low front seat and came around the car to open their doors.

"There's a parking spot right in front for this fancy automobile of yours," exclaimed Grace. "Who would've thunk!"

Who indeed, thought Aaron, bemused. This was a tactical decision of Jana's just earlier that morning. Chad took it upon himself to ensure the spot was kept free. He had a good vantage point while shining glasses from behind the bar. It was Chad, too, who alerted the restless group waiting inside of the arrival of the guests of honor. In seconds they took seats at tables that were strategically turned away from the door.

Marlo cheerfully greeted Aaron, Grace, and Lois and took them to a cozy table. She positioned Grace and Lois so their backs were to the rest of the room. Aaron was able to peruse the room, brilliantly disguising his thrill, holding his smug smile in place.

"So, what brings the three of you out tonight?" Marlo asked with caring charm, her emerald ring catching the candlelight, casting a simmering green glow. Aaron raised dark eyebrows, turning his heavy torso to Lois.

"Why, it's Grace's birthday, and only the finest restaurant in Bear will do!" Lois said, with a glorious smile, breathless. Grace placed a palm to her chest, her mother's beautiful sapphire and diamond ring gleaming on her finger, then nonchalantly waved her hand, dismissing the kind remark. "Pshaw, an old woman like me, birthdays are so familiar I can't count them anymore."

"Happy birthday! Girl, I only can dream of looking as good as you when I get older. And I'll just have to see later what miracle Enrique has whipped up in the kitchen to top off your meal," Marlo added with a big wink. "Would you like to hear the specials?"

As Marlo started her oratory on the dining creations, a group of people at the table in the corner stood and started to clap. Then another in the opposite corner. Then another. Passing several moments, patrons at all the tables in the restaurant except Grace's were standing and clapping.

Grace and Lois looked at each other as Aaron, too, stood to clap. Then it struck Grace what was happening. She recognized all those faces around the restaurant. They were clapping for her. Then, after everyone was standing, they started to sing *Happy Birthday*. It was a soft pleasant sound of real beauty. Grace was awestruck. Tears streamed down her face.

Lois's head tilted as she grasped what was happening. Instead of standing, Lois kneeled at her Auntie's knee like she'd done thousands of time. Quietly she whispered a message, hardly able to get out the words so overjoyed for her aunt and overwhelmed by the compassion of community. "Auntie Grace, Happy birthday. I love you."

Just then Grace spotted him over Lois's head as he walked to her from across the room. James. Grace was speechless, clinging to him with a strength that belied her age. Holding her gently, he stroked her hair. "This party's for you, Auntie Grace, and for all celebrations you should've had more of through the years. And dearest Auntie, you're *not* getting senile," he added with a gleam.

Magic. There was no other way to describe Bear, Wyoming, that evening. The dinner was sublime. The toasts were heartwarming and hilarious, the friendships ever deepened under the spell of the vast Gros Ventres. Camaraderie abounded and the yarns drew more grand as the wine flowed freely late into the night. For each twinkling white light brought a new laugh, tall tale, or slap on the back. Community.

"I can't even begin to think how Grace and Lois are feeling right now." Driving home in the wee hours, Eva bubbled with ceaseless energy.

Steve smiled, words not relevant.

"Oh, and Grace loved her gifts—and the detailed map of the old Russia, such a thoughtful idea." She relived every moment of the night like a bride would her wedding day. "Why, I haven't known them that long in the scheme of life, and if I feel this way, what could Grace and Lois, or James, possibly be thinking?" Then she gasped, pausing. She closed her eyes and let out a long anguished sigh. Steve glanced at her, and then back at the road.

"Oh, Steve, will you forgive me?"

"Well, I suppose I do," he chuckled. "Do you mind sharing with me what it is I'm forgiving you for?"

"I feel the fool. Here I am new to Bear even after two years." Eva winced, "New to all these people."

"How do you figure that?"

"It's just that I'm not from here, you know?"

"Eva, you most definitely are from Bear."

Ignoring his comment, she went on. "I'm absorbed in their lives and, well, probably think I'm a bigger part of it all than I really am. You've been here all along. This is your territory."

Reaching out for her hand, he brought it up to his lips, palm side up, his million-dollar smile wasted in the darkness. "You were the missing link, dear Eva." Knowing her well, Steve could sense—no, *hear*—her emotion. Quiet. The acknowledgment landed.

Momentarily stunned by the accolade, Eva closed her eyes. Did she belong? Was she taking root in the soil of Bear without rejection? Living a real life? Growing here?

"This night was a long time coming. One not to be forgotten. It was needed. And to happen, it needed you, Eva. Bear needs you."

His words covered Eva with the warmth of a pieced quilt, each stitch made with tireless love. She needed Bear. She *needed* to be needed, to be part of a community. Could she be in the right spot, right now? Was she no longer waiting for "someday"? No longer waiting for one more thing to find happiness. She was ready to live every moment. Isn't that the reason our heart works so hard pumping life for our body?

Leaning into the headrest, Eva held Steve's hand firmly in hers, feeling the pulse in his wrist. Lifting it to her heart, she felt an immediate sense of comfort blanket her at that moment. Indeed, the very moment that matters, the present.

Epilogue

Prague, Czech Republic

The boys raced on the cobblestone street, their pace unhindered by the uneven stones. Martin held Rita's hand as they watched the vibrant pair. Music cascaded across the courtyard of Prague Castle, the well-dressed street musicians playing the oboe, violin, and bass. Young Martin tentatively leaned to toss a few euros into the open violin case.

Delighted in their charity, the boys skipped back to the safe protection of their parents. Looking down at Rita, Martin pulled her close as the boys ran to gaze over the City of One Hundred Spires, trying to count each one, knowing from their father that there were more like four hundred steeples. Prague, the old city now anew, stood proud and shone bright as the sun glittered across the Danube River.

"This is the best week of my life. It's a dream come true. To have you, the boys, here in this city. My city. The city of my father, my mother." Tears rolled down Martin's face, so overcome with emotion. Rita wiped his tears tenderly, her giant man, her shield.

"It was my revolution, the Velvet Revolution. We came out from the university and shook our keys in the street to symbolize the unlocking of doors. The noise, it was a miracle. First Berlin, then us. A new beginning. Thank you for being here."

"My dear Martin, for such a brute of a man—and I'm not complaining—you're so compassionate." Rita slid next to Martin as close as she could maneuver, feeling protected by the man she married, his muscular bulk twice her size.

"Ah, Rita, it's interesting what a new furnace and some paint can do for a marriage, yes?"

"Yes, pretty much." Rita smiled, recollecting his noble conversation and how he acquiesced to fix the home front before going abroad.

Briefly interrupted by the boys, who pulled on their sweaters and asked for euros for ice cream, the couple kept their connection. "Ah, yes, life is good," Martin muttered to himself.

Paris, France

The bittersweet reality would be unbearable without purpose. Debra leaned on the bridge railing and soaked in the sites of the East Bank. She closed her eyes and the sun warmed her face. *Oh, Lord, this is too hard to bear. How can I continue? How can this be real? Let it please be a bad dream in a good place.*

Roy's sickness was harsh. It took his life in four months. The cancer stole him from her, his body not responding to treatment. What about her hope? What about all those other people who are cancer survivors? Sorry, they said, it wasn't meant to be for him. Or her. Debra was in Paris without Roy. A widow. This was supposed to be their dream trip, a celebration of their love, a childhood wish come true.

Interrupting her grief, Sue, Debra's lifelong friend, put an arm around Debra. "Roy would love this, Debra. Even more, he's watching you from heaven. He's damn proud you picked yourself up and came to Paris."

Debra could only answer with a pursed smile and a flood of tears on her face, leaning on her friend for support.

"Look at your kids over there, Debra. The girls are living, you know, and watching you. Your example to talk about Roy and put one foot in front of the other is a testimony to your love for Roy, to them, and to yourself. They say, you know, that you should live until you die. It was a noble idea to bring the whole crowd to Paris in Roy's memory." Sue paused. "Go ahead, cry like crazy, honey. You need it."

Debra did just that as she watched the breeze carry the last of Roy's ashes into the Seine.

Central Arizona, Prescott Hills Detention Center

Lauren took a deep breath and closed the book. The forty-five men ranging in age from early twenties to upwards of fifty were completely still, watching her intently. No one spoke. The silence overpowered any notion of clapping. They all wore the same prison-issue jumpsuit, yet Lauren knew they were as different inside as they were dressed alike on the outside. Did she detect a few rather loud gulps? Did she reach just one buried emotion? She scanned the room, and toward the back of the hall a twenty-something man barely nodded in a signaling gesture. Now it was Lauren's turn to gulp and hold in emotion. She closed her eyes to center herself and stood.

"Thank you all. You've been an attentive crowd. Next week I plan to read

Keats, and I'll take recommendations from that point. If there are any preferences you have, please write them down on the papers by the door before you exit. Until next time." She waved, unsure of her voice for any longer.

She closed her book, *Shakespeare's Sonnets*, careful to tuck in the piece of paper with two handwritten columns. Lauren didn't unfold the paper; she knew that on one side was written "I don't like Brad being at the detention center" and on the other side was written "Be part of Brad's life, I love him." What she had in her life, what she wanted more of in her life. To think that being fired by her coach put her into action.

Reading poetry at the center gave Lauren a way to pass the time until Brad paid his dues to society. She loved the kid. He was her brother, after all. He had a love for literature that went beyond that of most people, and he wanted to be a Shakespearean actor one day. Lauren knew he had it in him. These weekly readings were her way to encourage him while at his lowest and most discouraged. *Sort of like believing in him more than he believes in himself.* That sounded rather familiar. She just might need to call Eva.

Tarrytown, New York, IBM Headquarters

Her lawyer, Sam, barely out of law school, was competent, bright and even a little handsome. He reviewed the papers with a slow determination and a nod that she thought must be keeping time with his reading. Putting down the papers, he looked to Sarah and at the people around the table. "All is in order, Sarah. Including your requests." Sarah could tell he wanted to say 'and then some,' but he kept that to himself.

"So, what are the next steps?" Sarah wanted to whoop. *Oh my God!* She peddled her growing business to IBM, of all companies. And they want it! Gracious, Gracious, Gracious. The name of her future self kept running through her head. The compensation she would receive for the deal was obnoxious. Granted, it was fair by corporate standards, and IBM did right by her company. Dream come true. Cash for her personally, cash for her new charity foundation.

In eighteen months, after the building was complete, Little Rock, Arkansas, would have a new family center. It would cater to adult women and men to foster positive relationships, plan social activities, and offer counseling. The best part was the nonpublicized safe haven for women and children who need protection. The rooms would be fresh and clean, computer-equipped as part of the contract, and the beds would have soft, cotton bedspreads. No tears could pool on old piled polyester, that memory not to be repeated.

Sarah took in a breath. Yes, this was good. Action. Change. Impact. Move forward.

Bear, Wyoming

Applause thundered like a storm ravaging the roof of the restored barn. Finishing their piece, *The Dance of the Mountain Lions*, the children were mesmerized, paralyzed by the response from the audience. Kara, seventeen, and her young brother, Kyle, seven, were the last act. It was opening night at the new playhouse, Possibilities. The joint sentiment from the audience and rookie performers was palpable. There wasn't a dry eye to be found.

For the grand finale, Kara choreographed and danced a remarkable number mixing modern Martha Graham–style dance with traditional ballet en pointe. Her grace and strength moved the crowd. Her grasp of modern dance interwoven with ballet was a marvel. Kara's costume was a simple brown unitard that covered her from shoulder to toe. The passion Kara displayed filled the barn, painted the canvas. Kyle was her trusted and trusting companion. It didn't take much coercing to get her little brother to cooperate.

"Be on stage? Pretend to be a mountain lion? Just watch you and move around just like a lion? Wear a cool costume? Sure!" He mimicked and countered her body motions with all the vivaciousness of a seven-year-old boy.

The honest moves of a child imitating—no, *being*—a mountain lion brought down the house. The contrasts between the siblings were so great that they became harmonious counterpoints, moving creatures across the stage, painting their dreams. Young and old. Boy and girl. Grace and courage.

As the applause roared, Rosalyn grasped Charlie's hand. His head bobbed up and down with pleasure. He took a deep breath, unable to speak, glad he happened to meet Eva to push him into action.

This is it, he thought to himself. We can just make it up to create endless possibilities.

Acknowledgments

Writing *What if You Made It Up?* was a long private journey. The day my company announced it was going to be sold to another corporation was the day I started writing the story about Eva. It took me more than four years of early Saturday mornings to write the first draft. I did this mostly in private, telling very few people. I was worried that I wouldn't finish with all the other forces pulling on my time. But I did it. And I'm grateful to those who believed in me.

To publicly acknowledge is a wonderful honor. My dear friend, Ann Pateros, who read the terrible first draft with diligence, gave me feedback and encouragement to continue. My friend and coach colleague, Jackie Johnson, read it with a gentleness and wisdom that still carries me today. Not only did Jackie read the book, she listened to my tireless talk about the book on a monthly basis and held me accountable to myself in the difficult trip to publish the story. One of my sisters, Karlyn McPartland, took the manuscript on a weekend camping trip with her church youth group and read it as a reader and critic. It was two friends from high school, Julie Mooberry, my lifelong friend, and Patti Bower, a talented editor, who pushed me into action. In addition, I want to acknowledge the Coaches Training Institute in Palo Alto, California, and Quantum Coaching, a program in Boulder, Colorado, run by Ron and Sue Kerstner. The techniques I learned from these amazing people are adapted in the coaching vignettes.

My children, Kent and Claire, were curious that I was writing a book and rather excited for me to finish to see what would happen. At the beginning of my publishing anxieties, Claire gave me a hug and said, "Mom, I'm so proud of you and your ideas." Kent told me on the phone from university, "I look forward to reading your finished book." That says it all.

To you amazing readers who selected this book to read, I sincerely thank you. I appreciate the time you invested in the story and the characters, and I appreciate you taking a chance on a new author. I hope that you enjoyed the story of Eva, her trials, coaching calls, new friendships, and the beautiful fictional locale of Bear, Wyoming. It would be a delight to meet you at Grizzly Tracks coffee shop, hike with you in the Gros Ventres, and then meet for a delicious dinner at The Sicilian Ball. Never stop dreaming!

Reflection and Discussion Questions for *What if You Made It Up?* by Kathleen Kolze

1. Eva's profession as a life coach is woven into the story. Has your opinion of life coaching changed from before you read the book? If so, in what ways?

2. Eva stresses to her clients, self, and friends that everyone has a choice in life. What do you think about life choice from the perspective of having choices on how to respond to events in our lives when we may not think we had any choice? Is there an example in the book where Eva made a choice that surprised you? What about in your own life? Would you make the same choice again, or would you choose differently given another chance?

3. Eva embraced the new relationships she forged with Jana, Heidi, and Marlo. What is it about these four diverse women that allows their friendships to work?

4. As complex people, we can get caught up in making things harder than necessary. In your own life, when might the question "What if you made it up?" be a useful exercise?

5. Being a confident, professional woman, Eva can hold her own and work a room. What do you see in her vulnerabilities and self-perception that caused her to have at least two emotional meltdowns in the book (after her second speech to the women's league and after seeing Steve in Jackson with the "woman in red")?

6. Share your feelings about Gianni—his family history, management style, friendship with Jana, and landing in Bear. How is he typical, or not, from immigrants you've known in your own family or friendships?

7. Eva coached her clients about being in the moment, to be present with an idea, person, or thought. This idea is not new; rather it is ancient and is only spoken of more in the last years. What is your perception of how practicing being present can affect the actions in your life?

8. What character did you relate to the most? Was it one of the women— Eva, Jana, Heidi, Marlo, Grace, Lois? Or one of the men—Steve, Sander, Gianni, Dale, Aaron, Enrique? What was it about the character that resonated with you?

9. A sense of community in Bear is shown through the consideration of characters (i.e., reading at the library) and local events such as the opening of The Sicilian Ball and Grace's surprise birthday party. What makes this spe-

cial? Is it the groups of people or the atmosphere of community? What might be the similarities or differences? Where is your "community"?

10. Eva's dogs, Dash and Scout, are integral to her life and part of her environment in her home and, therefore, her work. What is your sense of an animal as part of someone's life? How would Eva's story be different if told by Dash or Scout? Do they have a unique view?

11. Thinking about an animal's perspective, what does this open up for you? How would your pet, a neighbors' pet, or childhood pet speak about you and your actions? Is it a tender feeling or does it raise an "ouch" for you? How could you take this perspective and improve the way you "be" with others?

12. When reading the epilogue, what touched you in the short summaries about Eva's coaching clients—Martin, Debra, Lauren, Sarah, and Charlie? Do you think Eva made a difference for them, or might they have come to the same actions without her as their life coach?

13. Simple questions and a listening mind and heart just might make a difference to others. Is this something you would want to take on with a person in your life? With whom and for what reason?

14. After reading the book, what is the one idea that you want to take into your own life? How will you keep yourself accountable for a week? A month? A year?

Is there someone in your life who would benefit by reading this book? Is it because they would enjoy the book, or do they need something more, less, or different from you? You decide and then take action.

Did you enjoy reading *What If You Made It Up?* by Kathleen Kolze?

Visit her website online at www.kathleenkolze.com and read about new projects and upcoming events.

Let her know if you are interested in having her call in to your book club, speak at an event, or coach you or your team!

About the Author

Kathleen Kolze has worked in global corporations for twenty-five years. She is a certified Emotional Intelligence Coach and Certified Professional Co-Active Coach, and is accredited with the International Coach Foundation. This all came after a career change from information technology, where she had roles from analyst to chief information officer. She holds a BS in computer science and mathematics. Her passion at work is to share the simplicity that awareness of personal choice and continuous development can improve your quality of life.

Kathleen resides in Illinois and has been married to Bob for more than twenty years. She has two children, Kent and Claire, and, until recently, had golden retrievers including Dash and Scout. They are the only reality-based characters in her first novel and will live on in fiction!

Kathleen loves to travel as much as possible and has lived across the American Midwest, in Northern California, and in Europe. She is an avid walker, quilter, and student of ballroom dance. When possible she dabbles in perfecting culinary delights using just a *little* too much olive oil and garlic.

CPSIA information can be obtained at www.ICGtesting.com
Printed in the USA
LVOW050733030912

297078LV00003B/2/P